Crestfield

Can't find my way home

This book is a work of fiction. Names, characters, places and incidents are products of the author's imagination or are used fictitiously. Any resemblance to actual events or locales or persons, living or dead, is entirely coincidental

ISBN   978-0-692-92058-9

Edited by Junior

Technical support by Randi & Matt

Cover design by Dezi

Crestfield

Crestfield is a small town. As a matter of fact, it has always been a small town and I suppose it always will be. Great or small, doesn't really matter to me, because it's my hometown and I wouldn't trade it for all the tea in China. I was born and raised in Crestfield and I have absolutely no complaints, and for me to do so would be just plain wrong. Having said that and moving forward, the last time my sister, Dezi, visited from California, I had this strange and overwhelming urge to find out what the west coast was all about. I've accumulated over three weeks of vacation days and I figure that'll be more than enough time to go watch the sun set over the ocean; or does it set in the ocean? Well, it's one of those.

The Mayor has approved my request to take some time off and go kick up a little sand on the sunny beaches of California. Just to be honest and so you know, the Mayor is my uncle, Ajax McCool. Yes, I know you're thinking that I'm receiving a gratuity I don't deserve or something to that effect. Well, the fact is Crestfield is usually as quiet and peaceful as a moonlit cornfield on a midsummer's night. And we have two very capable part-time police officers ready to fill in for me. Chances are I wouldn't be missed at all. That doesn't sound so great when I say it, but it's the truth. The problem I'm dealing with at the moment is making sure my dad is taken care of while I'm away. My sisters, Madison and Randi, live here in town and they can take care of Dad. It's just that I don't want them feeling like their big brother is taking advantage of them. And I suppose I should mention the fact that my dad is a handful.

"Junior, who are you talking to?"

"Myself Dad, I'm talking to myself."

"Well, if you ask me that's not a healthy habit to get into. In fact, the folks I've seen talking out loud to themselves have all been ready for the funny farm."

"Dad, you haven't been able to see for well over ten years now."

"You know darn good and well what I meant. All

I'm saying is that talking to one's self is not a healthy habit to get into. That's all."

"Ok, thanks Dad, I'll try to remember that. 'One's self', are you kidding me?"

"No, I'm not kidding. And you don't have to be able to see a person to know they're talkin' to themselves. Just this last Thursday or was it Friday? Anywho, I was listening to Jim Zabel cover the girls' state basketball championship. I'm pretty sure it was Everly against Union-Whitten. Did you know that both teams scored over a hundred points in that darn game? Doesn't seem possible, but every bit of what I just told you is true and factual. Anyway, Zabel was announcing the game one minute with all the zest and fire you'd expect from him and then the next thing you know he'd drifted off into outer space and was talking to himself. I hope one of the listeners let him know afterwards that he sounded like a crazy person. Yep, heard it with my very own ears Junior, and old Jim's probably in a nuthouse as we speak."

"Dad, you might be the one that belongs in a nuthouse."

"Junior, why would you say something like that to your own father?"

"For starters, because the game was not played last Thursday or Friday."

"Ok Mr. Know-it-all, when was it played?"

"Dad, the game you're talking about was played last year. I believe it was early in November. That's eight months ago, and you think the game was played last week?"

"So I got a few days mixed up. No matter, because right about now I'll bet ol' Jim is somewhere playin' with a ball of yarn."

"Playing with a ball of yarn? Dad, how do you come up with this stuff?"

"I don't know the answer to that question. You know why I don't know the answer?"

"No Dad, I don't know why you don't know the

answer to that question."

He turned his back to me.

"Dad, why don't you know the answer to the question?"

"Because I don't have to know the answer to the question. You know somethin' Junior; everything doesn't always have to be exactly accurate to be the truth."

I didn't say anything.

"Yeah, that's what I thought. You can't figure out why what I just said is true, but you know it is. Don't you, Mr. Shell Answer Man."

"Yes Dad, there's some truth in what you just said."

"So you do admit that Jim Zabel could be somewhere playin' with a ball of yarn."

"No Dad, I don't admit that at all. But I do admit that you could talk the hair off a politician."

"Junior, I hate it when you use my sayings against me. If you can't come up with somethin' original, then don't say anything at all."

"Dad, I'm going to turn your radio on so you can sit and relax and listen to some music. Do you want me to get you a bottle of pop or maybe a beer?"

"Yeah, a bottle of pop would be great, but I can't listen to any music right now. I don't wanna miss Jim Zabel's afternoon sports talk show."

"What the heck. What happened to the ball of yarn he was supposed to be playin' with?"

"Go away, Junior. You're pestering me and I don't appreciate it one bit."

I just shook my head as I walked over to the fridge to get my dad his bottle of pop. I heard him snickering behind my back.

When I walked back and handed him the bottle, he said thanks. I could tell he was struggling, trying not to laugh out loud. Sometimes I wonder if life is just a big game to him or if he's serious or if he's off his rocker. I guess it doesn't really matter, because he's my dad and I love him just the same.

I walked out back and sat down on the porch, I immediately started talking to myself. Out loud, of course. Only took about ten seconds for Dad to yell, "Funny Junior. That really is pretty damn funny. Now stop it!"

I think after our little exchange you might begin to understand how contrary, stubborn, and just plain difficult my dad can be. It's not all his fault; that is if you assign fault to human behavior that isn't always nice, polite, and pleasing. Sorry about that, sometimes I just start rambling on about stuff that I should probably keep to myself.

Anyway, about ten years ago my mom and dad were run off the road by a sick, hateful man. We'll leave his name out of this. My mother died that night. My dad survived, but he suffered some severe head trauma. So, as you know, he was left blind and somewhat brain damaged. He has days when he seems as normal as a bird in flight. Then there are days and sometimes weeks when he just isn't firing on all eight cylinders. I'd say it another way, but trust me it does make sense coming from a guy raised in the Midwest.

So, that's my dad and now I think you have a good idea why it's difficult for me to think about leaving him behind, just so I can go on a vacation. Ok, I know what you're thinking. I've already asked him if he wanted to go with me. And he was painfully clear when he said, 'No way am I going out to California with all them fruits and nuts that live there. And I would never consider going anywhere without Maggie, that's for damn sure.'

Right on cue Maggie ran out and sat down next to me.

"Hi there girl, how're things today? She barked and let me know everything was just fine. Maggie is my dad's true blue, faithful to the end, German shepherd guide dog. She is also his confidant, fortune teller, and best friend. Strange thing is, all five of us kids know that there are times when Dad prefers to be with Maggie rather than us. But for whatever reason, we don't mind.

Crestfield

I suppose we're all aware of the fact that parents feel different about their children than they do about their friends. And I guess that includes dog friends, too.

2

I sat with Maggie for a long time before I felt the strange stillness in the air. I pulled myself from my fugue state and looked out at a dark, forbidding sky. It had rained for days on end and the grass in Dad's back yard was deep green, and long. I contemplated going out and mowing the lawn before the weather moved in when a very distinct smell wafted across my bow. I didn't have to think twice or dwell on the aroma because in an instant I knew what it was. There is no mistaking the earthy tang of freshly cut grass. Funny thing is I didn't hear a mower, yet the smell was abundant and nearby. I decided to go have a look-see.

I walked around the back of Dad's garage and yelled for Maggie to come with me; at first, she balked at the idea. I thought *that's kinda strange*. We crossed over maybe five or six backyards when I saw old man Hopkins sitting on his riding mower. The mower wasn't running. He just sat and stared west into the distance. I was going to ask him what he was looking at when a gust of wind filled up the hood of the sweatshirt I was wearing. I followed his eyes and looked west and then I immediately knew why Mr. Hopkins had been staring, and what he'd been staring at.

The swirling gray funnel cloud seemed to stretch across the entire sky. I mean from left to right and top to bottom. The point at the bottom dipped and stabbed down at the earth like an anteater's tongue. It just kept moving and flicking and sucking and then moving again. The great gray hulk was like a heavyweight boxer bobbing and weaving, eagerly waiting to land his next knockout punch. I turned to yell at Mr. Hopkins to get inside when I realized he'd already jumped off the mower and run. He didn't go in his back door as I thought he'd do. He ran straight for the storm cellar doors and kicked open the hasp with his right foot and as he lifted the left side he turned and waved for me to come down into his storm cellar. He was yelling, but I couldn't hear a word he said. The calm that had hung in the air was now a fever pitched vicious howl. The roar in my ears was crippling. I was frozen, trapped in a nether world and incapable of moving any part of my body. Mr. Hopkins shouted and waved harder still and I stood there like a stone.

Maggie barked; I didn't move. Again, and again she jumped up and pushed me with her front paws. She finally knocked me down and then I came to my senses. I knew I had to get Dad down in the cellar. As I stood to run I saw the storm door fly out of Mr. Hopkins hands. He tried one last time to get me to come with him to a safe place. Maggie led the way as we ran crossing three back yards in a matter of seconds. I looked at Dad's back porch and he was standing there frantically waving his arms. He was yelling for me to come inside.

I looked behind me and the great gray beast was licking at my heels.

"Dad, I'm right here. I'm ok, go back in the house," I yelled with all my might.

He heard me and waved one last time before he turned and held the back-door open. Maggie beat me to the porch and I watched as the wind buffeted her and Dad from side to side. Then a titanic gust hurled them inside the house. The back door violently swung to and fro on its hinges before it slammed shut. I was only a few feet from the house when I leaped for the porch. And as I flew through the air, out of the corner of my eye I saw a large green blur heading my way. I turned to see what it was.

3

Crestfield hospital/my sister, Madison

Junior has been unconscious for just over twenty-four hours now. Obviously dreaming, he's been babbling with unrivaled energy. He's famous for the array of bizarre situations and characters he creates in his dreams, so the possibilities are wide open. Junior's vital signs are excellent, so Doc Mayland has told everyone not to worry. Well, evaluating and then treating abnormal behavior is what I do for a living. My experience in psychiatry has been that a person being unconscious for a prolonged period of time is cause for dutiful concern. Suffice it to say that the good doctor and I don't agree on this matter.

I'm Madison, the oldest of Junior's three sisters. Junior and I share some traits, but physical appearance isn't one of them. Yes, we're both moderately tall, but that's where the similarities cease to exist. Junior is a blue-eyed toe-head. And like my dad, I have hazel eyes and brown hair. Junior is famously slow to act and usually leans towards a much more conservative approach to life than I do. I'd tell you more, but at this time there's really no point. And I'm in a hurry. Want to go sit with Junior for a while, see how he's doing. After seeing Junior, I have to go rustle up some supper for my dad and me.

Since the tornado roared by town a day ago, it seems that I've done nothing but run here and run there. And of course, I ran from my car through the hospital towards Junior's room. And the closer I got to his room, the louder the laughter I heard became. When I walked into his room, I was met by three gum smacking candy stripers. They were standing in the middle of the room with their hands covering their mouths, staring and giggling at Junior.

"What in the world are you girls doing?" I asked in a heated voice.

Crestfield

The tallest of the three young ladies stepped forward. Her red hair was tied in pigtails and the lipstick and make-up she wore looked as if it had been applied with a large paint brush. After a few hard thought seconds, she worked her gum with a pop and said, "I'm sorry ma'am, but we're not really doing anything. It's just that he's so funny. He acts like he's in a wrestling match. And every minute or so he yells out crazy stuff–"

"What! No! Noohhhhhh!" Junior yelled and then moaned, as he flailed his arms and turned from his left to his right side.

"See what I mean. He's been going on like this for nearly half-an-hour now," she said, as her two compatriots nodded their heads in agreement.

"Ok, I understand. But the show is over now. And how come the three of you have so much time to stand around and giggle?" I asked in my authority voice.

"We have a lot of time because our shift was over a half-an-hour ago," the pigtailed redhead said in a practiced nasty little school girl voice.

Nothing else was said as the three of them filed out of the room. And of course, along the way they each gave me their version of a snotty little know-it-all face. Then, as soon as they were out in the hallway, they let loose with a big guffaw. I guess they felt it necessary to let me know they were young and in charge. *Teenagers...*

I sat down and studied Junior for a moment. And other than a bruise across the right side of his face and some gauze covering his ear, he appeared to be fine. But it was what I couldn't see that gave me great pause. I hadn't been sitting in the room long when I heard a few familiar voices coming my way. The Chief of Police, my Uncle Tommy, and the Mayor of Crestfield, my Uncle Ajax, were coming to see Junior. And of course, along for the ride were the two enlightened rogues, my dad and his dog, Maggie. The moment they entered the room Maggie rushed to Junior's side and barked and barked; Junior did not respond. Dad followed the sound of Maggie's barking and when he reached her, he dropped to a knee and asked her to stop barking and listen to him. And of course, she did.

"Maggie girl, it's ok. Junior is fine and he'll be out of here before you know it. I know you only want to help, but your barking does get a little bit annoying. Ok? So, can you stop for a while?"

Maggie looked at Dad, her black muzzle cocked to the side. And after he finished talking, I swear that her sparkling amber eyes were saying, 'because you asked, I'll stop barking for a while, but I'm worried about Junior.'

And as sure as you're born, Dad said, "I know you're worried girl. I'm worried too."

I turned and one at a time my uncles said hello and gave me a hug. And just as I was about to speak, Doc Mayland walked into the room. It's eerie to me how much the doctor looks like Gary Cooper. He gave all of us a short wave, which is commonplace in the Midwest. He didn't say a word as he slowly walked straight to Junior. Doc Mayland grabbed Junior's left wrist and began counting to himself. After a half- a-minute or so he turned and said, "Evening folks. Well, Junior's doin' fine and I believe it's just a matter of time, maybe a few hours before he wakes up. Try to be patient with the patient." Then as quickly as he'd entered the room, he left.

My Uncle Tommy stood in the corner of the room in his usual relaxed manner. Unlike the rest of us, Uncle Tommy has black hair. To me he usually looks like a bear casually standing in the forest with his legs crossed and his arms draped over a tree limb. Now my Uncle Ajax, well, he's a totally different animal. Try to picture a frenetic, chubby little otter with sad green eyes. Yep, that's my Uncle Ajax.

For some reason, after the hugs and hello's, everyone turned to stare at Junior. And right on cue he let out a disturbing yell. What he said was not clear to any of us. That's not really what mattered. What mattered was how desperate he sounded.

Dad immediately asked if anyone in the room understood what Junior had said. And Uncle Ajax replied, "I think he said, 'he rob me.'"

"Yes, that's close to what I heard, but it sounded like he may have said, 'a hob-knee.' And I have no idea what a hob-knee is. He talks like he had a fever," Dad said, as he scratched the back of his head.

"Dad, he does have a fever," I informed. "Right now, Junior is trying to fight through the turmoil in his mind so that he can wake up. And it doesn't really matter what he says or what we think he said. Maybe we'll find out when he wakes up. Until then, there's no point in worrying about it. The journey he's traveling through in his mind is probably quite stressful. So, almost any response he has should be considered normal," I said.

I guess the others agreed because for the next several minutes not a word was spoken. I think we were all anxiously waiting to hear what Junior would say next.

4

My hospital room

I heard noises so I opened one eye to survey my surroundings. I could see a blur or two, maybe even three or four. They seemed to be silently moving around me. *Am I being held against my will? Maybe I've been taken hostage by pirates and I'm on some vessel heading for far away exotic islands, and of course, treasures. No, that can't be because I don't think they keep dogs on pirate ships and I just heard a dog bark. Should I open my other eye? No, I'd better wait and see just who it is that has me tied to this bed. Let's see if I can roll over.* I rolled over. *Wait a second, I'm not tied down at all. Ok, I guess I'll open my other eye and see where I am and who I'm there with.* I opened my other eye and someone was shining a light in it. I reached out and tried my best to push the light away.

"Can you please stop that? The light is hurting my eyes."

"What'd he just say?" someone asked.

"I don't know, but he is definitely waking up," the guy holding the light said.

He's wearing a white coat. Gee whiz, I hope I'm not dead. Nah, he said I was waking up. Why was I sleeping? Maybe I'd better say hello.

"Hello, who are you and where am I? Please tell me."

"Hello Junior, Doc Mayland here. How do you feel?" he asked.

"I guess I feel ok. Who are you? And what did you just call me?"

"I called you Junior. Would you rather I call you Jack? These days nobody calls you Jack," said the man in the white coat.

"I don't know and I don't know anyone by the

name of Jack. Say, what's going on here? Are you holding me here against my will?"

"No, of course we're not holding you against your will. Junior, don't you recognize me?"

"No, I don't recognize you. And why do you keep calling me Junior?"

The man in the white coat turned away from me so that he might speak to a man sitting in a chair close to the bed I'm in. There was a large black and tan dog sitting next to the man.

"Jack, would you say that Junior is a kidder? Would he pretend not to know who I am?" the man in the white coat asked the other man.

"Junior - a kidder? Not likely. Let me try."

"Junior, it's your dad. I guess you can hear me just fine. Can't you? Nod your head yes if you can hear me."

I nodded my head yes.

"See Doc, he can hear me, he obviously knows who I am."

The man in the white coat turned to me again and said, "Junior, do you recognize your dad and his dog Maggie?"

"No, I don't. And why do you insist on calling me Junior? I don't know anyone by that name."

"Young man, if your name is not Junior, then what is your name?"

I just knew these people were messing with my head. I didn't know why, but I knew they were. Then the man in the white coat repeated, "Young man, what is your name?"

I started to panic as waves of extreme confusion exploded in my head. *Stop for a second. Ok, you can handle this. Just relax and tell them what your name is. Go ahead and tell them what your name is. Wait, what is my name?*

I started trembling inside, I tried to get out of bed, but the man in the white coat and another man in all white held me down. A lady with a white hat sat down next to me. Then a bee stung me on the arm and my eyelids became incredibly heavy. I had to do something and fast. I stopped struggling for a moment and did my best to gather all the energy I could. And as I slowly drifted away on the pirate ship, I reached out with my right hand to touch the man in the white coat.

"Help me. I don't know what my name is. Please help me. What is my name?"

"Doc, what did he just say?"

"I don't know Jack, I just don't know."

5

My hospital room/my best friend, Ricky Reed
"Madison, is Junior ever going to remember who he is?" Ricky asked.

"Yes Ricky, I believe he will. Doc Mayland said Junior's speech and cognition were well within what would be considered normal."

"What does that mean?" Dad interrupted.

"Well, it means that other than memory loss there doesn't appear to be any physical damage to the brain that would keep Junior from co-existing with other people."

"Co-existing? Dang it Madison, he doesn't even know who the hell we are. And worse yet, he doesn't know who the hell he is," Dad huffed.

"We know that, Dad. Listen, there are many types of amnesia. Junior is suffering from what is referred to as traumatic amnesia. In lay terms, he was struck on the head and that caused physical trauma to the brain. And when you get hit on the head by a riding mower flying through the air at a fairly high rate of speed, well, it's going to do some damage. Thank heavens Junior was only hit by a fender. Had he been hit by the body of the mower I don't believe he would have survived," I said.

Maggie began to whine and then she sat up and looked me square in the eye. I wondered if she understood what I was saying. Dad stroked the side of her face and softly said, "It's ok girl. That's the way I feel too." Then she laid her chin on his lap and was quiet.

"Junior is going to go through a period of memory loss, but I believe the memory loss will be temporary. If we take our time and slowly introduce him to familiar people and surroundings, I believe he will eventually remember who we are and, of course, who he is. We have to do everything we can to treat him in a non-threatening manner. If he feels any aggression on our part, he could be drawn back into the limbo-state in which he now exists."

"Maddi, you know I've seen this in the movies. Some guy gets hit on the head and forgets who he is. Then he gets hit on the head again and wah-lah, he remembers who he is. Maybe we oughta try hitting him on the head," Ricky said.

"Ricky, I'm sorry, but that only happens in the movies. I'm confident that hitting Junior on the head would only prove to exacerbate the situation."

"Madison, I don't wanna axstitate nothin'. It's just that I'm gettin' worried my best friend and the Junior we all know and love is never coming back to Crestfield," Ricky said with a lump in his throat.

"Ricky, Junior doesn't have to come back to Crestfield," Dad said in a comforting tone.

"Why not?" Ricky asked, bewildered by the moment.

"Because he never left, he's right there in front of you."

"Jack, that's not really what I meant."

"Ricky, Dad and I both know exactly what you meant. Try to think good thoughts. Junior will come back, I promise. It's just going to take some time," I said, in the most reassuring voice I could come up with at the time.

6

I opened one eye, but this time there was nobody else in the room. So I went ahead and opened the other eye. I surveyed the room for a few minutes. While I was looking around, I realized that the side of my head was aching, I didn't know why. Then I noticed there was a needle stuck in my left arm, and it hurt. So I sat up and was ready to pull the needle out when a red-headed girl wearing a red striped hat over pig-tails walked in the room. She looked at me and I looked at her and then she screamed and ran out of the room. I didn't have to wait long before a lady wearing an all-white hat ran into the room.

"Junior, I'm nurse Meadows. Are you ok? Is there something I can do for you?"

"I don't know. Um, yes, I guess I'd like this needle taken out of my arm. And then I'd like to get up out of bed."

"Well, no, you can't do that just yet. But the doctor is on his way. He'll be able to help you. Please, can you just wait a few minutes 'til he gets here? Please."

I demanded that I be set free so that I could speak with the captain of the ship when the doctor I think she was talking about ran into the room.

"Hey, I know you. You were here the other night. Stay away from me. Don't you dare put me to sleep again."

"I'm sorry Junior, but it was necessary. I didn't want you hurting yourself or anyone else for that matter."

"I'm not going to hurt anybody. All I want to do is get this needle out of my arm and get up out of bed."

"Junior, we'll do all of that, but first I want to know how you feel."

"Well, other than this giant headache and not knowing who the heck I am, I'm fine. And could you please stop calling me Junior."

"Ok, I can do that. Is there another name you'd like me to call you?"

"Uh, we've already been through this. I don't know what you should call me. Ok, so tell me why you insist on calling me Junior?"

"I call you Junior because everyone calls you Junior. You are the son of the man that was here with the dog. Your dad's name is Jack McCool. I guess at some point it got confusing with people calling both of you Jack. So, I'm assuming that to let everyone know which person they were talking to, they started calling you Junior. Does that make sense to you?"

"Yeah, I suppose it does. Say, why am I here? And why don't I know what my name is?"

Well, the doctor was patient enough to go through the whole story with me. Right down to the fact that I'd left a pretty good-sized dent in the fender of the riding mower that hit me. He said the mower continued on and took a large chunk out of the corner of my dad's house.

"You say the mower belongs to a neighbor of mine. I hope he wasn't on it, is he ok?"

"Yes, Mr. Hopkins made it down into his storm cellar in time; he's ok. Funny thing is, it was you he was concerned about. I guess caring about others is what makes some folks good neighbors."

"Yes, I think you're right. Well, Doc, when do you suppose I will remember who I am?"

"Junior, there's just no telling, but I'd say you're on the right track. May take some time, but trust me when I say you have a lot of concerned family and friends that would probably do almost anything to help you along the way. Ok, I've said enough. Jolene, can you please remove the IV from his arm. Junior, I'm going to let you walk around the hospital a little bit. There will be a nurse or two with you all the time. Don't over-exert yourself. I think the only way for you to figure things out is to ask questions. So if you want to know about something, ask. I'm going to contact your dad and the Mayor so that they can come to the hospital and be with you, might help you remember things."

"Doc, is there a reason you're going to tell the Mayor about me?"

"Yes Junior, I'm going to tell the Mayor about you because he's your uncle. And he'd want to know. And, if there's anybody in this world that can let the rest of the world know that you're up and about, well, it's him."

"What's the Mayor's - I mean, what's my uncle's name?"

"His name is Ajax. And believe me when I say, you're in for a treat."

"Ok, if you say so.

The doctor stayed in the room with me while the nurse removed the IV. Then he and the nurse each grabbed an arm and helped me stand up next to the bed. I was weak and shaky as all get out. For a moment or two I thought I was going to pass out.

"Doc, I know I insisted that I get up out of bed, but I gotta sit down for a little bit."

The doctor didn't say a word, he just nodded his head to the nurse and then they helped me lean back against the bed.

"Thanks, that's better. Can I just have a minute or two to get my head on straight?"

"Junior, you take all the time you need. We're in no hurry and you shouldn't be either."

"Doc, why am I so dizzy?"

"The blow you received to the right side of your head broke the eardrum in your right ear. Your equilibrium has been compromised. It's going to take a little time. But I think if you will be patient and slowly reacquaint yourself to the world around you, you'll be up and walking in no time at all. Today might be pushing it some. How do you feel now?"

"I feel awful because you people have been so kind to me and I've been nothing but short and demanding of you. I'm really sorry for behaving the way I did."

When I finished apologizing, I heard the doctor say there was no need to apologize. Then the room and everyone in it began spinning around me.

"Listen Doc, I'm getting dizzier by the second and I'm feeling sick to my stomach. I think I'd better lie down. Is that ok?" I asked, completely humbled by the moment.

"Sure, I'm going to put both arms around your upper torso. Hold on tight and together we can get you back into bed."

I was very weak, but I held on as tight as I could as the doctor lifted me back onto the bed. Then he and the nurse lifted my legs up onto a cloud that happened to be floating by. When my head finally hit the pillow the nausea I had been feeling lifted. I remember looking up at the nurse for a moment before my vision tunneled into a pinpoint. And then the nurse and everything around her went pop, and I slipped into darkness.

7

After my failed attempt to get out of bed, space and time seemed to drift by like dust in the wind. And every time I opened an eye there was a different person or group of persons loitering in my room. Metaphorically speaking, my room had become Grand Central Station, or is that a bromide?

Anyway, some of the folks talked to me, while others just talked about me. And somehow, someway, possibly through osmosis I slowly began to know who these people were. And therefore, who I am, or at least who I was as it pertained to them.

Then one day I opened an eye and decided to take a chance and open the other eye. I made up my mind that I was going to keep it open. There sitting with the dog was the man the doctor had told me was my father. He was the one constant. In fact, it seemed to me that he never left my side. So I got kind of brave and decided to say something to him. After considering all angles, I went ahead and said hello. But before he could say a word, the dog barked at me.

"Junior, it's ok. Don't be alarmed, she's just happy to hear your voice, and so am I. How do you feel? Something I can do for you? Junior, please don't go back to sleep. Talk to me, please?"

"Sure, ok, I'll talk to you. I won't go back to sleep. I have a lot of questions to ask. Is that ok?"

"Ask away. Anything you'd like to know or want to talk about."

"Well, for starters, why does the dog have that harness on?"

"Oh, that's a great question. And it's a question that is going to take me a while to explain. No, it won't take long because there's really no point in beating around the bush. Junior, I'm blind, have been for many years now. At first, I had a terrible time owning up to the fact that I could no longer see. Then a wonderful thing happened to me. You know what that wonderful thing was?"

"No, I don't know. What happened?"

"You and your best friend, Ricky Reed, went up to a farm in Minnesota where they train dogs like her. And you brought this wonderful animal back to me. Her name is Maggie."

After he said her name, the dog looked at him and then at me. She gave me a short little hello bark before she came to the side of the bed. She put her front paws up on the bed and nudged her nose under my hand so that I would pet her. I did and she was wonderful to touch. And before I knew it, she had jumped up on the bed and was licking the side of my face. There was no doubt she knew me. I just wished that I could remember her.

"See, she's crazy about you and all of your sisters, and of course your younger brother too. Believe me when I say she saved my life."

"You know what? I do believe you," I said.

My dad went on to tell me all about each of my siblings. And, I might add, in wonderful detail. And when he finished, I was extremely overjoyed that I had a brother and sisters. Then he went into detail about my uncles and what they do for a living. For some reason, I knew that one of my uncles was the Mayor. How I knew - I'm not sure. Then he told me about this guy named Ricky Reed. Dad said Ricky is a tall skinny guy that is funnier than all get out. And that he looks like a puppet named Howdy Doody. My dad said this Ricky guy and I have been best friends since we were little kids.

"Dad - is it ok if I call you Dad?"

"Of course it's ok. What else would you call me? On second thought, don't answer that. Yes, you should call me Dad."

"Ok, Dad, what I was wondering is... well, do I have a girlfriend?"

"Yes, you do. I'm sorry, I was going to tell you all about her. Lily is away, went to Paris to meet with leaders from around the world to negotiate a way out of the war in Vietnam."

"Lily, I like that. Dad, can you help me out, who is at war? And why are they at war?"

"Junior, the United States is at war with the communists from North Vietnam. Why we're at war is a question I can't answer. I just wish we'd hurry up and win the war so our young men and women could come home. That's what I wish."

"Say, didn't you tell me that my brother is in the army?"

"Yes, Buck is in the army. Thank goodness, he's stationed in Germany. He's training to be an air traffic controller. I talked to him a week or so before the tornado hit town. He told me he plans on re-enlisting. Scares me to think about it, but he says he owes it to our country to help out in any way he can. I was too young for one war and too old for the next. Tell you the truth, it's no skin off my back. I'd a given it hell had I gone off to war, but I didn't. Maybe I was lucky at that."

"Dad, there's a question in the back of my mind that I want to ask. Only problem is, right at the moment I can't seem to reach that question."

Dad and Maggie both cocked their heads to the side, wondering what I meant.

"Dad, I don't know if it's just me or maybe it's too warm in this room. Anyway, I'm so tired I can hardly keep my eyes open. Would you mind if I close my eyes and lay back for a minute?"

I couldn't hear exactly what he said, but it felt sincere and nice. I remember touching the dog for a second or two before I sailed away.

Can't Find my Way Home

8

My dad

I opened an eye and the man and his dog were still sitting there. I suppose they were both wondering where I'd been. Well, the last I remember somebody was driving me down a highway through the middle of some beautiful rolling hills. Occasionally the countryside would flatten out and there would be a bright white farmhouse; and of course, there were big red barns too. All the houses were surrounded by row after row of lush, deep green corn fields. As we drove, I stuck my head out the window and gazed at the mysterious queue on the horizon where the blue sky and the green earth shake hands.

Then I looked straight up and there were a few small puffy white clouds slowly rolling by; looked like the clouds were being pulled across the sky by a kite string. Stretched my neck out the window looking for the little boys and girls that must have been pulling the string, but I couldn't find 'em. I remember taking in a big breath of air and tasting the sweet yellow corn that was growing all around me. Then, for some reason I became so excited I could hardly sit still. I guess I was going to fly somewhere; because everywhere I looked there were airplanes. Didn't know where I was going, but I knew I was gonna go.

Suddenly the car I was in came to an abrupt stop. I looked out the window and there sitting in a tree all by his lonesome was a canary. The little bird was just as handsome as can be. He was the color of a blazing golden sun. He was wearing a little black hat, and his wings and tail were black too. I said, *"I'll bet somebody's out looking for that little bird."* Anyway, I was sure I was talking to myself, but I was wrong. I couldn't see the person driving the car, but I definitely heard him say, "Junior, that's not somebody's pet. That's a type of wild canary called an American goldfinch. Why, I'll bet you can't find a tree without a goldfinch sitting in it."

Well, as soon as he was done talking I made a point of opening my eyes as wide as I could. And he was right. Everywhere I looked there sat one of those beautiful little birds. Over and over they sang - *per-chik-or-ree, bay-bee, chik-chik-chik, per-chik- or-ree, bay-bee, chik-chik-chik*. And right out loud I said, "Sure sounds like a canary to me."

"Junior, are you talking to yourself again?" someone in the car asked.

I looked around, but there was nobody in the car with me. Then somebody said, "His eyes are wide open, but he's still asleep. Wake up Junior, please wake up."

My eyes were wide open, but no matter how hard I tried I could not wake up. I went from excited about going somewhere to being frustrated beyond words. I finally begged for help.

"I want to wake up. Please help me."

Then I heard a soft comforting voice that for some reason felt very familiar. I asked myself, *who is talking to me*? I know that voice. It was delicate yet reassuring. It was definitely a female; who is she? Then I remembered the question I wanted to ask my dad. And as supple and warm as can be my mom once again urged me to wake up.

"Junior, you can do it. Everyone is here for you. You don't have to hurry, just relax and let yourself wake up," she coaxed.

I did relax and then with only a tiny bit of effort my eyes opened. There were so many people in the room I couldn't count them all. My dad and Maggie were sitting next to the bed. And my sisters, Madison and Randi, were standing at the foot of the bed. Doc Mayland and the nurse were standing behind my dad, and over in the far corner of the room stood Ricky and my Uncle Tommy. Then I looked in the doorway and my Uncle Ajax yelled, "Junior, it's about doggone time you woke up. Where have you been? And why didn't you take little Jax and me with you?"

Can't Find my Way Home

Everyone laughed right out loud with him. It's kind of late in the game for me to explain who little Jax is, but I'll try. Little Jax is a doll that my uncle carries around with him; at all times. You could say the doll is a friend, but the doll is actually more like his alter-ego. Yes, it's a little bit strange; maybe even a whole lot strange. There's more to the story, but for now I'll leave it at that.

9

My hospital room

As you already know, with the help of my mother, I woke up. And when I woke up, I remembered who everyone was, and of course, who I was. At first, I tried to explain where I'd been, but I could see by the looks on their faces that my story was just a little too bizarre for them to relate to. So, I ended up just saying that I'd been in a dream world. Madison immediately chimed in.

"Well, I guess nothing has changed."

Everyone got a kick out of that. She was pretty much right. I do live in a dream world, but not all the time. Didn't take long for my dad to ask me how and why I suddenly decided to wake up. When I told him Mom had helped me wake up he started crying. I haven't gone into that part of my dad's behavior with you, but let's just say that it came with the severe brain damage he suffered in the accident. Everyone there has heard my dad cry before, so there wasn't a big fuss or anything. And as usual he stopped after only a half a minute or so. After I woke up, I spent another three days in the hospital. Guess they wanted to make sure I really was ok. Took pictures of the inside of my head, and I think when they saw that my head was empty, they decided to let me go home.

I spent two weeks at home recuperating before Doc Mayland gave me the ok to fly out to California. I made arrangements with my sister Dezi to meet me at the airport in San Francisco, and boy was I excited. Ricky was going to do a two for one. He was gonna drop me at the airport and then continue on over to Davenport to spend the weekend with his aunt and uncle. My flight was supposed to leave at ten in the morning and arrive in San Francisco at one in the afternoon, local time. The night before I was leaving, everyone showed up at Dad's and we had a nice family get-together. I was given letters each of them had written to Dezi. Along with the letters I had at least a dozen small gifts I was supposed to deliver. I told them I wasn't the U.S. mail, but as usual nobody listened.

Bright and early the next morning Ricky parked on Maple Street, right in front of my apartment. When he walked sideways through my front door, he gave me the usual wave and howdy pardner. Guess I haven't told you about the way he walks. Well, he walks sideways; and I mean all the time. His left shoulder is always leading the way. When he's walking along, it kinda looks like he's talking to somebody and that somebody is at all times to his right. He says he doesn't walk that way, but he says a lot of things that aren't quite accurate. Only took us a few minutes to load my stuff into the trunk. I was going to get in the car, but Ricky was staring at me.

"What is it Ricky?" I asked.

"Junior, do you wanna stop by the diner before we get on the road? You could get a cup of coffee and a bite to eat. You know California is a long, long ways away," Ricky said, as if I was going to walk there.

"No thanks Ricky, I'm fine. But I think we have time if you want to get some coffee."

"Uh, no thanks Junior, you could float a boat on all the coffee I already drank at the diner."

"What! Wait a second. You mean to tell me you already went and had coffee without me? What about how far it is to California and such?"

"Well, Junior, I figured I wasn't goin' to California, so I might as well go have some coffee and a bite to eat; didn't mean nothin' by it."

"You know what Ricky?"

"What?"

"I'd say chicken butt, but... Oh never mind. You ready to go?"

"Sure am, just been waiting on you is all," he said, as free and easy as a cool breeze.

I had promised my dad that I would drop by before I took off for California. Ricky drove us over to Dad's.

He and Maggie were sitting on the front porch waiting for us. Ricky and I waved at Dad and somehow, he knew and waved back. Not sure if Maggie waved or not, but to me it looked like she might have.

"Hey Dad, how long have you been waiting out here?"

"As a matter of fact, Maggie and I walked out the door just before you drove up. Listen, I know you have a drive and a long flight ahead of you. I just want you to promise me you'll call as soon as you get to Dezi's house. Ok?"

"Dad, I told you last night that I will call as soon as I get there. Everything is going to be ok. Why are you so worried?" I asked

"I don't know Junior, I just am."

He stopped and pet Maggie while he visited that strange dark world of his. And then he said, "Junior, I know you'll be ok, but for whatever reason I don't think a handshake will cover what's going on inside of me today. So, can you give your dad a hug before you go?"

"Gee whiz, of course I can give you a hug."

He stood up and I gave him a big hug and when I let go of him he began to cry. I looked away for a moment and Ricky was crying too. And when I looked back at my dad he had one hand over his eyes and the other hand was waving for me to go.

"Dad, I can't leave you here like this. I'm going to be ok, I promise."

"I know, Junior. Please, go and have fun. In fact, have the time of your life," he said as he forced out a small smile.

"Thanks for smiling, Jack. There's no way I could have left with you carryin' on like that," Ricky said, as his chest heaved.

Dad was silent and contemplative. I thought for sure that he was going to start crying again. Then as if a light switch had been flipped on he suddenly laughed out loud and hollered, "Junior, you just make sure to call me when you get there. Now I want both of you knuckleheads to get the heck out of here. And that's an order."

Dad barked out the order with such great vigor, I think Maggie felt obligated to followed suit. And so she did.

Crestfield

10

To the airport, California here I come
We took off out of Crestfield and headed for the airport in Des Moines. To tell you I was excited would be quite an understatement. I could barely control the buzz I was feeling. And as we drove through the rolling hills, it seemed to me that I had never experienced a nicer day. I fell asleep for a bit but woke up when I heard a big airplane go roaring over our heads. Ricky looked over at me. I guess he was checking to see if I was awake.

"Junior, you ever been in an airplane?"

"No, I haven't. Have you?"

"Yeah, it was a spooky experience. They're bigger inside than you think. You know with all those rows of seats it takes a long time to walk to the back where the bathroom is."

"Is it scary? I mean what's it like when you look out the window?" I asked, a little concerned.

"Well, all I remember is looking out the window and seeing people walkin' around. Wasn't too scary, just a little."

"Wait a minute, from inside the plane you could actually see people walking around?"

"Sure could, lots of them."

"Where'd you fly to?"

"Wha-da-ya mean - where'd I fly to?"

"You were in a plane, weren't you?"

"Sure was."

"Well then, where'd you go?"

"Didn't go anywhere, paid a nickel at the fair and just walked through an old airplane."

"Gosh! You know what Ricky?"

"What?"

"Never mind. You'd think after all these years I would have learned. But, I guess not."

"Learned what, Junior?"

"Nothing Ricky, nothing at all. Hey, that sign we just drove by said airport next exit. Geez this is exciting. You better slow down a little bit."

"Hey, who's peelin' this pig? I got us this far, didn't I?"

"You sure did Ricky, you sure enough did. And thank you."

"Junior, you know you don't have to thank me. This is fun, almost as much fun as walking you through that old airplane at the fair trick."

"Why I oughta! You know what Ricky?"

"What?" he asked in a worried voice.

I hesitated; I wanted him to wriggle on the hook for a little while before I reeled him in.

"What?" he asked again.

"I was just going to say that you're a lot smarter than you look."

He didn't say anything back. I guess he was running what I'd just said through that crazy head of his. He came to a stop at the parking lot and took a ticket out of the machine. He pulled into a parking place close to the terminal. We both got out and stretched and then he looked over the car at me.

"Junior, that smarter than I look thing you just said wasn't a compliment, was it?"

"If you think about it, well, it could be."

He didn't say anything; he just stuck his index finger against his temple and blinked his eyes the way the scarecrow in the Wizard of Oz did. Then with a twinkle in his eye he smiled and said, "Let's go inside and find out what airplane is taking you to Cal-i-for-ni-a."

"Sounds good to me, in fact that sounds mighty good to me," I said, as a big smile spread across my face.

11

Strangers in the Des Moines airport

"Hey Grasshopper, lookie what just walked through them doors, two unsuspectin' – gen-u-ine corn-fed dummies."

"Grits, Vladimir is 'spectin' us ta come straight home. Please don't go gettin' any of dem crazy ideas in yo headt. You gonna get de two of us in trouble."

"All right, you listen ta me and you listen good. Don't be frettin' 'bout any crazy ideas you think I might be havin'. And b'sides, ol' Vladimir ain't here, is he? And what he don't know won't hurt him. You get my drift? So right here and now I'm the boss. Is that clear?"

"Sure, but–"

"Ain't no buts' 'bout it. Y'all just do what I tell ya!"

"Sure Grits, sure ting."

•

"Gosh Ricky, I'm not sure I've ever seen so many people hurrying to get somewhere. Hope they know where they're going, cuz I sure don't."

"Me neither," Ricky said in his lost voice.

"Ricky, just look for American Airlines and I'll take care of the rest."

Eventually we ran into a police officer and asked him. He was more than helpful; in fact, he walked us all the way to the American Airlines booth and introduced us to the agent. She was awful nice and took care of everything. She checked my suitcase through to San Francisco and stamped my ticket. Then she told me exactly where to go to wait for the plane. I kept the small carry bag with me. Then Ricky, Officer Fowler, and I walked all the way to a far corner of the airport. That's where I was supposed to board the plane. Boy, excited doesn't do justice to the way I was feeling.

•

"Grits, why is dat cop wit dem. I don't like dis one little bit."

"Yeah, me neither. Well, let's just wait and see. And b'sides, we ain't done nothin' wrong."

"Grits, the stuff we're carryin' 'round could get us sent to prison for a long, long time."

"Stop your frettin'. We're gonna check this stuff through in a minute or two. And if you think about it, would you rather have the cop with them? Or would you like him looking for guys like us?"

"I s'pose you right. Let's go check dis stuff trough, den I'll stop worryin'."

"Grasshopper, before we check the stuff through, gim-me some."

"What if yo uncle finds out some a dem is missin'?"

"There's thousands here. You think he's gonna take the time to count 'em all?"

"No Grits, I guess not."

"Ok, so gimmy some."

"Gimmy a couple of minutes, I'll go in de batroom, I'll be right back."

Grasshopper went in the bathroom and when he came back out he said, "Ok. Grits turn yo back to me and put yo hand out."

"Oh, right, good thinkin'. Thanks. See, now that didn't hurt so much did it?"

"No Grits, I guess not."

"All right Grasshopper, listen up, here's what we gonna do."

12

Ricky and I sat waiting for someone, anyone, to say it was time to board the plane. Finally, at a quarter to ten a woman wearing a blue airline uniform walked in front of all the people waiting to fly out to California. I was so excited I was ready to jump out of my seat.

"Folks, I'm sorry, but we're going to have a slight delay; seems that the taxi carrying our pilot to the airport has broken down. Another taxi is on its way. The delay should only be a half-an-hour or so. Thank you for your patience. I'll come out for you as soon as he arrives. Thanks again," she said in a sincere voice.

"Shoot, Ricky, I was ready to jump up and holler yahoo. Say, when'd you tell your Aunt Trixie that you'd get to Davenport?"

"Well, I said I'd be there by noon. We're supposed to go have lunch with my uncle and his new boss. But I can wait a little longer. It's only about a two-and-a-half-hour drive. It's a straight shot across highway eighty."

"Ricky, you're already late. Listen, this is nuts. You don't have to sit here and wait."

"I can make it in two hours, easy."

"No Ricky, I want you to pick me up at the airport when I get back from California. And you won't be able to if you try to make it in two hours and get in an accident. Please go now. I want you to get to your aunt and uncle's house safe and sound."

"Are you sure, Junior? Cuz, I'll wait here 'til tomorrow if you want."

"I know you would, Ricky. Yes, I'm sure, but thanks. And thanks again for getting me here. Listen, I'll send you a postcard of one of those beaches full of girls in bikinis. How's that sound?"

"That sounds great to me. Ok then Junior, go have a good time. And make sure you tell Dezi I said hey."

"I will, I surely will."

"Ok then, I'll see ya later, pardner. Have a good time."

He waved and then walked about ten steps and stopped. He turned and looked at me.

"Hey, wait a minute. You have time for that coffee now. Why don't you go get yourself a cup of coffee or a coke or somethin'? No, you wait here, I'll go get it. Whada-ya want to drink?"

"Well, now that you mention it and since I have time, I think a big cup of coffee would be great. I could use something to make sure I'm wide awake. Don't want to miss looking at the people walking around down on the ground."

"Junior, you're not still mad at me for pulling that airplane trick, are ya?"

"No Ricky, I'm just kidding. I'll take one large coffee, please."

"Junior, I don't want to break a dollar. Have you got any change?"

"Sure, here Ricky."

I gave him fifty cents and said to myself, *what a cheapskate.*

•

"I told you the guy that looks like a puppet was just dropping the other guy off. Wait here."

"Ok Grits, but if ya tink he wise to ya, don't do it."

"He'll never know what hit him."

•

"Good morning sir. What would you like?" the young lady behind the counter softly asked.

"One large coffee, please," Ricky said.

She poured the coffee and politely said, "Here you go, that'll be forty cents for the large."

"Gee whiz, your coffee sure is expensive," Ricky the cheapskate said.

"Well, I suppose so. But the coffee we have does come all the way up from Columbia. Taste it and see. It's awfully good," she said.

Ricky took a sip and smiled before he took another sip.

"Boy, you're right. This is mighty good tastin' coffee. Thank you," Ricky said, as he set the hot coffee down.

He made sure the young lady was watching as he dropped a nickel in her tip jar. Then he began searching high and low for the cream and sugar, and a napkin or two. I watched as Ricky walked sideways back to me. He flinched and said 'ow' every time the hot coffee spilled on his hand. And he said 'ow' a lot.

"Junior, you're gonna love this coffee. Guess where it comes from?" he said, as he licked the fresh burns on his hand.

"I don't know. Where's the coffee come from Ricky?"

"Come on Junior, guess."

"I don't know - just tell me where it comes from?"

"Ok, this coffee comes all the way up from South Carolina; got an aunt and uncle that live there too. Go ahead and taste it."

I put in one packet of cream and one sugar, and stirred a bit before I tasted the coffee. Ricky was right about it tasting good. But I had my doubts about where the coffee came from. Ricky stood smiling at me while I took a few more sips.

"Junior, do you think that'll be enough. I can wait here and get you another if you want."

"Ricky thanks, but this is going to be more than enough. Now I want you to go. And I want you to promise me you'll drive slow and safe."

"I don't know about the slow part, but I promise I'll be safe."

I set the coffee down next to my seat and shook hands with Ricky. I walked with him for a little bit and then at the exact same time we stopped and looked at each other and said see ya.

Can't Find my Way Home

He slowly turned away and as he did, he gave me a sad little wave. I waved and watched him walk sideways 'til he was out of sight.

13

"Oh holy hell Grasshopper, he wasn't buying the coffee for hisse'f. It's for the other guy."

"Heck Grits, now what we gonna do?"

"Change of plans I guess, but we'd better get over there, cuz that guy drinkin' the coffee is gonna go down hard."

"You only put one in like we planned, right?"

"No, I wanted to make sure, so I put two of 'em in. We're gonna need a wheelchair. Go find one and I'll meet ya over by the guy with the coffee. Y'all'd better hurry cuz he's already startin' ta nod out."

•

I sat and sipped the coffee 'til it cooled down a little. Then I took a couple of big gulps. I felt great and my mind was so laid back I didn't have a care in the world. Seemed everywhere I looked people were darting about like water bugs. I thought to myself, *what's the big hurry.* Then as if all the people in the terminal heard me talking to myself, they all slowed down to a sloth-like crawl. I don't know how much time passed before I realized that for some strange reason I couldn't feel my arms or legs.

I started to worry which turned into panic when I asked myself, *how am I going to make it to the airplane.*

I turned to ask the guy sitting next to me for help. He had dirty blonde hair and a scruffy beard. He had a lengthy pink scar that started above his right eye and went right through his eyebrow and ended up going an inch or two down his right cheek. He got creepy close to my face, as if he was examining me. He said something to me, but I couldn't understand him. His breath was rank with alcohol, and he had crooked brown teeth. I was going to tell him to go away, but I couldn't get the words to come out in the right order. I guess he decided to help me because he and someone else put me in a wheelchair and rolled me away smooth and quiet like an oiled-up ball bearing.

•

"Grasshopper, take him into that first stall. It's a little bigger than the rest. Think it's for people like our buddy here. You know folks that live in wheelchairs," he said, as he laughed out loud.

"Grits, good Lord, what you just said is blasphemy. 'Tain't funny even a little bit," Grasshopper said, as he cringed, waiting for the lightning bolt to strike.

"Grasshopper, you can keep yer big mouth shut and yo opinions ta yo-se'f. As far as yer blasphemy goes, I don't give a damn."

"Ok, but remember dis one ting. De Lord never takes a day off. Sure as you born, he's a watchin' you."

Grits grabbed Grasshopper by the collar and pulled him nose to nose close.

"I don't give a damn about the Lord or what y'all say. You understand?"

Grasshopper didn't answer him. So Grits bent Grasshopper's face over the toilet and repeated.

"You understand?"

"Yes, yes Grits, I unnerstands."

Grits slowly let go of Grasshopper.

"That's better. Now hurry up and find his plane ticket. I'll get his wallet."

Grits grabbed the wallet and the first thing he did was open the sleeve where a man would keep his paper money.

"Hot! Damn, hot damn! There's pert near eight hunnerdt dollars here. Hot! Damn."

"Gosh Grits, looks like dis fella is goin' out ta San Francisco. Gots a round trip ticket. Heck, dat's all the way over ta California."

"Yeah, he was goin', but he ain't goin' no-mo. Now I'm the one that's goin' ta California.

"No, please don't say dat Grits. What am I gonna do wit dis guy?"

"Well, you cain't leave him here. They'll find him

sure as daylight. People gots ta believe he went ta California. Here, open his mouth."

"Whatchya doin' Grits. Oh Lord, please don't. No!"

"Grasshopper, if I have to stick yer got-damned head in that toilet again, I'm gonna. Now do what I just told ya ta do. Ok, that's better. See, I ain't gonna hurt him. Just gonna pour some of this here whiskey down his throat."

"Stop Grits, he's chokin'."

"Do as I say. Ok, that'll do 'er. Gonna leave the bottle in his pocket, don't you dare drink none. Now you put him on that plane and take him with you. He can use my ticket."

"What, I cain't do dat Grits."

"That ticket you have of mine is only good fer taday. So, you're gonna take him with ya."

"How'm I s'posed ta get him on de plane?"

"Roll him up ta the plane and ask the stewardess ta he'p ya get him to his seat. Just say he drank a bit too much. You know on account he's deathly 'feared a flyin' and all. It'll work, they ain't gonna turn away a passenger that's got a ticket and ain't done nothin' wrong."

"Ok Grits, what do I tell Vladimir? He's gonna be waitin' fo us. But dere ain't gonna be no us, cuz you went ta California."

"Tell him I had a family emergency."

"A family emergency, what family? You ain't got no family in California."

"You let me worry about Vladimir. I'll take care of that when I come back."

"When you comin' back?"

"Well, when the money runs out I'll fly back. Or maybe I'll find me a job out there and just stay. Don't make me no never mind, cuz I'm a goin' and that's all there is to it."

"Lord, have mercy on my wicked soul. Ok Grits, den I guess I'll be see'n ya later."

"Don't look so gloomy. Things'll work out. Here, I'm gonna give ya fifty bucks, happy now?"

"I s'pose."

"Let's see who I'm gonna be. Well, now that's catchy. Grasshopper, you're lookin' at the new and improved, Jack Anderson McCool - Jr."

Grits delved a little further in a different section of the wallet and found another I D. One that made him shiver inside.

"Hellfire, this guy's a cop! I can't believe my busted ever-lovin' luck. This guy is a got-damned cop! Grasshopper, as soon as ya get back you gots ta get rid-a-him."

"Grits, what you talkin' 'bout? Get rid-a-him. You mean kill him? Good Lord, I cain't do dat. What am I gonna do?"

"Just tell Vladimir this guy's a cop, he'll know 'xactly what ta do with him."

"Ok Grits, but what you gonna tell people when dey look at his identification and den dey looks at you?"

"I'm just gonna tell 'em I run out a razors and so I growed a beard."

"Ok, but what you gonna tell 'em when dey ask how you got dat big ol' ugly scar 'cross yo face."

Grits hit Grasshopper in the throat with his right fist. Grasshopper fell to the floor with his hands around his own neck, choking and gasping for air. Then Grits kicked him in the stomach. And while Grasshopper lay there in a pool of his own drool, Grits yanked the fifty dollars out of his hand.

"I'll be seein' ya Grasshopper. You better do what I done told ya. You get this cop and yo-sef back ta where y'all belong. You hear me - boy!"

Grasshopper just nodded his head.

"What! I cain't hear ya."

Grasshopper knew that if he didn't answer he'd be kicked again. He gathered enough strength to squeeze out, "Yes, Grits - I'll get us back."

Crestfield

Grits grabbed the small carry bag and hustled out to board the plane bound for the west coast.

14

Dad calls San Francisco to talk to my sister, Dezi
Several hours had passed since the airplane Junior was
on landed in San Francisco. And still no phone call. I tried
over and over calling my daughter Dezi, but the phone just
rang and rang. She was supposed to pick Junior up at the
airport. I couldn't take the not knowing, so I called the
airport. First, I talked to a nice young lady with American
Airlines. She assured me that Junior was on the airplane
and that he had picked up his baggage in San Francisco.
Then I was patched over to airport security. That's where I
finally found my daughter, Dezi. She was there in the
office asking the same questions I had been asking.

"Dad, please don't yell at me. I've looked
everywhere in this airport and he's just not here."

"When did you get to the airport?"

"Dad, I called to see if the flight was on time. And
they told me it had been delayed and that it would arrive at
about one-thirty our time. My friend, Tarrah, drove me and
we got here at exactly one-thirty. I was so excited I ran all
the way from the parking lot to the baggage claim, but
everyone was gone. I guess the pilot made up the half-hour
by flying a little faster or something."

"Is airport security looking for him?"

"Yes, of course they are Dad. They've been
searching everywhere. They're doing everything they can,
but they're as confused as we are. Dad, don't worry, we'll
find him. Hang on for a minute Dad, one of the security
officers just came in with something. Oh no, please no, oh
Dad!"

I could hear the phone being jostled around, but
Dezi wasn't answering me when I called out her name.
Everything was quiet, too quiet. Then a man that said he
was with security asked if I was the father of the young
man that supposed to be on the flight.

"Yes, I'm his father. What's wrong?"

Before the gentleman could answer me, I heard Dezi in the background. She was weeping and crying so hard that just hearing her made me start crying. And each time I heard her heave and shudder, I did the same. My heart was pounding out of my chest. Then I screamed into the phone, "Somebody tell me what's going on!"

The gentleman I'd been talking to finally answered me.

"I'm sorry Mr. McCool, but one of our airport custodians has found a small carry bag. It has a dozen or so envelopes in it that are addressed to your daughter, Dezi. I can only assume that your son would never leave something as important as those letters behind."

The thoughts that raced through my mind cannot be accurately described. I was mentally going in circles, and each circle ended up right back where I'd started. Junior would never, I repeat, never leave Dezi's letters anywhere for any reason. I was lost and quietly weeping when someone touched me on the shoulder. I jumped across the kitchen. Because my hearing is extra sensitive, it's near impossible for a person to sneak up on me. A year ago, I had a similar thing happen I screamed, "Stay away from me! Get back! Who are you?"

"Dad, it's me Madison. Randi is here too. Geez, what's wrong? What has you so spooked? Dad, come sit down. Why is the phone off the hook? Hello, is anyone there?"

"Yes ma'am, I'm agent Clint Walker with the San Francisco International Airport Security. There's a young lady here named Dezi, are you related?"

"Yes, I'm her older sister. Does this have to do with our brother, Jack McCool?"

"Yes, I'm afraid it does. I don't know how else to say this other than your brother is missing."

"What do you mean? Missing?!"

"Please ma'am, don't yell. We're doing everything we can to find him."

"I'm sorry, please continue and don't leave anything out. I want to know everything that you know."

"Ok, we know he arrived because he boarded the plane in Des Moines. And when he arrived, he picked up his suitcase. What has us confused is his canvas carry bag was found on the floor in one of our bathroom stalls."

"What?! Junior would never leave those letters behind. Oh dear, is my sister there?"

"Yes ma'am, but she is quite distraught. Do you want me to try and put her on the line?"

"Of course I do."

"I'm sorry ma'am, but she won't come to the phone."

"Then take the damn phone to her. Put her on and I mean right now!"

"Hello," Dezi said in a shattered voice.

"Dezi, this is Madison. Ok, I know things don't look great at the moment. But you and I both know Junior, and we both know how capable and dependable he is. He'll show up, I just know it. Dezi, did you explain to the people with security that Junior had a recent episode of memory loss?"

"Yes, I did Madison. But everything keeps coming back to the fact that if he was wandering around here, we would have seen him but he's not here. And I want to know where he is. Madison, if I had just gotten here a few minutes earlier I could have found him. Oh, God..."

"Dezi, please don't cry. Please don't cry. Dezi, this is not your fault. Dezi, please answer me. Dezi! Answer me!"

"Ok, I'm here. What should I do? What do you want me to do?" she asked as her voice trembled in desperation.

"Dezi, let me talk to Dad and Randi for a moment. Don't go away, do you hear me?"

"Yes, I'll stay right here."

"Dad, Dezi wants to know what she should do. And frankly I'm not sure what she can do."

My younger sister, Randi walked over to me and spoke in an experienced and forceful voice. She is, by the way, a police officer.

"I gather from what I've heard and what Dad has told me that Junior is missing. Dezi needs to stay active and hunt for anything that might lead to Junior. Tell her to stay connected to the people with the airport security. Tell her to give them every contact phone number there is. That means all of our numbers and the Crestfield Police Department number too. The more information that is shared the better the chances are of finding him. Tell her that right now sadness and confusion are a normal first step where it concerns a missing person."

Madison cut Randi off at that point.

"Randi, you can tell her. I think the more familiar voices she hears the better."

"You're right, give me the phone."

Madison and I listened as Randi explained everything to Dezi. And the longer she spoke, the more at ease her voice became. And the more relaxed each of us became.

Randi ended the conversation by saying, "Dezi, call any of us if you need to or even if you just want someone to talk to. Got it? Ok, good. Junior is going to show up and you can take that to the bank. Yes, I know he is. Try not to worry, we're going to find him. Yes, ok, bye."

When Randi got off the phone with Dezi, she immediately called Davenport so that she could tell Ricky what had happened and as expected, he went berserk. Randi yanked the phone away from her ear and pressed it against mine.

Over and over Ricky screamed, "This is all my fault. If I'd just stayed there with Junior, I know he'd be ok. I'll bet he forgot who he is again and now he's lost and wandering around asking people for help. But they can't help him because they don't know who he is. Why didn't I just stay in the airport with him? Oh Lord, help me."

"Ricky, this is nobody's fault. We have to stop thinking in those terms. It won't help anything or anyone to throw blame around. Yes, it's possible that he has somehow lost his memory again, but we have to be strong and believe in Junior. I do, and I know you do too," I said.

"But—"

"Ricky, listen to me. Junior has plenty of identification with him. If he's lost, somebody will call us and let us know where he is. And when they call, all of this will be over and done with. Ok? Don't worry, we're going to find him," I said in as reassuring a voice as I could.

"Jack, I'm driving back down to Crestfield, right now!" he screamed, before the line went dead.

15

Unknown distant airport
Grasshopper rolled Junior through the terminal and out to the bus stop. Vladimir was there waiting for him with an intense eye and too many questions.

"Vladimir, I don't know why Grits took off. He said he had family problems."

"Family problems in California, no I don't believe this is true. I will deal with Grits when he comes back. And he will come back. Now, who is this man and why is he unconscious?"

"I don't know who he is, and as far as him bein' unconscious, well, Grits opened a couple of de capsules and put de powduh in dis here guy's coffee."

"Did you steal from him?"

"No Vladimir, I din't take anyting, not one penny. Grits took dis guy's wallet and his plane ticket so's he could fly out ta California. I's sorry Vladimir, but I tried ta talk Grits outa it. He hit me and kicked me. I's sorry, please don't be angry wit me."

"So, Grits thinks he is boss now? Do you have the barbiturates?"

"Yes, dey's in de baggage claim."

"You go get drugs and then come back and wait for me. I will take care of this guy."

"Vladimir, please don't hurt him."

"He is a problem. I must get rid of problem, who would care if I kill him?"

"Please Vladimir, I would care. Don't kill him, please don't kill him," Grasshopper begged.

Vladimir stared down at Grasshopper, his dark eyes rolling left and right, the deep furrows along his face flexing as he roiled in deliberation. Grasshopper stood silent, completely unaware of the fact that he was holding his breath. Vladimir turned full circles as he studied his surroundings. Then as if a fire had suddenly been lit in his mind, he narrowed his eyes at Grasshopper. He wriggled his talon-like-fingers as he pointed towards the terminal.

"Ok, I just get rid of him. Now go and not to worry. This guy is not your brother. He is no concern of yours. Now go!"

16

Bus stop on Airport Boulevard
"Sir, I can't understand you, why are you here? Are you supposed to take the bus somewhere? What's wrong? Can you tell me what happened?"

"Hobnee, hobnee," I garbled.

"I'm sorry, but I can't understand you. Ok, let's try something else. What's your name? Can you tell me your name?"

"Hob-nee, rob-mee, bob-nee, hob-bob-ee."

"Ok, got it. What's your last name?"

"Mic, mic, mac, mac, kill try kill-in. Mac, kill-in, mic-kill-in. Hobnee, heh, hell, help me."

"Ok, I'll help you. But help you do what?"

A low slung black sedan screeched to a stop at the curb. A tall man with sinister clearly written in the craggy lines on his face jumped out of the car and hurried over.

"Hey! You go away from this man, leave. Go away, now!" Vladimir yelled as he pulled a revolver from the inside pocket of his trench coat.

"Sir, you do not have to tell me twice. I am leaving, goodbye."

•

"Pearly, where'd y'all find him?"

"What do you mean, where did I find him? What kind of asinine question is that? I found him right here."

"Yes, but where'd he come from?"

"He was at the airport. Then some guy with a heavy Slavic accent drove him down here and dumped him in. Shameful, it's just plain shameful."

"What'd the guy dat done pushed him down here look like?"

"He wears a long black trench coat and he looks like he probably started shaving when he was about five. He's evil Odell, nothing but pure evil."

"Mercy, don't sounds like nobody I knows. What you gonna do wif dis white boy?"

"Odell, I'm going to help him. You can see for yourself that he's badly hurt and can't move."

"Well, dat old Timex ain't worth nutin', but his shoes is new. They'll fetch me at least a couple dollar, easy."

"Odell, if you so much as lay a hand on him I will break every bone in your body. Now help me put him back in the wheelchair. This has got to be one of the cruelest things I've ever seen done to a body. What kind of monster would push a man into a concrete culvert and then just leave him there. This sure is a wicked world we live in. Let's see if this chair will still roll. Good it does."

"Pearly, where you gonna take him?"

"Well, first I'm going to get him back up on the sidewalk. Then I'm going to roll him to the Jackson County free clinic. He needs immediate medical attention. That laceration across the side of his head has got to be cleaned and sutured."

"What the hell you talkin' - sootyerd?"

"Sutured, s u t u r e d, sutured you big dummy."

"I still don't know what the hell you talkin' 'bout?"

"Sewn up - with the proper kind of needle and thread, that's what I'm talking about."

"Oh, dat kinda sootyerd."

"Odell, help me - would you please."

"And what is I gonna get out a dis?"

"Well, let me see. I know if you help me then you won't have to stay in the clinic and get yourself sutured. You understand what I mean, you big black jellybean."

"Yes'm I sho-nuff do. Ok, let's us just go."

•

"Pearly, where'd you say you found this man?" Doctor Miller asked.

"He was pushed into the culvert over by the Salt. A crueler act I have yet to see."

"Yes, well, Pearly, there's something you need to understand. I'm going to sew him up, but state law mandates that I report this to the police. They're going to want to talk to him. And I want you to understand that he may be involved in a crime of some sort. Or, he may know the person or persons that did this to him."

"Oh doc, do you have to report this?"

"Yes Pearly, I do. Try to understand, it's the law."

"I understand doc. For now, let's just get him fixed, ok?"

"You got it. Loretta, please take this young man and prep him for surgery."

"Doc, I feel somewhat responsible for this gentleman's welfare. So, can you please keep me informed as to his whereabouts?" Pearly asked.

"You're welcome to stay here and talk with the police yourself," Doctor Miller suggested.

"Uh doc, I think I'll take my leave. The police and I don't necessarily get along, if you catch my drift. I guess I'll be watching from afar," Pearly said, as he backed up to the clinic door and vanished.

17

Jackson County free clinic/enter the police
"**I can't get him to wake up**. He's got one eye that's kinda open. Hello sir, can you hear me? Nope, he's out cold," Officer Reed Tucker said.

"Lord he reeks, he smells like he drank a shit-load of cheap-ass whiskey. Must have got himself drunk and then fell down and busted his head open," Sergeant Ronny Detwiler offered up.

"Doctor Miller, do you know this man's name?" Officer Tucker asked.

"No, I don't. He has no identification. The only thing in his pockets was the broken bottle of whiskey."

"Well, since he has no identification, by law he is considered a vagrant. And we've been trying hard to move all the vagrants out of the city. Doc, he has to appear in front of the judge. When do you think he'll be able to be moved out of here?" Officer Tucker asked.

"Hold on there, he has a name," Pearly said from behind the police officers.

"Well now, if it ain't our dear old friend, Pearly Cisco. We've been lookin' for you Pearly," Sergeant Detwiler said.

"May I inquire as to your motivation for knowing my precise whereabouts," Pearly asked.

"We were told that you've been stealin' bottles from the Winn-Dixie again," Sergeant Detwiler said as he moved towards Pearly.

"Officer, I assure you I have not stolen nary a bottle. All the bottles I possess are legitimately acquired. After finding said bottles, I return them to the store for a mere pittance. And at the same time my efforts help clean up our fair city. My small business venture is quite legal," Pearly said, waiting of course for the officer's rebuttal.

"Pearly, you're full of shit. Ok, you said you know

this guy's name. How is it that you know his name? And why don't you do somethin' about that damn hair of yours?" Sergeant Detwiler asked as he removed the handcuffs from his belt.

"My hair is free to do as it pleases. In fact, it is the only thing about me that is truly free. Now, as far as this gentleman is concerned, he offered his name to me when I first made his acquaintance," Pearly said with a nod of the head.

"Yeah, well, I still think you're full of shit. Ok, do yourself a favor and don't argue with me. Just stick your hands out nice and peaceful like. Good. Pearly, you're under arrest for petty theft. And you can save your damn story for the judge," Sergeant Detwiler said without any hesitation.

Pearly didn't argue with the sergeant. He knew the drill; he'd been arrested many times. So, he just smiled as Sergeant Detwiler fastened the handcuffs. Officer Tucker spun Pearly around and sat him down on Doctor Miller's stool, so he could ask him a few questions.

"Pearly, how do you know this fella? And, did you see what happened to him?"

"I don't know him. I found him sitting in the wheelchair at the bus stop by the airport. He was desperately trying to communicate with me. And no sir, I did not see what happened to him," Pearly acknowledged.

"Go on," Officer Tucker urged.

"Well, it was at that time that he told me his true and legal name."

"Pearly, I'm beginning to think that you're holding out on the Sergeant and me. Now, for the last time, what is his gosh darned name?" Officer Tucker demanded.

"His name is Bobby McKillin. Unusual, but it is none-the-less his name. I have just come from the library wherein I completed my research. Killin or Cill-Fhinn as it is in Gaelic is in reality a small tourist village in Scotland. The prefix Mc was added to the name to denote that he and his clan are descended from highlanders. In America the name is pronounced exactly as it is spelled, McKillin," Pearly said with an upright snap of the head.

"Too bad you just told us that little story. You know why you shouldn't have told us that story, Pearly? I'll tell you why. Because you and I both know you are not welcome in the library," Sergeant Detwiler said with some force.

"On that point Sergeant, you are mistaken. Mrs. Beasley welcomed me into the establishment today. We have made amends," Pearly said with another snap of the head.

"Pearly, I don't understand. Why are you so captivated by the library?" Officer Tucker asked.

"'Ignorance is the curse of God; knowledge is the wing wherewith we fly to heaven.' That, in a nutshell, Officer Tucker, is why I am so captivated by the library," Pearly said.

Then with his nose in the air Pearly stood up, snapped his head back, and came to attention, still handcuffed of course.

"He's full of shit. Reed, take his big black ass out and put him in the squad car. Doctor Miller, I'll come back for Mr. whoever tomorrow morning. He and Pearly can tell their stories to the judge," Sergeant Detwiler said with a shake of the head.

18

I opened my eyes and stared into a dark room. I lay there for a moment or two trying to figure out where I was. The room I was in smelled clean, but not in a good way. I sat up and then I immediately lay back down. My head was throbbing something fierce. Felt like I'd been hit with a sledgehammer. I put my hands up to my face and nothing seemed to be sore or broken. I continued probing when my hands came to a huge bandage that was covering my right ear and the side of my head.

I decided that despite the pain, I had to get up and find a light switch. This time I rolled over on my stomach and then I turned and put my feet down on the floor; it was cold. I lay there for a minute or so, I had to get my bearings straight. Then I pushed with my hands and stood facing the bed, *so far so good.* Didn't want to fall and make things worse. I turned to the side and slowly walked a step or two towards the foot of the bed. I felt along the mattress 'til I reached the round metal bed frame; it was ice cold. *Ok, I'm doing fine.* Then I saw light creeping around what had to be a door frame. I thought, *must be a switch next to the door.* I was feeling my way along the wall towards the door when the lights came on.

A young nurse with her red hair in pig-tails was standing in the doorway. She stared at me as though I was a monster or something. Wasn't long before she started screaming bloody murder. I began backing up, why, I don't know. Then I put my hands up in front of me to signal that I wasn't going to hurt her. She screamed even louder. Then she ran out the door. I braced myself for what might come through the door next. I thought to myself, *maybe, just maybe, these are the people that hit me with the sledgehammer.* I was relieved when a young man wearing a white lab coat ran into the room. I assumed he was a doctor. He immediately said, "Don't be alarmed, I'm here to help you."

I wanted to say ok, but nothing came out.

"I'm Doctor Reese Miller. I sewed up the laceration you had on the side of your head."

He was a pleasant enough looking guy. Slender build with light brown hair and eyes; didn't seem like he was a threat at all. In fact, I thought to myself, *I think he's telling me the truth. Ok, I need to say something, because now the doctor is staring at me like I'm some kind of idiot.*

I managed to squeak out, "Hi." That was just before the room started spinning.

Next time I woke up I was back in bed staring up at a short stocky guy with dark hair and eyes to match. He was wearing a blue uniform of some kind and the look on his face was not as welcoming as the doctor that I'd seen earlier.

"Good morning, I'm Sergeant Detwiler. So, I hear you decided to sneak out this morning before I could come get you. Normally, I wouldn't mind it if you left, but for some reason I think I need to keep tabs on you. How're you feeling? You had one heck of a fall. Can you tell me what happened? Who did this to you?" he asked in a not-so-friendly way.

"Um, I don't know," I said.

"You don't know what?" he asked.

"I don't know anything. Can you please tell me what happened to me?" I asked.

"Say, he's kinda polite. Imagine that sarge, a polite alcoholic," somebody said from behind the sergeant.

I craned my neck as much as I could. I was trying to look around the sergeant to see who was talking. Then I looked over the sergeant and there was this tall skinny guy with red hair and blue eyes. He looked familiar in an unfamiliar way.

"I'm an alcoholic?" I asked in earnest.

"Ok, buddy you can stop with the act. Doc is this guy ok to be moved?" the sergeant asked.

Then the doctor that had run into the room walked over to me. He felt my pulse and then he shined a light in my eyes.

"Yes, I believe he's good to go."

"Ok then, let's get this show on the road. Officer Tucker, can you help Mr. McKillin out to the squad car. Don't think we need to cuff him yet. We'll wait 'til we get there. We can cuff him before we take him in," the sergeant said, as he chuckled a bit.

I thought to myself, *what'd he just call me?*

"Excuse me; what did you just call me?" I asked.

"Ok, listen, Mr. whoever you are. You can stop with the, I-don't-know-my-name act. Let's go," he said, as he and the tall guy named Tucker led me out to a light blue police car. There was something written on the door of the car, but I didn't have time to read it. The tall guy pushed my head down as he shoved me into the back seat.

"Watch your head," he warned.

Officer Tucker drove as we headed east into a sizzling, burnt orange morning sun. I scooted over and looked out the rear passenger side window as we drove by a huge, glistening, blue-green lake. And for whatever reason, watching the water lap against the shoreline made me feel good.

"Gosh, that sure is a big lake. Say, can you tell me where we are?" I asked.

The sergeant turned all the way around and looked at me as if I was an idiot. "We're in a car, that's where we are." Then he looked over at Officer Tucker and said, "He thinks that's a lake."

I thought, *that's two times in one day that I've been looked at as though I was an idiot.*

"Please, can you just tell me where we are, please?" I asked almost pleading.

"You know something sarge, I think he's being honest with us." Then Officer Tucker looked back at me and said, "That's not a lake."

"It's not?" I asked

He abruptly said, "No, it's not."

"Then what is it?" I asked.

"That is the Gulf of Mexico."

"It is?" I responded in disbelief.

"Yes, it is. What else don't you know?" he said, as he chuckled to himself.

"Well, I don't know where we are. Please, can you just tell me where we are?" I begged.

"We're in Jupiter."

"Where?" I asked again.

"Jupiter, where'd you think you were?" Officer Tucker asked as the two of them squinched their faces at each other.

"I don't know where I thought I was. Where is Jupiter?" I asked as both police officers stared back at me.

"Where's Jupiter?" said the sergeant.

"Yes, where is Jupiter?" I asked again.

"Jupiter is in Mississippi, where the hell else?" the sergeant said as though I was an idiot.

Then he turned to Officer Tucker.

"Reed, aren't you from Nebraska?"

"Yes, why?" asked Officer Tucker.

"Well, because I'm originally from Jersey and he don't sound like he comes from the east coast. But he does sound like somebody that comes from your neck of the woods. You know Kansas or one of them square states. Say, Mr. whoever you are. You don't sound like you're from around here. So, where are you from?" he asked in an aggressive tone.

"I don't know where I'm from," I said in a voice that I didn't recognize.

"Man, you better lay off the liquor for a while," Officer Tucker said, as we pulled into a parking lot surrounded by concrete walls.

Officer Tucker got me out of the car.

"Stick out your hands." He snapped a pair of handcuffs on me and I thought to myself, *I must be a criminal, but I have no idea what I've done wrong.*

19

Police station – Jupiter, Mississippi

I was marched through a small hallway with walls the color of a robust seashell. We turned a corner and walked through what appeared to be the back of a police station. I thought I was going to see a judge. As Officer Tucker pushed me, Sergeant Detwiler said, "Hey Betty-Sue" to a middle-aged woman wearing lipstick that was such a deep dark red it was nearly black. She winked back at him as she pushed up her brassiere.

"Hi Ronny, court is gonna be late taday. I guess ol' Judge Jones done got herse'f stainky out at the goff co-urse laz night. Shelton had ta go pick-er up and take-er rich ass home," she said, just before she lowered her headset microphone to answer an incoming call.

"Jupiter po-lice - how can I he'p y'all?"

We continued towards the very back of the police station. Then I was led down a dark stairway. The further we went down, the greater the sense of doom became. When we finally reached the bottom of the stairs, I peered into a large jail cell full of ill-tempered faces. To describe one as unique to the next would be absurd. They were all brothers in ruin, desperate to find their way.

The moment Officer Tucker opened the cell door they stopped what they were doing. He pushed me in and the smell alone was absolutely repulsive. I gagged and put my hand over my mouth and nose. And they stared back at me with the same regard.

"Ok, Mr. no name, try to behave yourself," Officer Tucker said, as he shut the cell door behind me.

I backed up against the bars and felt the side of my head. I guess it was a reaction to the thought of further damage. Two guys right next to me called me some awful names. They were walking towards me when someone yelled, "I think the two of you had better sit back down."

I didn't see who had sent out the warning, but I sure was thankful that he did. I looked in the direction that the voice had come from. And sitting in the corner was, in my estimation, the biggest human being in the world. He was waving at me to come over to him. I hesitated, as I think any sane person would. Then he said, "Young man, don't be afraid. Please, come and sit down."

I moved at a snail's pace. And when I got close, the man sitting next to the giant got up and ran away. The closer I got the more bizarre the huge man became. He was wearing what was possibly the largest jumpsuit in the world; it was turquoise in color. His hair was coal black and the front was standing nearly a foot straight up over his forehead, at the very top stood a proud soft serve swirl.

"Hello again," he said to me.

"Um, hello. Do I know you?" I asked.

"The proper answer to your question would be yes and no. Yes, we have met, but no I don't believe we have ever been formally introduced. My name is Pearly Cisco," he said, as he stuck out his massive right hand and wrapped it around mine like a swaddling blanket around a small doll.

"I'd tell you my name, but I don't know what it is. I'm sorry," I said, as I stared down at his glistening black patent leather shoes.

"'What's in a name? That which we call a rose by any other name would smell as sweet.' You'll have a name soon enough. Now, let's get to the business at hand. You've been through some horrific treatment by others."

"I have?" I asked.

"Yes, you most certainly have. At present, how are you feeling?" he asked in the sincerest voice.

"I suppose I'm ok, I just wish I knew how I got here. Can you tell me how I got here?" I asked.

"Young man, I wish I could tell you how it is that you have come to this part of our great country. But alas, I don't know. Listen, enough of that. For the immediate future, you need to know what to say when you're in front of the judge. She can be quite unreasonable at times. And today may be one of those times. It is rumored that the judge is suffering from a colossal hangover. So be quiet, don't say one word. Only speak when spoken to. First she is going to ask you where you're from. And you are to tell her you're from Saturn."

"Did you say Saturn?"

"Yes, don't be alarmed. Saturn is the next town directly east of Jupiter."

"Oh," was all I could come up with.

"Next she will ask if you are employed. You tell her that you are seeking employment. And will be gainfully employed within a fortnight."

"Did you say a fortnight?"

"Yes, a period of two weeks. Promise her you will have a job within two weeks."

"What happens if I can't find a job?"

"You will be escorted back to this den of iniquity to wait for your next chance to promise to find employment. Do what I've told you and then we'll stay out of sight for at least two weeks, ok," he suggested in a friendly manner.

"Excuse me, but I'm grateful and all that you're helping me. I'm just wondering why?"

"Why you say, because I believe that we should 'strive to love all, trust a few, and do wrong to none.' And to leave you to the jackals would be wrong. That, in a nutshell, is why I'm helping you."

"Thanks. Did you come up with that?"

"No, I only wish I were so clever. That, my friend, was taken from William Shakespeare."

"Oh," was all I could muster.

I was about to ask him my name when an officer of the law wearing a different uniform than the police officers I'd seen earlier shouted through the bars, "Ok, everybody up, those that aren't able to stand will be left for tomorrow's calendar. Now, you know the drill. Get in line; we'll take five at a time. Understood?" he said.

I stood to get in line when Pearly picked me up and carried me to the front of the line. The others quickly moved out of our way. We walked single file up a different stairwell than before. And when we reached the courtroom we were told to sit on a bench and listen for our name. The first named called by the bailiff was Bobby McKillin. I looked around, but nobody got up.

"That's you," Pearly whispered to me.

"Oh," I said, dazed and confused.

I got up and walked out into the courtroom and stood at a lectern. I said good morning to the judge and she looked up from her paperwork. She had gray hair that had been dyed to a perplexing purplish hue. I think at one time she may have been a looker, but time and stress had taken quite a toll.

"Young man, I don't want to hear you speak unless you are spoken to."

"Yes ma'am, I'm sorry ma'am," I said.

She jerked her head up again and mumbled something under her breath.

"Mr. McKillin, where are you from?"

"Saturn, your honor, it's the next town east of here."

She sat up real straight and as a few people in the courtroom giggled, she locked eyes on me.

"Are you some kind of comedian?"

"No ma'am, I'm very sorry. I just thought you should know is all."

"Why, everyone knows where Saturn is. Young man, I'm tempted to send you back into that jail cell. Now just answer my questions."

"Yes, ma'am, I will."

"Not now! Wait 'til I ask them."

I started to say ok, but I felt tension in the room. So I looked over at Pearly. He put his finger to his mouth and shook his head no.

"Mr. McKillin, from what I see and from what the arresting officers have told me there is every chance that due to your alcohol abuse you have suffered permanent damage to your brain, and in particular, your memory. This court believes you are suffering from a form of Korsakoff's syndrome. Do you know what that is?"

"No ma'am, I don't."

"No, I don't suppose you would know. Ok, Mr. McKillin do you have a job?"

"No ma'am, but I've been looking real hard, and it just keeps gettin' tougher every day. Right now, there just isn't a job out there for me, but I know someday there will be."

"Um, I don't believe I've ever come across anyone quite like you. Are you sure you're from Saturn? Because it sounds more to me like you're from Mars."

Everybody in the courtroom got a kick out of that one; even the judge smiled a little.

"Ok, Bobby McKillin; by the way is that your real name?"

"Yes ma'am, I suppose it is."

Someone directly behind me started to laugh when the judge slammed her gavel down and stared into the courtroom before she stared at me.

"Mr. McKillin, you are free to go, but find a job, and I mean soon."

I stood gazing at her for a minute. I was wondering what kind of job I was going to get. I continued standing there when I heard the gavel come crashing down again.

"Mr. McKillin, most men run when I tell them they can go. Is there something wrong with you?"

"No ma'am, well, maybe…"

"Bailiff! Escort him out of this courtroom. And keep him going 'til he's out of the building."

Before the bailiff started towards me he read the next name. "Jefferson Abraham Cisco, you're up."

I was pushed all the way out onto the sidewalk, and left there. I waited for maybe five minutes before the giant named Pearly came strolling out to me.

"Hey, you said your name was Pearly."

"Bobby, my name is indeed Jefferson, but my nom de plume is Pearly." Then he smiled real big at me and said, "My friends call me Pearly due to the juxtaposition of my obsidian colored skin and my glistening snowy white teeth."

"Oh," I said, as he dazzled me with a smile.

"Bobby, enough of that, for now we are off on an adventure. Then we will do a little research into the 'Korsakoff's syndrome,' the moniker the court has so abruptly pinned on you."

"What do you mean?"

"Follow me," was all he said.

"Pearly, can I ask you a question?"

"Because I believe questions are the currency of knowledge, yes, you may."

"Um, ok, are you sure?" I asked.

"Yes, pilgrim, I'm sure."

"Ok, how tall are you?" I asked.

Pearly thought for only a moment before he said, "I am over twenty hands in height."

"What?"

"Seven feet," he said.

"Gosh, that's way up there. Wow, ok, do you know how much you weigh?"

"That my friend is a question to which I do not know the exact answer. Because I live from day to day my weight can fluctuate greatly. But I'd venture to say that an accurate guess would be that I weigh just over twenty-three stones."

"Stones?" I asked.

"Yes, stones. Twenty-three stones would be just north of three hundred pounds. And if I am able, I shall soon add to that number. Bobby, are you hungry?"

"Gosh, now that you mentioned it, I'm starving."

"Follow me, I believe we shall dine on pizza this evening. What is your favourite?"

"Well, I'm not sure, but right about now I think

any topping would do. So you can choose," I said as I licked my lips.

"Good, but unfortunately my friend, we will have to take whatever pizza we can get."

"What?" I asked, still bewildered by the moment.

20

Back in Iowa/Dad calls Madison

Dad called my office at the Paige County Mental Health Facility. He was searching for solace. It had been nearly seven days since we last saw Junior. Dad was fraught with anger and depression. Under the circumstances, an outbreak of both emotions was understandable. I was going through a similar range of emotions. Through the tears and the occasional fit of rage, he expressed his confusion and disbelief where it concerned Junior vanishing into thin air. He could not come to grips with the fact that Junior may have made a mistake. What my dad was saying is this: Junior has always been the last person to act or react whenever a difficult or dangerous situation was concerned. He is slow and careful to a fault.

What I'm trying to say is that Junior is so overly cautious about the world around him, it is nearly impossible to believe he would do something that could threaten his own well-being. Yet, that seems to be exactly what has happened. Now, as I explained to Dad, there are two sides to every coin. And the side that none of us wants to look at is the fact that Junior is extremely trusting of others. And it's this trust that has me shaking my head.

It seems obvious to me that his trust in those around him is what may have backfired. All of my training tells me there is no golden bridge to relief when it comes to the sudden absence of a loved one. There is no best or right way to deal with unexpected grief when it concerns the disappearance of an adult, or the loss of a child. So, I did my best to listen to my dad and then let him know that the struggle he is experiencing is ok. Then I reminded him that the struggle Junior is now going through is worse than anything we might be feeling. After explaining this part of the problem, Dad for whatever reason became calm and almost happy. I couldn't understand why, so I asked him.

Crestfield

His response was one that I wish others could grab hold of when they're trying to deal with depression. Dad had somehow found a positive in his search for emotional relief. I'd never considered telling one of my patients to look for the proverbial silver lining, but maybe I should have. Anyway, when my dad said goodbye, he was almost giddy with positive vibes. Why? Because he knows that Junior is always, and I mean always, the optimist. And that gave my dad a renewed sense of hope and purpose. I sat for quite a while thinking over the conversation with my dad and decided to call long distance and do my best to cheer up Dezi. Well, the moment I said hello I could tell Dezi was already in good spirits. Why? Because my dad had beaten me to the punch. He called Dezi before I did. He had come up with a plan of attack. And it made too much sense to ignore.

I don't want anyone to get the idea that we were all suddenly in heavenly bliss, but we were feeling better than we had just hours, maybe even minutes before.

21

Dad calls San Francisco to speak with Dezi
"Hello Dezi," Dad softly said."

"Hi Dad, how're you doing?" Dezi asked in an even softer voice.

"I suppose I'm ok, how about you?"

"I'm ok... Dad, the airport security called me a little bit ago. Do you know why they called?" I didn't respond. "Ok, so they called because–" Dezi tried to answer me. I cut her off at the pass.

"I know why they called. They wanted to let you know that because Junior traveled across state lines, it's now a case for the Feds. Dezi, thanks for letting me know, but I don't believe we're going to need any of those people."

"Dad, we need help. Why don't you think we need them?" she asked as her voice quivered like a lost little girl.

"Dezi, please don't cry. All you do is make me want to cry. And crying won't help either of us, or Junior. Listen, my gut tells me that Junior never set foot in that airport, or for that matter California. I think he's still on this side of the country. Where? I don't know. But that's what my gut is telling me. And I trust my gut."

"Dad, that makes me feel worse than ever. Cuz, if I had been here on time we'd know whether or not he got off the plane. And now I don't know what to do."

"Stop your worrying; because I'm gonna tell you what to do. You're gonna do what the airport security should have done in the first place. You're going to go to the police. You ask to speak with a detective named Olmstead, his first name is David. Anyway, you ask him to keep an eye out at the local cheap motels. I think what happened is somebody stole Junior's wallet and plane ticket. How they did it, I don't know. But like I said, my gut tells me that's what happened. The person that stole his stuff is probably as dishonest as they come. And, I'll bet he's dumber than a sack of hammers. My gut tells me that sooner or later he's going to make a mistake. And we have to be waiting for him when he does. What kind of mistake is he going to make? I don't know. But he's going to, that's for damn sure. I know Junior is trying his hardest to get back home. He just can't find his way. So, if you really want to help Junior, you need to get yourself over to that police station. And I mean today. Ok, Dezi, you have a job to do."

"Oh good, now I feel like I'm helping, thanks Dad."

"Great, that's the little tiger I know. You be sure to call me after you talk to the detective. And think positive, you got it? Ok, yes, I love you too. Bye," I said, just before I said a prayer.

22

Jupiter, Mississippi
"Pearly, why are we standing here in the back of the restaurant? I mean we need to go in and sit down. Then a waiter or waitress will come take our order."

"I'm sorry Bobby, but Gino's is what would in England be called a take-away kind of pizza parlor."

"I don't understand."

"Bobby, may I ask you a simple question?"

"Yes, of course."

"How much capital do you now possess?"

I thought *how much money do I have?* I reached into my pants pockets, front and back, tried my shirt pocket too. Then as my head drooped, I understood why Pearly had asked me the question.

"Pearly, you don't have any money either, do you?" I said.

"Regretfully, no I don't."

Then he walked by a row of trash cans and took the lid off of the trash can furthest from the back door. He turned to me and said, "But we're in luck, because today is free pizza day."

He reached in and pulled out a pizza box. He opened the lid and I looked inside. There was nearly a whole pizza in the box.

"Pearly, you mean we're going to eat the pizza that someone else has left behind?"

"Yes, Bobby, that is exactly what we're going to do. Now stop thinking and hold this box."

He put the box in my hands and as I held it open, he reached in and took a half-eaten slice out. And within seconds the pizza disappeared. He ate the whole thing in one bite. Then he reached in for another.

"Bobby, you can stand there holding the box all day and night. But I guaran-dam-tee you none of the pizza will jump into your mouth. So, if you really are hungry, you had better grab a piece and eat it while you can."

He ate the second piece nearly as fast as the first. Then I realized that if I didn't grab a piece, and soon, there wouldn't be any pizza left to grab. After picking up the piece of pizza, I hesitated for a moment and looked at Pearly. He smiled and gave me the high-sign so I dug in. The pizza was pepperoni, and it was fabulous. As we ate, I asked Pearly how he knew to try that certain trash can.

"I know because I have obtained many a pizza at this establishment."

"But how do you know when to come here?"

"That Bobby is one of the many reasons why I keep this small notebook with me at all times. I have a schedule I adhere to. I am, in the world of psychology, considered an obsessive-compulsive person. In fact, I'm so retentive that the mere thought of free styling can make me quite ill. What I'm saying is I work best on a schedule. Now, if you'll come with me, I shall attempt to check off the second item on my agenda. Please, follow me."

We walked around to the east side of the restaurant. Pearly looked in the corner of a big window, knocked twice, and then he offered up a short but crisp whistle. He stepped back to me and waited. A half-a-minute or so went by and then someone on the inside knocked twice and whistled back.

"Come Bobby, Dionysus is smiling upon us this evening."

I thought, *dio-who* as we walked back to the rear of the restaurant. The moment we reached the row of trash cans a petite young black woman glistening with sweat walked out the back door and gave Pearly a hug. After the hug, she looked me up and down and then up and down again.

"Pearly, who dis?" she asked with a frown.

"Mahidabelle, I'd like to introduce you to my new friend, Bobby. Bobby, this is my beautiful baby sister, Mahidabelle."

I gave a small wave and said hello before I stepped forward to shake her hand. And she stepped backwards and put her hands behind her back.

"Go on Belle, please say hello. He is not the gnawing type," Pearly urged.

"I ain't shakin' hands wif or sayin' hello ta no white boy. A colored girl could gets hersef kildt doin dat."

"Baby sister, it is time you let go of those ill begotten, antiquated attitudes. Now, do what Moms would have wanted you to do. Go on, mind your manners and shake hands with this young man."

She stepped towards me as though I was poison. The look on her face was a combination of fear and hate. My shoulders drooped a little and I actually took a step back. I think she understood that I was feeling as apprehensive as she was. And slowly she moved towards me and brought her right hand out from behind her back. And when she was close enough to shake hands, she stopped. Her shoulders drooped a little as her hand touched mine. She said, "Hello, Bobby, I's pleased ta meets ya."

Her voice was so soft and sweet that I just had to smile. As I smiled, she did too. Then we both looked down at our hands and let go of one another. That's when a strange sensation came over me. I couldn't help but notice that her hand was as rough as sandpaper. I wondered how that could be. Well, I found out how, and in a hurry.

"Belle, you get your ass in here and finish them damn dishes," a short roundish guy wearing a white paper hat yelled out the back door.

He stepped a little further out and when he saw Pearly, he changed his tune a bit.

"Oh, hey Pearly, I didn't see ya standin' there. Um, Belle, when you're done talkin', we need to get them dishes done."

He offered up a half-smile and just before he closed the door, he gave me a, *who the hell are you* look. I noticed that Pearly wasn't smiling, not even a little bit.

"Pearly, don't pay no never mind ta Gino. He just

takin' care-a-bidness," Belle said, as she reached for Pearly's massive hand.

"Thank you, Belle, I'll pay you back as soon as I can. Bye sweetie," Pearly said, as he swallowed her up in his arms and gave her a monumental hug.

Belle smiled at us as we looked over our shoulders and walked away. We continued down a dark alley.

"Where to now?" I asked.

When we reached a crack of light from the back of a house, Pearly opened up his massive paw and showed me a five-dollar bill.

"Now, we shall make our way to an establishment wherein I may purchase an elixir to soothe my ever-increasing dehydration."

"A what?" I asked.

"As Bacchus might say, an elixir, something to heal thyself. Then we'll do a little research as to your malady."

Who, what? I thought. "Whose malady?" I asked."

"Your malady Bobby, the one the court has deemed to be Korsakoff's syndrome."

"Pearly, just tell me where we're going and what we're going there to get?" I asked.

"We're going to Ricky-Tom's to purchase an alcoholic beverage. What is your preference?"

"I don't know that I have a preference," I said as I looked up at Pearly.

"Yes, well, I can see that you're addled. Ok, good, that's part of the research. You have three different beverages to choose from. The first of which is Mad Dog twenty, twenty. The second is Thunderbird. And the third, which is my favorite, is Ricky-Tom's private reserve."

"Well, if the third one is your favorite, then that's what I want too."

"Fair enough, now we need to walk at a fair clip. The liquor establishment is on the south side of town. However, on the bright side of things, it is also near my humble abode."

Can't Find my Way Home

I followed Pearly and his shining shoes into the night. And for some strange reason I was very content.

23

Hurtwood plantation – Saturn, Alabama

"**Vladimir, you've checked all the hospitals** on both sides of the border?" Cotton Hurtwood asked.

"Yes, Mr. Hurtwood, the man has vanished. He may be dead. Was long ways down to bottom of culvert," Vladimir said.

"Ok, bring him in."

"Yes, Mr. Hurtwood," Vladimir answered.

"Grasshopper, come in," Hurtwood said, as he slowly stroked his white Colonel Sanders goatee. "Please sit down," he said, as he pointed to a chair sitting directly in front of his massive three-hundred-year-old dark oak desk.

"Yes, Missuh Hurtwood," Grasshopper said, as the beads of sweat on his brow began to drip into his eyes. Playing on Grasshopper's mind was the fact that many people have gone in to speak with Cotton Hurtwood, but not all of them have come back out.

"Grasshopper, Vladimir tells me that Grits decided to go to San Francisco. Was this a decision he made on his own or were you part of that decision?" Hurtwood asked as he reached into a box of Cuban cigars he'd just received as a gift.

"No suh, I never, I begged Grits not ta go, but he wasn't takin' no fo an ansuh."

"Who is this man that you drugged, robbed, and then brought back to Alabama with you?" Hurtwood asked as he cut one end off the cigar.

"I don't know who he is or was, honest," Grasshopper pleaded. The sweat continued to pour from his body and his bowels began to ache.

"Grasshopper, I sent the two of you to Canada to do a very simple job. You wrecked the rental car you were given and so I had to fly you back from somewhere in the middle of this country. Then you bring with you a man that does not belong here. There will be people looking for this young man. I don't like people snooping around, because eventually they start asking questions. I don't like questions. Now, moving ahead, you don't really expect me to believe that you don't remember his name, do you?" Hurtwood said, as the scowl on his face tightened.

"Um, Grits did say his name. It was just such a strange name dat I cain't remember what it was," Grasshopper said as Vladimir silently moved from the rear wall and stood next to him.

Vladimir put his hand on Grasshopper's shoulder and squeezed 'til Grasshopper cringed in pain. And then slow and deliberate he said, "Grasshopper, you know the name, but are afraid to say. Mr. Hurtwood and I are becoming impatient with you. Say man's name so I do not have to hurt you. Say it now!"

"His, his, his name is Jack something or othuh. I swears ta ya dat's all I knows."

"Grasshopper, do you know why you work for me? I'll tell you why. You work for me because when my daughter was a child, your mother took good care of her. Subsequently, my daughter expects me to take care of you. But when you create problems, it makes me think that allowing you to live and work here might be a mistake. Do you understand? Mistakes give me headaches," he said, as he nodded to Vladimir.

"Grasshopper, Mr. Hurtwood would like to be left alone. Please come with me."

Grasshopper began to weep and then he dropped to his knees and begged, "Please don't kill me, please, I'll do bettuh. Please don't kill me."

"Grasshopper, Vladimir nor I are going to kill you," Hurtwood said as his dark eyes narrowed onto Grasshopper the way a Hawk would look down at an unsuspecting chubby squirrel. "We need you. Do you know why we need you?"

Grasshopper blinked and shook his head no.

"We need you to find this Jack or whatever his name is. Now, I want you to go out and find him, and the sooner the better. I can't have any loose ends. When there are loose ends, people start asking questions, and I don't like questions. Do you understand me?"

"Yes Missuh Hurtwoodt, I unnerstands. And I promise dat I'll find him. I'll start ta lookin' fo him first ting in de mornin'."

"No, you will start now - tonight," Vladimir said, as he pushed Grasshopper out of Hurtwood's office and slammed the door shut behind him.

"Vladimir, you know you should probably have gotten rid of the man when you had the chance."

"Yes, I have thought of that many times. But there were so many eyes and ears I could not take the chance. Not to worry, I have heard that he does not know his own name. The fall must have given him amnesiac."

"You mean amnesia, Hurtwood said.

"Yes, amnesia is the word. Not to worry, we will find him. And then when all the eyes and ears sleep, so shall this stranger," Vladimir said.

"He could wake up any day and remember exactly who he is, we cannot take that chance. We have to eliminate him, and soon," Hurtwood said as he lit his cigar.

Hurtwood rolled his wheelchair back from the desk. Vladimir offered to help him. Hurtwood's response was razor-sharp.

"I don't need any help, thank you."

24

Outskirts of San Francisco
"Lady, you can kiss my grits," Grits said before he just had to hoot at how clever he was.

The young buxom brunette wearing a mini, mini-skirt and high heels picked up her purse and stared down at Grits. He lay on the motel bed just as smug and content as can be.

"You have to pay for services rendered," she said as her head bobbed from side to side.

"Yeah, well, I didn't like the services," Grits said back.

"Look, if you don't pay me right now, Leon is going to come looking for you, and trust me, you do not want Leon looking for you," she said with daggers in her eyes.

"Listen, Candy, or whatever the hell yo name is, I ain't 'fraid'a no Leon. Got it? Now, you go tell Leon he can kiss my grits too."

The young lady was obviously in the life. She knew there would be hell to pay if she reported back to Leon that she'd been ripped off, but she was dead broke and there wasn't a John in site. She knew there was no other choice. Leon was not a happy camper when she gave him the news.

"He said for me to kiss his what? Where'd you say this cracker with the big scar is?" Leon asked.

"He's down at the Seaside Inn, room ten. His name is Grits Wetmore," Candy said hoping Leon would rush out.

There was no rushing Leon. He took his sweet time punishing poor Candy. When he was done, he said, "Now you get your money-maker out there and make some godt-damn money."

•

Grits walked back to the motel with his belly full of Chinese noodles. He was fat and very happy. When he rounded the corner and looked across the street at room ten, all was quiet.

"Ain't no Leon gonna scare Grits Wetmore. Not today, not never," he said to himself.

As Grits walked by the office, he heard someone whistle. He looked over and the young man named Allen that had given him the room key the night before was waving him in. Grits walked into the office to see what the young man wanted.

"If I were you, I would not go back to your room right now," Allen said.

"Why the hell not?" Grits blurted out.

"Because Leon is in the room waiting for you with his employed leg-breakers," Allen reported.

"Hellfire, shit, got-damn-it all ta hell; does he know who I am?" Grits asked.

"He most certainly does. I know that because while I was taking a towel to the guy in room twelve, Candy came in here and stole your name off of our registry," Allen said.

"And how do you know that?" Grits asked.

"I know that because she told me so. She said I'd better stay out of the way because Leon was gonna hurt you real bad. And if I got in the way, the same would happen to me. Now, you can see that I'm taking a chance just talking to you. Listen, I went and got your suitcase. It's here behind the front desk. You're paid up for the night, but if I were you, I'd find somewhere else to stay. Leon will not stop 'til he finds you. He has some awfully mean guys that work for him. They'll beat you senseless," Allen said, experienced in the matter.

"When did Candy tell you this?" Grits asked.

"She came and told me right after she walked out of your room. Boy was she pissed. You left right after she did and I figured I'd better go get your suitcase while the getting was good, if you know what I mean. Anyway, Leon will check every motel on the circuit. You'd better leave the area, and in a hurry. And I'd think about using a different name if I were you," Allen said as Grits walked behind the front desk and picked up Junior's suitcase.

"Ok, listen Allen, how do I get outa here without Leon seein' me?" Grits asked as he shook his head.

"Here, go through the back door. You keep walking west to the frontage road. Go north from there; Leon doesn't work north of here. There will be several motels in Pacifica; it's a few miles further on up the road. There is a city transit bus, but Leon will check the bus stop for sure. You'd better get going. And if I were you, I wouldn't come back," Allen warned.

Grits didn't say thanks or goodbye, he just walked through the back of the motel and kept right on going.

Crestfield

25

Jupiter, Mississippi

Pearly and I continued walking straight south at a brisk pace. My watch stopped running, but I believe it was about an hour later when we reached the corner of Sea Shell Avenue and Airport Boulevard, which were in turn adjacent to the culvert where I'd been dumped. I knew this because Pearly told me so. Now standing in front of Ricky-Tom's, Pearly said to hold tight and that he'd only be a few minutes. Well, I waited all of a minute or two before Pearly came out with a paper bag in each of his massive hands. He stuck his hands out and said, "Pick one, any one, and it shall be yours."

"I'll take the one in your right hand."

He handed me the brown paper bag with the rather large bottle in it. I just stared at the bag. So Pearly said, "Go ahead and pop the top. I want to witness this event. Please take a big swallow."

I didn't even look in the bag. I just unscrewed the top of the enclosed bottle and took a big swallow, which in turn caused me to sputter, choke, and gasp for air.

"Whooo-weee," involuntarily sailed out of my mouth. Afterwards it took a few shakes of the head to get my eyesight back.

"My, that's strong. Is it wine or whiskey?" I asked.

"I'd say wine, but I'm not sure about the physical make-up of Ricky-Tom's private reserve. However, I do know that the alcohol present within is twenty-four percent. Which, by the by, is about how many hours it will take for the feelings you shall be experiencing to go away.

"Ok, if you say so. Pearly, which one did you get for yourself?"

"The same as you my friend, yes, I have the same as you. I only asked you to make a choice to see if you were experienced in such matters. And I would say that you're not, which by the way, I have duly noted. Now, we should be off and heading for my abode. Drinking in public is frowned upon. And I might add, forbidden by local law. Bobby, please follow me."

As I looked down into the culvert, I said, "Pearly, why are we going down there? I thought you said we were heading to your house?"

"I'm sorry Bobby, but if I'm not mistaken, I believe I said abode, yes I'm certain of that. Please, follow me," he said, as we headed away from the spot where I had been dumped.

We continued under a bridge and into the teeth of the storm drains that were connected to the culvert. As we walked, I noticed that up ahead there were lights bouncing off the walls. And connected to the lights were voices, lots and lots of them. The closer we got to the voices, the more familiar they became. And as my eyes adjusted to the diminished light source, I saw nothing but disheveled men, and I mean everywhere my eyes traveled. These were, without question, most of the same men I'd seen in the Jupiter jail.

I didn't receive as many dirty looks as I had earlier that day; maybe because I was walking with Pearly? We came to a stop next to a makeshift camp and next to the camp was a circle of bricks and large rocks with old tires and chairs around it. There was a small fire slowly burning in the middle, and just above the fire there was a metal grate with one large pot sitting atop.

Someone from the shadows said, "Hello there Pearly, how'd the po-lice treat ya today?"

I looked into the darkness of the corner where the voice had come from and out hobbled a man with a scruffy little dog sitting on his shoulder. The man was wearing a pair of green overalls, over a light blue plaid shirt. He had a brown beard that reached clear down to his stomach. I must have been gawking because he said, "Young man, where I come from it is ok to gaze, but starin' at someone is considered rude."

Crestfield

My mouth had been open as I stared and I immediately shut it. I then opened it again to say, "I'm very sorry if I offended you. It's just that I have never seen such a long and full beard. It must have taken nearly a lifetime for you to grow a beard that formidable."

"Well, not quite that long young man, and thank you for apologizin'. Takes a big man to say he's sorry, and o'course, mean it."

"Bobby, meet Scooter Coffey and his dog Ralph, who is, by proxy, the mayor of our fine little underground parish, which we refer to as the Salt. The Salt is a crossroads for men seeking information and a helping hand," Pearly said, as the man with the beard stepped towards me.

He moved the cane he held in his right hand to his left so that he could shake hands. And as we shook hands, the little dog jumped from his shoulder and stood next to my ankle and growled.

"I'm pleased ta meet ya Bobby," he said, as he gave me one heck of a firm handshake. "Don't pay no 'ttention to Ralphy, he's just pretendin' like he's protectin' me. Stop that Ralphy. Have you been in Jupiter long?" Scooter asked.

"Well, no sir, I don't believe I have. But the truth is, I really don't know," I said, as Mayor Ralph continued to growl.

"You don't say, well, we have many a feller come down to the Salt that don't know where he come from. I suppose it's ok, long as you know where you're goin'," he said, as his eyes moved from the bandage on my head to the paper bag. "Bobby, do you suppose there's enough in that bottle so's you could share a little with a poor old veteran down on his luck?" Scooter asked.

"Oh, yes sir, I have plenty enough. Here ya go, be my guest. Have a drink on me," I said.

Scooter took a long pull from the bottle and said thank you when he handed the bottle back. I figured I must be the only whooo-weee guy there was in the Salt.

"Pearly, why do you call it the Salt? I mean what is the Salt?" I asked.

"Bobby, follow me and I'll show you," Pearly said, as he headed through the storm drain.

I followed him for another fifty yards or so. When we got to the end of the tunnel, we turned a full ninety degrees south and walked out into an area with overhead lighting that surrounded what looked like a park of some kind.

"Pearly, is this a park?" I asked.

"Sure is. Full of people nearly every day, but at night it's pretty much all ours. The city put this park here because it's so close to the Salt."

He walked around a wall that had to be at least seven feet high; all I could see was the soft serve swirl on his hair go by. I ran around the wall and looked at a theatre bowl of some kind.

"Do they give performances or plays here? Sure looks like the perfect place for it."

"Yes, they do Bobby. And some Saturday night we'll come watch one, from a safe distance of course. Ok, here we are."

We walked around a concession stand. And when I looked up, I was stunned. There in front of me was the largest body of water I had ever seen.

"This must be the Gulf that the police officer told me about this morning. Gosh, I never. Now I get it, you call it the Salt because it's salty. That's it, isn't it?"

"Yes, but there's more to it than just salt. Bobby, where we are standing is one small part of a great alluvial fan. You see there are lots and lots of tributaries that are fresh water. The water that flows from the north empties into the Gulf, and then it becomes salty. You understand?" he asked.

"Yes, I do. There must be thousands of rivers and lakes behind us, but you wouldn't call them the Salt because they're not, they're fresh water. I understand now and I sure do like it. Look at the moon's reflection bouncing off the water. Pearly, is there somewhere we can sit down, I'm feeling a bit woozy and my legs are tired from that long walk we took. Think I could lay down right here and fall asleep," I said, not really sure of where I was.

"Bobby, I have an extra army cot back down in Scooter's corner. I don't fit on it, but now and then it makes for a good chair. Will a cot do?" he asked.

"Sure will, I think I'll go get it and bring it up here and sleep outside tonight."

"Oh, that does sound wonderful Bobby, but it is not to be. You see, the folks in this fair city, the ones above ground, well, they don't like seeing the dregs of society sleeping on their nice little beach, or in their park. As a matter of fact, they don't like seeing us anywhere. I'm sorry Bobby, but those are the facts," Pearly said in a sad voice.

"That's ok Pearly, and I understand, but can I stay out here a little longer?"

"You can stay as long as the stars above shine on your heart," he said.

"You mean I can stay out here as long as there are stars, but when the sun comes up I'd better not be here."

"Yes, that is what I meant, 'tis not in the stars to hold our destiny, but in ourselves.'"

"Was that Shakespeare?"

Pearly nodded his head yes as we sat down near the shore line. We sat for a long time watching the water move with the ebb and flow of the tides.

"Ssay Pearly, would it be ok if we went back inside and ssat by the fire. I wanna let Scooter have another drink or two. And I'm beginning to have a hard time holding my head up."

"Sure, and it would probably be prudent to arrange your sleeping situation when we get back inside. I want to make sure you know which spot is yours. Some of the men can become very agitated if someone takes their presumed spot. Ok, let's go."

"Pearly, let me take one laz look at the moon and

the shtarz. There'sh shomethin' magical about starsz reflecting off water. You know Pearly I can't -*hiccup*- 'magine why everyone in the world doeshn't live here. Ok, well, thanksh, we'd better go back while I can shtill walk," I slurred.

I stumbled back inside and handed Scooter the bottle. Then I stood and watched Pearly set up the old faded green army cot.

"Ok pilgrim, this is your area, all three by six feet of it. Would you like to lie down now or do you still want to go sit by the fire?" Pearly asked.

"Yesh, I think the fire would be niiish. And I'd better get back there before Shcooter drinksh the whole bottle," I said, joking of course. I sat down on an old truck tire and stared into the fire. Then Scooter and Ralphy sat down next to me.

"Bobby, have I got a treat for y'all." He reached into the pocket of his overalls and pulled out a transistor radio. "I don't play it too often, wears out the bat-tree. But I figure tonight is as good a night as any for wearin' out a bat-tree."

He turned it on and worked it 'til he found an A.M. station out of Biloxi. And the music that floated from that simple little radio was wonderful. And as song after song played I said to myself, *I guess mushic really doesh shooth the sshoul.*

I said it because now there were a lot more men sitting by the fire. Some had their eyes closed, some sang with the music, while others just silently swayed back and forth. The music was appreciated and uplifting. Then a new song by The Winston's started playing, I think the name of the song was "Color Him Father". When the song started playing, the singing and the swaying stopped. I think every man around the fire now listened with his heart rather than with his ears. The song told the story of a man that cared for and loved his step-children and their mother. And as I listened, depression reached into my mind and then it clutched my heart and refused to let go.

Crestfield

Sure, the message was a good one, but all I could think of was, who am I, and where is my father? Is he as lost as I am? When the song ended, I got up and handed my paper bag to Scooter and quietly retreated. I lay down on my cot and wrapped my arms around my head and wept as the sadness enveloped me. There seemed to be no end to my confusion. Where is my mother, my father, my family, and who am I? As I drifted into oblivion, I searched over and over, but the reality was that for every question I asked, there was no answer.

Can't Find my Way Home

26

San Francisco

After Dad called me, I threw a sweater on over my Grateful Dead t-shirt and ran to the bus stop. I rode the bus downtown and walked several blocks before I found the police station, which ended up being the easy part of my trip. The hard part was trying to get in to see Detective Olmstead. Everyone kept asking whether or not Olmstead knew I was coming and why I wanted to see him. After a lot of questions, I finally found out where the detectives were housed. The problem was, without first scheduling a meeting, nobody was going to let me see or meet with any of the detectives; they were 'too busy.' Well, Dad said for me to get the job done and by gosh that's what I intended to do. So, I went outside and sat down and thought about how I could get in to see Olmstead.

I didn't have to think about how to get in for very long, because the answer to my question nearly ran me over.

"Oh, sorry about that," said a kid riding a courier bike that was obviously more bike than he could handle.

After he apologized, I looked at the kid and said to myself, *here's my ticket in to Olmstead.*

"Hi, what's your name?" I asked.

"Uh, my name's Billy, what's yours?" he asked as he parked the bike against a light pole.

"I'm Dezi. Say Billy, you must be the youngest courier in the city. How'd you get the job?" I asked with a smile.

"My dad owns the company. So during the summer he lets me make a little money by helping out. I don't deliver any of the real important stuff, but that's ok with me," he said.

"Billy, do you ever deliver letters or stuff to the police?" I asked with a bigger smile.

"Sure do, all the time," he said, as he puffed out his chest a little.

"How about the detectives?" I asked.

"Yep, in fact that's where I'm headed, why?" he asked.

I was going to make something up and try to appeal to his manhood, but he was just a boy. So, I ended up telling him the whole story about how Junior had disappeared. And about my dad telling me to come down and talk to some detective by the name of Olmstead. Well, after he listened to my story and being pretty savvy for his age, he made me an offer I couldn't refuse.

"Ok, you go to the company party with me this Saturday, and I'll get you in to see Olmstead. Deal?" he said as he stuck out his hand.

We shook hands.

"Deal," I said as I tried talking myself into believing that this scrawny boy with the squeaky voice and longish hair was Robert Redford.

After I said deal, Billy replied, "Bitchen, the guys are gonna be stoked when they see I have a date, this is radical." Then he quit the small talk and put his hand to his chin as he thought for a minute.

"Ok, when I walk in the door, I'm gonna say special delivery for Detective Olmstead. The guy at the front desk will point to Olmstead's desk. If he's a big shot, the guy will say which office he's in. Anyway, I'll hand you an empty envelope and you take it to Olmstead. After that you're on your own, ok?" he said with a boyish but sincere look in his eyes.

"Ok, I can handle that," I said, as we started into the building. "Billy, before we go, I just wanted to thank you for being so helpful. And even if it doesn't work, I'll know you tried," I said, just before I gave him a little peck on the cheek.

Billy gently touched his face as he turned a bright crimson. Then he said, "Never been kissed before, well, that is except by my mom, thanks."

Can't Find my Way Home

We walked in and proceeded up two flights of stairs and after some last second confidence builders, bold as a bull we walked in and Billy announced that he had a special delivery for Detective Olmstead.

Some guy about two rows of desks away pointed to the back and said, "First office on your left."

I took the empty envelope and walked back and looked through the glass window into the first office on the left. There was a handsome young guy sitting behind the desk; I wasn't expecting that. I walked in and when he looked up, I could tell by the look on his face that he knew who I was. I was going to apologize for barging in when he stood up and said, "Hi, I'm Dave and you must be Dezi. Come in, here sit down, I've been expecting you.

"Gee thanks, how'd you know who I was?" I asked.

"Your dad gave me heck on the phone for not doing my job. Then he gave me a detailed description of the person that was coming in to see me. He said you were smallish but not too small. He said you have brown eyes, and that your hair was usually brown, and that you have an Elvin face. Well, he was exactly right. And that is how I knew who you were. Now, tell me how you got in here."

I explained about Billy and the rest and as I talked, he smiled. Then we went through the whole story about Junior disappearing and then he made me feel like all the trouble I went through to get in and see him was well worth the while.

"Dezi, I've already got my fingers out in the community. Right now I'm looking for a stranger in town that doesn't know his way around. San Francisco has eyes and ears that most people don't know about. I believe your dad is right about your brother not being on that flight."

"You do?" I asked.

"Yes, I do. Just isn't possible for him or anyone else to disappear like that, unless of course they wanted to disappear. Your brother does not strike me as that kind of person. Listen, your dad gave me a detailed description of your brother, but he didn't tell me how he was dressed, said he couldn't remember what Junior was wearing the day he left. I found that to be kind of strange, but–"

"I'm sorry, but my dad couldn't tell you what Junior was wearing because my dad is blind."

"Oh, I see. Well, that certainly explains a lot," he said, with a nod of the head.

"It does?" I asked, a little confused.

"Yes, I didn't go into too much detail with you about the way your dad described you and Junior, because nobody could remember that much about what a person looks like. Except for maybe a blind person. They have a picture in their head that is far clearer and crisper as to the physical appearance of not just people, but for the most part almost everything around them. We, I mean those of us that can see take too many things for granted. Ok, so now that I understand that part. It will help a whole bunch if you can tell me what kind of suitcase your brother carried with him," the detective asked in an overstated serious voice.

I sat and thought about it for a few seconds and the answer was in my head, I just couldn't corral it. Then I knew why the answer was evading me.

"Oh, yes, now I know. Junior doesn't have a suitcase, but Dad does. It's a royal blue plaid thing with a few lines of light gray stuck in. Kinda sounds crazy, but my dad is very fond of plaid. He said it didn't matter if he couldn't see it. He just wanted to make sure we could find him in a crowd. Yep, I would bet my bottom dollar that Junior packed his stuff in Dad's old plaid suitcase."

"Dezi, you never know, something like an old plaid suitcase just might help find your brother. Ok, listen, I have a call to go out on right now, but I'm going to be calling you every other day or so. Just to keep you informed. Now, I want you to keep an eye out, but if you should see someone carrying that suitcase, do not, I repeat, do not go after them. You immediately call me, ok?" he asked.

"Yes, I'll call you. Say, it's awful difficult for me to get here to the station, so I was–"

"Dezi, you call me and I'll either come get you myself, or I'll send a car. Got it?" he asked as I nodded my head.

We exchanged a lot of phone numbers and then when we were finished, he looked at me and said, "Your dad thinks the San Fran PD doesn't know or care about your brother, but he's wrong about that. We do know and we do care."

I smiled and thanked him for all the help. That was just before he walked me down to the street. When I walked outside, Billy was there waiting for me with a big smile on his face.

"So, how'd it go?" he asked in an energetic voice.

"It went great, I not only found him, but he was really nice about everything. He's going to help me find my brother," I said in an excited voice.

Billy reminded me of my promise so I gave him my address and phone number.

"I know that area. You must live in one of the painted ladies. Gets kinda confusing finding a house over there. What color is your house?" he asked.

"It's light blue, gray, and white. When you look from the street there's a green and white one on the left side of my house and a white one with red trim on the right. You can't miss it," I said.

He told me to dress casual and that he'd pick me up at six for dinner and then we'd go to the party. He was so happy and as he rode away, he just smiled back at me. I did my best to hide my worry and smiled as I waved goodbye to him.

27

The Salt – Jupiter, Mississippi

I woke up the next day with the headache from hell ; just breathing hurt. And every breath I took felt like it might be my last. I slowly looked around and Pearly and Scooter were gone, I was all alone. I couldn't tell what time it was because my watch was broken and I was underground. I tried to sit up, but there was no way. I felt so sick to my stomach, but for the short term I managed to keep most everything down. Of all things, I think my neck hurt the most. Didn't take long before I figured out why. I'd been sleeping on my paper bag and of course the bottle was still in it. I thought I'd given my bottle to Scooter the night before. I just had to get up and find a bathroom, but there wasn't one. I lay there and stared at the concrete ceiling 'til I fell asleep again.

The next time I opened my eyes it was late in the day. I knew it had to be late because it was so dark in my corner. I forced myself to sit up, and then I headed out to the park. I passed walls made of cardboard and some made of corrugated tin or aluminum. I walked by whispers and even a few outright threats. When I finally made it up to the park, I stayed hidden and carefully looked around for a bit. I watched a man pick up a small boy and head for the parking lot. Two women chatted up a storm as they walked behind him. One of the ladies was pushing a stroller. When they reached the street, I thought the getting was good. Now too dizzy to walk, I crawled to the concession stand and went into the bathroom, I clung to the toilet for what seemed like an eternity. When I stopped heaving, I skulked over to the sink and pulled myself up and with one eye peered into the mirror. I didn't recognize the guy looking back at me. I turned both the cold and the hot faucets on and was attempting to wash my face and hands when someone yelled, "Hey! You get the hell outa here!"

I was so startled I jumped sideways and then fell to the floor, and hard. When I looked in the direction the voice came from, I got sick and had to crawl back to the toilet. There was nothing I could do, I was sick and that's all there was to it. When I finally got to my knees, I tried again to see who had hollered at me, but my eyes just wouldn't focus. So I said to the air, "I'm sorry, soon as I can, I'll leave. I really am sorry." I rolled over and dry heaved and mumbled I was sorry a couple more times.

Next thing I know, Ralphy was licking my ear. Then I heard someone say, "Gal-durn-it Bobby, you surely are a sad sight. Don't believe I've ever fixed my eyes on a man as miserable as you look right now. Here Bobby, take my hand and I'll he'p you get back down to the camp."

"Is that you Scooter?" I asked just before I dry heaved again.

"Sure is, come on Bobby, take my hand. There ya go - that's it. Now, if you cain't walk, I'm gonna have to send Pearly down to carry y'all out. Thing is, I don't expect Pearly to come back to camp for at least another couple hours. Can ya do this fer me?" he asked in a fatherly voice.

"I'm sorry Scooter, but I don't think I can make it. You can just leave me here. I'll get back down to the camp somehow," I said, as I fell back down and rolled to my back.

"No Bobby, we gots ta get ya out now."

I tried to answer Scooter, but my mouth and brain were suddenly out of order. I lay there and prayed that I wouldn't be moved or disturbed.

"Listen, Bobby, I have an idea. Ok, well, it's not like you're gonna jump up and run away, but y'all need ta stay here," Scooter said.

I lay there on the floor in the bathroom for a long time. How long? I really don't know. Then somebody picked me up and put me on a flat board with wheels. All I heard was wheels rolling on concrete as I was whisked back to my cot. The bottle was gone and in its place

Scooter had given me a fat little Teddy Bear to lay my head on. I was about to conk out again, but Scooter sat me up and made me drink what he said was bromo-seltzer. Then he lay me back down and put a sheet over my shoulders.

I woke up a few times that night, but for the most part I slept 'til the middle of the following day. When I finally was able to sit up, I heard a few men laugh at me.

"Bobby, I'm sorry to say this, but you look like hell. But, 'it is better to be a diamond with a flaw than a pebble without,'" someone said.

I thought, *has to be Pearly*. I looked over, and thankfully, it was.

"Was that Shakespeare?"

"No Bobby, that was one of my other favorites, Confucius," Pearly said with a big smile.

I rolled over to my side and then I dropped my legs down on the concrete beneath me. I was now sitting up and as I rubbed the sleep from my face and eyes, I blinked several times before I could actually focus on anything. The first thing my eyes rested on was Pearly's waterfall hairdo and his gigantic smile.

"Well, Bobby, I have wonderful news for you," Pearly said with an even bigger smile.

I didn't say anything because my mind told me there was nothing wonderful about being this sick. I had the hangover from hell, no family to go to, which meant I was pretty much lost in space. And I hadn't yet forgotten the misery the song had caused a couple of nights ago. Having said all that, I could tell Pearly was eager to give me what he believed was good news.

"Ok, Pearly, I guess if there's something you think is wonderful that has occurred during the last two days, I'd like to hear what it is," I said just to be polite.

"Bobby, you are understandably quite miserable. And I suppose I am to blame for some of the misery. But something good really did come out of all this."

I didn't respond.

Can't Find my Way Home

"Ok, I plied you with the alcohol in the belief that along the way and of course afterwards I would be able to discern whether or not you were indeed suffering from Korsakoff's syndrome. And my compatriots and I all agree that you are not, I repeat, you are not suffering from any alcohol related illness."

"I'm not, how do you know?" I asked.

"I, we, know because an experienced consumer of alcohol would have wanted more the same night. And he would not have suffered from the effects of the alcohol the way you did. In short, you don't know anything about serious drinking, you can barely take even the smallest drink without choking, and you certainly have not built up any tolerance to the effects of alcohol. That means during or after consumption. You my friend are, when it comes to drinking alcohol, an apprentice. A beginner's beginner," Pearly said with a big smile.

And when Pearly finished, I heard someone say, "Here, here."

I looked behind me and it was Scooter. He and Ralphy walked out from the shadows. Ralphy jumped up on my lap and nudged me with his nose so I'd pet him; and I did. "Hi-there Mayor," I said, as Scooter sat down next to me.

"Bobby, Pearly has told me the entire story about findin' you at the bus stop. We both agree that at that time your memory was still intact. And we also agree that at the time you were heavily sedated or drugged. That's the good side of all of this," he said, as I shook my head and thought, *how could what Scooter just told me be the good side of anything?*

"Bobby, it has to have been after you were at the bus stop that you lost your memory. And trust me, being throwed or shoved down twenty feet or so into a concrete culvert and landin' on your noggin has to be, the when, the where, and the why y'all don't know who y'are," Scooter said.

I started to interrupt him but was asked to please

listen for a bit longer. That's when Pearly told me what he considered to be the best news of all.

"Bobby, we have a new source of help for us hoboes. And it's through this new source that I believe you will find out who you are," Pearly said.

I thought he must be talking about a miracle drug or something; I was wrong, dead wrong.

"So," Pearly continued, "After we get you cleaned up and back to your healthy self, I'm going to escort you to the on-duty psychiatrist at the new facility and get you the help you need. Bobby, I know you're a good person and I'd love to have you around as a friend, but the simple truth is, you don't belong down here with us."

I was kind of sad when he said I didn't belong, but somewhere in the back of my mind I knew he was right. And the more I thought about finding out what was wrong with me, who I am, and where I came from, the more excited I became.

"Pearly, maybe we can go tomorrow," I asked as much as demanded.

"Bobby, I know you're eager to go and going tomorrow is a first-rate idea. But alas, the psychiatrist is only there the third Thursday of the month. I know this because I went to see him. He told me he travels to clinics that crisscross the entire state. I'm sorry Bobby, but he won't be back there again until next month," Pearly said.

My hopes were dashed. I tried my best to think positively about things, but Pearly could see the sadness build as the hope faded.

"Bobby, surely you can linger in hope for a fortnight or two for something that could have a profound effect upon the rest of your life," Pearly said with genuine optimism bursting from every word.

"Yes, yes, I can wait. Pearly, was that 'linger in hope' thing Shakespeare or Confucius?" I asked.

"No, Bobby, that was nothing more than the meek mutterings of plain old Jefferson Abraham Cisco."

"You know something Pearly?"

"What's that Bobby?"

"There is nothing in the world that is plain about you," I said before I heard Scooter laugh and say, "Here, here."

"Say Scooter, how'd you get me from the bathroom back down here to the camp?" I asked.

"Ralph and I went across the boulevard and asked old Joe at the fillin' station if I could barruh the mechanic's creeper. He was mighty nice and said yes. Then old Joe and I come over and put you onboard and rolled you down here. Maybe when you get a chance, you could go over and thank him," Scooter asked.

"I sure will, and thanks," I said, as I thought about how many good people there are on this earth that never get acknowledged for their kindness and good deeds.

28

Outskirts of San Francisco
"Cain't believe I'm runnin' from some got-damn pimp named Leon. *This is a whole bunch a horseshit,"* Grits said to himself as he trudged along the side of the frontage road.

And as buses and cars passed him he continued to swear under his breath. He'd walked a fair piece and he knew it. Then as luck would have it, a kind passer-by in a black sedan saw Grits and pulled over and opened his passenger side door. Grits hoisted the plaid suitcase and ran like the dickens and when he got right next to the open door, the driver stepped hard on the accelerator and sped away leaving Grits on the side of the road.

"Hellfire, boy when I catch up with you, you're gonna wish you hadn't done that. Oh hell, who am I kiddin'? I ain't never gonna catch him," Grits once again said to himself.

Grits continued walking for another quarter of a mile. He could now see a few of the roadside motels Allen had told him about. He quickened his pace and thought of how nice a shower and a nap were going to be. Then he heard the noise of car tires running over the gravel on the side of the road. His instincts told him to jump out of the way.

After he jumped out of the way he looked back thinking it must be another smart-alec driver. It wasn't. It was a car with a row of lights on top. He thought, maybe he should just keep on walkin', when he heard a voice from a loudspeaker say, "Stop! And walk back to my car." He turned and set Junior's suitcase down and walked back to the car. By the time he reached the car, the driver was standing outside waiting for him. The officer was tall, square jawed, and formidable. Grits did not like encounters with law enforcement.

"Hello officer, are you the local po-lice?" Grits asked.

"No, I'm California Highway Patrol. Where are you headed?"

"Well, I was told that there was some nice motels along this here road. So, I set out ta walkin'. Haven't broken any laws, have I?" Grits asked in a cushy, smart-ass voice.

"Yes, you have. Do you see that sign right there in front of you?" the officer said as Grits turned to read. "It says no hitchhiking allowed. And the sign is there for your safety. We've had a lot of people hit by passing cars walking down this road," the officer doggedly said.

Grits studied the officer for a second. He stared into the mirrored glasses the officer was wearing and smiled as he said to himself, *I look just like Jiminy Cricket.* Then he looked at the officer's badge that read, R. Duncan, blah, blah, blah.

"I'm sorry officer Duncan, but I ain't been hitchhikin'. Did someone say I was?"

"Yes, a man no more than five minutes ago told me you were hitchhiking. He says you stepped dangerously close to his car when he drove by you. Is that true?" Officer Duncan asked.

"Why no Officer Duncan sir, it ain't true a'tall. I just been walkin' with my head down."

"Can you show me some identification?" Officer Duncan ordered more than asked.

"Sure thing," Grits said as he wondered which identification to use.

Allen had told him that maybe he should think about using a different name. But that was meant for pimps and such. He was going to use Junior's identification but at the last second decided to show the officer his Alabama identification.

"Mr. Wetmore, it says here you're from Alabama. What brings you all the way out to California?"

"Actually Officer Duncan, fer the most part I

growed up in the Florida panhandle, then I moved ta Alabama. Been saving up fer a couple of years so's I could come out ta your fair state. Just wanted ta see what it looks like when the sun sets in the ocean rather than poppin' up out of it. I ain't gonna break no laws or nothin'."

"Ok, listen to me and listen well. I don't want to see you out on this road again. You find a motel and stay in it. Understand?"

"Yes sir, I do understand. Thanks for being so understandin'," Grits said to Officer Duncan's back.

The highway patrol car sped past him and when it was out of sight, Grits waved a finger at it.

"Jeepers, these cops ain't no different from the others, gotta be pushin' me around and such. Always tellin' me what I can and cain't do and what I oughta be doin'. I'm gettin' sick and tired of it. One of these days I'm gonna let some damn cop have it. But not taday, I gots ta get me over ta one of them motels and stay outa sight for a day or two," Grits said as he picked up Junior's suitcase.

Grits continued walking all the way to the furthest motel north there was. He didn't feel any need to make it easier for old Leon to find him. Grits felt safe and secure when he checked in to the Blue Pacific Motel. He had no idea he was being closely watched by the man in the black sedan.

29

The Salt

Pearly gently shook me and said, "Bobby, I'm sorry to have to wake you so early, but if we are to make it to work on time, we need to get out on the road. There will be many soldiers out there vying for the same job. Come quickly, we must hurry."

I got up and had just barely wiped the sleep from my eyes when I noticed that Pearly was wearing overalls, a faded brown short sleeve shirt, and battle-scarred work boots.

"Pearly, where's your shiny shoes?"

"The shiny shoes as you call them are for play and leisure activities; thusly they have been stored in Belle's home. I am now wearing my work garb. An employer looking for men willing to put in a full eight hours of work would not appreciate my leisure attire," he said, as he started walking away.

I said *ok* to myself as I ran in the darkness trying to keep up with Pearly's gigantic strides. He wasn't running yet he was moving at twice the speed I was.

"Um, Pearly, do you think you could slow down a bit?" He didn't respond. "Ok, can I ask you where we're going?"

"We are on our way to Belle's for coffee and grits. After a quick bite to eat, we will go stand in the queue and hope to procure employment with 'A HIC,' The Alabama Highway Improvement Corps."

"Alabama? What in the world? How long is it going to take us to walk to Alabama?" I asked completely confused by what I'd just been told.

"Bobby, my fair-haired friend, the Salt and Belle's home are on the border of Mississippi and Alabama. In fact, had you walked fifty yards due east from where you slept last night you would have been in Alabama. Our camp is located on the border between the two states. And thusly it gives us an edge when it comes to employment opportunities on both sides. Come Bobby, please, we must not dawdle."

I followed at a steady jog until we reached a row of clapboard sided shanties, all of which were identical in size and their drab gray color. The light was on over the front door of number nine. And as we approached, Belle stepped out of the door onto the small knotty pine roofed gallery. She wore a plain brown cotton dress that reached her ankles, a dingy blue apron, and an off-white kerchief was tightly wrapped around her head. She must have known the situation quite well because she ushered us through her meager front room into a kitchen barely big enough to hold herself, let alone Pearly and me. She sat me down at a small table in the corner of the kitchen.

"Mornin' Bobby, do y'all prefuh salt and black peppuh o red eye gravy?"

"Morning Belle, I'm sorry, what?" I asked.

"What do y'all prefer on yo grits?" she repeated.

"Um, I don't know. Not sure I've ever had grits," I said with question marks in my eyes.

Belle took a step back, she had an academy award winning astonished look on her face when, "Unh, uh," popped out of her mouth. Then she said, "Did I hears you right? Y'all ain't nevuh had grits? Where you from, white boy?"

"Belle, it is considered quite rude in this country to refer to someone of Bobby's persuasion as a 'white boy.' From now on please try to use his given name," Pearly asked.

Belle softly said, "Ok, I'll tries."

"Thank you. Belle, I believe Bobby would love some of your award winning red eye gravy on his grits," Pearly said with a smile.

Belle set a gigantic bowl of grits in front of me. I mean the kind of bowl that I'm sure at one time belonged to a troll. Then she handed me a teaspoon and offered up,

"De small spoon gonna make it seem like dere's mo grits dan dey really is, white - uh, Bobby."

"Thank you," was all I said as I dug in and then smiled. I was starving.

Belle stepped back from the small table where I was eating and tended to something on her stove.

"Gosh Belle, this is awfully good. Where'd you learn to make this?" I asked with my mouth full.

"Why, everbody in de sout knows how ta make grits. But mines is a little diffrent. My secret is de buttuh you might be tastin'. And, a'course a few other tings dat I ain't tellin' nobody," she said, as she pursed her plump red lips into a ring of fire.

"Well, these are, without question, the best grits I've ever tasted, I think," I said, as I gave Belle a big smile.

Then I took a sip of the coffee she'd set down in front of me. It was rich and tasty, not bitter. I thought about the coffee for a little longer and for some reason it tugged at my memory banks. I shook off the confusion and asked Belle how she got the coffee to taste so smooth.

"It's de chicory I adds; takes de bittuh clean out'a coffee."

"Sure is good, thanks," I said when I realized that somehow I'd forgotten about Pearly; that is 'til he spoke up. "Belle, I have two dollars left from the five that you shared with Bobby and me. Here you are, and thanks again," Pearly said as he handed the money to Belle.

He'd been standing and eating before he placed his empty bowl in the kitchen sink.

"Bobby, you need to hurry. We haven't much time to spare," Pearly urged.

"Pearly, I ain't takin' dis here money. Y'all gonna need dis money to quench yo thirst when ya gets done woikin'," she said, as she handed Pearly a brown paper bag. "Dere's a samich and a piece a bean pie fo each a ya. And Pearly, I knows you, don't you dare eat dis 'til lunch. Now woik hard and den comes by fo pizza dis evenin'."

Crestfield

I was nearly finished when Belle held her hand out to take my bowl. When she looked at me, her eyes sparkled like black marbles floating in a cup of cream. And when she turned her back to me, I found myself staring at how tight the fabric of her dress was across her bottom. Then, as if she could feel my eyes on her, she turned and tilted her head a little and smiled. I'm pretty sure I turned a little red; maybe a lot of red. Then Pearly threw his shoulders back and said, "Ok Bobby, we need to get moving, 'all wealth is the product of labor.'"

I didn't ask.

Belle stood in the light of the gallery and waved as Pearly and I lit out into the darkness. I turned and looked back at her one last time and when I did, she winked at me. I thought to myself, *gosh, I wonder if anyone else has ever winked at me.* I knew it was too dark for her to see me wink, so I waved.

30

San Francisco
"Hello."

"Hello, may I please speak with Dezi?" the man on the other end politely asked.

"May I ask who is calling?" I politely enquired.

"I'm sorry, this is Detective Olmstead with the San Francisco police department."

"Oh, hello, I didn't recognize your voice. Um, this is Dezi," I said.

"Oh, good, I thought that was you, but I wasn't sure. Listen, I just got off the phone with the California Highway Patrol. I have some good news, and I'm sorry to say, a bit of bad news."

My heart sank when he said bad news. He must have felt my distress over the phone.

"No, Dezi, it's not that kind of bad news. Listen, I put out a notice to all law enforcement in the entire bay area to be on the lookout for anyone that might seem suspicious and or carrying a plaid suitcase. Well, an officer named Duncan stopped a man walking on a frontage road south of Pacifica. He was carrying a plaid suitcase. The bad news is the bolo hadn't been sent out. He let the guy go."

"He got away!" I yelled in a most desperate voice.

"No Dezi, he didn't get away. The officer has given us a physical description, and we know his name, where he's from, and we just found out where he is. I'm heading there right now."

"Oh, take me with you, please take me with you," I begged.

"Dezi, I'm sorry, but that is out of the question. It's not allowed and it's too dangerous. We don't know anything about this person. We can't have the public involved, it's just too risky. You understand, don't you?"

he asked in a kind yet professional way.

"Yes, I suppose I understand. Ok, but will you please call me after you arrest him?" I asked.

"Dezi, I will call the first chance I have. I'm sorry, but I need to leave. Ok, I'll call you, bye," he said in a hurried voice.

I set the receiver back down. I was going to call Dad when the phone rang again.

"Hello," I said.

"Hello, Dezi, is that you?" someone asked.

"Yes, who is this?" I asked.

"It's Billy, you didn't forget about our date did ya?" Billy asked in a disappointed voice.

"No Billy, I didn't forget. It's just that…"

"It's just that what?" he asked.

I thought to myself, *Billy has wheels and he knows this town better than most.*

"Billy, no I haven't forgotten, it's just that there has been a change in plans."

"What the heck does that mean?" he asked in a desperate teenage voice.

"Billy, just come and get me. I'll fill you in on the particulars when you get here, ok?"

He gave me a soft ok. As soon as I got off the phone with Billy, I called Dad. He was so excited to hear something, anything, as long as it concerned Junior. I gave him my word I'd call the minute they arrested the guy that was carrying Junior's suitcase; Dad reminded me that it was actually his suitcase. Funny the way things work out sometimes. We all poked fun at Dad when he first bought that silly old garish suitcase, yet now it appears that the ugly suitcase might be the ticket that brings Junior home. At the end of my conversation with Dad, he hugged me, in my mind of course. And he reminded me that since we'd eliminated the negative and accented the positive, good things were happening. Then he got back to business and told me he was going to go through the phone tree and let everyone know there was a break in the case.

Can't Find my Way Home

There were good vibrations running through us, and I just knew we were gonna find Junior. When we said our goodbye's, Dad told me to keep my chin up. I'm just beginning to understand what that really means.

The moment I got off the phone with Dad, I ran into my bathroom and put on a little make-up, for persuasion purposes. Didn't wear any make-up at all for a couple of years, but I'm a little older and wiser now and I realize that, now and then, there's nothing wrong with looking like a lady. I looked in the mirror for a moment and thought *that oughta do-it*. Then I ran to the kitchen and got the phone book out. I started looking up all the motels in and around Pacifica; there were more than I thought possible, a whole lot more.

31

Saturn, Alabama

Pearly and I walked down an old country road on our way into the town of Saturn, Alabama. By the light of the moon I could see the tops of trees, and lots of them. When we reached the staging area, we could only see a few other men; it was still dark. We got in line and with each passing minute, more and more men showed up. And when the sun finally woke up and smiled at us over the eastern horizon, there must have been fifty men in line.

Then a rock-jawed guy wearing a gray flop hat and a dark blue jacket with the name Armstrong stenciled on the left breast walked up and said, "Taday we'll be workin' in two's. So, if ya wanna work, find a pardner and stand next ta him." Then Armstrong started down the line and as he passed by, he'd tap the man nearest him on the shoulder and yell, "Ok, y'all get in the truck." He continued 'til he got to Pearly. He stopped and gave me a long hard look. "Pearly, where in the hell did you find this guy? Look at him, half his head is covered in bandages. What's the matter with him?"

"There is nothing the matter with him boss. Just had a cauliflower ear repaired is all. Believe me he's strong as an ox," Pearly said as he looked Armstrong straight in the eye.

"Ok, Pearly, but if he cain't pull his weight, it's gonna be twice the work fo you." He looked me up and down again before he said, "Ok, y'all get in the truck."

"Let's go Bobby. The truck will fill up fast, we need to find a seat and stay in it."

As we were getting in the back of the truck, a guy handed Pearly a flat nosed shovel and he gave me a burlap sack and a pair of gloves. He continued until the back of the truck was full. Soon after the truck was full, it lurched forward and we headed out of town.

Can't Find my Way Home

The sun was shining on all the men riding in the back; I knew we were heading west. I peeked through the windshield and I could see what had to be the same wooded area Pearly and I had walked through on our way into town. We finally came to a stop and the moment we did, somebody yelled for everyone to get out, and quick as can be the back of the truck was empty.

I heard Armstrong yell for the men to line up shoulder to shoulder with their partner.

"Ok, we are gonna clean this got-damn road up so's it can be blacktopped. I want ever damn one of them rocks you see shoveled up and put in them sacks. You get a sack full you carry it back to the truck and get yo-se'f another sack, ain't nothin' to it. I see ya loafin' you gonna get sent ta packin', with no pay. You got it? Ok, then y'all get busy."

Pearly turned to me and asked me if I wanted to shovel or hold the sack.

"Pearly, I'll start off with the shovel. And then we'll switch every time we fill up a sack, that sound fair to you?" I asked in good faith.

"Yes Bobby, quite fair, now listen carefully. You find a steady pace, don't try filling up the sack with one shovel full. Old Armstrong doesn't mind if you go a little slow, but he does mind if you stop. Do you understand me?"

"Yes I do Pearly. So let's give it a try," I said as I scooped up my first shovel full of rocks.

We headed straight down the road like all the others. When the first sack was nearly full, I asked Pearly how long the road was.

"Bobby, my fair-haired friend, this road heads northwest all the way into Mississippi. We'll stop when we get to the border, but that will be seven miles of sand, dirt, and rocks."

"We can't pick up all the rocks for that many miles today. That's crazy," I said.

"No, we can't, but we won't be expected to do it

all today. This job we're on is going to mean steady work for at least a week or two. We're going to be in the money come Friday afternoon."

"Pearly, how much do we get paid?"

"Bobby, it will be ten dollars per day in cold hard cash plus a ten-dollar voucher that can be redeemed at the Hurtwood company store. Bobby, this is a private road owned by Cotton Hurtwood. The Hurtwood family has lived on this land for over three hundred years; at one time, they owned many slaves. We passed by this morning, but it was still far too dark to see. On our way home, you'll get to observe just how grand an antebellum estate can be.

"Doesn't that mean pre-civil war?" I asked.

"Yes, it does. Every now and again, when they entertain or have a large southern style party, Belle is hired to work at the Hurtwood plantation. I'll have her tell you all about the place this evening when we have our supper. At the present, we'd better get busy because Armstrong's driver, Mr. Teerlink, is giving us the evil eye. We do not want to get on his bad side," Pearly said with a tired smile.

Pearly carried the sack full of rocks back to the truck. And as I stood leaning on the shovel, I stole a look over my shoulder at the driver named Teerlink. He was nearly as big as Pearly. He stood with a menacing glare in his eye; the look on his face reminded me of a wounded weasel. There just wasn't a nice thing about him. He looked my way and for a moment our eyes met. I quickly turned away. I said to myself, *no matter what, I am not making eye contact with that man again.*

Thank goodness Pearly came right back, and then we switched jobs. The sack became so heavy so fast I couldn't believe it. That's when I first realized that the shoveling was the easy part.

We worked like mules for the next four hours, and I thought my back would surely break. Teerlink finally pulled the lever on an air horn at noon, and I for one, could not have gone another five minutes. I was hurting beyond words and the moment Pearly looked at me, he knew.

"Bobby, you stay here and I'll go retrieve our lunch from the cooler."

I tried to talk but nothing came out, so I just nodded my head ok. I walked away from the road to a big shade tree and sat down. Once I was on the ground, I took off my gloves and looked into my hands. The skin had blistered up in several places and they ached clear to the bone. I stopped and thought about it for a bit and I felt horrible. You see, Pearly didn't have any gloves at all. There weren't any big enough for him. I thought he must have blisters the size of silver dollars.

He came back with the paper bag Belle had given him in the morning and a dixie-cup for each of us. I just had to ask him, "Pearly, you're not wearing gloves. Are your hands ok?"

"My hands are conditioned for this kind of labor. They're fine, but thanks for asking."

He handed me my sandwich and I took the waxed paper off and the slices of bread were each as thick as a piece of cake. I took a peek inside the sandwich and there was what appeared to be a type of minced ham, onions, and a few dill pickle slices, all covered by a dark and pungent mustard.

"Pearly, what is this I'm about to eat?"

"Belle calls it country delight. It's made from ground ham parts. Go on try it, I believe you shall surely enjoy it."

I took a bite and it was different, but good. As I ate, I realized that I was so hungry I would have eaten almost anything. But this country delight sandwich was just plain delicious. I was nearly halfway done with my sandwich when a guy walked by pulling a small cart with a bucket filled with water sitting on top. Somehow, I'd forgotten how thirsty I was. I handed him my cup he filled it and gave it back to me. The water was ice cold and I gulped it down. I stuck my cup out and he filled it again. He did the same for Pearly before he moved on down the line.

"Gosh, Pearly, I sure did need a break. Didn't realize just how doggone thirsty and hungry I was. I've got to remember to thank Belle when we see her this evening."

Pearly didn't say anything back; I looked over and he was sure enjoying his lunch. I took the last bite of my sandwich and had a drink of cold water. I lay my head back on the ground and watched a fluffy cloud float by.

"Bobby, don't forget your bean pie. It will be a treat like no other you've ever tasted. Here you go, now enjoy yourself."

I took a bite of the pie and it was just as Pearly said, like no other I'd ever tasted. I think.

There was a hint of cinnamon and nutmeg, and the beans were sweet as can be. The crust was buttery soft and flaky, and as I took another big bite, Pearly just smiled back at me. After I swallowed, I said, "Pearly, do we have to go back to work?"

"Yes, Bobby, we do. But I think you would agree that 'a crust eaten in peace is better than a banquet partaken in anxiety.'"

"Yes, I think so," I said, as I thought about what he'd just told me. "Where'd you get that one?" I asked.

"That my friend came from a fable written by a slave who lived in ancient Greece. His name was Aesop," Pearly said just before he ate his entire piece of bean pie in one great bite.

Pearly laid his head down, and I did the same. I turned to my back and set my last bite of pie on my chest. I must have instantly fallen asleep because I was immediately dreaming of rolling hills and singing birds. I was just beginning to whistle along when I felt some kind of disturbance. I woke up and saw a guy running away with my pie. I jumped up and chased him 'til I got to the truck. The pie thief was hiding behind Teerlink. He peered out from behind him as he chewed the last of the pie, and then one at a time he licked his fingers.

"You just ate my pie, you miserable jerk."

"I did no such thing. The pie I just et, was just a

sittin' on the side of the ro-uhd. Somebody must not a wanted it, is all."

"That was my pie and you know it!" I yelled.

Teerlink had been looking at this other guy, and then he turned and put his hand against my chest and said, "If you've got a problem with Alvin, you're gonna have to settle it some other time. Because right now it's time to get back to work." He blew the horn right in my ear and then he yelled, "Lunchtime is over, now get them sacks filled!"

The pie thief named Alvin just laughed as he walked away. When I turned to go back to Pearly, he was standing right behind me.

"Come on Bobby, you'll have to take this up somewhere else. This is not the time nor place. Our day is half over with, and we need the money."

Pearly was right, but I was still fuming inside. The idea of somebody so desperate that they would steal a half-eaten piece of pie was beyond my comprehension. Eventually I let it go. My thinking was he must have been starving and I really didn't need the rest of that pie, but it was awfully good. We worked like dogs for the rest of the day. Teerlink finally blew the horn at quitting time. We trudged back to the truck, crawled in, and flopped down. About halfway back to the staging area I looked over, and the pie thief was talking up a storm with the guys next to him. They stared at me like a bunch of wild hyenas.

Oh, that pissed me off. The moment the truck came to a stop Pearly grabbed me by the arm and dragged me away.

"Bobby, I know you want to wrangle and go to squabbling with Alvin, but now is not the time. Come on Bobby, we have a long way to go."

We started down the road, but I still wanted a piece of Alvin. After a few minutes, I calmed down and figured I was probably way too tired to fight, so I let it go. We walked back through the woods we'd come by in the morning and as we passed by the last copse of Georgia pines, my mind immediately snapped a picture. I felt like I was looking at an expensive postcard. There in front of me was the most beautiful home I think I'd ever seen. Truth is, it didn't look like a home, it looked more like a gathering of beautiful white castles all neatly sewn together. I said to myself, *that must be what Disneyland looks like.*

From the white picket fence in front of the property to the house must have been a half a mile. There was a circle drive that led in to the home and, of course, back out. Each of the roads was lined with magnolia and cherry blossom trees in full bloom. The grass from the street to the house was a green so deep and lustrous it didn't look real. The great white structure had pillars across the front and a second story veranda that ran around the entire home. There were large black storm shutters on each side of every window. And even from the road, the front door looked the size of three. There were trellises going up the sides of the home filled with flowering ivy and four chimneys on the roof.

I came back down to earth and noticed there were men and women working on the flower lined walkway that stretched from the road all the way to the house. I'd forgotten about Pearly, but only while I stared and wondered. Then he let loose with a sharp whistle and an older colored man with large white mutton chops and a shining black pate looked up from what he was doing. He stood and dusted off his bright red jacket before he strolled on over to us. I wondered if Pearly actually knew him. When the man was next to the picket fence, he reached over and shook Pearly's hand.

"Well, I'll be. If it ain't ol' Pearly Cisco come a callin'. How you been Pearly?" he asked with a smile.

"I've been fine Riley, just fine. Working a little harder than I like, but I don't believe hard work ever did a body any harm."

Pearly stopped for a moment because Riley was staring at me. Riley started to say something when Pearly said, "Riley, I want you to meet a new friend of mine. Riley this is Bobby McKillin; he's come to stay with me for a while."

Riley continued to stare for a long time before he actually stuck his hand over the fence.

"Well, Bobby, I'm pleased ta meet ya," he said as we shook hands. While we shook hands, he was staring at Pearly, and finally he said, "Pearly, where in de wide worldt did you find dis here white boy? You feelin' ok? Maybe y'all needs ta see a doctuh."

"Riley, I'm in good health and I don't need to see a doctor, thank you. It's a long story, but Bobby is good people and I'd like him to think the same about us, if you get my meaning."

"Yes'm, I gets yo meanin' it's just dat..."

"Say, Riley, I don't see you folks out here that often. Are you getting ready for a party of some kind?" Pearly said to change the subject.

Riley peeled his eyes off me and said, "Yes'm, we sho-nuff is, s'pose ta be ovuh two hunnerdt people coming to see Miss Hurtwoodt. I guess you knows she just won herse'f a seat in de state senate."

"Yes Riley, I read all about that. Papers said she won with her daddy's money. Doesn't surprise me though, that's how most elections are usually won, with money, that is."

"Yes'm, I s'pose you right 'bout dat. Guess, I won't be runnin' fo no senate, or anytin' else fo dat matter," Riley said, as he and Pearly shared a good chuckle. "Listen, I'd better get back on dem daff-o-dils. Comes by again Pearly, and please tell Belle dat Riley say hello. She sho is a sweet ting."

"I'll tell her this evening. Ok, Riley, it has been a pleasure. Don't work too hard," Pearly said.

"Nice meeting you," I said to Riley's back.

After we'd walked further on down the road, I stopped and said, "Pearly, can I ask you a personal question?"

"Sure Bobby, go right ahead."

"Do all the black people hate me or am I just

imagining this?"

"No, they don't hate you Bobby, they are afraid of what might happen if they trust you. And they're a bit leery of your intentions."

"Did you say my intentions? I don't have any intentions. Why can't they just trust me?"

"Bobby, try not to take their attitude as a personal attack, it is not. Because they have so little, most people of color have learned not to trust anyone, even their own. 'Learning to trust is one of life's most difficult tasks.' I read that somewhere and I believe it to be true. Remember Bobby, you are the new kid in town. Give folks a little time; eventually they'll warm up to you. Ok?" he asked.

"Yeah, ok."

"Well, enough of that, Bobby, let's go have some pizza."

"Yes, that sounds great. And I can't wait to see Belle."

Pearly gave me a strange look after I said it.

"She's expecting us, and I want to thank her for the nice lunch she made," I said in response to his look. He studied me for just a moment more and then turned and headed down the road.

32

San Francisco

Billy knocked on my door at six o'clock on the dot. I looked at him through the peep hole. He stood twisting and fidgeting while he whistled a familiar tune. What is that song he's whistling? Oh, I know, it's rain drops keep falling on my head. What a nut, it's not even raining. Ok, I'd better get this over with. I opened the door real fast and Billy jumped back off the porch. He acted like nothing happened.

"Hey Dezi, you look nice, ready to go?"

"Yes, and thank you. Just a minute, I gotta get my purse."

"Um, Dezi, it might be a good idea if you bring a jacket and a hat," he said in a weird way.

"Billy, have you forgotten that it's summer. Why would I wear a jacket and a hat?"

Then he pointed out to the street. Parked right in front of the house was a vintage convertible with the top down. The car was sitting under the street light, and it looked like a picture you might see in a magazine. The car was a shining two-tone; looked like black coffee and cream. It was stunning.

"Gee whiz, Billy, is that your car?" I asked in a small voice.

"Nah, it's my dad's car, but he said since this was my first date ever it was a good time to take the Bel Air. Isn't it pretty," he said in a way that told me he was as impressed as I was.

"It's more than pretty, it's… Oh, I know what it is, it's handsome. Yes, handsome is what I would call it. Billy, come in while I go get a sweater and a scarf," I said as I ran to my bedroom so I could rummage through the closet.

I grabbed three sweaters and a bright red scarf

before I stood and looked in the mirror. I put the scarf on and then put one sweater at a time up in front of me. *Yep, this is the one*, I said to myself.

I ran back out to the front room and Billy was still twisting and fidgeting from side to side.

"Billy, you're going to wear out the rug you're standing on."

"Oh sorry, guess you can tell I'm pretty nervous. Ok, well let's get going."

On the way to the car I thought that if I could keep his mind busy he might forget about how nervous he was. He opened the door for me like a gentleman and when he shut the door, it sounded heavy, but well-made and tight. He ran around and jumped in behind the wheel and before he stuck the key in the ignition, I asked him what year the car was.

"Oh, it's a fifty-five Chevrolet Bel Air. Listen to this," he said as he turned the key.

The car's motor came to life with a smooth yet throaty roar. Then he revved the motor a little and I could hear the thrust of the exhaust reverberating off the pavement.

"Oh, that sounds nice. This is going to be fun," I said as I tried to figure out how to tell him what it was that I really wanted to do. "Billy, listen, I need to tell you something very important before we go." He surprised me and turned off the motor.

"Thank you, ok, just before you called I was talking to the detective named Olmstead. He said they found the guy that stole my brother's suitcase. He's on his way now to arrest the guy. Billy, would it be ok with you if–"

"Where is the guy that stole the suitcase?" Billy blurted out.

"He's in a town called Pacifica. Do you know where that is?" I asked.

"Oh boy, do I know where it is. When my friends and I want to have some fun, we go there and rent a room in one of those cheap motels. Then we get some military guy to buy us beer."

"Billy, I'm sorry to interrupt, but—"

"No buts, we're on our way. This will be a lot more fun than going to some company party. Oh boy this is exciting. Let's go," he said, as he started the car again. This time he reached over and turned the radio on before he put the car in drive, then he whipped a U-turn and we sped away heading south.

"Oh Billy, I can't thank you enough. Going to your party would have been ok. It's just that…"

"I know Dezi, and you don't have to thank me. This is too important, and to be honest, well, I want to see the creep that stole your brother's ticket and suitcase and stuff. Maybe he'll tell 'em where your brother is," he said with a sincerity I didn't think a boy of his age was capable of.

We headed down the 280 and before you know it, Billy was speeding like a racecar driver.

"Billy, I know you want to get there in a hurry, but it'll take more time if you get stopped for speeding," I said as my scarf nearly blew off my head.

"Ok, yeah you're right. And my dad would kill me if I got a ticket. He might kill me anyway for not showing up at the party. Oh well," he said with a harried look. "Dezi, when we get there, I'm gonna start on the south end of town and then head north. I suppose when we see a cop car, we'll know to stop."

"Yes, that sounds like a good idea. Oh, I hope something good happens."

"Dezi, what do you mean by something good?"

"Billy, I really don't know. I guess almost anything, as long as Junior is not hurt in some way."

Billy didn't say anything at that point. He just knuckled down and kept the car heading south towards Pacifica. We didn't talk and then he leaned over and turned the radio off. For whatever reason, I understood why he did it. We were too transfixed on what was up ahead to think about music. Finally, I saw an exit for Pacifica, but Billy drove right past it. I was going to say something to him but held my tongue. He took the next exit. Once we were down near the old highway, Billy seemed to know what he was doing and where he was going.

We inquired about the detective at five different motels; and we struck out five times. Then we saw a motel all lit up like something special was happening. Billy pulled into the parking lot and went into the office. I looked at the clock in the car and it was much later than I had expected. I guess we must have fiddled around at my house for a long time. Either that or it took longer to drive than I thought. In any case, it was nearly eight o'clock when Billy walked out of the office with a frown on his face.

"They've got all the lights turned on in an effort to get people to stay the night. I guess business has been awfully slow lately. Um, Dezi, this is the last of the motels on this little part of the road. There's some more up ahead, maybe three miles or so. You wanna keep going, don't you?"

"Yes, yes, I do, it's just that I thought we'd find the detective by now. I hope he hasn't already come and gone," I said in a depressed voice.

"Dezi, don't get down. We haven't been looking that long. Let's go find our guy, ok," he said in a determined way.

"Yes, ok," was all I could muster.

We drove north and it was dark as can be. It was so dark that it felt as if we were out in the sticks on some old country road. I couldn't see the ocean, but I could still smell it. We drove over a rise and there were at least three more motels, all of them dark. In fact, they were so dark it looked to me as if they were closed for the night. The wind was whipping around my head and my lips were so dry and chapped I just had to put something on them. And as I rummaged around in my purse for my chapstick, Billy screamed, "There they are!"

I looked up and 'they' didn't really fit the bill. There were at least five police cars. Two had Pacifica on the door and one said Sheriff. There was a California Highway Patrol car parked right next to the last car; it had San Francisco Police on the door. Then I saw something that made my heart begin racing so hard and fast I could barely breathe - an ambulance with the back-door open. Billy drove by the motel and then parked on the street. I got out and snuck around two policemen and then I ran as fast as I could towards the ambulance. I just had to see who they were going to put in the back. I made it halfway across the parking lot when a policeman grabbed me around the waist and picked me up. "Hold your horses there young lady. This is a restricted area."

"Let go of me!" I shouted as I wriggled to free myself. "Let me go!" I hollered as he held on even tighter.

Billy ran up and pulled on the policeman's arm; that was a mistake. However, the policeman did let go of me. But before you could say boo, he and another policeman had Billy face down on the asphalt. It did offer me a chance to get away, and I took it. I ran towards the back of the ambulance and watched as two men rolled a gurney into one of the rooms. I was almost to the room when someone grabbed me again. I started hitting the person that grabbed me as hard as I could.

"Dezi, please don't hit me. Dezi! Stop that, it's me, Detective Olmstead."

I looked up and sure as heck it was him.

"Oh detective, I'm sorry, it's just that I have to know that's not my brother. Please tell me that's not my brother!" I cried.

"Dezi that is not your brother! Dezi, listen to me. That is definitely not your brother."

"Then who is it?" I screamed.

"All I can tell you is, it is not your brother. Now, please calm down. Please?" he asked.

I calmed down and then I thought of Billy. When I

looked back, Billy was handcuffed and lying face down on the asphalt with a big black hobnailed boot on the back of his neck. "Oh, what have I done, I have to help him," I said out loud.

Detective Olmstead grabbed my hand and pulled me towards Billy. "Dezi, is he with you?" he asked.

"Yes, Billy's with me, I'm sorry. Detective, he's a good guy, please let him go," I begged.

Detective Olmstead slowly walked over to the policeman that had his foot on Billy's neck.

"It's ok officer, he's one of the good guys. You can let him up now."

The policeman gave the detective a hard look before he took his foot off Billy. Then Detective Olmstead helped Billy to his feet; Billy gave the policeman a look. The policeman got his key out and begrudgingly took the cuffs off. Then Billy turned to the policeman and started to say something, but I think he thought better of it and just said thanks to Detective Olmstead.

I don't know why, but I wrapped my arms around Billy. "Thank you for trying to help me. You're a really brave guy, you know that?" He didn't say anything until I kissed him on the cheek. Well, actually, he didn't say anything then either. He just turned red. We walked away from the others with Detective Olmstead.

"Dezi, do you remember me telling you to stay away. Well, had you been here at the wrong time, there's no telling what might have happened to you or your friend here for that matter. Dezi, a very violent crime took place here this evening. And we have just begun this investigation. Now, all I can tell you is that I can't tell you anything. Does that make sense or do I have to spell it out?" he asked with a whole bunch of frustration in his voice.

"I'm sorry, it's just that... Did you find my brother's suitcase?" I asked in desperation.

"I can't tell you anything right now. Please, Dezi, I'll call you when I know more about what happened here.

Now, the two of you need to go home and I mean right now," he said in a very convincing tone.

Billy and I started to walk away when the detective said, "Billy, that was a brave thing you did; a dumb thing, but nonetheless a brave thing. Dezi, I will call as soon as I know what happened here. Now go home."

Billy drove slow and steady on the way home. We didn't talk much, but for whatever reason I felt better about things. Why, I don't know. When we got to my house, Billy turned the car off and just stared into space. Then he said, "Dezi, I wish we would have caught that s.o.b. Do you think that was him they loaded in the back of the ambulance?"

"I don't know what to think, but I do know that it wasn't Junior, and that's a good thing. And I know that you tried your best to help me this entire evening, and I want you to know I appreciate all that you did. Thanks," I said, just before I leaned over and kissed him two times on the cheek.

He turned red again and then he looked me straight in the eye, "Thanks. Dezi, would it be ok if I called you again?"

"Yes, of course you can call me again."

I got out of the car and waved as he drove away. He was smiling and I thought that was a good thing, a very good thing.

33

Outskirts of San Francisco

Grits showered and then he put on Junior's slacks, silk shirt, dress shoes, coat, and tie. He looked in the mirror at himself and although he had on nice duds, all he could see was the ugly raised scar across his face. He mumbled to his reflection; *imagine my own damn brother cutting me like this. Someday I'm gonna pay you back, and paybacks are a bitch, Alvin.*

Grits decided to go get a bite to eat, maybe some of them tacos he'd heard so much about. Next to the motel there was a Mexican bar and grill. Grits sat at the bar and munched on salsa and chips before downing six tacos. He drank three beers and had himself two shots of tequila. Before he drank the second shot of tequila, he raised the glass and toasted Junior, "Here's to you, you got-damn cop. I'm here in sunny Cali-for-ni-a, and havin' me a good ol' time. And I ain't leavin', least not fer at least another couple weeks. Thanks, and I hope y'all're enjoyin' stainky old Alabama."

Grits was still talking to himself when the bartender said, "Are you talking to me?"

"No, I ain't talkin' ta y'all. Say, listen, can I buy a bottle ta go?"

"No sir, it's not allowed, but there's a liquor store on the corner north of here. You can get whatever you want there."

"Well, thanks, I appreciate that and here's a whole dollar for the tip."

"Gee, thanks," the bartender said in disgust.

Grits walked to the liquor store and decided to splurge a little.

"I'll take a pint of that there whiskey with the turkey on the front."

On the way back to the motel he decided to call a

service like he'd done the night before. He whistled a woo-wee after he took a drink of the fine whiskey he'd bought. And then he said to himself, *this right here is the life, and I deserve it.*

He unlocked the door, stepped inside, and then shut and locked it. He said to himself, *a rich man like me gots to be careful.* He reached to turn on the lights when he saw the end of a cigarette brighten as someone took a drag and then blew out the smoke. Grits reached for the door handle, "I have a gun pointed at your back. And from such a short distance I don't believe I would miss."

Grits pushed the light switch up to the on position, but nothing happened. Then the man sitting next to the bed slowly turned the switch on the small desk lamp. Grits looked at a dark-haired man wearing a black trench coat. The man waved his gun at the bed and said, "Sit down."

Grits sat down, but did not say a word.

"Do you know who I am?" the man with the gun asked.

"Yes, I know 'xactly who you is. How'd you find me?" Grits asked in confusion.

"Was not difficult task, you leave a trail of bad odor everywhere you go. Now, do you know why I am here?"

"I suppose my uncle sent you, Nikita!" Grits said in frustration.

"So, nephew, you do know who I am."

"Yes, you're the ugly twin brother of that damn Vladimir. You cain't make me do nothin' I don't wanna do. This stuff is mine now, the clothes, the plane ticket, and the money. And I ain't givin' it back ta nobody, not now, not never."

The tall man with the five o'clock shadow stood and slowly moved over to Grits. He got right up next to his ear, "Grits, you can come back with me or you can go swim with fish. It is up to you. I will be paid either way. Now, what is your choice?"

Grits raised his voice, "I ain't goin' no–"

The gun crashed against Grits's face with a thud. And before he could get his hands up to protect himself, he was hit again. Now looking up at the dark man, he felt the blood begin to drip down his nose. The man named Nikita walked to the bathroom and came back with a towel.

"Here, hold this tight on eye. The bleeding will stop. Now we must go but before we leave, I want you to know how lucky you are that Nikita found you and not Leon. Instead of just bleeding you would be dead. Leon came to kill you. Like I said, you leave a trail of bad odor."

Grits looked at Nikita, "Leon was here?" he asked in a confused voice.

"Yes, Leon was here. In fact, he is still here, and that is why we must leave."

Grits stood up and mumbled as he walked to the bathroom and turned on the light. Leon was lying in the tub with the shower curtain over him. Grits lifted the plastic curtain and began to choke and sputter. Leon's throat had been slit from ear to ear. There was more blood than Grits had ever seen. As Grits stared into the tub, Nikita slipped the lamp cord over Grits's head and pulled the cord tight around his neck. Grits's arms and legs flailed in a frantic effort to free himself. Nikita pulled the cord tighter, and as he choked the life from Grits, Nikita said to himself, *I will be paid more if I bring him back, but I want to end his miserable life right here and now. He is much trouble for me.*

Nikita squeezed harder still and the blood vessels in Grits' eyes burst. Then, as his life began to swim away, Grits mustered up one final electric jerk before he was dropped to the bathroom floor.

34

Jupiter, Mississippi
Pearly and I made good time, I sure was hungry. We were only three blocks away from Gino's Pizza Parlor when we walked by a building with at least a dozen Harley Davidson motorcycles parked out front. But it wasn't the motorcycles that grabbed my eyeballs by the throat. It was the flashing brilliant blue neon lights on the roof of the building that read, **Sam's Broken Bone Tavern**. My mind flashed right along with the sign and it told me to go have a look-see. So I started to walk over to take a peek in the window. I made it about two steps before Pearly grabbed me by the arm.

"Bobby, this is not a nice place. We need to leave, right now."

"Ok, it's just that I want to read what the sign in the window says. Pearly, I'll only be a minute." He let go of my arm and I walked over and read the handwritten sign. It said, "needed: one, honest, hard-working white man, apply inside."

I walked back to Pearly with my head hung low. I wasn't sure what to think or say.

"Pearly, I'm sorry I read that sign, but mostly I'm sorry I didn't listen to you."

"Bobby, 'hell is empty and all the devils are here.' Since you've come to this small corner of the world you've witnessed human behavior so retched and vile that no sane man or woman could possibly believe there is a god, or for that matter a multitude of gods that could have created us, that is, mankind. Yet, that is exactly what we have all been told to believe. It seems that at every turn in this social experiment we've been a part of, some of those around us have failed. It really is a wonder, a true miracle that we're not all worshipping the devil himself. Yet, knowing all of that, I choose to believe that if I'm patient enough, long enough, someday I will witness the silver lining that life at times does reveal."

I stood looking at Pearly, but he didn't look back. He had his head hanging down looking at the sidewalk. I wasn't used to seeing him so glum, and I knew I had to do something to bring him back to the happy side of life.

"Gosh darn it Pearly, what you just said was so powerful I want to write it down. You know, so I can share it with others. But for the life of me, I don't think I could remember how it went. So, if you can excuse my poor memory, I have an idea." He lifted his eyes up to mine. "Why don't we go search for the silver lining and maybe eat some pizza along the way."

He paused for a moment as the sparkle in his eyes returned. "Bobby, I couldn't have said it any better, let's go," he said with a smile.

We sauntered up to Gino's, the back of the restaurant, that is. Pearly checked the farthest trash can from the back door, but there was no pizza. So he eased over to the side window and gave it a couple knocks, and then he let loose with that little whistle of his. A few seconds later the back door opened and out walked Belle and Gino. I thought to myself, *uh oh, this is not a good thing*. Gino walked straight to Pearly and I thought he was going to yell at him or maybe ask him what he was doing, but he fooled both of us when he said, "Pearly, listen, I know that sometimes Belle leaves you pizza. And I suppose I understand why. An empty belly is the same the world over. So, tonight I thought it'd be nice if you and your new friend here came inside and ate. What do you think, you feel like sitting down and having some pizza and some fresh garlic bread with your spaghetti and meatballs?"

Pearly fell to a knee. Weary and humbled, he softly said, "The hand of Providence has touched my very soul, thank you." Within a heartbeat, Belle and Gino were patting him on the back and coaxing him to come inside. Funny thing is, even down on one knee, he was still taller than both of them. And as I watched Pearly get to his feet and walk with Belle and Gino into the restaurant, I whispered to myself, *thank goodness there really is a silver lining.*

Gino looked back and waved me inside. "Here, you two gentlemen come inside and wash up. And when you're ready, you can sit at my table. Please, come in," Gino said with a smile.

Belle told us to follow her. She took us to the employee bathroom. Pearly stopped in front of the door, bent at the waist, and as he swung his right arm forward, he said, "After you, kind sir."

I went in and started scrubbing my face and hands. And before the soap lathered up, I took a long look in the mirror. I had several days if not a week's worth of beard growing. I said to myself, *doesn't look like Scooter, but it's more hair on my face than I think I've ever seen.* Of course, I didn't really know, and I guess at the moment I didn't care. I dried off and tucked my shirt in and stepped outside the bathroom to tell Pearly it was his turn. He'd already washed up in the sink next to where Belle does the dishes. He was sitting at the table next to the kitchen. When he looked up at me, he had a piece of garlic bread in one hand and a fork in the other. He was eating a salad and smiling at the same time. I sat down across from him and dug in. I started with a piece of pepperoni pizza and then I filled a plate with spaghetti and meatballs. Then a strange thing happened. Gino came out of the back of the restaurant with two wine glasses in one hand and a bottle in the other.

"Before you say anything Bobby, I already know about your first bout with alcohol. And it's time that you learned to drink responsibly. Now, I want you to slowly drink just one glass of wine. Trust me, it will make the meal much better."

He didn't give me time to argue, he just poured each of us a glass of wine and then he said something about our appetite. We both dug in and I don't believe a word was said for at least a half-an-hour or so. I ate a big plate of spaghetti and was right in the middle of a piece of pizza when I realized I was getting full to the point of being uncomfortable. I picked up my glass of wine and sat back and relaxed for a little bit. I looked around for Belle, and Pearly knew what I was doing.

"Bobby, I told Belle to stay away from us."

I started to ask him why.

"Bobby, you have a serious situation about to happen, and it's one that I believe you are going to have to handle on your own."

He could tell I was confused.

"Is this about me wanting to see Belle?" I asked.

"No, Bobby, this is about the guy that stole your piece of pie. His name is Alvin Wetmore, and I don't believe a lower form of our species exists. He has found himself a mark, which, by the by, is you."

I must have still had a dumbfounded look on my face.

"Bobby, you are the patsy, the person Alvin believes he can take dominion over."

"You mean he thinks he can own me or something like that?" I asked.

"Yes, owns would be an excellent way of looking at this. What I'm saying is that he is going to come after you again and again. Unless of course you do as some people say and nip this in the bud. Do you understand what I'm saying?" Pearly asked as he looked me square in the eye.

"Yes, I do. I can't have him, or anyone else for that matter, thinking that I'm a coward or afraid. So, what do you think I should do? I mean, I know I'm probably going to have to fight him, but how do I go about that? Should I just walk up and slug him or should I announce to everyone that I'm not afraid of him or what?"

"Bobby, there are many ways to go about this, but I think a little cunning would prove to be apropos. Oh, trust me, you are going to have to fight him, but I think it would serve you well to do this on your terms and not his. If you walk up and start the fight he'll involve others. And then it will be you, and of course me, against everyone else. I think you would agree that neither of us would do well in that scenario. So, I have a plan of attack, one that has served in military battles since the beginning of time. Bobby, you and I will outflank Alvin. We will draw him in to our camp. He'll be alone and that will give us the advantage. Now, I said advantage, but you will still have to fight. Here's what we're going to do."

I listened as Pearly explained the strategy in detail. When Pearly finished, he looked over in the corner and Belle was there, patiently waiting.

She walked straight over to us.

"Hi, Bobby, sorry I lef you sittin' here all by yo lonesome. It's just dat Pearly toldt me ta stay 'way fo a bit. Din't mean nuttin by it. Hopes you unnerstands?"

"Yes, of course I understand Belle. Listen, would it be ok if we left Pearly here and went out back alone." I said, not understanding how she might take what I'd just said.

Belle put her hands up to her face and then I realized why she might be a little embarrassed.

"I'm sorry, Belle; I didn't mean it like that. What I meant was if we could go out back so that I could talk to Gino. I want to thank him."

Belle looked at Pearly and then she grabbed my hand and pulled me into the kitchen.

"Bobby, you can thank Gino in he'uh," was all she said.

Gino looked up from what he was doing and gave me a nice smile before he asked what it was I needed.

"I'm sorry to bother you Gino, and I don't need anything. I just wanted to thank you for being so kind to Pearly and me. On the way here I was beginning to think there were no nice people left in this world, and then you invite us in to eat. Gosh, that was awfully nice of you. So, Pearly and I say thank you very much. If there's ever anything I can do to repay you, well, you just let me know. Thanks again," I said.

"Young man, your thanks is all I need as payment. Can't do this every night, but I think maybe a few times now and then won't hurt. Listen, I've got a whole lot of leftover pizza, garlic bread, and spaghetti. I was hoping you two would take it back with you and share it with the others. You know wherever it is that you live or stay or well, you know."

"Gino, the guys will really appreciate this. All I can say is thank you one more time."

Gino and Belle loaded the two of us up with pizza boxes and containers of spaghetti. And then he topped it off with the bottle of wine that he'd opened for our meal. Pearly and I said our goodbyes and then turned to go back to the Salt. We only made it two steps when Belle ran up and hugged her brother. Then she looked at me for a moment before she looked at Pearly. He smiled and nodded his head and Belle ran over and hugged me. And then when she let go of me, she kissed me on the cheek. I couldn't see myself, but the heat of my skin told me that I was as red as a ripe maraschino cherry.

When Pearly and I finally made it back to the Salt, Ralphy met us with a 'how you doin' bark.' Ralphy and the guys in the camp hardly spoke as they ate. When they finished eating, each and every one of them thanked us; sure made my heart feel good, especially when Ralphy thanked me.

When I lay down that night, all I could think of was the silver lining. I drifted off to sleep in a hurry, but just before the sandman came to visit, I thought of the impending fight.

35

San Francisco
Nikita drove back into San Francisco; he believed the authorities would look south, not east. He crossed the bridge over into Oakland and headed further east 'til he reached highway 99. From there, he drove the three hours straight south to Fresno. Before he locked up the black sedan, he lifted the trunk lid and took the plaid suitcase out. He noticed that the pint of Wild Turkey he'd put in the trunk was still nearly full.

Bright and very early the next morning he drove to a private airfield outside of Clovis. This time when he opened the trunk, the pint of whiskey was empty. After he loaded the luggage into the plane, he asked the pilot for help. They picked up Grits and threw him in the back of the plane. And then Grits was summarily gagged and hogtied. He was so polluted he never opened an eye.

The pilot made the flight from Clovis to an airfield outside of Mobile, Alabama in just over six hours. The plane landed and then taxied to a nearby hangar. Cotton Hurtwood and Vladimir were there waiting. Grits, now quite awake, writhed from side to side in an effort to communicate to his uncle just how poorly he'd been treated.

"Nikita, please untie him, but after you do, hold him down and for God sakes do not remove that gag. I am not in the mood this evening for screaming and such nonsense."

Nikita and his twin, Vladimir, exchanged only a look before they put Grits on the concrete. They removed the rope that connected his feet to his hands and with his hands still tied behind his back and his ankles still tightly bound together, Grits hopped and flailed in a circle before hopping towards the open hangar doors.

"Please go stop him and then load him in the back

of the truck," Mr. Hurtwood said in a repulsed voice.

Nikita grabbed Grits by the back of the shirt and dragged him towards the panel truck that was parked outside. When he had Grits outside and next to the panel truck, Vladimir reached in the back and brought out a flame fused model Louisville Slugger. Grits made a futile attempt to scream, but it was of no use. Vladimir hit Grits in the lower back with a tremendous blow. Grits screamed into his gag. The second blow landed just above the right ear and Grits struggled no more.

Grits woke up an hour later in the stables. He was still gagged. His uncle was sitting in his wheelchair next to him.

"Grits, now if you scream, I'm going to let Vladimir hit you again. Do you understand me?" he asked as Vladimir wrapped both hands tight around the handle of the Louisville Slugger.

Grits had had enough and nodded his head.

"Ok, Vladimir, please remove the gag from his mouth. I warn you Grits, do not scream," his uncle admonished in a clear and forceful tone. "Ok, that's better. Now you listen to me and listen well. You are my sister's child and I am obligated to treat you with some dignity. But when you do things that can hurt all of us, your mother included, well, I'm inclined to believe we'd all be better off without you around." Grits started to say something. "Stop! Grits, this is your last chance. One more screw up and you'll be out on the streets with your brother, Alvin. Do you understand me? After today, your behavior and the consequences thereof will be out of my hands. Now, you have brought a young man here that will eventually cause others to ask questions. Do you remember me lecturing you before you left for Canada?" Grits didn't respond. "I said, do you remember!" Grits nodded his head. "That's better. Now, I have a job for you and you'd better come through for me or... Listen, I want you to go out and find this man, this police officer, and bring him to me. Do you understand?!" Grits's eyes opened wide as he nodded yes.

"I previously sent Grasshopper, but he has not been able to find him. So, now there will be two of you working together. You must find this man." Mr. Hurtwood sighed and stared at Grits. "Ok, go get cleaned up, and then come to my office. I'll tell you where this policeman is and how you're to get him to come here. Do you understand me?" Grits nodded his head yes and then asked if he could be excused.

"Yes, go get yourself cleaned up, you're a mess. I expect you to be in my office in one hour. Now go," his uncle said.

"Vladimir, please, I need my medicine. Take me back to my office."

Vladimir set the bat down in the corner and rolled Cotton Hurtwood out of the stables. Along the way, Vladimir pled his case.

"Mr. Hurtwood, Nikita and I can go tonight and kill this man. We know where he is."

"No Vladimir, someone might see you. We can't take that chance. Everyone knows you work for me."

"But Mr. Hurtwood, the only people that would see are homeless. No one will listen to them if they talk."

"No, I want no witnesses and no questions. That's final."

"Mr. Hurtwood, how are they to get him to come to plantation?"

"They're going tomorrow morning. They will tell him that they know who he is, and that they have his possessions, including his money. He will not be able to resist. Trust me, he will come and then you and Nikita can eliminate all three at the same time."

Vladimir smiled and said, "Khorosho."

36

The Salt

Pearly was already up and dressed to leave when Ralphy started licking my face. Then Scooter shook me.

"Good mornin' Bobby, I'm sorry ta have ta wake ya, but there's something I need ta tell ya."

I sat up and tried to move, but every muscle in my body ached.

"Gosh Scooter, I can hardly move, can you wait 'til after I crawl to the bathroom?"

"No, Bobby, this it too important. Listen, there has been a guy asking all over the Salt 'bout ya. He's come by three times in the last two days. He goes by Grasshopper. I'm not sure what he is; what I mean is, he's hard ta describe. I don't know if he's black or white or well, whatever else there is. Some of the guys say his mama brought him here from the Caribbean. Anyway, he works for the Hurtwood family, and Cotton Hurtwood is nobody to mess with. All the men here believe that you'd better lay low for a while. So, I talked it over with Pearly and he thinks maybe you can stay with Belle. You'll find out this mornin' when you go for grits. Ralphy and I might not see ya for a while so good luck today in yo fight."

"You know about the fight?"

"Sure do, Pearly told all of us last night. Several of the men are gonna try and get on the work crew taday. They want to be there ta he'p y'all. Bobby, I know Alvin Wetmore. He is nobody ta take lightly."

"All over a stupid piece of pie," flew out of my mouth.

"Bobby, this is not about a piece of pie."

"It's not?" I said, totally confused.

"No, this is 'bout who you was 'fore y'all come to the Salt. Now listen up! Alvin always carries a knife and he is gonna try ta kill ya with it. Do you understand?"

"Yes, now I do. Gosh, I didn't know about the knife or the killing stuff. Scooter, you and Ralphy and all the men have been so good to me, well, I don't know if I can ever thank you enough. Listen, I'll be back to the Salt before you know it. Take care of yourself, oh and that goes for Ralphy too."

We shook hands but I don't think Scooter felt it was enough. So he let go of his cane and gave me a big hug. Kinda felt like I was leaving to go fight in a war or something.

Pearly came out of the shadows and waved his arm at me.

"Time to move, you know the routine."

"Yes, but I have to use the bathroom first. I'll only be a minute."

I ran out to the park area and into the bathroom as fast as my aching back and sore legs would carry me.

•

"There he is Grasshopper, why don't we just handle this on our own. We'll be on my uncle's good side if we take care a' this ourselves."

"Grits please don't. Dat's not what we was told ta do."

"I don't care what we were told ta do. This guy has caused me a lot of pain and misery. I'm gonna go ahead and kill him right now." Grits pulled out the knife he'd brought with him and started to move when Grasshopper said, "Grits get down, dat dog will see's ya and start ta barkin'."

"Then I'll kill the damn dog," Grits said as he held up his knife.

"No, you ain't killin' no dog. He didn't do nuttin' ta you," Grasshopper said with a conviction Grits had never heard.

"Well, I didn't know you was such a dog lover. Ok, I won't kill him taday, but maybe I will someday. And don't you ever boss me like that again," Grits said as he slapped Grasshopper in the face.

•

Pearly followed Ralphy across the back of the park by the concession stand and met me as I walked out of the bathroom. Ralphy nudged me with his nose, so I pet him.

"Bobby, you may think me a worry wart, but from here on out you need to be more careful about where you go. Please, these people that are looking for you are not to be taken lightly. They could be here as we speak."

"Oh gosh Pearly, it's only just the two of us. And besides it's still dark out. I mean if we can't see anybody then it stands to reason that nobody can see us."

"Bobby, let's just go. Darkness is the tool of the wicked. Please Bobby."

"Ok, let's go, bye Ralphy. Say Pearly, where'd you hear that darkness thing?"

"Didn't hear it anywhere, it's just what I believe to be true."

"Geez, you've been coming up with some good ones lately."

Pearly said nothing as we headed to Belle's for breakfast. When we were within eyesight of her clapboard home, I had a strange sensation come over me.

"Pearly, you must have spooked me because I've had the strangest sensation since we left the Salt that someone is following us."

Pearly peered into the darkness behind us, but there was nothing there to see.

"Bobby, if someone has followed us, they now know where Belle lives. We need to hurry and get inside."

As she'd done the day before, Belle was standing on the porch waiting for us. She smiled until we were right up next to her. Then she saw our faces and the concern in her eyes made me feel just plain awful.

"Belle, please, we need to go inside," Pearly said without hiding his concern.

"Why Pearly, what in de world is wrong? I ain't never seen ya look so fraught wit worry."

"Belle, this is all because of me. There's really no

need for either of you to worry. You see, I have to fight a man today when we go to work. Yes, that's what this is all about."

"Well, if dat's what dis all about, den why Pearly starin' out my winduh?"

Pearly stopped looking out the window and walked over to Belle. "Little sister, there is no need for you to worry. What Bobby has just told you is the truth. However, he has left out a vital part of the situation we're now in. Belle, please give us our grits. I'll explain the rest while we eat."

Pearly explained to Belle the entire mess I had made for them. She listened as she prepared the same lunch for us she made the day before, except this time she added a cornpone cake for each of us. She worked at a steady pace and I know on the inside she had to be worried, but she never let on. We finished eating and before we left, Pearly went outside and searched around the clapboard building. He came back and said, "All clear, time for us to get moving."

We both hugged Belle, but this time we said our goodbyes in her front room. As she waved goodbye, I saw the worry in her eyes. I felt awful.

•

"Grasshopper, why-da-ya think them nigguh's is takin' care of that cop. Just don't make no sense."

"I don't know Grits, but dey not our concern," Grasshopper said in an obvious attempt to get Grits from thinking about hurting Belle.

"Why I never, Grasshopper, you tryin' ta protect yo people, ain't ya. Well, ta hell with that. Them there nigguh's get in the way, then they gonna be sorry."

Grasshopper said nothing.

"Damn it, Grasshopper, I don't need ya on their side. And if y'all're against me, well, you'll get yours too. Come on, we gots ta follow. I know where they're goin', but we gots ta make sure."

Grasshopper followed Grits, but in his mind, he

wanted to hurt him. Over and over he whispered, *someday, somebody is gonna hurt you real bad for being so mean and nasty. Someday you gonna get yours, someday Grits!*

•

Pearly and I hurried down the same old country road we'd trekked the day before. But this time I knew what things looked like, in the light of day that is. When we finally reached the staging area, I recognized at least two of the men from the Salt. We nodded our heads but made no attempt to speak to one another. Those were the directions Pearly had given us. So we kept to ourselves. Wasn't more than ten minutes before Pearly and I saw Alvin walk up with at least a half a dozen guys around him. I didn't like the odds, but I really had no choice in the matter. Pearly and I stood near the front of the line and when Armstrong walked by, he gave us a nod. "The two a you did a nice job yesterday, go ahead and get in the truck." We didn't have to be told twice and jumped in the back. We sat up next to the cab and watched as the truck filled up; four of our guys were picked and got in. Then we watched Alvin and his posse get in the back. They wasted no time; I mean the moment they got in they gave me the stink eye. I looked at Pearly and he leaned over to me and with his hand over his mouth he whispered, "As sure as a rose has thorns, a confrontation awaits." I didn't ask where he got that one.

•

"Let me go talk ta Teerlink, I'll let him know that Mr. Hurtwood wants the cop."

"Ok, but remember Grits, we not sposed ta spook him. Tell Teerlink all ya want him ta do is keep an eye on de guy, ok?" Grasshopper said, knowing that Grits never listened to him.

"I know what I'm doin', you stay outa this. If things work out, Teerlink won't have ta follow this guy. See, what y'all don't know is, I told Alvin I'd pay him if he killed the cop. He's gonna kill him taday. And when he does, my uncle will give me back the clothes and the money. You just watch and see."

"Oh no, you shouldn't have involved Alvin. I haves a real bad feeling 'bout dis," Grasshopper said.

"Shut up Grasshopper, stay here," Grits ordered before he slipped over in the darkness to speak to Teerlink.

•

We drove to the spot where we'd quit the day before and everybody jumped out. This time instead of Armstrong giving us the directions, it was Teerlink. When he finished talking, he gave me a look that made my skin crawl. Pearly noticed and whispered, "You're fighting Alvin, not Teerlink."

Pearly knew I was sore as heck so he let me do most of the shoveling. I was slow but steady with the shovel and Teerlink left us alone. We took a short water break at ten, Alvin didn't make a move. Then we both knew it was going to be during lunch when he'd come after me. When the horn blew for lunch, Pearly and I walked together to the cooler and got the lunch Belle had made for us. Then we found a shady area away from the road just like we'd done the day before. We sat down and ate and for a moment or two, I relaxed and forgot about the fight. I finished my sandwich and cornpone and started eating my piece of pie. Pearly stood up and signaled our friends from the Salt. Then, as he walked away, he reminded me to put a sack in my back pocket and keep another close by. I put the pie on top of a sack and lay down and closed my eyes; well, at least from a distance it looked like my eyes were closed. I heard footsteps coming my way. I took a peak and sure enough, it was Alvin. There were three guys with him that stood by the truck, and, of course, Teerlink was there. I watched as Alvin moved closer and closer. Then two of the guys from the Salt started fighting. I heard Alvin's friends yell fight, fight as they ran away. I thought Alvin would go for the pie, but he reached down for his knife instead. He never knew what hit him. I swung the sack of rocks as hard as I could and caught him square on the side of the face.

Crestfield

He crashed face down in the dirt and tried to get back up. I swung hard and hit him again. He leered up at me as a river of blood spilled from his nose and mouth.

I guess you could say the animal instinct to survive came to life in Alvin. He scurried on all fours away from me. He reached into his pant leg and pulled out his knife. I swung the sack at him but I missed. He immediately lunged at me. I felt a sharp burn as he drove the knife deep into my left shoulder. I swung the sack again and delivered a mighty blow to his chest. He backed away again. I dropped the sack of rocks and he charged like a bull. I did what Pearly had told me to do and reached for the sack hanging from my back pocket. And as he threw himself at me, I grabbed the hand with the knife in it and wrapped the sack around the knife; I felt the same burn I felt earlier, but I managed to pull the knife out of his hand. Now I held the knife. My first instinct was to kill him, but that was not the plan. I threw the knife as far as I could and then I turned to Alvin and we squared off. My hand was bleeding, but it worked just fine as I moved in close and bear hugged Alvin. He squirmed trying to get away and then he bit down hard on my left arm. I howled as I threw him to the ground. I leaped on top of him, and I must have hit him three or four times before he curled up in the fetal position. He was screaming with all his might for help, but I didn't stop. I continued to hit him about the head and neck 'til someone grabbed me from behind and pulled me off him. I stood for a moment as if I was done fighting and then I broke loose and with everything I had I kicked Alvin in the ribs. I was blind with rage when I heard him gasp for air. I was not going to stop and nobody was going to make me.

"Bobby, stop. Teerlink and Armstrong are on their way over here." I struggled for a moment longer. "Bobby, it's me Pearly, you need to stop."

Teerlink was ahead of Armstrong and when he ran up he swung wildly at my face. I managed to duck the first punch, but he caught me with the second.

I hit the ground like a sack of potatoes. I managed to get back up to my knees when I heard Teerlink yell, "You sum-bitch, I'm gonna kill you."

He raised his right hand and then the next thing I know he was frantically clutching at his neck. He was desperately trying to free himself from the choke hold Pearly held him in. Pearly squeezed for a moment longer then let go and with a thunderous right hand he knocked Teerlink to the ground right next to me. Teerlink was out cold and convulsing. Spittle and foam began to froth from his mouth. My mind told me that Pearly had killed him. We froze when two gun shots rang out. Armstrong stood with a revolver in his left hand and yelled, "Pearly, get back! You hear me, get back."

Pearly moved back and I screamed, "Alvin started this whole thing! He had a knife and was going to kill me! Then your man Teerlink took sides and hit me and said he was going to kill me!" I was still yelling when two of our guys from the Salt walked up to Armstrong and swore that they'd seen the whole thing. And that I was telling the truth.

"Where's Alvin?" Armstrong asked.

The two guys carried Alvin over to us.

"Look inside his right pant leg and you'll find the sheath that he had his knife in," I said.

One of the men pulled up Alvin's pant leg and sure enough, there it was. He took it out and when he turned it over Alvin's full name was carved into the back. I told them where I'd thrown the knife and one of them took off out into the brush to look. Armstrong was down on a knee checking on Teerlink.

"Well, he seems to be breathing ok, but that don't mean things are good with me. Shit, I trusted the two of you. Shit, got-damn it all ta hell. Pearly, why'd you have ta go and hit Teerlink? Shit, oh to hell with it. Ok, you two are out of here." Armstrong reached in his pocket and pulled out two twenty dollar bills. "Here, now you've been paid, don't come back here again. You hear me?"

Someone ran up when Armstrong stopped talking and yelled, "I found the knife, it's got blood on it. It's just like he said," as he pointed at me.

"You know something Mr. Armstrong? I believe a good attorney could cause this company a lot of grief. I've been attacked with a knife while working for you. Then one of your employees for no apparent reason hit me and knocked me to the ground. I suppose I should go see an attorney."

Armstrong looked at me for a long time. I think he was trying to see if I'd back down. I had him on the ropes and he knew it.

"Ok, wise guy. Here, this oughta do it," He said, just before he reached in his pocket and pulled out several of the company store vouchers.

I reminded him that it was attempted murder. He reached in his pocket and handed me two more twenties before he said, "Don't push it, young man. The people you're messing with have a lot a power. They'll run you over and not think twice about doin' it. Now, if I was you, I'd get while the gettin' is good."

Pearly looked at me before he grabbed my arm and started dragging me away. We took off down the road and didn't look back. Took a long time before either one of us said a word. We knew there were going to be repercussions, and lots of them. This time when we walked by the antebellum plantation, something didn't feel right.

It wasn't near as enchanting or handsome or appealing as it was the day before. I apologized several times to Pearly, but he didn't say anything back. I thought I'd lost the best friend I had. At least that's what I thought 'til Pearly suddenly stopped walking.

"Bobby, you need to have those wounds cleaned and bandaged."

"I don't care about the wounds. I shouldn't have brought you into this, it's all my fault."

"Bobby, this is not your fault. I could have stayed away today. And I believe you would have acquitted yourself just fine. You did a very brave thing today."

"Yeah, but you did come with me. And now you've lost the job you were counting on."

I walked away from Pearly for a little bit and sat down on a large boulder. I reached way down inside myself for an answer to our problems, but nothing came to me. I had to do something and fast. Then a crazy idea came to me; I said to myself, *this just might work, but I can never tell Pearly.* I stood up and took forty dollars and the vouchers out of my pocket.

"Here Pearly, you keep this money, you earned it. As far as the vouchers go, well, I'll bet Belle could sure use them."

He looked at me but didn't say a word.

"Pearly, you know we have to part ways for a while. I can't go back to the Salt and even though I'd like to stay with Belle, it's too dangerous. I can't involve either of you in this. I want these people that are trying to find me to believe that I've fallen off the face of the earth. Listen, I know where to find you and eventually I will. But for now, I'm going to go someplace where nobody will ever find me."

I stuck my hand out and Pearly looked at me real hard before he shook my hand.

"Bobby, this is where I'm supposed to say parting is such sweet sorrow, so on and so forth, but I'm just not in the mood," he said as he hung his head.

We started walking away from each other and after maybe five steps, I yelled back at him, "Tell Scooter and Ralphy and all the guys at the Salt thanks! Oh, and give Belle a hug for me, please."

Pearly gave me one last smile and then we both turned and put our heads down and started walking in opposite directions. I wasn't sure where Pearly was going, but I knew where I was going. I headed straight for Gino's.

Crestfield

37

San Francisco
I waited three whole days for Detective Olmstead to call.
I was becoming more anxious by the minute. Then I came
up with a plan that I thought might work. I called the
number he'd given me and told the guy that answered the
phone I was returning a call from Detective Olmstead. The
guy hesitated for a minute before he said, "Just a minute,
let me see if he's here."

I stood in the kitchen holding the phone for at least
ten minutes and counting. I was tapping my knuckles on
the kitchen counter when the line went dead. Someone had
hung up the phone. I thought to myself, *ok, the guy that
answered figured out that Olmstead didn't really call me.* I
was late for work so I hurried in and threw on my work
clothes and ran out the front door. I ran down my steps and
right into Detective Olmstead.

"Whoa, hi Dezi, say, where are you going in such
a hurry?" he asked.

"I'm going to work and I don't want to talk to you.
You gave me your word you'd call. I told everybody back
in Crestfield that there was a lot of new information as far
as Junior was concerned. Why didn't you call me?" I
yelled more than asked.

"Dezi, look, there was a lot we had to do that
night. We, being the San Francisco PD, the coroner, the
highway patrol, and now the FBI. Dezi, let's go inside and
I'll explain as much as I can."

"No, I'm gonna be late to work. You had several
days to call, but you didn't. I, I trusted you," I said as I
started to cry.

"Dezi, please, let's go inside and I'll call your boss
and explain. Then I'll give you a ride to work. Ok?" he
offered in a soft voice.

I stood and thought about things. I wanted to know

anything and everything there was, but I was still sore at the detective. Instead of saying anything, I just jumped back up onto the porch and opened the door. I went all the way through the front room and into the kitchen. Detective Olmstead followed me. I sat down at the kitchen table and he picked up the phone. I gave him the number and he made good on his promise to call and explain to my boss. Then he sat down.

"Ok, now listen, I can tell you some of what I know, but not everything. Do you want me to start or do you want to ask questions?"

I blurted out, "Who did they load up in that ambulance?"

"That is something I can tell you. His name was Leon Beauchamp. He was born in Compton and raised right here in Oakland. He had a business he ran south of Pacifica."

"A business, what kind of business? And how does that concern Junior or the guy that stole his stuff?" I asked in real time confusion.

"Dezi, he was a pimp, do you know what business I'm talking about now?"

I was embarrassed and just said, "Ok, just tell me how this Leon Beauchamp is involved."

"A few of the people that worked for Leon told us this guy didn't pay one of his gals. So Leon went looking for him. From what we found at the crime scene, it looks like Leon waited in the guy's motel room; well, the guy came back. Leon had a knife and a gun on his person and still lost. The guy we're looking for must handle himself quite well. And the way he disappeared afterward, tells us he is a pro."

"Ok, you said you know who he is, and where he's from, so tell me," I demanded.

"Dezi, I think you already know that I can't divulge that information. If it makes you feel any better, the FBI is on his trail as we speak. They'll get him, that's for sure," he said in an effort to calm me down.

I was so frustrated I was shaking.

"What about Junior? We still have no idea where he is," I said as I trembled with a growing fear.

"Dezi, I'm sorry, I wish I could tell you where your brother is. I really do."

He looked at me and he could tell I was not satisfied with his answer.

"If it makes you feel any better, the guy we're looking for is definitely a pro. He didn't do anything to hide Leon's body and that tells us if he had done something to Junior, well, it may sound awful, but I'm sure we'd have found him by now. Do you understand?" he asked.

I was confused and really didn't understand the reasoning. And so, I just came right out and said, "No, I don't understand."

"Dezi, I'll put it in very blunt terms. If this guy had killed your brother, well, someone would have already found his body. Crazy as it sounds, and I don't want to give you false hope, but we still believe your brother is alive," he said as he folded his hands together on top of the table.

I stood up and because I didn't know what to say, I just motioned for him to follow me. I walked back outside and stopped right in the middle of the sidewalk.

"Can you please just take me to work, I'm still late."

"Come on," was all he said.

He opened the door for me. He was driving his unmarked - everybody knows it's a police car. He drove me to the bar where I work. But before I got out, I made him promise to call me, and I meant every day. I stared him down 'til he said ok.

That night when I got home, I called Dad and told him everything. It was four in the morning in Crestfield. I could tell Dad was tired, but there was more to it, he was sick with worry. I called both of my sisters. I made them promise to go see Dad that same day. My sister, Madison, had no problem with what I'd asked her to do. She gave me her word she'd go see Dad. But my baby sister, Randi, broke down and cried. She told me from worrying about Junior, the whole town was sick. I guess the trust, the fabric that holds people together, was being torn apart. And neither she, nor anyone else, knew how to sew things back together again. When I hung up the phone, I wasn't sure if my calling had been a good idea. I was left feeling so cold and lonely. I got into bed and tried to think of good things. Things I knew Junior would enjoy. And I did my best to think of the silver lining.

I finally fell asleep and I dreamed I was with Junior. We laughed and had such a good time during the dream I just knew that somehow, someday, our entire family would be together again. When I woke up, I had a plan, a very good plan.

38

Jupiter, Mississippi

I got to Gino's and hid out back by the trash cans. Well, actually, before I hid, I lifted the lid on the last trash can; there was no pizza. It must have been nearly six thirty when Gino finally walked out the back door. I gave a soft little whistle and Gino looked over at me like I was some kind of nut.

"Bobby, what in the world are you doin' over there?" he asked.

"Gino, I didn't want Belle to see me. Listen, I need a small favor."

"Ok, how much money do you need?"

"No Gino, I don't need any money. I need to shave and get cleaned up is all. I'm going to go for a job interview and I can't go looking like this."

"No, you can't. I don't know how you got all bloody, but you're gonna need a new shirt. I'm gonna go inside and have Belle run a little errand for me. Stay out of sight, and when you see her take off, come in."

I ran across the street and hid behind a tree, it was still light out. I felt alone and awful as I watched Belle walk down the street. I ran over and Gino was waiting for me at the back door.

"Come on in Bobby, I've got a razor for you and I found a shirt you can wear. It's not fancy, but it's clean. When you get done washing up, I'll put what bandages I have on that shoulder and your hand. Geez, how'd you get cut up like that?" he asked with genuine concern.

"Gino, it's a long story. Would it be ok if I told you about it some other time?"

"Sure-thing Bobby, sure, as long as you're ok."

I nodded my head to let him know I was ok. Then I got started with the shaving. It was much more difficult than I thought it would be. I had to use scissors to cut a lot of the beard before the razor would even get down to my skin. After I finished shaving, I took off the bandage that had been on my head. The hair had started growing over the wound and I didn't think anybody would notice. I washed my hair twice before I washed my face. I was filthy. I put some mercurochrome on the stab wound on my shoulder and the slice on the palm of my hand. Gino came out of the kitchen with the clean shirt and helped me bandage up the wounds. The shirt he gave me was a dark blue work shirt; wasn't fancy, but like he said, it would do the job. I put the shirt on and then combed my hair. When I looked at myself in the mirror Gino said, "Hey, you clean up pretty good. Bobby, where is this job interview?"

"It'd be better if I didn't tell you."

"Ok," was all Gino said back to me.

"Here Bobby, I hope you don't mind, but I wrote a recommendation for you. Says all the right stuff and that I'd like to keep you, but business hasn't been so great lately."

"Gino, I don't know what to say, except thank you. Listen, I need to get out of here before Belle comes back. Ok if I go out the front?"

"Sure, listen, good luck and I want you to come back and see us now and then. I guess you already know that Belle's crazy about you."

"She is?" I asked while I stood there like a big dope. "Gino, how do you know?"

"I just know; anyone would know if they saw her face when you come around. In fact, all I have to do is mention your name and she smiles. Too bad you gotta go, just come back, ok?"

"Yes, Gino, I give you my word I'll come back. Ok, well, I'll see ya, and thanks again for everything."

I headed down the main drag and it only took me about five minutes to get to my destination. I said to myself, *you need this job, so be the best, and the most honest white boy in town.* I walked by two Harley's and into the tavern. It was dark and dank inside. As my eyes adjusted to the lack of light, I could see that the walls were covered with pictures of motorcycles. I walked in a little further and there were stairs going up the right side of the room. I had no idea there was a second story inside the tavern.

The place was much, much bigger on the inside than it looked from the outside. There were four nice pool tables at the far end of the room. And there were two guys with long hair standing next to one of the tables. They set their cue sticks down and stared at me. I thought about when Scooter told me it was rude to stare. Then I realized that I was staring too. The guys were both wearing denim vests with shrunken heads on the left breast. On the right, 'Headhunters' was stitched in bright blue letters. I turned my head and my eyes walked the length of the bar; the bar was long. Then I nearly melted. There was a lady standing at the end of the bar looking at me. She had the most stunning big brown doe eyes I have ever seen. That is, that I think I've ever seen. I walked towards her and the closer I got, the more beautiful she became. She was tall, but with her auburn hair up and kinda big and puffy she looked to be well over six feet in height.

"Can I help you?" was all she said as she casually ran her eyes across me.

"Well, yes ma'am, I mean I hope so."

"Would you like to sit down and have a beer or maybe something a little stronger?"

"Um, no ma'am, I–"

"Ok, around here nobody calls me ma'am, and if you're selling religion, you've come to the wrong place."

"No ma'am, I'm not selling religion," I said as I started to sweat.

"Ok, listen, come over here and sit down. I don't really care what you're selling or not selling."

I sat down and she leaned over and said, "Why are you here? And don't call me ma'am."

"I'm sorry; I'm here to apply for the job."

"Geez, why didn't you say so in the first place?"

One of the guys yelled, "Need some help?"

"No, I don't, so get back to your game."

She turned and walked away and when she came back, she laid an application and a pencil down on the bar in front of me. "Fill it out and give me a holler when you're done."

I wasn't even sure I knew how to write, but when I picked up the pencil, it felt ok, so I printed my name. So far so good. Then I made up a birth date and a social security number. Coming up with a permanent address was a tough one. I swore I had a driver license and then I signed my name on the bottom of the application. I set it and the recommendation Gino had written for me on the bar. She walked over and started reading the application to herself. It didn't take her very long to go over everything that I'd just sworn to. Then she started reading Gino's recommendation. When she was finished she looked me over again with those big brown eyes of hers. I was kinda spooked, but in a good way.

"Well, I certainly trust Gino, and he thinks you're stand up. Says here you're from Omaha, is that right."

I said yes, and then I hoped to goodness that she wasn't from anywhere near there.

"I'm from the Bronx, you know where that is?"

"Um, I'm sorry no. But I'll bet it's a nice place."

"You're funny, you know that. We don't ever have any guys like you come in here. You're polite and kinda shy and, I hope, genuine. I like it. Ok, here's what the job entails. Several years ago, we decided to start moving our products ourselves. That is, we go and pick up all the booze. Doesn't matter if it's beer in a keg or booze in a bottle, we go pick it up. We cut down our overhead by quite a bit. Well, last week our driver started a prison sentence. He's going to be gone for a few years. So, can you drive?"

"Yes ma'am. I'm sorry, yes I can," I lied.

"Yes, but can you drive a big truck?"

"Yes, I believe I can," I lied again. "I'll do my

best, and I'm a quick learner."

"Ok, well, when Joey gets back I'll have him take you out so you can drive the truck."

"Oh, that's great, thanks. Um is Joey the boss. I mean you think he'll give me the job?"

"No, I'm the one that will give you the job. I'm the boss."

"Oh, I didn't know. So, who is Sam?"

"Sam is short for Samantha. I'm Sam, and I'm the boss. Joey is my husband, but he's not very good at the business end of things. So, I run the tavern and he rides his motorcycle."

"Oh," fell out of my mouth.

"Listen, I don't want it to sound like he doesn't help, because he does. He just helps make sure people don't get out of hand and so on. Do you understand?"

"Yes, I guess he's the security?"

"That's a nice way of saying it, yes he's the bouncer. That is, he and Haystack."

"Did you say, Haystack?" I asked.

"Yes, he only works nights. He'll be in pretty soon. You won't be able to miss him. Would you like a cup of coffee while you wait?"

"Please, a cup of coffee would be great. Thank you."

"Huh, I like you. It's going to take me a little time to get used to someone saying please and thank you all the time. That's a good habit to be in. Somebody taught you right," she said.

She filled a cup of coffee and floated it over to me. "I added a touch of cream and sugar?"

"Ok, thank you. That will be great."

She sailed away from me, and that's when I noticed that she was wearing a jump suit something like Pearly would wear. Except hers was bright blue like the neon sign on top of the building. Oh, and Pearly's jumpsuit didn't fit him anything like hers fit her. She bent over and reached in a cooler and then turned and gave me a wispy smile as she walked out from behind the bar. She carried two beers like batons in a relay race to the guys playing pool. Then she floated back with their empties. I don't think my eyes ever left her, they couldn't. She was like a magnet and I was stuck right to her. There came a moment, maybe two or three, when I didn't care about the job. I didn't care because my mind screamed, job or not, rain or shine, I'm coming back to this tavern. I was enjoying my bliss when someone with a deep, scratchy, and irritating voice said, "Who's the mouth-dribbler?"

I turned around and a guy walked through the front door that spooked the stuffing out of me. He had light brown hair down to his shoulders and a beard that covered his face right up to his eyeballs. He filled the entire doorway when he walked in. He had to weigh at least three hundred pounds. He had on bib overalls but no shirt and no shoes. I blinked a couple of times, because it was like seeing a character walk right off the funny pages. He smiled, but he had no teeth that I could see.

And behind him was the guy that called me a mouth-dribbler. He was probably six feet tall, but wide like a semi. He was wearing the same clothes the guys playing pool were wearing. His hair was long like the big guy's. He got up real close to me and I noticed one eye was blue and the other was brown. Then Sam said, "Joey, just once in your life I wish you would try to be polite. And he's not a mouth-dribbler. Bobby McKillin, meet my husband, Joey Lombardi. And this is the tavern's bouncer, Haystack." She signed something to Haystack and then she gave the two of them a hard look and said, "Now say hello and shake his hand, please!"

I stood up and Haystack shook my hand; his hand felt exactly like a catcher's mitt. He mumbled something, so I mumbled back. "He can't hear ya, he's deaf and dumb," Joey said as he shook my hand. As we shook hands, he looked me right in the eye. It was kinda like looking at a cobra, well, what I think it would be like to look at a cobra. Joey had a strong grip, and he knew it. He watched me squint with pain as his vice-grip began to crush the bones in my hand. I said hello, nice to meet you, as I tried to let go, but he wouldn't let me let go. Finally, Sam said, "Ok Joey, he gets the idea."

Joey let go of my hand and laughed a little and in his scratchy voice he said, "Nice ta meet ya kid. You sure got yourself one heck of a name, never heard of anybody by the name McKiller."

"No Joey, it's McKillin, got it Mc-Kill-in," Sam repeated.

"Ok, well, why are you here Mc-Bobby?"

"I came to apply for the job," was all I said.

"Well, it's about damn time somebody had the guts to come in here. I mean, it's not like we're gonna bite your head off or nothin'."

One of the guys playing pool blurted out, "Hey, Joey, I tried to apply for the job. You told me to go to hell."

"Yeah, I told you to go to hell because the sign says one honest guy. Not some dumbass biker like you," Joey said as the three of them laughed at what must have been an inside joke.

He turned to me and gave me that look of his again. Then he said, "Bobby, are you hungry?"

"Well, yes, I suppose I could eat."

"Good, because I'm starvin'; and we ain't goin' anywhere 'til I get me some food in my damn stomach."

Then Haystack growled something to Joey, but I didn't understand any of it. Then Joey said, "Oh hell Haystack, you're always hungry."

"Hey Mc-Bobby, follow me."

He started walking towards the back of the building and after we walked by the bathrooms, he turned left into a small office. He pointed to a chair and told me to sit down. Then he walked around a desk, sat down, and pulled open a drawer. Haystack stood in the doorway, I mean the entire doorway. Joey pulled a sandwich out of the drawer.

It was wrapped in plastic. He threw it across the room to Haystack. Then he asked me if I wanted ham or beef. "Beef would be fine, thanks." He tossed me the sandwich. Then he opened another drawer and pulled out some little packets of mayo and mustard.

"We sell the sandwiches here in the tavern, but the ones out front are stale, just picked these up this mornin'. Go ahead and dig in." I opened the package and put a little mayo on one half of the sandwich and I put mustard on the other half. I took a bite and the sandwich was awful. I mean cold, dry, and just plain awful. I smiled and took another bite. To be polite I kept eating, or maybe it was out of fear.

"Bobby, would you like a beer?" Joey asked as he threw a bottle to Haystack.

"No thank you, remember I have to drive."

Joey laughed, "One beer ain't gonna hurt no-body, geez, where'd you say you're from?"

"Um, I'm from Omaha."

"A cornhusker hah, well, I'm from Jersey and we always drink before we drive. You know, to calm the nerves. You ain't no preacher are ya?" I didn't answer him. "Heck, well, ok, but when you get all parched and thirsty, don't say I didn't offer you one."

I forced down the first half of the sandwich and watched Joey throw another to Haystack. I think he mumbled back a thank you before he walked over and spit some tobacco in an old coffee can.

"Where does he keep the tobacco when he's eating?" I asked Joey.

"Damned if I know, but he has that chaw in his mouth day and night," Joey said as he took out a sandwich. He ate the sandwich in about four bites. That was between the two beers he guzzled down. Joey suddenly stopped eating, picked up the phone, and then he waved for me to go out and sit with Sam. I thought, *I'd love to sit with Sam.*

I walked back to Sam and sat down on the same stool. Sam moseyed over to me and leaned against the bar.

"Listen, Bobby, I know you're probably in shock, and nobody would blame you if you ran out of the place and never came back. But, you'd miss out on some good people. Joey is rough around the edges, but on the inside, he's a really, really nice person. And if you get on his good side, you'll have a friend for life. Ok, now that I've lectured you, are you going to hang around for a while?"

"Yes ma'am, I'm sorry, yes Sam. I'm going to stay because the truth is, I have nowhere else to go."

"What about your house, you know the one on Neptune."

"So, you know."

"Yes, I checked. There's no house there."

"I'm sorry; truth is I don't really have a home. I hope you're not going to fire me."

"No, Bobby, I'm not going to fire you. Least not 'til you have a chance to prove you can drive the truck. Then if you can't drive, I'll probably fire you," she said as she smiled at me.

"Gosh, thanks so much. You're an angel."

"Bobby, I'm no angel, but I'm not the devil either. Ok, you do your best driving and then we'll see if we can't find a place for you to sleep," she said with a warm smile.

"I don't need much room, just a little is all," I said, ready to break down right in front of her.

She stuck her hand out to me and started to say something when Joey yelled, "Hey, Mc-Bobby, follow me."

I gave Sam a look and jumped up and followed Joey outside. We kept walking 'til we were behind the building. There was a one ton Chevy truck with a cargo box. For some reason, I wasn't worried. I felt like I'd either driven one or I'd been around trucks before.

"Ok, listen Bobby, there's not enough room in the cab for the three of us. So, I'm gonna have Haystack go with you. He'll show you where to go. You want me to back the truck out for you?"

"No, I can do it. Joey, are you sure about this? I

mean, how's Haystack going to tell me which way to go?"

"Bobby, you didn't listen to what I said, you need to listen better. He's not gonna tell you, he's gonna show you. Get it?"

"Ok, I guess so. All right then Haystack, let's get a move on," I said with gusto.

"Bobby, he can't hear you, remember? Ok, just point and gesture and that kinda shit. He'll get the idea. And when he points and so forth, you'd better get the idea. Get the idea?" Joey said with a grin.

"Yeah, ok." I answered before I yelled real loud and pointed to the passenger side door.

Haystack understood and got in the truck. Joey stood and watched as I backed the truck up and then turned it around. He gave me the thumbs up. I waited for Haystack to show me the way. I felt good, really good, driving the truck. It was like I was somebody and that I mattered. Haystack pointed to the right and we took off down the road. Drove a block or so. Then I pulled over to the side of the road and got out. Haystack looked at me like I was a nut or something. I walked around and moved the outside mirrors into what I thought were the best positions for me to see out of. Haystack smiled at me when I was on his side of the truck. I got back in and we jammed down the street. He motioned to me that we were going to go straight for a long time. Then he reached over and turned the radio on. It came to life with a bang. There was a speaker on his side of the dash. He put his hand on the speaker and smiled. I guess he could feel the vibration. I turned the radio down a little and he just looked straight ahead. He gave me signals all the way to the back of a huge warehouse. He rolled his hands in a circle. I guess he was telling me to turn the truck around. I did and he gave me a thumbs-up. As he got out, he motioned for me to turn the motor off and sit tight. So I did. Haystack was gone for a few minutes before he came back to the truck and pointed in the warehouse. A lanky guy with long hair just like the rest of them came walking out.

"How y'all doin'? I'm Chet; I work for Sam and Joey. I guess you are takin' over for Denny. Too bad about that, ok, well, we've got a couple of crates to unload so we'd better get to it. Oh, hey, it's nice ta meet ya," he said, as he shook my hand. Chet started walking, so naturally I started walking; I was going to help him. Chet stopped and gave me a hard look. Then Haystack grabbed my arm and shook his head no. So, I just stood and waited by the back of the truck.

Wasn't long before Chet came back driving a forklift, straight at us. He unloaded a small wooden crate and then Haystack motioned me to help him slide it to the back of the box. Then Chet came back with a couple more. As Haystack and I moved the last crate, I could hear metal clanking inside. When we were done, I stopped to read what was printed on the last crate we put in the truck. It had Czechoslovakia printed on one corner. I said to myself, *I thought we were picking up kegs of beer?* I asked Chet what was in the crates. He gave me a very sour look before he said, "Motorcycle parts." He hesitated a second or two. "If y'all wanna keep this job, I'd stop asking questions and just do the work." Chet waved to Haystack to shut the door on the back of the truck. Then he turned, shook my hand, and said, "Nice meetin' ya Bobby; hope ta see ya again, well, bye now."

Haystack spit a black stream of tobacco by the side of the truck and then he smiled at me and motioned for us to go. That's when I realized he did have a few teeth; they were just black was all. We made it back and when I pulled around to the back of the building, Sam was waiting for us. Haystack went straight to her and signed something. She smiled real big before she turned to me and said, "Bobby, Chet and Haystack say you did just fine. You got the job."

"Gosh that's great," I said as I looked at the back of the truck. "Are we going to unload the truck now?"

"No, it's late and the night crowd will start pouring in pretty soon. Haystack will lock up the truck.

Come on Bobby, I'm gonna show you where you will sleep, but first you need to have a beer. You earned it."

I thought to myself, *it'd be rude to say no to a beer. And I suppose one won't hurt me.* "Ok, thanks Sam," I said, feeling pretty good about myself.

We went back in the tavern and the place was starting to fill up. There were more long-haired bikers wearing Headhunter vests, most of them were men. Sam sat me down in the corner away from the crowd. I drank the one beer and did my best to enjoy it, but I was incredibly tired.

I must have nodded out for a moment or two. Sam shook me and said, "Come on sweetie, you need to get some sleep."

I followed her across the room and up the stairs. When we got to the top, we turned left and Sam stopped. She unlocked a door and reached in and flipped a light switch. I looked around her into a small room that was directly over Joey's office and she whispered, "This was an office at one time, but Joey hated going up and down the stairs. It's small, but there's a closet, enough room for a bed, and best of all a bathroom. Tomorrow we can go get you a single bed at one of the thrift stores. Tonight, you're going to have to sleep on this old army cot. Is that ok?"

"Sam, it's better than ok. And believe it or not, I'm used to sleeping on a cot. Thank you so much, you have no idea how wonderful having a room, a bed, and a bathroom is. You really are an angel."

"Bobby, I'm no angel. Ok, well, sweet dreams," she said as she walked out.

I sat down and took off my shoes. I hadn't taken them off for at least a week. I wiggled my toes and thought, *gosh that feels good.* I turned the shower on full blast. I took off my clothes, but I left my underwear and socks on.

I jumped in the shower and the warm water splashing off the back of my neck felt so wonderful, it made me want to sing. There was an old bar of soap in the shower and I scrubbed and sang 'til I was too tired to move. Then I sat down in the shower and let the water fall on my head as I washed my underwear and socks. I was sitting there just letting the water bounce off my head when Sam yelled, "You're gonna need a towel."

I turned the water off and when I pulled the shower curtain to the side there was a towel, a toothbrush, and a pair of pajamas sitting next to the bathroom sink. I grabbed the towel and started drying off. I happened to look over at the pajamas and they started spinning like a barber's pole. I was dizzier than heck so I closed my eyes for a few seconds and the spinning stopped.

I figured I was just overtired. I put the pajamas on and when I looked in the mirror, the spinning started all over again; me and the pajamas. I closed my eyes and walked out of the bathroom. I reached in and turned the light off and then I went back in and brushed my teeth in the dark. I stood up and took a look in the dark, nothing happened.

I thought, *of course nothing happened you idiot, it's dark.* I limped over to the cot and said to myself, *maybe it's the blue plaid on the pajamas?* Just to be on the safe side I decided not to wear the pajamas again. I lay down and when I closed my eyes, a little golden bird sang to me as I sailed away on a pirate ship.

Can't Find my Way Home

39

Saturn, Alabama

Grits just could not stop needling his twin brother, Alvin. And Grasshopper could not stop thinking about how much trouble they were going to be in when they left the bar. All three of them knew that eventually they'd have to face the music.

"Alvin, you sorry sum-bitch. I sent ya in ta do a job, and y'all got your ever-lovin' ass kicked by a damn corn-fed cop. Now what are we gonna do?" Grits asked.

"Grits, know what y'all can do? No, well, I'm 'bout ta tell ya. You can kiss my grits, that's what you can do. You ever been hit in the face with a sack a rocks. No, I didn't think so. Well, let me tell ya, it hurts ta high heaven. How was I s'pose ta know he was gonna use a damn sack full a rocks? And besides, if you hadn't robbed the poor son of a bitch in the first place none a this woulda ever happened!" Alvin hollered as he got off of his bar stool and took a wild swing at Grits. Grasshopper jumped between the two of them and looked at the bartender for help.

"Hey, you two got a problem with each other, take it outside!" the bartender yelled.

"Please, y'all sit back down and listen for just a minute, please," Grasshopper begged.

The twins slowly sat back down.

"Dat's better. Listen, Armstrong is gonna tell yo uncle fo sho. Grits, we was just s'posed ta talk to de guy. And Alvin, instead a fightin' y'all coulda just told de cop dat we have his belongin's. Now we needs ta get back and tell yo uncle befo dat damn Armstrong get dere, please," Grasshopper begged again.

"Ok Alvin, you dumbass, finish yo drink so's we can get the hell outa here," Grits said with a bunch of attitude.

Crestfield

"Y'all finish yo own damn drink. I don't have ta go with ya. Uncle Cotton ain't allowed me around his place in months. Sides, this here is all y'all's fault. I ain't the one who robbed and then brung that got-damned cop here," Alvin said with more truth than attitude.

Grits got to thinking and decided that he'd better be nice to his brother, at least for a little bit.

"Ok, Alvin you got a good point there. I guess you can hide out somewhere's 'til this blows over. But if Uncle Cotton sends them Russian twins after y'all's ass, well, good luck. I guess you ain't never been hit and choked and so forth by them. Trust me, it ain't no got-damn fun," Grits said with a double-edged smirk.

Alvin thought about the Russians for a second or two. "Ok, I'll go, but only if y'all buy us a bottle to drink on the way.

Grits looked at Grasshopper and he didn't have to look twice. Grasshopper knew he had to acquiesce, "Ok Grits, I can buy a bottle."

The two brothers got up and at nearly the same time they said, "Shit howdy."

"You know what brother, by the time we gets ta that stainky old plantation, I'm gonna be feelin' no pain," Alvin said to Grits.

The pint of whiskey was procured and the three of them set out for the plantation. Grasshopper worried the entire way. Once there, Grits said they should go out to the barn before going in to see their uncle. They were going to need to make sure they had their ducks in a row. Well, they made it to the barn and it was either the second or maybe the third time Grits refused to let Alvin have a drink when Alvin picked up a pitch fork and threatened to stick Grits.

"You dirty low-down skunk of a brother. You brought out a knife and done this to my face that day we got kicked out a school," Grits said as he touched the ugly raised scar across his face. "And now ya threatenin' me with a got-damned pitchfork," Grits said as he raised the bottle for a drink.

Grasshopper jumped in between them again and pleaded with them to stop.

"Ok, I'll stop," Alvin said as he turned the pitchfork around and touched the tip on one of the barbs. "Mercy, that there's pretty damn sharp."

"I knew you didn't have the guts ta stick me," Grits said as he took another drink.

Alvin bent over to put the pitchfork down and then swung the pitchfork by the barbed end and hit Grits square in the mouth with the handle. The pint bottle shattered as Grits was knocked to the ground in the corner of the barn. Grits sat on his rear end and reached up and touched his hand to his mouth. He stared at the blood on his fingers as rage boiled up inside of him. Then he reached back and picked up the Louisville Slugger Vladimir had left in the corner the day before. He stood up and Alvin tried to turn the pitch fork around, but it was too late. The barrel of the bat hit Alvin along the left side of his head and he was immediately knocked to the ground. He struggled to his knees and looked up at Grits while he desperately tried to focus his eyes. The next blow hit Alvin dead square on the back of the neck. He toppled over face first to the ground and didn't move, not even a twitch. Grasshopper ran and turned Alvin over and held him on his lap. He put his ear next to Alvin's chest and then he lifted Alvin's head up and put his ear next to Alvin's mouth. Then he looked up at Grits and shook his head no. Grasshopper let Alvin slide down on his lap a little and stared at Grits.

"What you starin' at me fo? Wake him up. I won't hit him again. I just wanna give him a piece a my mind. Wake him up, I say."

"Grits, I cain't wake him up, nobody can, I tink his neck broke, he dead, you kildt him," Grasshopper said as he began to weep.

"What the hell you talkin' 'bout, killed him. I barely hit him, give him to me," Grits said as he knelt down and picked his brother up in his arms. "Alvin, please wake up I say, you hear me, I said for you to wake up," Grits said as he stared at Alvin and shook him from side to side. Grits listened for his twin's breath; once, twice, three times and then he looked up into the darkness and howled like an injured dog.

Grasshopper's mind went straight into overdrive as he tried to understand what had just happened and how to make it go away. Grasshopper knew what he could do, but it was risky to the point of life threatening. He told himself there was no other choice. He left Grits in the barn and rushed to the plantation and entered through the back door and into the kitchen. He stopped and stood in the dark listening for his boss or the Russians. He heard nothing and continued down the hallway and then he climbed the stairs. He softly knocked on the first door to the right of the stairs and Hurtwood's daughter, Razor Hurtwood, said, "Is that you sweetie. I'm not dressed, come on in." She giggled a bit at what she'd just said.

Grasshopper walked in and she was about to caress him, but she could see by the way he stood and the look on his face that something was wrong, terribly wrong.

"What is it darling; you look as if you've seen a ghost. Honey, please tell me what's wrong," she said as she shut her bedroom door.

Grasshopper knew he had a decision to make, tell her the truth, or keep her out of the mess and make something up. He chose the latter and said that Alvin was in the barn and was too drunk to make it back home. So, he wondered if he could borrow her car to take him there.

"Why sure, you can use my car, but you don't have to be so secretive about the whole thing. Daddy knows Alvin is a dirty little nuisance," she said as she fumbled in her purse. "Here, take the keys. I have to go back to Montgomery tomorrow morning, so when you get back, come on up and stay with me for a bit, please," she said as she handed Grasshopper the keys to her Jaguar.

"Ok, could be a little while, Alvin lives all de way over in de holler by Grand Bay. Thank you; in case it takes

longer, I'll leave de keys in de car. See ya, bye now,"
Grasshopper said before they shared a short kiss.

Grasshopper drove the car around to the barn with
the lights off. When he walked in, Grits was still holding
Alvin.

"Come on Grits, he'p me put Alvin in de trunk,"
Grasshopper said as he touched Grits on the shoulder.
Grits brushed Grasshopper's hand off his shoulder.

"Please, Grits, if we don't move his body you are
gonna be charged wif murder. Please, Grits," Grasshopper
said before he opened the trunk of the car. "I brought a
blanket wif me, here we need ta wrap him in it, come on
Grits, please," Grasshopper begged one more time.

Grits slowly got to his feet and stood and watched
as Grasshopper laid the blanket out on the ground. He
stood stoop shouldered and did nothing. So Grasshopper
picked up Alvin by his arms and dragged him to the edge
of the blanket. Then he rolled Alvin on and kept rolling
him 'til he was wrapped up tight. Then he looked at Grits.
"Please Grits, I cain't lift him into de trunk by myse'f."

Grits finally complied and grabbed the end of the
blanket at Alvin's feet. Grasshopper counted to three. They
lifted and softly put the body in the trunk. Grasshopper
shut the trunk and got in and started the car. Then he got
back out and walked around and helped Grits get in the
passenger side.

Grasshopper drove and talked to Grits about all the
ways they could handle the situation. Over and over, Grits
blamed Junior. He wanted to go to the police and tell 'em
the new kid in town killed Alvin. Grasshopper had other
ideas.

"Grits, we cain't blame him now. People saw him
leave de woik area. And mo impotant, dey saw us together
at de stagin' area. Dey saw us in de bar, and de liquor sto'.
Nobody will believe de cop killdt Alvin, unless a course
we can get people ta believe dat Alvin still alive."

"I don't understand," Grits said as the guilt on his
face turned to confusion.

"Grits, y'all gonna have ta stay in Alvin's crib fo a day o two. And from a safe distance wave ta yo neighbors a couple a times. Nobody will know de diffrence. You two have de exact same voice, build; you even walk de same."

"Yeah, how'm I sposed ta cover up this damn scar on my face?"

"You know that flop hat Alvin wears in de summer. It has ta be in his bedroom or–"

"Hey, you know that just might work. I know 'xactly where the stupid hat is. I'll just throw it on and keep my head down. This just might work. Thanks Grasshopper, oh but what are we gonna do with his body?" Grits asked in a tempered voice.

"Well, we waits a few days. Let's say dis Tuesday night, ok? We go late at night and puts him in de Salt near where de cop live. Den if somebody find him, we can tell de autorities dat de cop had a fight wit Alvin and dat he prob'ly de one dat dun kildt him. Wha-da-y'all tink?" Grasshopper asked.

"I think it sounds like our only real option is what I think. Yep, by God, that's what we'll do," Grits said as they drove up in front of Alvin's tiny clapboard bungalow.

Grasshopper backed up to the front door and they quickly carried Alvin inside. They decided to put the body in the closet. Grasshopper reminded Grits to be ready Thursday night. He said goodbye and drove away in the darkness.

Grits opened the closet door and grabbed the flop hat. He put the hat on and then looked down at his brother.

"Alvin, how'd all this go wrong. I'm sorry; Lord knows I's sorry. I hope someday y'all can forgive me. Alvin, please forgive me."

Grits walked out to Alvin's little kitchen and opened the fridge. There was one bottle of beer and a half empty bottle of cheap wine. Grits took them both out and sat down at the table. He started with the beer and sat there in the dark for the rest of the night.

40

Grasshopper didn't go back up to Razor's bedroom. He figured he already had enough problems. And he knew that if Cotton Hurtwood ever found out about his daughter and him, well, he'd be dead. He hid out in the barn and watched Razor drive away. She had an important job; she was now a State Senator. And he knew that it was just a matter of time before she would latch on to somebody else, somebody with money and power, and of course, white skin.

Grasshopper waited 'til Mr. Hurtwood was up and medicated before he knocked on his office door. He wasn't sure if it was Vladimir or Nikita that said come in. He told them everything about the previous day, which is everything except for the fact that Alvin was dead. He explained that they tried to tell the cop that they had his belongings, identification, and money. But they could not shake Pearly.

"Mr. Armstrong has already told me what happened, but I'm glad you have come to me and told me the truth. Where is Grits? And why didn't he come with you?" Hurtwood asked.

"Grits has gone to de Salt. He bound and detoimined ta bring dis guy to y'all," Grasshopper said with as much confidence as he could muster.

"Ok, well, you look like you need some sleep. Rest up and then go bring this man to me," Hurtwood said as he waved Grasshopper out of his office.

Grasshopper walked out and kept going 'til he heard the door shut behind him. Then he snuck back and listened as Mr. Hurtwood spoke to the Russian twins.

"Vladimir, I think you had better take over. This has gone on long enough. Do whatever it takes to find this police officer. Ok, Nikita, you can go ahead and administer the rest of my medication, please?" Hurtwood ordered more than asked.

Nikita brought out the kit and got the syringe ready before he tied Hurtwood's arm off. He did as he'd been told a dozen times and slowly introduced the 'medication.' He removed the rubber hose and watched as Cotton Hurtwood drifted off to never-never land.

41

The Broken Bone Tavern

I woke up and wasn't sure what time it was, but I felt as though I'd slept for a week. I was still very sore from the work with the road crew. I hadn't thought about it, but I must have been a little sore from the fight with Alvin Wetmore too. I sat up on the cot and could smell coffee. I ran to the bathroom and when I looked in the mirror, I started spinning again. I turned the light off, took off the pajamas, threw my clothes on and went down the stairs. When I got to the bottom, Sam said, "Well, it's about time, sleepy head. You know it's after nine o'clock? I guess I forgot to tell you that your job starts at eight every morning. I'll excuse you this time, but don't let it happen again."

"Good morning, Sam. I can't see you, but I know you're here somewhere," I said as I strained to look across at the bar.

Not sure exactly why, but it's a strange thing to walk through a tavern in the morning. And to be honest, if not for the coffee, I'd rather have stayed in bed. I strained my eyes looking for Sam before I walked out a little further, and then she popped up from underneath the stairs and said, "Come sit down at the bar and have some coffee. We need to talk about a few things."

I wasn't sure what a few things meant, but I guess I was ok with whatever she wanted to talk about. I sat down and she poured me a cup of black coffee. I didn't say a word for at least five minutes. I just sat and soaked up her beautiful face while I sipped on the coffee.

"Ok cowboy, we have a little job to take care of this morning. Seems that somebody told me they didn't really have a home, but they forgot to tell me that they didn't really have a valid driver license either. When was the last time you went to the Mississippi Department of

Motor Vehicles? Well, I'd say never. Now, you get to go stand in line, pass the damn test, and then get your picture taken; and I mean today. Do you understand me Bobby, or whatever your name really is."

"I was feeling so good about a minute ago, and I was going to thank you for the towel and well, everything else. But now it seems that I'd better apologize before I start thanking you. Sam, I'm really sorry, but I really had no other choice."

"Ok, you can stop right there, Mc-Bobby," Joey said from somewhere behind me.

I turned and watched Joey walk out from underneath the stairs. I thought, *what the heck, is there a hidden room under the stairs?*

"Ok, I owe both of you an apology, but first please let me explain. I don't really know who I am, or where I'm from. In fact, I don't even know if Bobby is my real name."

They both looked at me before they walked over to a table and pointed for me to sit down. I did and then I told them the whole doggone story. I mean from the beginning to the end. When I was done, neither of them said a word. I think they were trying to decide if I was nuts or telling the truth or both.

"Does anyone know you're here?" Joey asked in a very determined way.

"No, I cleaned up at Gino's and walked out. I did tell him I was going for a job interview. That's why he wrote the recommendation. But I didn't tell him where the job was or what I would be doing, because I didn't even know what this job was, or what I'd be doing. There isn't a soul in the world that knows I'm here, well, except for Chet and Haystack, and of course the two of you."

Sam and Joey looked at each for longer than I was comfortable with, but I guess they had the right. Finally, Joey said, "Go comb your hair, and do whatever it is you need to do. Then come back down here. I have a birth certificate for you to show at the DMV. Get your damned license and then we'll get you started. You know something, Mc-Bobby, if you had gotten in a damn wreck last night, Sam and I could a lost the bar. Don't you ever do something to endanger this bar again, you hear me?" Joey said with force.

"Yes, and I'm sorry. Sam and Joey, you have my word, it will never happen again."

"Ok, go get ready," Sam said.

I ran up the stairs and got myself ready to go. Then as I was running back down the stairs, something crossed my mind and I said to myself, *I have no idea what the rules of the road are in any state, let alone Mississippi.* When I got down stairs, Sam and Joey were gone. I thought, *what the heck*, so I walked outside. Sam was there waiting for me in what looked to be a brand new bright blue Corvette. I opened the door and got in and just had to ask her about something.

"Boy Sam, this sure is a beautiful car. You know I've noticed that from the sign on top of the tavern to the vests all the guys wear that everything is blue. Is there a reason for that?" I asked.

"Took you long enough. Yes, almost everything is blue because of the blue-eyed dog. That's dawg, d a w g," she said with a smile.

"Um, what blue-eyed dawg?" I asked.

"Why, Joey of course. Have you ever seen another dawg that has just one blue eye?" she asked in earnest.

"No, I guess not, but remember, I'm not really sure about anything that I might or might not have seen before," I said in earnest.

"In all seriousness, the blue-eyed dawg is Joey's club name. Sometimes the guys just call him dawg. Either way, it fits," she said with a smile.

"Yes, it does," I agreed before I decided to leave it at that.

We drove to the DMV and I stood in a line for just over a half-an-hour. I finally got up to the window and the gal sitting behind the counter says, "Are y'all renewin' or gettin' yo first license?"

"Um, I'm not–"

"This is his first license," Sam said from behind me.

"Oh, is this y'all's mother?" the girl behind the counter said as she looked over at the gal working next to her. They had a good little giggle at Sam's expense.

"No, I'm not his mother, but thanks for the compliment. I'm gonna let my mother know how kind you were. Maybe you know who my mother is?"

The girl behind the counter smacked her gum real loud and said, "Ok, who is your mother?"

"My mother is Deborah Landis; do you know who that is?" Sam said without smiling.

The girl behind the counter gave me a piece of paper and said, "Sir, please fill this out and then go on over ta winduh eight. They'll give you the written test. Thank you, and if you need any he'p, please be sure to come on back. You don't have ta stand in line, just walk right on up. Ok, well, good luck," she said before she shut her little window, put her head down, and walked away.

I walked over to a table, sat down, and filled out the form with Sam's help, of course. Then, as we walked over to window eight, I asked Sam who Deborah Landis is.

"Take a look at the bottom of the form you just filled out," Sam said.

I looked down at the bottom of the DMV application and read to myself, "Deborah Landis, Executive Director - Department of Motor Vehicles for the State of Mississippi."

I looked at Sam and asked her if the Landis lady was really her mother.

"Nah, but that little smartass doesn't know whether or not Ms. Landis is my mother. She's probably in the bathroom wondering if she's going to have a job tomorrow. That'll teach her to keep her smartass comments to herself. Look, I can't go in the test area with you. So, get as close to that hallway over there as you can, and if you have a question, whisper it to me."

I passed a vision test and the written test without any help from Sam. Then I took a driving test, in the Corvette. The test guy was impressed with the car. Said he'd never been in one before. I passed the driving test too. I stood in one more line and had my picture taken. I was given a temporary license, and for the very first time since hearing the name Bobby McKillin, I felt like a real person.

42

San Francisco

Detective Olmstead called me each evening for a week straight. Every single time I answered the phone, I prayed he would have some new information to share with me; he told me nothing. I decided to go ahead with my own investigation. Each afternoon my friend, Tarrah, drove me downtown and dropped me off in front of the police station. I stood and watched and waited for Billy to show up. On the third day, I was so frustrated I went ahead and asked one of the other couriers about Billy. I found out that Billy had been disciplined by his father for not going to the company party. So I wrote a note and asked the guy to give it to Billy. The note simply said, please give me a call. I wrote my name and number down and hoped.

Two days later Billy called. I was getting ready for work so I just asked him if he could meet me the next day at two o'clock in front of the police station. He gave me a definite yes, and an apology for not calling sooner. We met the next afternoon.

"Hi Dezi, listen I really am sorry for not calling, but my dad grounded me. He told me that females are the bane of society. I don't know what a bane is, but he ordered me to stay away from you. But I'm here now," he said as he parked his bike.

"Billy, thanks for coming. Listen, now that you've told me what your dad thinks of females, I'm not sure I should tell you what I had in mind."

He gave me a strange look before he said, "My dad will get over it, but I won't. We have to find your brother."

I jumped at him and hugged him real hard. When I let go of him, he smiled and said, "What, no kiss?"

"I'm sorry Billy, not now. Look, here's my plan. I have to find out what the guy's name is that stole Junior's stuff. And then I have to find out where he's from. Because I think that's where Junior is. Does that make sense to you?" I asked as Billy stared down at the sidewalk and fidgeted. "Billy, what's wrong?"

"Well, I knew that's what you were going to ask me to help you with. So, I asked Jude if he'd help. The problem is, he wants money," Billy said as he looked up at me with a frown.

"Who is Jude? And how much money does he want?" I asked, knowing I had no money to give to anyone for anything.

"Jude Robertson, he's the special courier for the police department. He runs their stuff all over town. Anyway, he has access to all the files. He can get the info, but he wants fifty bucks for the name and another fifty for where the guy lives."

"A hundred dollars," I asked in shock.

"Yes, a hundred dollars. Jude made a good point when he reminded me that if he got caught, he'd definitely lose his job," Billy said as I started to cry.

"Dezi, it's ok. I've made arrangements to get the money. We can pay it back in installments."

"You mean Jude is going to let us pay him back a little at a time?" I asked.

"No, Jude is too big a jerk to go for that. So, I asked a bane I know real well to loan me the money. She said ok," he said with a sheepish grin.

"What bane is this?" I asked.

"My mom. Other than you, she's really the only other bane of society I know," he said as he looked down at the sidewalk in front of him.

His hair was tangled, and he had food stains on his shirt, and he said I was a bane of society. But for whatever reason, I wanted to give him a kiss, so I did. He turned beet red, again.

"Ok, now listen Dezi, this is how it's going to work out. On Friday, I'm going to meet Jude at Candlestick. He's using my ticket to go watch the Giants.

Anyway, when I give him the money and the ticket, he's going to give me the name and address and stuff."

"Billy, what if Jude lies and just makes up a name?" I asked, concerned about the money, etc.

"Oh no, I made sure he can't do that. See, I have a failsafe plan. He has to make a copy of the notes with the police letterhead on it. And if he lies or makes the stuff up, then my friend Biff is gonna beat Jude up. Biff said he'd do it for five dollars. Jude knows Biff and he doesn't want to get beat up. What do you think, I mean, does it sound like a good plan to you?" he asked.

"Oh Billy, that sounds wonderful. I just don't know what I'll do once I get the name and stuff. What if the guy lives in New York or Europe or someplace far away? I mean, how am I gonna get there?"

"Dezi, we can worry about that after we get the information. Remember, we need to look for the silver lining," he said with a smile as he got on his bike. "Ok, I'm back on the job, so I gotta go make some deliveries. I'll call you Friday night and let you know what happens. Won't be able to use the Bel Air, but I'll find a way to bring the stuff by on Saturday morning. Is that ok?" he asked.

"Yes, that is wonderful. Gosh Billy, you're the best," I said as I gave him a peck on the cheek.

He looked like a rose with eyeballs as he rode away.

43

Hurtwood plantation

Cotton Hurtwood watched the sun set from the west side of the second story veranda every night. It was his time to forget about business and so forth. Nikita knew that his boss would not like being disturbed, but he had no choice.

"Sir, sir," Nikita said to his sleeping boss.

He gently shook Hurtwood and when his eyelids opened Nikita said, "I'm sorry sir, but there are two law enforcement agents here to see you."

"What, what, what's going on?" Hurtwood asked in a drug induced stupor.

"Mr. Hurtwood, I'm agent Lipscomb," a tall black man wearing a dark suit said, "And this is agent Cummings, we're with the FBI." Both agents flashed their badges. "We need to ask you a few questions. Would it be ok if we went back inside?"

"The FBI, why in the world would you want to ask me questions? Nikita, can you show these people to the door," Cotton Hurtwood said with a note of southern arrogance.

"Mr. Hurtwood, I assure you that at some point you're going to have to talk with us. We only have a few questions," Lipscomb repeated.

"Nikita show them to my office, I'll be down shortly," Hurtwood said in disgust.

Nikita walked away with the agents and Vladimir handed Hurtwood a fifty-dollar bill and a small mirror with fancy scrollwork along its edges. On it lay a small, neat line of snowy white powder.

"Vladimir, I hope this does the trick?" Hurtwood creaked in a craggy voice after the powder was gone.

"It will. Sir, if you do not know the answer to a question or you are unsure, then say so. And no matter how simple the question may appear, only give them known facts," Vladimir said as he rolled his boss to the elevator.

"Vladimir, when we get down to my office, immediately offer the agents some coffee. And of course, bring me some."

"Yes, sir, it is already done. Nikita has your coffee waiting."

"Thank you, please stay in the room. Just in case of, well, just in case," Hurtwood said as he began to wake from his slumber.

Hurtwood was rolled into his office and moved behind his enormous desk. He took a sip of the coffee that was sitting in front of him. He did all he could to compose himself. When he looked up at the two agents, he realized for the first time that one of them was a female. The agent named Cummings had an extremely keen look in her eyes. She was tall and had dark hair and eyes. She was beautiful. As he studied the female agent some more, he realized that the likeness to his own daughter was uncanny.

"Please, sit down," he said to the agents.

"Thank you, but we won't be that long," said Lipscomb.

"Please, I insist," Hurtwood repeated.

The agents looked at each other for a moment and then they sat in the chairs provided by Nikita.

"Would you care for some coffee or maybe something else, perhaps water?" Nikita asked.

Lipscomb looked at Cummings and she shook her head no. Then he looked at Nikita and said, "We won't be that long. Thank you, but neither of us need anything to drink at this time."

Nikita walked back and stood next to the hallway door behind the agents. Vladimir stood next to his boss.

"Well, how can I help you?" Hurtwood asked.

"We would like to speak to a man that uses your address as his home address. We assume he either works for you or he is family. His name is Grits Elmo Wetmore," Lipscomb said in a hollow and rehearsed dry voice.

"Has Grits broken the law?" Hurtwood asked as his eyes narrowed onto agent Cummings.

"We believe he is involved in a," Lipscomb stopped and looked at agent Cummings. She only glanced at the other agent for a moment before she said, "We only need to know his relationship with you and his whereabouts. Then we will need to speak directly to him," Cummings said in an experienced voice.

"Grits is my sister's son. Now and then he does odd jobs for me, well, actually he does them for the household. He has a fifth-grade education and is what would be considered a functioning illiterate. As far as his whereabouts are concerned, he lives in a makeshift room we have out in the stables, which he calls the barn. He comes and goes, but at the present I don't believe he is here. I have no idea where he could be. You are welcome to go out and check the stables. In fact, you are welcome to search the entire home if you'd like. Please, can you tell me a little more about why it is you're here?" Hurtwood asked as the amphetamines gave him a sudden jolt.

"Has Grits told you about his recent visit to California?" agent Cummings asked.

"California?" Hurtwood said in a rehearsed lost voice.

"Yes, we believe he was in California this last week. So, you know nothing about this?" she asked.

"No, I don't," Hurtwood said as he looked at Vladimir and then Nikita. "Do either of you know anything about Grits going to California?" The Russians shook their heads no but did not say a word.

"Agent Cummings, this is very odd. You see, Grits has no money that I know of. Nor does he have the wherewithal to be on his own or take a trip of such magnitude. Are you sure it was him?" Hurtwood asked.

"Yes, we believe so, but that is one of the reasons why we need to speak with Grits. Ok, we would like to see his living quarters. I'm going to give you a card with phone numbers where we can be reached. The moment you see Mr. Wetmore or know of his whereabouts, I want you to call. Doesn't matter day or night, do you understand? Oh, and one other thing, where does his mother live? That is Grits Wetmore's mother," agent Cummings said in a very clear voice.

"She lives in Mississippi, Choctaw Ridge, to be exact. I can guarantee you Grits is not there. He is not welcome, but I do have my sister's address and phone number," Hurtwood said as he wrote down his sister Scarlett Wetmore's information on a note pad.

Hurtwood tore off the small sheet of paper and handed it to agent Cummings as she handed him the card with the FBI phone numbers. Nikita showed the agents the small room in the stable where Grits slept. They rummaged through his meager belongings for about ten minutes and then left the property. After the FBI agents drove away, Nikita went directly to Hurtwood's office.

"I want the two of you to find Grits, and then I want you to kill him. Do you understand?" Hurtwood demanded as the Russians nodded their heads yes. "I want you to put his dead body in the trunk of your car and drive him as far away from here as you can. Then we'll concentrate on this police officer. I don't know why the agents didn't ask about him. I wonder if they even know he's here. Are they clever enough to keep that information from us? Perhaps they really don't know. That would certainly bode well for us. Do either of you know where Grasshopper is?" In unison, the Russians shook their heads no. "Well, he might be of help, don't harm him; at least not yet. Ok, enough of that - find Grits. I don't want to see him again. Vladimir, before you leave, there is a section of the railing that is ready to give way on the south side of the veranda. Write a note and have Riley take it to our carpenter so he can repair the railing." Vladimir gave a nod yes. "Nikita, I do not like this sudden energy I'm feeling, please administer a larger dose of my medication," Hurtwood ordered more than asked.

44

Grasshopper snuck up slow, his heart beating like a kettle drum in his ears as he peered into the window. At first all he could see was his own reflection, then movement. He ducked out of sight and hoped he had not been seen. He slowly lifted his head and watched again as the young lady moved about. He asked himself; *maybe I should just knock on de do. No, she might know who I is and hit me wit somepin'. I wish I was a brave man, I'd just walks right in and tell her de truph about tings. But, I'm not a brave man. What am I gonna do?*

Then right out loud Grasshopper asked himself, *"What am I gonna do?"*

"I knows what you ain't gonna do nigguh, you ain't gonna be peekin' in no mo winduhs, dat's fo damn sho," the unknown giant said, as he picked Grasshopper up with one hand.

Grasshopper started to scream, but no sound came out. The giant had pressed his other massive hand over Grasshopper's nose and mouth. Now instead of trying to scream Grasshopper struggled for a breath of air, none was forthcoming. He squirmed and struggled, his vision turned gray, then black as he was carried inside the home.

"Odell, who is dis boy?" Belle asked.

"He de hi-yelluh boy dat woiks at dat slave plantation over yonder in Al'bama. You know dat Hurtwoodt place. I tink he go by Grasshoppuh?" Odell said to Belle as they both looked down at the captured peeping tom.

"Unh uh, what's we gonna do wit him?" Belle asked.

"Well, I'm gonna let him wake up den we can decides what ta do wif him," Odell said.

Grasshopper began to stir before he slowly opened

his eyes. There, looking down at him, was the giant that had taken the air out of his world. He wanted to run and hide, but he knew that if he jumped up or made a sudden move, he just might be killed. So, he ran through his head what his options were. He decided on the truth.

"I'm sorry ta have snuck up and looked in dat winduh. It's just dat I had ta gets a message ta y'all 'bout de new kid in town," he said as he put his hands up to protect against any reprisals.

"What new kid you talkin' 'bout?" Belle asked as she walked out from behind the giant.

Odell grabbed Belle by the arm and walked her into her bedroom and whispered, "Bell, he talkin 'bout dat white boy Pearly done foun' down at de culvert by de Salt."

"You means Bobby," Belle whispered.

"His name is Bobby?" Odell softly asked.

"Yes, everbody know his name Bobby. How's come dis hi-yelluh nigguh don't know?" Belle asked.

"I don't know, Belle, how you know his name Bobby?" Odell asked with a little attitude.

"I knows cuz Pearly call him dat. And dey comes ovuh fo grits, dat's how I knows. And don't you give me no truck on dis," Belle said with a roomful of attitude.

"I can gives you all de truck I wants to. What you doin' hangin' wif a white boy?" Odell asked in utter disgust.

Belle put her hands up to her face and then covered her eyes as she began sobbing.

"What's wrong, Belle?" Odell asked.

Belle stomped her foot down and yelled, "I hang wit him cuz I likes him. I likes him a whole lot!" Belle said with fire in her eyes.

At first Odell took a step back and then he moved over and put his arms around his little sister.

"Mahidabelle, it ok, I's sorry. Lord have mercy, I had no idea you liked a white boy. You and Pearly sho-nuff confuse de stuffin' right outa me. Unh - uh, hangin' wif a white boy. If dat don't beat all," Odell said as he gently rocked Belle in his arms. I guess dis world we lives in changin'. What's next, a colored president?" Odell said with a chuckle.

"Now Odell, don't go gettin' all crazy on me; a colored president. Can you imagine dat? Ok, let's us go see what dis hi-yelluh want wif Bobby. Oh 'fo I fogets, don't let on dat we know his name Bobby," Belle warned.

"Ok, we won't let on 'bout yo boyfriend Bobby," Odell said with a chuckle.

Belle smacked him on the arm and then she pulled him back out to the front room. Grasshopper was now sitting in Belle's favorite sewing rocker.

"Boy! You better get yo ass out my damn chair, and right now," Belle admonished.

Grasshopper jumped up out of the chair and began explaining why he was there. He told Belle and Odell that he and Grits had followed Pearly and the white boy to her home.

"We din't want de little dog to see us, so we couldn't pass de message on ta de white boy. Can y'all tell him fo me?" Grasshopper asked.

"We don't know where he at," Belle said.

"Don't nobody know where he at, but you can give us de message. Den if we sees him, we can pass it on," Odell affirmed.

"Tell him ta go to de Hurtwoodt plantation. Day o night, won't mattuh," Grasshopper said.

"Tell him ta go dere fo what?" Belle asked.

"Oh yeah, dey have some of his belongin's, not sure what dey have, but dey have somepin'," Grasshopper said.

"What's in all dis fo you? You sneaky little hi-yelluh nigguh," Odell charged.

"Shit! Ain't nothin' in it fo me. And dat's de Gods truph," Grasshopper said as he looked back at Belle and Odell for some redemption.

"Ok, well, chances are we ain't never gonna see

him, but if we do, we might go-'headt and tells him. Say, what you do out at dat slave plantation, anyway?" Belle asked.

"I do small jobs, like dis here, and I he'p out wif de gardenin' and horses and such. My mama uzed ta woik fo Missuh Hurtwoodt. She took care a his daughtuh; you know de one dat's a state senator, her name Razuh Hurtwoodt. And trust me, razuh is right; she could cut you to de quick, she gots a sharp tongue. Anyway, dat's about all dat I do," Grasshopper said in a humble voice.

"Dey still has de coloreds pick cotton out at dat slave plantation?" Odell asked.

"No, Missuh Hurtwood don't like de cotton bidness. Says most a his land is fallow. I believe he buys and sells tings, you know import - export. What he buys and sells, I don't know," Grasshopper said.

"Ok, well, we gonna let you go dis time. But I'm tellin' ya right here and now, if I sees ya anywhere near here again, I'm gonna kill ya, you unnerstands me, boy?" Odell said as he pressed his huge index finger deep into Grasshopper's chest.

"I unnerstands," Grasshopper said as he started for the door.

Belle had other ideas and grabbed his arm and stopped him.

"What Odell dun tol' you go fo everbody dat live o woik at dat slave plantation. And 'speshly dat nasty ol' man Riley, you unnerstands me, boy?" Belle said as her head bobbed from side to side.

"Yes, ma'am, I unnerstands. I will certainly tell dem ta stay 'way from yo crib," Grasshopper said with a noticeable tone of dread in his voice.

Odell opened the door and Grasshopper stepped out, then started running as fast as his legs would carry him. He never once looked back.

"Now what we gonna do Belle?" Odell asked.

"We not gonna do nuttin', but when I sees Pearly, I'll tells him. Den he can decides what oughta be done. Fo now, Pearly say it impo'tant dat Bobby stay 'way and dat nobody know where he at," Belle said, knowing full well there was nothing in the world she would rather do than see Bobby.

45

Grasshopper ran all the way back to the plantation. He had a deadline to meet. That is, picking up Grits at Alvin's crib and then finding somewhere near the Salt to dump the body. He took the long way around through the backwoods so that he wouldn't be seen. Then he entered the old slave quarters where he had lived for the last twenty years or so. He walked in and didn't turn on the lights. He didn't want to be seen. He sat in the dark and his mind scurried back and forth trying to come up with a way to find a vehicle to carry Alvin to the Salt. He needed some fresh air so he walked outside and plopped down on the porch swing. He didn't hear the footsteps from behind and to the side of him.

"Hello Grasshopper," Nikita said as he lit a cigarette. "We've been waiting for you. Where have you been?"

Grasshopper started to answer but was cut off by Vladimir.

"Grasshopper, we don't like being lied to. Do you know why I say this? No? We've been to Salt and after many questions, we have determined that you lied when you said Grits was there."

Grasshopper started to explain and once again he was cut off.

"Grits is not at Salt and has not been there for several days," Vladimir said as he slowly struck a match and lit a cigarette.

"But he was dere, we was both dere," Grasshopper said in truth.

"Grasshopper, we have been told not to harm you, but we have also been told to find Grits. Now, if you can't help us, then you are of no use to us. Mr. Hurtwood will want Russians to get rid of problems. Are you a problem?"

Nikita asked. And before Grasshopper could spit out an answer, Nikita yelled, "Do you understand me? Where is Grits? Tell us now!"

"Ok, I'm gonna tells ya, but I gots ta have me some inshoance dat y'all ain't gonna hoit me," Grasshopper said.

He had the Russians over a small barrel and they knew it. It was really all very simple, without Grasshopper they didn't have Grits. Nikita thought of a plan he believed would work so he asked.

"Grasshopper, do you like Grits?"

"No, I hates his ignorant cracker ass. He is de meanest, well, he is one a de meanest people on dis here oith," Grasshopper said with a scowl.

"What if Mr. Hurtwood tells you himself that we won't hurt you. Then will you help us with Grits?" Nikita asked.

"Ya mean, gets rid of Grits, permanent like?" Grasshopper asked.

The Russians both nodded their heads yes.

"Ok, I'll do it, but only if Hurtwoodt gives me his woid I won't be harmed. Dat's my deal fo y'all," Grasshopper said as he stuck out his chest.

"Deal," was all Vladimir said.

They walked around the slave quarters and got in Vladimir's low slung black sedan. The drive from the slave quarters took all of ten seconds. Hurtwood was waiting near the stables. Grasshopper got out and pleaded his case to his boss. He wasn't near as Cavalier under Hurtwood's scrutiny.

"Grasshopper, you have my word that you will not be harmed in any way. I want Grits taken care of, that's all. Now, Vladimir and Nikita, you have witnessed this agreement. You are not to harm Grasshopper. He is going to help us. Now go get Grits," Hurtwood ordered.

Nikita pushed Hurtwood through the back of the house and into his office. Then he joined his twin and Grasshopper. Along the way, Grasshopper decided to tell them about what Grits had done to Alvin. They never said a word, but they did smile on the inside as they thought, *this will be Khorosho, both idiot brothers gone in one fell swoop.*

They drove up the path in front of Alvin's home with the car lights off. Grasshopper knocked on the door and Grits peeked out through the front window before opening the front door. They both hurried inside. Once inside, Grasshopper had to tell Grits about the Russians. Grits was livid, and as his temper flared, he slapped Grasshopper across the face. Grasshopper fell to the floor and Grits was on him in a flash. Grits began to pummel Grasshopper with haymaker punches. Grits stopped for only a moment because his hands ached. Then he reached down and began strangling Grasshopper, and for the second time that day, Grasshopper's world turned black.

Grasshopper woke to the gentle sway of an automobile, smoothly rolling down a country road. He looked up and realized he was in the back seat of Vladimir's car. All was quiet as Grasshopper came back to life. He looked in front of him and the Russians were staring straight ahead. Then he heard the pounding from the trunk of the car.

"Nikita, is dat Grits I hears?" Grasshopper asked.

Nikita did not answer. He just turned and nodded his head yes.

"Goodt," was all Grasshopper said.

Vladimir drove the car into the stables. He was being extra cautious because the FBI had been to the plantation asking questions, too many questions. Vladimir carried a bound and gagged Grits into one of the stalls. He sat him up against the wall before securely tying his hands and feet to the metal chair he sat on. When Nikita pushed his uncle into the stable, the gag was removed. Grits let out a banshee yowl before his Uncle Cotton softly told him it was ok, and not to yell anymore. Grits slowly let the dread he felt leave his body. Surely his uncle would never harm his sister's child.

"Grits, Grits, you have been up to no good again. Grasshopper tells me you killed your own brother. Is this true?" Uncle Cotton asked.

"It were an accident!" Grits screamed.

"Accident or not you have been warned too many times. And now you are a known murderer. I can't have a murderer living at the plantation. What would people say?"

"Why, they ain't gonna say nothin', cuz we gonna get rid a the body," Grits reasoned.

"Yes, we are. And that will make two bodies in all," Uncle Cotton said.

When the reality hit Grits, the screaming could be heard for quite a distance. So, Vladimir put the gag back in Grits's mouth. Grits squirmed, and his eyes bulged as his head twirled on his neck like a lasso. That was just before he passed out.

A few minutes later he woke and his uncle told Vladimir to remove the gag.

"Grits, please try to be brave. We will make this as painless as we can. Do you have anything that you'd like to say?" Uncle Cotton asked.

"What're you gonna tell my mama?" Grits begged.

"Why, I'm going to tell her the truth," Uncle Cotton said.

"The truth, what do you mean the truth," Grits bellowed.

"I'm going to tell your mother that you went to California, of course," Cotton Hurtwood said as he motioned to Nikita.

Grits started to scream, the gag was quickly replaced. Grits watched Nikita push his Uncle Cotton out of the barn. He violently shook his head no as he watched Grasshopper slowly walk in the barn. Grits stared down at Grasshopper's hands. He was carrying the flame fused Louisville Slugger. The last thing Grits Wetmore ever saw on this earth was the rage in Grasshopper's eyes, and of course the barrel of that bat.

Crestfield

Vladimir drove, Nikita sat in the front, and Grasshopper sat in the back. They drove for hours before they finally reached their destination. So that the twins would be near their mother, Grits and Alvin Wetmore's weighted bodies were driven deep into the great state of Mississippi and were quietly thrown off the Tallahatchie Bridge.

46

Tavern
I'm grateful to have a job, a place to sleep, and a bathroom, but each morning when I open my eyes, I have the blues something awful. There's just too much missing in my life. Mostly, my family and I guess, me. That may sound strange, but truth be told, I do miss me. Pearly said a couple of times that above all else, 'to thine own self be true.' Well, I'm beginning to understand what that actually means. And trust me, it's a lonely world when you don't know who thine own self is. I wake up at seven every morning and trudge about for a while. After I get dressed, I go downstairs and have a cup of coffee with Sam. Then we head over to a small diner nearby for breakfast. The owner's name is Billy-Joe-Bill. Men and women having two names is commonplace in the south, but having three names and two of them the same is, in my opinion, a bit over the top. Once in a while, Joey and Haystack join us for breakfast, but they're usually still sawing logs. They don't get to bed until early in the morning. As a matter of fact, sometimes when I come downstairs, they're still up. I don't know how they do it. After breakfast, I work like a dog cleaning the tavern. My first week I got to know both of the night bartenders, Jay-Don and Mickey-Lee. They're stand up guys.

They do their best picking up the tavern before they leave each night but believe me, when I start mopping, there are still smells and things stuck on the floor that can't be described. I do the best I can. It's a dirty job, but a job, nonetheless. Maybe you remember me talking about Sam and Joey popping up from underneath the stairs. Turns out that's where they keep all the empty bottles. After I finish the floors, I carry all the empties out to the truck. I usually take a break at about ten and play a game or two of checkers or cards with Sam.

Crestfield

Playing cards comes natural to me. I think there's a good chance that I played cards in my other life. That's one of the things I wonder about all the time; my other life. After I get tired of trying to figure out who the heck I am and where I came from, I think of Pearly, and Belle, and Scooter and Ralphy. Gosh, I miss them. No, that's not the whole truth; the truth is I miss them and I feel guilty for running out on them. I hope they understand that I had to leave.

After lunch each day, I make the rounds in the truck. I drop off empties and pick-up more full bottles. The full ones sure do get heavy. And one evening each of the last two weeks, Haystack and I have gone to the warehouse where Chet works and picked up crates of motorcycle parts. They open the crates at night so I never get to see the parts. Truth is, I don't care to see them. I'm getting tired of seeing motorcycles. Mostly, I'm tired of cleaning up after the people that ride them. They're nice to me and all, but I really don't fit in with them.

At night, I stay upstairs in my room as much as I can. At first, the noise from the tavern was overwhelming, but after a day or two, it just became a slow constant buzz. I have one window in my room and I keep it open at all times. The noise from the outside helps dissipate the noise coming from downstairs. I suppose the worst thing I deal with is the amount of smoke that finds its way up the stairs; not sure, but I don't think it's all cigarette smoke.

It was the second evening I was living here when Sam came up and sat with me for a while. I sure do like her company. Anyway, she brought me some magazines and three books to read, and a pen and notebook. She said writing stuff down would help when I was feeling blue. Not sure how she knew, but she knew. She sure is a thoughtful person. I found out that writing the stuff down does help cope with the relentless life void that follows me like a sunless shadow, everywhere I go.

47

Dezi's home – San Francisco

Saturday morning at about nine o'clock somebody rang the doorbell. I looked through the peephole at a short, chubby, cherub-faced young man wearing a Giants hat and a blue shirt. The shirt had S.F.P.D. stitched across the pocket. He was staring at a large brown envelope he held in his hands. I opened the door; I left the security chain latched.

"Who are you and what do you want?" I asked.

"I'm Billy's friend, Jude Robertson. Are you Dezi?" he politely asked.

"Yes, I'm Dezi. What do you want?"

"I have the information you asked for. Billy couldn't get here so he paid me five dollars extra to deliver the stuff. Can I come in?" he asked.

I unlatched the chain and opened the door. The kid walked in about three steps, took off his hat, and stuck out his hand. I took the envelope he held and immediately tore it open. From what I could see, the two papers inside looked official. The top piece of paper had a physical description of a man named Grits Elmo Wetmore.

I walked away from the kid and sat down on the couch to read the papers. It said this Grits person was twenty-seven years old, six feet tall, had blonde hair, blue eyes. And in dark print it said, **distinguishing features**: heavy southern accent, beard, and has a long raised-scar running through his right eyebrow and down his right cheek.

I turned to the second page and found myself staring at a picture of Grits Wetmore. It was the picture taken for his Alabama driver license. He disgusted me to the point of feeling ill. The longer I looked, the angrier I became. The rage boiled up inside of me and then without any warning I screamed as loud, as long, and as hard as I could. When I finally stopped screaming, I looked over in the corner and Jude was stuck to the wall. His eyes were bugged out and he was trembling.

"Hey Jude, don't be afraid. I'm sorry; it's just that my emotions got the better of me."

He slowly walked out of the corner. I had to find a way to relieve the anxiety in both of us so I asked him if the information was correct.

"Yes ma'am, it is, even the address is correct. I looked it up; there is a Saturn, Alabama. It's down on the Gulf of Mexico; people there call it the Salt. I hope you don't mind, but I called the Saturn Chamber of Commerce. A nice lady told me that the address given was a famous one. She said it used to be a slave plantation."

For some reason, he suddenly stopped.

"It's ok, keep going," I said.

"Yes ma'am, this Grits Wetmore guy lives at One Hurtwood Lane. The lady told me she didn't know exactly how big the property was, but she estimated it to be at least a couple thousand acres. It's a historical site," Jude said with a smile.

I could tell he was looking for approval so I smiled as I walked by him and opened the door.

"Jude, thank you. My family will appreciate what you've done for us. One thing before you leave, not a word to anyone about this. Do you understand me?" I said with my freaky, I'll-scratch-your-eyes-out face.

For such a little gal, I guess I pack a big punch, because over and over as he was running out the door, he promised never to tell a soul. I hollered one last thank you, not sure if he heard me.

48

Saturn, Alabama

Vladimir was about a half-a-mile away from the north entrance to the Hurtwood plantation when he saw the parked government car.

"Grasshopper, FBI agents are watching car. Get down and stay down," Vladimir ordered.

Neither he nor his twin brother, Nikita, looked at the dark gray automobile as they slowly drove by and entered the plantation. After he parked his car behind the stables, Grasshopper was told to stay in the car. The Russians exited and walked to the rear of the home and entered through the kitchen. They were immediately met by Hurtwood.

"Did anyone pay special attention to you during your drive?" Hurtwood asked.

"No sir, not one person made notice of car or people in car. But when we arrived, I saw FBI car with the two agents inside watching plantation with binoculars. I told Grasshopper to duck down and to stay down. He is still in car. Agents don't know about Grasshopper, we don't want him answering questions; he might say more than he should," Vladimir said as his boss and Nikita listened.

"Yes, you're right. Ok, well then, for now we will lay low and stay out of sight. An hour from now I will send Nigeriana out to feed and water the horses. She can tell Grasshopper to wait 'til the cover of darkness before leaving the car. It is late and the two of you need to sleep. Nikita, can you help me with my medication before you go to your room, please?" Hurtwood said.

Grasshopper stayed in the car 'til the cook, Nigeriana, came to get him. He was sleeping like a baby. When he woke up, he asked if the agents were still there. She left him in the car and came back five minutes later.

"Yes'm, dey out dere awright. Dey lookin' wif dem big glasses ya holds up to yc eyes. Sumpin' else you wants me ta do?" she asked.

"No Ana, you go on and do what you was toldt ta do. I s'pose I'mona wait here 'til it dark out," Grasshopper said.

Grasshopper waited 'til it was good and dark before he slipped out to his room. He left the lights off and lay down on his bed. As he fell asleep, he said, *Lord dis sho has been a long day.* He didn't notice the blood splatter all over his clothes 'til he looked at himself in the mirror the following morning. He washed up and then the first chance he had, he burned everything; everything that is except the bat. He hid the bat under the floorboards in his bathroom. He thought he might need the bat again.

49

Tavern

I came back to the tavern with a truck full of bottles late Tuesday evening; I had been working at the Broken Bone for nearly three weeks. The bartender, Jay-Don, told me that Sam had something for me, and that she was waiting for me in my room. I ran up the stairs and Sam was sitting on my bed. She had two envelopes in her hand. Without a word, she smiled and handed me one, so I opened it. It was my Mississippi driver license with my picture and everything. For a moment or two I felt like a real person. I stared at the license as I asked myself, *is that really me? It says it is. My name and my picture are right there.*

Sam could see I was struggling with my identity and said, "Bobby, I have something else for you." She reached under my pillow and handed me a thin bright blue nylon wallet with a red, white, and blue Harley Davidson on the front. "It'll keep your license from getting wrinkled and such."

I turned the wallet over a couple of times and then I looked inside. There was a twenty-dollar bill, two tens, and five ones in the wallet.

"Gosh Sam, it's not payday yet. What's all this money for?" I asked.

"Bobby, you know darn good and well money is for spending, it's used to pay for things. And I figured you're gonna need some money after you read this note that Gino brought here for you."

I'd completely forgotten about the other envelope. I opened the envelope and unfolded the paper that was inside. The first thing I noticed was how professional looking the handwriting was. The letter was addressed, Dear Bobby.

I thought right out loud, "That's me," as I looked over at Sam for a moment. I read the whole letter and when I was done, I looked back at Sam.

"Sam, could you do me a great favor and drive me to a mental health facility on Thursday?" I asked not understanding how someone might take what I'd just said.

Sam looked at me as she narrowed her eyes.

"Bobby, are you ok? I don't understand?" was all she said.

I explained about the new facility that many of the homeless were going to for help. Then I told her about the psychologist that was going to be there Thursday. And how he might be able to help me figure out who I was and where I came from.

She frowned a bit before she said, "Bobby, sure I'll take you, but I think getting your hopes up might be a bad idea. Why don't we just go and then if something good comes of it, well, then great."

"Yeah, you're probably right. Ok, I'll keep a lid on my emotions and just hope for the best. Listen, it says here that the facility is this side of Pascagoula, you sure you can take me?"

"Now that I think of it, no, I can't take you, but you can take us," she said as she smiled at me.

"What do you mean - us?" I asked.

"We'll take the truck. Bobby, you can help many instead of just one."

"You're right, oh my gosh you're so right. Listen, Sam, would it be ok if I went over to Gino's for a little bit. I want to make arrangements, you know to get the word out."

"Sure, I think we can get along without you for a little while," was all Sam said.

I read the note again. And when I got to the bottom I smiled because Pearly had signed the letter Sincerely, Jefferson Abraham Cisco. I tucked the letter in my pocket and ran all the way to Gino's. When I got there, I knocked on the side window and then I gave a short whistle. A moment later I heard a short whistle come back to me. I walked around to the trash cans and heard the back-door slam shut. I looked over and Belle was standing there wiping the soap off her hands. She looked up at me. "Well, what are you waiting for?" I said before she ran and leaped into my arms. We hugged and over and over she kissed me on the side of my face.

And as I turned red, I twirled her around a couple of times; she was light as a feather. I set her back down, but she jumped back up and kissed me again. "Oh Bobby, don't you evuh go runnin' off like dat 'gain. I been worried sick just a tinkin' 'bout-you. Where has you been?"

"Belle, I got myself a real steady job, but if not for Gino, and Pearly, and of course you, I'm not sure what would have happened to me. You are the best people in the world. A nice man and lady gave me a job, and although I knew I would miss you guys something awful, I had to go away. You understand, don't you?"

Belle stepped back from me and just stared for a little bit. She was smiling.

"Belle, what are you doing?" I asked.

"I'm lookin' at a white boy dat got himse'f all shaved and washed up. You sho are purdy," she said as she shivered.

"Belle, are you ok, you cold or something?" I asked, a little confused.

"No Bobby, I's just happy ta see ya is all," she said as she covered her mouth and looked up at me with her big dark wild eyes.

I told her all about the letter Pearly had written me. And when I was done, she said, "Bobby, I knows all 'bout dat lettuh. I toldt Pearly what ta write. And I toldt him you'd come a runnin', and you did. And now I's happy, cuz you happy."

"Listen Belle, I need to talk to Gino. Can we go inside for a bit?"

"Sho we can, come on lets us go inside."

I explained to Gino what I was gonna do on Thursday. Then I asked him if Belle could take the day off and come with us. She looked at me and then she looked at Gino. And when he said yes, she smiled so big and bright it made Gino and I do the same. Then she nearly jumped through the roof. I'd say she was kinda happy. I told her I'd come get her at her home on Thursday morning at eight. I was hoping she'd offer to make me some grits, and she did. I had to get back to work, but Belle said she would explain everything to Pearly that evening. Belle gave me a fierce hug and a kiss on the cheek before I left. I walked maybe ten steps toward the front door of the restaurant and then stopped. There was something I had to find out.

"Gino, thanks for everything. How'd you know where to take the letter Pearly wrote?"

"I didn't know Bobby, 'til a little bird by the name of Sam came and told me where to take it. She thought you were getting lonesome. And she thought that seeing some old friends might help. She is quite a gal, isn't she?"

"She sure is," I said, without realizing that I must have had a big grin on my face.

Belle gave me a look I'll never forget. It was like I was looking at a jealous young tigress.

I walked away with a strange kind of guilty feeling welling up inside of me. I looked back at Belle one last time and she smiled and then she cocked her head to the side and winked. I thought to myself, *whew, I guess that means everything's ok.* Two days later, I found out looks can be deceiving.

50

Dezi calls Dad from San Francisco

After I found out about this Grits Wetmore guy and where he lived, I called Dad. He was filled with so much energy I could barely keep him on the phone. He said he would call me right back after he talked to everybody. He was thinking about how we could all go down to Alabama to look for Junior. I guess I knew in my heart that everyone wouldn't be able to go, but then again - I really wasn't sure.

When I hung up the phone with Dad, I sat and waited for over an hour but got no call back. So I went about my day and hoped I'd hear from him; the sooner the better. About two hours later the phone rang, it was my Uncle Tommy.

"Hello Dezi, it's your Uncle Tommy. Are you doing ok?" he asked, knowing how tense things had probably been for me.

"Yes, I'm ok, I guess. I guess you talked to my dad about what to do?" I asked, not knowing what they'd actually talked about.

"Well, yes I did. He, or I should say we, didn't call right back because I've been on the phone with the Saturn Chief of Police. Just wanted to check on this Wetmore guy and it didn't sound too great. You see, he and his twin brother have just been reported as missing. The chief says he's had trouble with Grits and Alvin Wetmore ever since when, if you know what I mean. And he's willing to help us look for Junior, but he's kinda hampered at the moment. I guess the FBI is already there in Saturn. They don't want anyone interfering; they're also looking for Grits - and Junior as well. Dezi, try to remember, Junior has been gone now for over a month. He could be almost..." He stopped when he heard me sigh. "If it makes you feel any better, well, I believe Junior is still alive. Don't know why, but I do. So, the chief there in Saturn is going to check with the DMV and all the shelters in the area. He told me that if he gets even a sniff of information about somebody fitting Junior's description, he will call me. He said it will take a week or so for the information to travel through the entire state, but eventually it will. I believe if Junior is in Alabama, we'll find him," Uncle Tommy said.

"Yes, but what about going down there and seeing for ourselves?" I asked, kinda confused.

"Dezi, we're discussing that option. We're trying to decide who should go. So far and for obvious reasons your dad is out. Ajax is out because he, well, there's no telling how folks would respond to him; most people do find him to be a bit strange. Then there's Madison, we think because of her skill in speaking with professionals, she might be just right. I am definitely going and so is either Randi or Ricky," Uncle Tommy stopped talking again.

"Uncle Tommy, what's going on?" I asked.

"Oh shoot, well, it's your dad and your Uncle Ajax. They both just walked into the station. They're saying they want to go. Dezi, listen, my feeling is that too many cooks will spoil the stew. Let me talk to them and then I'll call you back, ok?" he said more than asked.

"Ok, bye, but don't wait too long before you call back, please?" I begged more than asked.

"I promise, I'll get back as soon as I can," he said before he said goodbye.

I was left kinda cold and confused. I mean, I think they were doing the right stuff. It was just that I felt so far away. I guess because I was.

51

Tavern

I woke up as excited as I've been in a long… well, for at least three weeks. I hurried and got dressed and went down to have a cup of coffee with Sam. She had on skintight bellbottom jeans and a bright blue button-down shirt; the front of which was neatly tied together above her naval. And she had on a pair of light brown work boots. She wasn't dressed like June Cleaver, but she sure was beautiful.

"Morning Sam, gosh, you sure do look nice this morning. Is something special going on today that I don't know about?"

"Thank you, and yes silly, something very special is going on today. Thought I oughta dress accordingly. Do you want me to go change?" she asked.

"Don't go changin' to try and please me, I like you just the way you are," I said as I stared into space.

"Bobby, you ok?" she asked.

I heard her talking, but I was someplace far, far away. I was thinking about when I first met Joey and he called me a mouth-dribbler. I looked at Sam again and then I closed my mouth.

"Yeah, I'm fine. I was thinking about that day I … Oh never mind."

She gave me a look and then she turned, walked over to the coffee machine, and poured me a cup of coffee. She was still a magnet and my eyes were stuck right to her. We drank our coffee and shared small talk before we walked out back to the truck. I opened the door for Sam and helped her up into the truck. I walked around to the driver's side and grabbed the handle next to the door and just as I was going to jump up in the truck, someone yelled, "Bobby!"

I looked back behind me and Haystack was giving

me one of his black toothed smiles. I knew he wasn't the one that yelled, so I started scanning the back of the tavern. Joey walked out from behind a crate and curled his index finger a couple of times at me to come over to him. I opened the door and looked in at Sam to explain and she waved her hand towards Joey. Just when I thought Haystack was the one that used his hands to do his talking, the two of them started doing the same thing.

"Morning Joey, is there something I can do for you?" I asked.

"Yeah, I guess you could say that. Listen, I'm goin' up to Joisey for a few days, got some business to tend to. So I wanted to tell you to take good care of Sam..." He didn't say anything else for an uncomfortable period of time; at least for me it was uncomfortable.

I looked him in the eye and then he reached in his pocket and says, "You're gonna need some duckets to fill up the truck and pay for shit while I'm gone. So, take this."

He pulled out a wad of paper money.

"No Joey, I can't take your money. This is my deal and I already feel bad enough for taking the day off. I hope you're–"

"Take the money, it's not for you, it's for the business, ok. Now, take duh money," he said, just like the gangsters do in the movies.

Then Sam yelled, "Take the money!"

After Sam yelled, Haystack walked over and gave me a black toothed smile and nodded his head. I didn't know what to say.

"Ok, geez, you three are like... well, I don't know what you're like. Ok, I'll take the money. Thanks, Joey," I said, as Joey shoved the money in my right hand. Then with both hands, he squeezed my fingers around the money 'til I winced.

"Have a good time, Mc-Bobby. I hope you find out who you are. Now get going."

I jumped up in the truck and waved to Joey and

Haystack as I pulled away from the tavern and headed for Belle's. The sun was up and there wasn't a cloud in the sky. And somehow, I just knew I was going to find out who I was. I don't believe I could have felt any better.

We rolled up to the row of clapboard homes where Belle lives and Pearly was there waiting by the front porch. Gosh, I can't begin to tell you how excited I was to see him. I ran around and helped Sam get out of the truck. I wasn't sure how Sam might react to Pearly and Belle, but in truth it didn't matter. They were my friends and as far as I was concerned, they would always be my friends.

"Hello Pearly, this is Sam Lombardi. She is the nice lady that gave me the job. Sam, this is Jefferson Abraham Cisco," I said with as much panache as I could muster.

Pearly was wearing his turquoise jumpsuit, his glowing patent leather shoes, and the soft serve swirl rising over his forehead was as proud as I've ever seen it. He bowed and then stuck his hand out and said, "Tis such a genuine pleasure to make your acquaintance. If you are a friend of Bobby's, then you are indeed a friend of mine."

"Well, a gentleman and a scholar. It is such a pleasure to meet you. I only wish that I had been introduced yesterday," Sam said as she gave me a stern look.

"Ah 'yesterday, all my troubles seemed so far away.' My fair lady 'yesterday is not ours to recover, but tomorrow will be ours to win or lose,'" Pearly said as he gave Sam a private little wink of the eye.

"Ok, the two of you can stop with the secret language. Pearly, was that Shakespeare?"

"Bobby, I believe that was the Beatles and then former President Johnson," Sam said.

"Ah, a lady after my own heart. Sam, may I inquire as to your education?" Pearly asked.

"Yes, you may. I graduated from New York University with a degree in economics. I moved on to Harvard law and then on a fellowship I traveled abroad and taught World Commerce at Cambridge. However, after just one short year, the Bronx was calling my name. And I did feel a bit out of place in Merry Old England. So, I came home and married Joey. And the rest, as they say, is history," Sam said as Pearly smiled and shook his head.

"Good Lord, and much to my delight, here you are in Mississippi hobnobbing with the riffraff. I am so impressed I'm speechless, and that, my fair lady is, in my case, the road less traveled," Pearly said as he slowly turned towards Belle's front door.

Sam and I did the same, I guess it was just a reaction or well, I'm not sure why we turned. But when we did, the three of us were facing Belle. She was glaring at Sam, hate tumbling down from her eyes. I ran over to hug her and she started bawling. When I was right up next to her, she slapped my hands away and ran back into the house. I turned to Pearly, "Good Lord, what has come over Belle?"

"Bobby, I haven't the slightest notion. I am as befuddled as you."

"I believe I know what happened. Pearly, would you please take me in and introduce me to your sister? I'd like to talk with her for a little bit," Sam said with a fractured smile.

"Of course, I will take you in and introduce you. Would you like me to stay there with you?" Pearly asked as if he was looking in a mirror.

"No, I don't believe that will be necessary," Sam said as she reached out for Pearly's hand. "Please, I think the sooner the better."

"Oh," was all Pearly said in response as he pulled Sam into the front room. Then he softly said, "Belle, this nice young lady would like to meet you. Would you please come out here?"

"No, I ain't comin' out," Belle said, the way a child might.

Sam put her hand up in the universal 'I'll handle this situation' and walked into Belle's bedroom. I had made it to the front door by that time and when I opened the door, Pearly put his hands up and then he just shrugged his shoulders. The look on his face told me he was as confused as I was. So, like a couple of big dummies, we stood staring at each other. Then Pearly gave the universal sniff with his nose and ran into the kitchen. I followed him in and sat down at Belle's little kitchen table.

"Bobby, I believe the grits are done, would you like to eat now?"

I just nodded my head yes. Pearly handed me a bowl of grits and my small spoon. He moved over and leaned against the wall with his giant bowl and silently started eating. Now and then we looked at each other, but we didn't say a word.

I can't speak for Pearly, but I know I was trying hard to listen for the girls. I think I heard a few peeps, but that's about it. Pearly had finished eating, and I was close to being done when Belle walked into the kitchen. She'd obviously changed her clothes and was now wearing white jeans, Sam's bright blue shirt, and Sam's light brown work boots. Sam followed Belle into the kitchen wearing a tie-dyed purple and pink t-shirt, and she had on white tennies.

"How're the grits?" Sam asked.

I wasn't sure if she was asking Pearly or me. I said they were great and at the same time Pearly said they were superb.

"Well, that's good enough for me. Belle, I'll have a bowl with a little sugar and a lot of butter, please," Sam said as if she and Belle had known each other their entire lives.

And it seemed like Belle already knew what Sam wanted because she had the bowl of grits in Sam's hands before Sam finished talking. I started to say something at the same time Pearly did. And both of the ladies held their hands up in the universal, be quiet, position. Pearly and I gave each other a look as we shrugged our shoulders.

And right when I thought we'd both had enough of the silent treatment, Sam looks at Pearly and says, "Pearly,

I told you about my education. Would you please tell me about yours."

It's difficult to catch Pearly off-guard, but Sam had certainly done it. It took Pearly a double take or two before he could respond.

"You certainly caught me napping with that one. Ok, the long and the short of it is that I graduated with honors from the well-known University of Jupiter; better known as the streets. After my time on the streets, I went to night school where I did in fact earn a high school diploma. Not quite up to par with your accomplishments, but I have given it my all. And someday when my ship comes in, I hope to continue working and learning at the university level."

For whatever reason, when Pearly finished, he and Sam looked at me. I guess they wanted to know about my education. I crash landed right there in front of them. I was sitting in a chair, but I felt as though I was looking up at everybody from a far corner on the floor. Belle came to my rescue.

"Bobby, I guess you and me de only ones wif mo impotant tings ta do dan goes ta sckooh," she said as she softly laid her hand on my shoulder.

"Listen, all of you. I feel awful because I don't know if I even finished the first grade. I assume that I did or well, whatever. My point is, none of my not knowing is your fault. And I know that you're all here right now to help me. So, if we don't get a move on, we're going to be late for the party," I said, trying to keep my chin up.

"Belle, you and Sam can sit up front with Bobby; I'll sit in the back. Bobby, I didn't tell you and you didn't ask, but I hope it's ok that I told the guys at the Salt that were interested to meet us at the filling station across the boulevard." I started to say something, but Pearly stopped me. "And Bobby, I think today would be a good time for you to thank old Joe for helping you the day you could not make it from the restrooms back to your cot. You do remember, don't you?" he asked with a wry smile.

"Yes Pearly, I remember all too well. And that's what I was going to ask you about when you so eloquently stopped me. Enough of that, awright y'all, let's get ta steppin'," I said, like the phony southerner I had become.

I helped Belle up into the cab and then she reached down and pulled Sam up. I opened the back for Pearly and reminded him to stay away from the very back of the truck because of the fumes that can get sucked in. He knew the drill and assured me he'd be ok. I jumped up in the cab and Belle sat so close to me she was almost on my lap. You could tell she was just as happy and proud as can be. We took off down the road, the girls were sharing glances. I've never really understood what it is they say with their eyes, but I know they can say a lot. Seems to me females are better at communicating than guys, even when they don't say a word.

We headed south towards the Salt and when I pulled into Joe's Sunoco station, there were at least a dozen guys from the Salt waiting for me. I thought, *thanks to Sam I drove the truck.* Old Joe came around the truck and asked if I needed the oil checked and then he gave me a long look, and then another before he said, "Dog-gonnit, I remember you. Boy you sure was a sight. You looked like the purest kinda misery there is. But I guess you done recovered, how you doin'?" he asked as he stuck out his hand. "I'm Joe, and I'm glad y'all got ta come over ta my station. Been slow taday, you want I should fill-er up?" he asked before I could get a word out.

"Yes, go ahead and fill her up. But before you do, I want to thank you for helping me that day. And you're right, I was a mess. Anyway, I'm Bobby and thank you," I said as Joe smiled and shook my hand.

I asked the ladies if they needed anything and then I jumped out and met Pearly at the back of the truck. The men started getting in the back and as each one passed me, he said thanks. Sure did make me feel good. Then I felt even better when three women and four small children were helped into the back of the truck. I went back to my open door to the cab and asked Joe what I owed him for the gas.

"Bobby, she took twenty-two gallon. That'll be three dollar and seventy-four cent."

"Ok, sure thing," I said as I pulled out my new wallet.

Didn't take but maybe five seconds before Sam got all up in my kitchen and yelled, "Bobby! Joey gave you that money for a reason. Now give me that wallet of yours," she ordered. So I handed over the wallet. Then she said, "Now use the money in your pocket that Joey gave you. Then I won't have to really get mad."

I reached in my pocket and pulled out the money that Joey had given me. I handed Joe a five-dollar bill.

"Joe, please keep the change."

"Why thank ya Bobby, that sho is kind a y'all."

I walked back to Pearly and told him that for safety reasons the rear door had to be shut and locked. He was good with that.

"Hey Pearly, I just thought of something, where is the place? And how do I get there?"

"Bobby, I've already discussed the directions with Samantha. She'll guide you from here," Pearly said as I shut the rear door and locked it.

Samantha huh, I jumped up in the cab and both gals smiled at me.

"Ok, Samantha, Pearly says you know the way. So, whenever you're ready, I'm listening," I said with a smile.

"Head west on Adams, then we'll need to head north. I'll let you know when," Sam said.

I headed straight west on Adams Avenue, which is Jupiter's main street. We passed by the police station and courthouse as we drove through the middle of town. Then we drove by the clinic where I'd been sewn up a few weeks back.

"Bobby, I don't think you've been here long enough to know, but all the streets that head east and west are named after presidents. And most of the streets that run north and south are the planets in our solar system. We just passed Earth Street and Sun Street is further on up the road, it's on the west edge of town. We will be turning right on Mercury Street," Sam said, the way a tour guide might.

I turned right and headed north as I was told. Only drove maybe a half-a-block when Belle says, "Keep goin' on up ta de Old Spanish Trail, den jump on it and heads west 'gain."

"Belle means state route 90 west. The Old Spanish Trail is the name the locals use for route 90. There was a time when the Old Spanish Trail stretched from the Atlantic all the way to west Texas. Belle, you understand and speak the vernacular much better than I do," Sam said.

"I do?" Belle responded.

"Yes, you most certainly do. You know the patois, all the cool colloquialisms. What I'm saying is you know the history of this part of Mississippi better than I do," Sam said.

"I do, don't I," Belle responded.

"Yes, you do. Belle, you're like having an encyclopedia all about Mississippi with us. And that's a comfort, at least for me it is. Thank you," Sam softly said.

"You welcome," Belle said as she sat up real straight.

I drove for only a minute or two in silence, but I just had to know so I blurted out, "Ok, when are the two of you going to tell me what happened this morning?"

Neither one of them even looked at me. The cab of the truck was deathly still before Sam said, "We have no idea what you're talking about."

"You know exactly what I'm talking about. Come on Sam, please. If I did something wrong or if I hurt someone's feelings, I want to know," I pleaded.

Sam gave me a frustrated glance before she turned to me and said, "Bobby, if you must know, it was a female thing. But, of course you didn't notice because you're a typical guy. Important things are said and important things go on around you guys and you don't even know it. There are times when I'd like to hit you men with a skillet, or maybe a broom. You know, try and knock some sense into you. But, I don't because I know in the end it wouldn't do any good."

Then Sam looked at Belle. "Belle, would it be ok with you if I tried to explain to Bobby?" Sam asked.

"'Course it would be ok, you don't has ta ax me fo po-mishin. Go on aheadt and tell him," Belle said with a smile.

"Thank you. Bobby, you didn't notice, but Belle and I were wearing the exact same outfits this morning. That to females is a big no-no. And I might add, that Belle had heard about me, but she didn't think you would actually go so far as to bring me along for the ride; remember, two's company, three's a crowd. Well, she didn't need me tagging along. So, she was wondering why I was there. And if that weren't bad enough, we were wearing the exact same duds. So, after we got acquainted, we decided to swap and change things around a little. Now, I hope you understand because I'm not going to explain anymore. Belle, are you ok with what I just said?" Sam asked.

"Yes ma'am, I tink you did just fine," Belle said with another smile.

I shook my head and admitted to the ladies that I would never have guessed. Then I apologized for bringing Sam. Oh, the look Sam gave me was priceless. We headed west on the Old Spanish Trail for maybe five minutes when I saw the road sign for the new Family Aide Center. A buzz began to spread throughout my body. I did my best not to get my hopes up, but deep down in my soul I was hoping that I would find out who I was and where I came from. I took the off ramp and headed west on a frontage road. The building was new and fresh in physical appearance. I stopped the truck close to the front of the building and ran to the back of the truck.

Can't Find my Way Home

When I slid the rear cargo door open everyone inside cheered. All the men jumped out first and then we helped the women and children get down out of the truck. There was an unsaid excitement brewing. Sam and I went in first and a nice young lady with a name tag that read Sally-Jo met us at the reception desk.

"Hello, and welcome to the new family aide center. How can we help you?" she said with a nice smile.

"Well, I, I–" I stuttered before Sam took over.

"What he means is we've brought men and women and a few children with us," Sam said as the entire group crowded in the building behind us. "We're really not sure what services you offer. But I'd say the men are definitely seeking employment. And the women are probably hoping you offer some assistance, you know in the way of food, medication, immunization, general healthcare, and so on, for their children, of course."

"Yes, ma'am we offer all of those things, and more," Sally-Jo said as I tried to interrupt her.

"Sally-Jo, can I–" I blurted out before I was talked over and pretty much ignored.

"We can help all of you, but first we need to get every person registered with the state. Please, everyone needs to come into the main room here and fill out the eligibility forms. It only takes a few minutes. And I can assist any of the folks that don't know how to read or write. Please, gather everyone up and we'll get started," Sally-Jo said as she went to retrieve the forms.

There was a very large table and enough chairs for everyone to sit at and fill out the forms. I wanted to ask about the psychologist, but I figured first things first. Most of the men and women had no address, no phone; some didn't know what day or year they were born. I mostly helped the men, while Sam and Sally-Jo helped the women and children. Pearly stuck to Belle like a magnet. I passed by them once for a moment and it didn't take long to realize that Belle could not read or write. I thought, *how could that possibly happen in this modern day and age?*

Crestfield

When the forms were completed, the men were taken to the employment section of the center. All the women were taken to a separate room where a nurse waited to examine the children. Belle looked a little lost but decided to join the women and children. I sat down at the table by myself and was feeling kinda glum. I wanted to know where the psychologist was, but there was no one there to ask. I was lost in space when someone tapped me on the shoulder. I looked up and Sam was smiling back at me.

Standing next to Sam was a man wearing a brown suit. He reached out to shake my hand and introduced himself.

"Hi Bobby, I'm Doctor Cooper," he said as we shook hands.

He had the kind of face and expression that would be perfect for a police lineup. Nobody would ever pick him for anything. He was that plain and unassuming. He was so calm, collected, and distant, it made me nervous. I thought, *I wonder if he knows what I'm thinking. He could probably care less. Ok, stop it. Just give him a chance.*

"Bobby, please come with me. We have a lot to do and so little time. Thank you, Samantha, we'll probably take a break at noon. Bye," he said as I followed him into an office that was obviously not meant for psychiatry of any kind.

There wasn't a warm looking couch anywhere. And to my surprise, it was still under construction. One wall was just bare two-by-fours with wires running helter-skelter through it. There was a desk and Dr. Cooper sat me down next to the desk and then he left the room and came back rolling a chair for himself.

"Ok, Bobby, I'm not sure what you've been told or haven't been told." I gave him a blank look. "Ok, what I'm getting at is this. I was hired as a marriage counselor. Ninety percent of the time I deal with spousal abuse and broken homes. And the other ten percent I spend with alcoholics."

Can't Find my Way Home

He could see the disappointment in my eyes and just when I was about to stand up and walk out, he said, "Bobby, I'm going to do my best to help you, so please bear with me." I shook my head but didn't say a word. "Bobby, I have a photo and a brief description of six different men that for whatever reason have been reported missing."

He could see that his mentioning a list of men certainly got my attention. I wanted to see the list immediately, but he had other ideas.

"Bobby, I know all you want to do is find out who you are and where you came from, but this list could actually make things worse." I started to fidget. "Hang on for a minute, please?" he asked. "Ok, before we go over the list, I want you to tell me everything you can remember. Go slow and tell me what the first thing was you saw or did here in this part of Jackson County."

He took out a notebook and said for me to begin at the beginning. And although at first, I wanted to scream, I started at the clinic where I awoke after being sewn up. I told him about jail and meeting Pearly and living in the Salt and so on. I told him everything I could. After about a half-hour of my talking, he stopped me.

"Bobby, your speaking ability is way above average. And I'm sure you understand it is not of this part of the country, which brings me to the list of names. I'm going to cut to the quick and show you a photo of each of the men on my list."

He opened the drawer to his right and took out a manila folder. He removed the top photo and showed it to me. I studied it for a little bit. The man in the photo and I looked kinda like each other, but not exactly.

"Ok, Bobby, don't make up your mind just yet. Let me tell you his name and then we'll see if it rings a bell. After I say his name, I don't want you to speak. Please, just listen and let the name sink in. After I say the name, I want you to say it over and over to yourself. Can you do that for me?" he asked in a polite and caring way.

"Yes, doc, I believe I can. Or at least I'll try my best."

"That's all I ask for. Ok, the first name is Delbert Hawkins. Say it to yourself, please?"

I said the name over and over in my head and I knew right away the name meant nothing to me. I just shook my head no to the doctor.

"That's ok, that's why we're here. And I'm glad you don't recognize the name Hawkins. He was born and raised right here in Pascagoula and he has a fifth-grade education. You were not born here and I would not be going out on a limb if I said you have more than a fifth-grade education. Ok, are you ready for the next person?" I nodded yes and he showed me the next photo. The guy had blonde hair and blue eyes. I mean we looked similar but not the same. He gave me the same instructions before he said the guy's name was Albert Anderson.

I said the name over and over to myself. Then I stopped cold. "Doctor that name does sound familiar to me. Could that be me?" I asked.

"Excellent, I'm glad the name sounds familiar, but no, it's not to be. Albert Anderson is a guy I knew in high school." He could see that what he'd done frustrated me. "Bobby, I said his name because I don't believe for a minute that you're from this part of the country. I think you're from the same part of the country I am. Do you want to know where I went to high school?" he asked with a big smile. I didn't ask. So he asked me again.

"Ok, doc, where'd you go to high school?" I asked with a little bit of attitude.

"I went to high school in Kansas, right in the middle of the state. Don't you see? It's a good thing," he said as I stared back at him. "My point is, I don't believe you're from the south." I continued to stare at him. "Ok, I have five more names all from this part of Mississippi. And I would bet my bottom dollar that none of the missing men is you." He showed me their pictures and he was right. I wasn't any of those guys. "Ok Bobby, let's try one more. This is a young man that is exactly your age, height, weight, etc. He's from the northern most tip of Mississippi. I'm only bringing him into this because his bio says he doesn't speak with a heavy accent. His Mississippi driver license photo and you do look somewhat alike."

He stopped and took the photo out and handed it to me. I studied it for a bit; the guy in the picture and I looked kind of like the same person.

Doc said, "Ok, here we go, his name is Cole Bellingham. Say the name to yourself."

I said the name over and over and over again. I wanted to be that person more than you'll ever know, but it didn't sound familiar at all. I was more dejected than ever and poor Dr. Cooper could see it in my eyes, and everywhere else for that matter.

"I'm sorry Bobby, maybe it's time we took a break. Go eat lunch and then come back. I have a couple more areas to explore. Try not to worry," was the last thing he said to me.

Try not to worry. I hate it when people say that to me. Try not to worry. Just saying it makes me worry. I walked out through the reception area and kept right on going to the truck. I went around to the back and sat down on the bumper. I was as low as a... I can't even come up with something clever that describes just how low I was. I sat and stared into the mid-day sun and as I started to sweat, I began thinking about the last month. It took a lot of effort just to go back to the beginning but when I did, something flashed in my head. I didn't tell him about the airport. Somewhere along the line it was either Pearly or Scooter that mentioned the airport, and more than once. Ok, I can tell the doctor about that when I go back in.

At that point, as it so often does, my mind started wandering. Then for some crazy reason, I flexed all my muscles, and hard. Then I probed my face, head, and neck. Then I stood up and took a deep, deep breath. For some reason when I sat back down, I smiled and said, *"What's wrong with being Bobby McKillin? He has some great,*

great friends. He has a job and a soft pillow to lay his head on at night. Sure, there's more to life than a name and a place to sleep, but how much more. Why don't I just be me and be happy. I guess it's because I don't know who me is, that's why you idiot. Geez, I can't believe this. Here I am talking to myself again. And—"

"And talking to yourself is not a healthy habit to get into," Sam said as she walked around the corner of the truck. She reached down and lifted my chin so she could look into my eyes. "Bobby, do you remember talking about not getting your hopes up too high. Well, I think you may have forgotten. And now the fall is further down than it was just a few hours ago," she said as she gently held my chin.

I was shaking my head no.

"Bobby, please stop shaking your head and listen to me. I heard you ask yourself what was so bad about being you, well, trust me there are worse things than being you. What if all you accomplish today is to help all these other people. Isn't that a good thing?"

I shook my head yes; she was right and I knew it.

"Sam, you're right, thanks for being here. I suppose being me, I mean the Bobby me, isn't so bad. And yes, there are worse things in this world, that's for sure. I'm feeling a little selfish for only thinking of myself when there are so many others that need help. I can talk and worry and talk some more, but nothing seems to change. And to be honest, I'm sick and tired of it. So why don't we go get some lunch and forget about things for a while," I said as I did my best to produce a smile.

"Sounds like a good idea. Bobby, before I forget. When I said that talking to yourself was not a healthy habit to get into, well, I might have been talking to myself too," Sam said as she snickered.

We gathered everyone up, that is everyone that was still in the center. Two of the men and one of the women had been given jobs in another part of the state and had left for greener pastures. I drove the rest of us to a

Krystal hamburger drive thru. Everyone sat in the back of the truck in the shade and ate in peace. The hamburgers are little square things, but I still think Pearly may have set a record that day. He ate ten hamburgers, two orders of fries, and he drank two sodas and a milkshake. He was a happy camper. Since the hamburgers were only eight cents, the total bill for all of us was just over five dollars. When I turned to Sam for my wallet, she refused to give it back to me. So once again I paid with the money Joey had given me.

We went back to the center after lunch. The women had dry goods, clothing, and state vouchers to retrieve. Most of the men were still searching for whatever jobs were available. I went back to see Dr. Cooper. When I walked in, I was a little surprised to see that he had a nurse with him; an elderly nurse with a mean look in her eyes. The doctor left the room and she gave me the once over. She started by inspecting the wound on the side of my head; she was kinda rough with me. Then she gave me a series of hearing tests. After that it was the old flashlight in the eyes thing, and of course she took my blood pressure. I thought we were done, at least I hoped we were done, but I wasn't so lucky. The last thing she did was make me pull my pants and underwear down and cough. I didn't think that was necessary, but she did. After the nurse left the room, I sat for about five minutes waiting for the doctor. I wondered what the tests the nurse had given me could possibly have to do with my loss of memory and self. I was frustrated to the point of no return and just shrugged my shoulders. Finally, the doctor came in and rolled his chair over next to me.

"Bobby, I know you're wondering what the physical exam was all about." I started to say yes, but he said, "Hold on for a minute with the questions. So, Nurse Meador tells me that other than a slight problem with the hearing in your right ear you're in perfect health. So, what does that tell me? It tells me that your mind and your body are sound and working together the way they should."

I knew that and he could see the frustration rising.

"Bobby, please listen for just a few minutes longer. I've been on the phone with a colleague of mine that has a lot of experience in cases exactly like yours. We've concluded that you are suffering from focal retrograde amnesia." He held up his hand. "Wait, please wait and listen. To simplify things, we'll call it RA. And there is very good news where RA is concerned. In most cases, it has been found to be temporary," he said with a smile.

"Doc, I don't mean to be mean, but what is temporary? Wait, I guess I should say how long is temporary? It has already been a month and I don't have the slightest idea who I am. And I've run clean out of patience. So, thank you very much for trying, but I'm just going to be Bobby and leave it at that."

Dr. Cooper looked at me and nodded his head just a little.

"Fair enough, that's fair enough. Bobby, I'm sorry I couldn't give you the answers you were looking for. I'm going to continue looking for men that match your description that have been reported missing or otherwise. I have your number and I'll call the moment I hear something. I'm willing to keep trying if you are," he said as he stuck his hand out to shake mine.

"I have something to say. When I first met you, I sold you short. I didn't think you could do anything to help me. And therefore, I thought that you wouldn't even try, but you tried hard. So, I owe you an apology and a thank you."

He shook my hand and smiled. I believe he smiled because all the effort he'd given me and my case had not gone unnoticed. I said thanks again and then goodbye. I was pretty sure I'd never see the marriage counselor again. Most of the people were already waiting out by the truck. There was lots of good news for all. Five more men had been given jobs and so they were staying there at the center. The two women that remained had found jobs in town, which meant they could help put food on their table each night. All of that was great, but not near as great as the smile on Belle's face. She had been accepted into an adult day school where she could learn to read and write. She was ecstatic.

I drove back to Jupiter with a truckload of happy people and I felt good about that. I wanted to ask Pearly more about the airport, but of course he was in the back. So, I figured when I dropped everyone off, I could go talk to Scooter. I wanted to go say hi to him and Ralphy anyway. Then I started wondering why Scooter hadn't come with us in the first place. I pulled the truck into Joe's filling station and let everyone out. The mood was good.

"Sam, I'm going to go down and talk to one of the men that helped me when I first came to the Salt. Will you be ok up here?"

"Sure, I'm fine. And I'd like a little time to go over the workbooks Belle has. You go on ahead and we'll be here when you get back."

"Belle, how about you, I hope you don't mind if I go down and visit with Scooter for a bit?" I asked.

Belle looked at me and then she looked over my shoulder at Pearly as he walked up. They both had distressed looks on their faces. I turned to Pearly and he looked down at the ground.

"Pearly, what's wrong? Is there some reason why I shouldn't go see Scooter?" He didn't answer me. "Pearly, please, you've always been straightforward with me. Is there some reason that I shouldn't go down and see Scooter?"

"Bobby, Scooter has been injured. That's why he didn't come with us to the family center," was all Pearly said.

"Injured how, what happened?"

"I think I should let Scooter tell you."

"Pearly, then I need to see him more than ever. Ok, I'm not going to stand around anymore. Sam, I'll be back in a little bit," I said as I started walking away.

"Oh no you won't!" Sam said before she grabbed my arm. "I'm going with you. I'm smart enough to know that something is wrong. Belle, I'm sorry, but I can't stay here right now. Pearly, please show me the way down to the camp," she ordered.

"I gots ta come wif you, if dat's ok?" Belle said to Sam as she reached out for her hand.

The ladies followed Pearly and me down into the heart of the homeless camp to see Scooter. After seeing the look on Pearly's face, I had a dreadful feeling running through my veins.

•

"Hi Dezi, are you ok?" I asked.

"Yes Madison, I guess I'm ok, it's just that well, I want to go with you to Alabama."

"I know you want to go, but we need to go now. It doesn't make any sense for us to wait."

"Madison, I could catch a flight tomorrow morning. I'd be there by early afternoon."

"Yes, you would and then someone would have to drive up and get you. And then drive back down here. And it would be an entire day more before we get started. Dezi, you're not the only one that wants to go. If we let them, every person in Crestfield would probably drive down to Alabama. Dezi, stay there, I promise I'll keep in touch. Ok?"

"Ok, but Madison, as soon as you hear something or find anything out, please call me, ok?"

"Dezi, you have my word that I'll call you."

"Madison, just find Junior, ok, bye."

"Bye Dezi," I said with a lonely heart.

We decided that Tommy, Ricky, and I were going to drive down to Alabama. Dad was upset about being left in Crestfield. But there was just no way we could look for Junior and take care of him. So, although he fought us tooth and nail, we just couldn't take him with us.

We had bickered back and forth about whether to fly or drive down to Alabama. We knew that flying would certainly get us there faster, and trust me we wanted to get there in a hurry. But, we felt like we might miss something along the way; you know, like Junior. And the cost of flying was prohibitive. We decided to drive Uncle Ajax's Imperial; that was another fight we had. Uncle Ajax made a good case for himself, but we knew there was every chance that people might look at him and clam up. And I should add that Uncle Ajax refused to leave little Jax, the doll he carries around, at home.

You might be wondering how we decided to bring Ricky and not my sister, Randi. Well, that was an easy decision. We needed Randi to stay in Crestfield because other than Uncle Tommy and Ricky, she was our most experienced police officer. Somebody had to steer the ship. Randi didn't fight us one bit, probably because she knew that Ricky was the person that drove Junior to the airport. And she knew that once we got to the address we were given in Alabama, Ricky might see someone he recognized from the airport in Des Moines. I know it's a mouthful, but that's pretty much the way things were decided.

So, we took off out of Crestfield at seven o'clock in the morning and headed straight east on highway 34. When we were close to the Mississippi, we headed straight south. We drove all day and that evening we crossed the Mississippi into Memphis and stayed in a nice hotel. We had three drivers and could have kept going, but Ricky had put a scare into Tommy and me a couple of times. So, we decided to stop for the night. When we got up the next morning, Tommy had a long talk with Ricky about his driving. Oh, Tommy didn't question the fact that Ricky was a good driver; it was the speed at which he drove. I mean, it really was a wonder Ricky didn't get six speeding tickets instead of just the two.

From Memphis, we took some of the less traveled, smaller roads and highways. Not sure why it made sense to us, but it did. Our thinking was that maybe, just maybe, Junior might use these roads if he was avoiding someone.

Crestfield

We drove into a strange little town just west of Mobile and filled up the car. We asked for directions to Saturn and the toothless guy that was pumping the gas said, "Now, why in the world would anyone wanna go down to Saturn. Hell, the Salt ain't even nice there. You got relations or a cousin down there?"

For some strange reason Ricky and Tommy looked at me after the man asked the question. Well, after he spit on the ground right in front of me, I decided to answer the question. I said, "Yes, as a matter of fact, we do have relations down there. Thanks for the gas, what do we owe you?"

He spits again, and then he looked at the license plate a couple of times. After he looked, he gave all three of us a pair of squinty eyes and said, "We don't take ta nothennuhs 'round heuh. I'd stay in that car of yers whenevuh possible if I was you. The gas will be two-dolluh and seventee-two cent."

So much for southern hospitality. I paid him as fast as I could. I hurried because I could see that Uncle Tommy wanted to belt the guy for being so rude. Tommy drove after I suggested it, and we got down to the outskirts of Saturn at just about supper time.

•

When Pearly, the ladies, and I made it down to Scooter's corner, I pulled the blanket partition apart and he was lying on my cot. Ralphy was sleeping right next to him. Scooter had his back to me; it seemed that every breath he took was heavy and extremely labored. He wasn't breathing like someone that's sleeping, but like somebody that's in pain. I said his name and after a short whine, he turned over. His face was swollen and bruised to the point that the only way I knew for sure that it was Scooter was the fact that there is only one beard in the Salt like his. His right arm was in a sling and a large cast had been applied to the arm in a position as if he were going to salute someone. I held his left hand in mine. I must have been shaking real hard because Pearly put his hand on my shoulder to steady me. I looked up at Pearly and he put his right hand over his eyes to hide the tears.

I turned and got down on my knees so that I could speak with Scooter and said, "Scooter, can you hear me?" He slowly nodded his head yes. "Can you talk a little bit?" He nodded again. "Scooter, what happened? Who did this to you?" He didn't say anything, he just looked at Pearly. I suppose it was a reflex, but I did too.

"Bobby, I should have told you from the start, but I just didn't have the heart. The Russians came down to the Salt looking for you. And–"

"What Russians!" I screamed.

"The Russians that have been looking for you since you got here."

"For me?" I said as I turned on a knee to face Pearly. "What do Russians want with me?"

"Bobby, I think you should stop for a minute and let Pearly tell you what he knows, please?" Sam said.

I had forgotten that the ladies were there behind me. I took a deep breath and slowly exhaled. "Ok, talk," was all I said.

Pearly started from the beginning, a part of the story that I'd not heard. He explained how the Russian put me in his car and drove me to the Salt and put me back in the wheelchair only to push me down into the culvert. I stopped Pearly at that point so I could ask him who the Russians worked for. Pearly did all he could to avoid telling me the truth. I couldn't take it anymore so I screamed, "Pearly! Do the Russians work for someone? And if they do, who do they work for?"

Pearly started to answer me, but Sam told him to stop. I looked at Sam and in an instant, I could see in her eyes that she knew about all of this.

"Sam, you kept things from me that you knew might help me find out who I am?" She looked away from me. "Sam! Answer me," I said as we all stared at her.

"Bobby, I didn't know any of that, but I do know the Russians. And I know who they work for. I know this because Joey and I work for the same person. His name is Cotton Hurtwood and just about everybody in this part of both states either works for him or at one time has worked for him. Cotton Hurtwood is the person that put the money down for the Broken Bone. We make our mortgage payments each month to him. That's all I know, and up to now, there was no reason to bring him into any of this. Bobby, I would do anything to get you home to your family. Anything," Sam said as tears welled up in both eyes.

I looked at Belle and she was already in tears when she said, "Bobby, I woiks fo Hurtwoodt too, but I dint know nuttin 'bout all dis mess."

"Belle, you don't have to explain to me. Pearly already told me that sometimes you work at the plantation. I understand and it's ok."

"No Bobby, it ain't ok. You see Gino and I boph woiks fo Missuh Hurtwoodt. He own evree bidness in town, po-lice and judges too."

I think I stopped breathing for a little bit at that point. Then I looked over at Pearly and he said, "Bobby, when you worked on the road crew, you were working for Hurtwood too. The working part of all this is no crime, but the personal injury is. Now, we have to find a way to get you in that mansion so that you can speak with Hurtwood himself. And that will take some doing," Pearly said with a note of trepidation.

I looked at Sam and she responded by saying, "Bobby, I promise you that when Joey gets back, we will find a way to get you in to speak with Mr. Hurtwood. That's as much as I can do."

"I tink dere is somepin else we can do," Belle said as she stepped over to me and gently caressed the side of my face. "Bobby, dere's dis little nigguh boy dat woiks fo Hurtwoodt. He go by de name Grasshoppuh. He say dey got somepin' of yo's. I tink maybe he can he'p us. Maybe Samantha can gets holdt a him. I tink it worph a try," Belle said.

"Yes, Belle's right, it is worth a try. Bobby, I promise we'll start working at this as soon as Joey comes back from Jersey," Sam said.

I had turned back to Scooter while Sam was talking. The pain he was feeling was worse than a physical thing. There was something in his eyes that told me his heart was ready to burst.

"Scooter, is there something I can do or get for you?" I asked. He just shook his head no. "Is there something you want to tell me," I asked.

He nodded his head yes. So I got down right next to him and he softly said, "I'm sorry fo givin' in Bobby. I told them yo name, now they gonna find you fo sho. I tried to be brave, but they hurt me real bad."

"Scooter, I understand. It's ok; I don't care what you told them. All that matters now is that you get better. Ralphy is going to need you to take care of him," I said.

Tears gushed from Scooter's eyes as he looked back at Ralphy. Then he covered his face with his left hand. The feeling, the awareness, was slow in coming, but come it did. I reached over Scooter to pet Ralphy, but he didn't move. And as I felt along the length of his body, I could tell that he'd been broken to pieces. His nose was so cold and without a warning the air rushed from my lungs and I heaved and wailed to the heavens. I fell to the ground, curled up, and tried to hide my face. No one moved, they just stood watching me as the confusion and horror in my mind increased. I was destroyed and inside my head I knew that I was the reason Ralphy was dead. I was a rat, end of story. I stayed curled up for a long time before I sat up on my knees.

I took one look at Scooter and Ralphy and I started slapping my face. At first it was just a slow rhythmic slap, left, right, left, right. Then I balled my fists and as fast and as hard as I could I punched myself in the face. Over and over the blows landed. I deserved it and nothing was going to stop me 'til I knocked myself out. I think I heard Belle yell at Pearly to stop me, but I'm really not sure who yelled. In any case, Pearly did restrain me from hitting myself and after a long walk with me hanging over Pearly's shoulder, we made it up to the filling station. He laid me in the back of the truck and the next thing I knew I was laying on my bed in my little room.

I suppose I had been sleeping, but I'm not sure. I was sure that I'd lost my mind and I would never be Bobby the sensible person again. I knew I was nuts, and I knew I was a rat, and that's really all there was to it. I sat up and something grabbed hold of me. I walked my useless-self down to the bar and told Jay-Don to give me a beer and a whiskey. He gave me a long look and I could tell he was going to say no. So I pulled all the money Joey had given me out of my pocket and slammed it down on the bar. Then at the top of my lungs I yelled, "Give me a damn beer and a shot of whiskey right now!"

Jay-Don looked over my shoulder and I heard Sam tell him to go ahead and give me what I asked for. I turned and watched Sam walk away. I guess she didn't want to see a loser get drunk.

I'd tell you all about what I drank and how much of it, but I don't remember. Funny how not remembering has become such a staple in my life. I guess I was dreaming, although I'm not really sure about anything anymore. Anyway, I was walking through a field chock full of milkweed and burdock, surrounded by sunflowers, bearded beggarticks and firewheels. The flowers were all talking to me at the same time. I couldn't understand them, but I didn't care. I walked a little further and my shadow passed over a small turtle and he jumped back into the pond where he lived. I walked only a step or two more and the sun on my back was so intense I had to stop and cool down. I lay down in the shade of a huge tree; it was a kind of tree I'd never seen before. Without any warning, all the leaves on the tree floated down and covered me. I got up and started walking again, but all the flowers and the milkweed and such were gone. Everything was now as brown and bare as an unsown field. I trembled a bit as Jack

Frost wrapped his arms around me. And as the snow began to fall on my shoulders, I shivered so violently I woke myself from my dream.

I looked next to me and there was someone there sleeping. I blinked and tried to focus, but all was a dizzy hangover haze. I lay back and then I watched as Sam slowly got up out of bed and as she walked towards the bathroom, she stopped and smiled at me. If she'd had wings she would surely have been an angel. She didn't have a stitch of clothing on and I don't believe I have ever seen anything so beautiful.

I lay my head back down and a moment, maybe two moments later, Sam was dressed and sitting on the edge of my bed.

"Sam, how long have you been in my bed?"

"All night of course. Why do you ask?"

"I'm asking because I have this feeling that I've done something terribly wrong."

"No Bobby, everything you did was just right," she said as she kissed her finger and then placed it on my lips. Then, as stately as can be, she stood up and walked out of my room.

Crestfield

52

Saturn, Alabama

Tommy, Ricky, and I were starving when we pulled up to
the police station in Saturn, Alabama. We were going to
get something to eat, but first we wanted to talk to the
Chief of Police. We walked in and just like the police
station in Crestfield, it felt low key and easy going. A
young man not wearing a uniform was standing at the front
desk. He was quick to want to please and very polite.

"Hello, can I he'p y'all with somethin'?"

We looked at each other for a moment and then
Tommy said, "If he's here, we'd like to speak with Chief
Brown."

"I see. Is he expectin' ya?"

"Yes, I suppose you could say that. I spoke with
him on the phone a day ago about a missing person,"
Tommy said as he fidgeted a little.

The young man started to say something when
someone from the back of the station yelled, "Ricky-Lee."
He walked back to the voice and then he came back and
pressed a button and the door that led into the station
opened up. He took us back to an office with a big sign on
the door that read: Saturn, Alabama * Chief of Police *
Asa Brown.

We went ahead and walked right in the office. The
chief was standing behind his desk with the phone in his
hands. He waved for us to have a seat; he said sure thing to
the person he was speaking with and then he set the phone
back down in its cradle. We went through the introductions
and the chief seemed like he was paying attention to our
names. He was a small man with quick eyes and a nice
speaking voice. Not sure what that means to men, but to a
woman it's comforting to hear a soothing and trustworthy
masculine voice.

"Well, you folks have come a fair distance to look

for your...," he hesitated.

"He's my nephew, and he's Madison here's brother, and he's Ricky's best friend. I know that is a little confusing, so to keep things simple, why don't we just call him Junior and leave it at that," Tommy said in good faith.

"That sounds like a good ideya," Chief Brown said as he stopped and looked around the room for a second. "And you say Junior has been missin' now for a little over a month?"

"Yes, he was supposed to fly to California June twenty second, but he never made it. So, as I told you on the phone, this Grits Wetmore guy that stole Junior's plane ticket gave Saturn, Alabama as his address to a California Highway Patrolman," Tommy said.

"Well, Tommy, ok if I call ya Tommy?"

"Sure," Tommy quickly replied.

"Ok, Tommy, Grits is a troubled person. And that's the best I can say of him. He's been in trouble since, well, since when. I told you he and his twin brother, Alvin, have both gone missing. Timing is kinda strange when you think about it."

"Yes, it is. Listen Chief, all we want to do is go out to the address he gave and speak with the folks there. Maybe somebody there remembers seeing Junior. We'd appreciate it if you could go with us. Do you know the people that own the home there?"

"Yes, yes I do. I'd say everyone in Saturn knows of the Hurtwood family. Ok, here's what we'll do. Y'all go ahead and get somethin' ta eat and get some rest. And in the morning, let's say at about nine, come back to the station here. And I'll drive us all out to the Hurtwood plantation. Does that sound reasonable?" Chief Brown asked.

"Yes, sounds like a good idea. Listen Chief, if you don't mind, I have a flyer I'd like you to put up here in the station," Tommy said as he handed a flyer with several pictures of Junior on it. Junior's name and the word 'missing' were in bold print.

The chief walked around us and hollered to the kid up front again. And the young man came running.

"Yes sir, Chief Brown."

"Ricky-Lee, I want you to make copies of this and put them up in the station. Put this one in the meeting room so that all the officers will see it." The young man stood looking at Chief Brown for a moment. "Go on boy, do what I done told ya," the chief said as the young man ran off.

We shook hands again and left the police station feeling like we'd accomplished something.

•

"Ok Cotton, you heard what was said. Do you have any special instructions for me?" Chief Brown said into the speaker phone that had been on during our entire conversation with him.

"Well, first thing I want you to do is get rid of those flyers of this missing person. I can't take a chance that someone has seen him. Next, remember you don't know a thing about anything. Asa, you can play opossum with the best of 'em. So go ahead and do it. We know where this person is now and I've spoken with Judge Jones, and she knows what to do. Asa, in a day or two you may have to make an arrest on a murder charge, but for now we can wait and see. All right, enough of that. Bring them out at about ten and not before, I want to be up and thinking straight when they get here. Ok, y'all know what to do, bye now."

•

On the way across town Tommy, Ricky and I put flyers of Junior up on every telephone pole we came across. And we put one on every storefront window we saw. We were doing our due-diligence and hope was running on high.

•

"Agent Cummings, don't you find it a bit strange that these people never leave the plantation?" Agent Lipscomb asked his FBI partner.

"Yes, it's more than a bit strange, it's very strange," Agent Cummings replied.

"How about our eyes on Alvin Wetmore's residence?" Agent Lipscomb asked.

"Pretty much the same, the agent there did talk with an older woman by the name of Riggins. She said she has seen both brothers in and around the home. Said they were still as mean and nasty as ever. She said they have probably gone fishing or hunting, which is consistent with everything we've heard about them, as far as the Russians and this Hurtwood guy are concerned. Well, I'm positive they're dirty; I can feel it in my bones. My guess would be that they're going to lay low 'til we and the rest of this goes away. What they don't know is we are not going away. At least not anytime soon," she said with a very determined note.

53

Tavern

After Sam walked out of my room, I fell asleep again and the dreams flew by. These were the kind of dreams that most people would consider to be nightmares. And in every single one of them, I was a no-good rat. I woke at about noon, I think. I sat up in bed and just knew I could never face Sam or Joey or Scooter or well, anybody again. I got dressed and slowly crept down the back stairs so no one would see me. I knew I looked a wreck and I didn't care. I started down the street, not knowing where my destination was. Over and over I said to myself, *you're a rat, you killed Ralphy, and you slept with another man's wife. You killed Ralphy, you slept with another man's wife, and you're a rat.* I had a real nice rhythm going when I walked up to the bus stop. I quit with my mantra and decided that getting on a bus and riding away from the truth would be a good idea. I sat down on the bench and zoned out as I watched the weeds grow between the cracks in the sidewalk. I was beyond depressed and felt like jumping in front of a truck or maybe off a cliff. I didn't hear or notice the car drive up and stop at the curb. I only heard the footsteps coming towards me because suddenly the footsteps had a voice. And over and over the voice was saying, unh, unh, unh.

"Unh, unh, unh lookie Reed, it's our old drunk friend that doesn't know who he is," Sergeant Ronny Detwiler said to Officer Reed Tucker.

The two Jupiter policemen that had arrested me when I first came to Jupiter had a ravenous look in their eyes that made me very uncomfortable.

"No, I have a name now. My name is Bobby McKillin. Don't you remember?" I asked.

"Yes, we remember. So, if that's your name, then you must have some identification that can verify what you just told us," Sergeant Detwiler said in an aggressive voice.

"Yes, yes I do. I have a valid Mississippi driver license," I said as I reached and put my hand in my back pocket.

There was nothing there, so I reached in the other pocket and then my shoulders slumped down. I watched as Officer Tucker took his handcuffs off his belt.

"Honestly, I have a license. A lady friend of mine has my wallet. Can't we go see her and then I can show you my license, please," I begged.

"Stick your hands out and don't make any sudden moves," Sergeant Detwiler said.

As Officer Tucker put the cuffs on me he said, "Well, at least you're still polite. You may be a drunk and so on, but at least you're polite." I didn't respond; just didn't seem to be any reason.

They put me in the back of the patrol car and when they got in and shut their doors, they sat for a moment before Sergeant Detwiler stuck his nose up in the air and sniffed. Then he turned and gave me a hard look.

"Christ all mighty, you smell worse than the last time we picked you up. Son, you got to lay off the booze," Detwiler warned.

They were both turned looking at me when Officer Tucker says, "Jesus, what happened to your face. Looks like you got hit by a train. Who did that to you?"

"I did, ok, so just drive would ya," I said.

Tucker whipped a U-turn and headed for the station. I deserved what was happening. After all, I was a dog killer, an adulterer, and a no-good rat.

•

"Yes, Cotton, he's here in our jail. He'll be up for the morning calendar. Please stop beating about the bush and tell me exactly what it is you want me to do."

"Eleanor, I'd like you to kill him. And for some reason I believe you probably could, with just your bare hands. But that would draw a little too much attention. So,

all I want you to do is find out where he lives. Just to be sure, I'll have someone follow him when he leaves the courthouse. Eleanor, I've got to make him go away, and the sooner the better. The feds have been monitoring the plantation for too long. And the longer they stay, the greater the chance of something going awry. Find out where he lives and I will take care of the rest. Thanks, and bye now," Cotton Hurtwood said as he hung up the phone with Judge Jones.

•

I sat in the corner in the same dirty jail cell I'd been in when I first came to Jupiter. There were two big differences this time from the last time I was here. For one, there was no Pearly to protect me. Two, I was going to have to spend the night before I could get in to see the judge. I could only shake my head when I thought of her. She will not be happy to see me again. But, this is the mess I've gotten myself into. I suppose I deserve it, being the rat that I am.

I turned to my right to stretch and the little skinny guy sitting next to me says, "What y'all in fo?"

"Well, it's kind of a long story, but the bottom line is, I don't have any identification. And they don't take kindly to homeless men wandering the streets of Jupiter," I said before it crossed my mind to ask him what he was in for. "Why are you here, I mean what'd you do wrong?" I asked.

"Din't do nut'in' wrong. Just don't have a job, is all," he said as he hung his head.

"Sounds familiar, say, I'm Bobby. What's your name?" I asked as I stuck out my hand.

"I'm Diego, and it's a pleasure ta meet ya," he said as we shook. "I ain't much when it come ta fightin' and such, but I tink a person better off here in jail if he gots a friend or two. You know dat ting 'bout dere's strength in numbuhs," he said with a shy smile.

"Yes, I believe you're right," I said.

We spoke with each other for quite a while. He

was nice to talk to and he knew an awful lot about Jupiter and the folks that live here. After they gave us supper, we were allowed to watch a little TV. I mean an actual real itty-bitty TV. It was hung up over in the top corner of the cell. When it came time for lights out, Diego came up with a good plan to keep anybody from going after one of us while we slept. He said we should sleep on opposite sides of the jail cell. That way we'd have a clear view of each other if someone was coming after one of us. I guess it worked, although I think I slept through the entire night. After all, I was still pretty darn hung over, and I was definitely still a rat.

Woke up in the morning when I heard an officer yelling at the top of his lungs for us to get in line. Diego and I both jumped up to get in line, but it was no use. We were in the back and there was no sneaking up in line, least not for the two of us. We waited and waited and were finally taken up to the courtroom in the last group of the day.

I knew the drill and sat down on the bench to wait for my name to be called. Funny how last time I was the first name picked and this time it looked like I was going to be last. I knew this because there were only two of us still sitting on the bench, that is, Diego and me. Then the bailiff called out, "Diego Hopper, you're up."

Judge Jones looked him over and then said, "Diego, you have been here too many times in the last few months. I thought I told you to get a job."

"I's sorry yo honor, but I cain't seems ta find me nut-in' permanent like. All de jobs is taken by folk's dat gots skills and such. I ain't gots none."

"Diego, it's, don't have any. Anyway, I'm going to let you go today, but the next time you come into my courtroom, it's going to be thirty days of hard labor for you. Do you understand?"

"Yes'm, yo honor, I unnerstands," was all he said as he hung his head.

"Diego, you're free to go," Judge Jones said.

Diego didn't wait to hear the gavel strike. He sprinted out of the courtroom and never looked back. The bailiff hollered, "Bobby McKillin."

Seemed like he put a little extra hot sauce on when he said my name. I walked over and stood in front of the lectern. The judge had the strangest look in her eyes. She looked at me the way I think an eagle would look down at a fat little rabbit.

"Well, Mr. McKillin, you're not going to say good morning?"

"Good morning your honor," I said like a rabbit.

"That's more like the drunken fellow I had here in my courtroom several weeks ago. How have you been, Bobby?" she asked, her head cocked to the side and her eyes glaring down on me.

"I've been—"

The gavel hit so hard it made my shoulders quake. My mind asked, *why would she do that?*

"Mr. McKillin, I don't want you to speak unless I tell you to speak. Do you understand?" she yelled across the empty courtroom.

I wasn't going to take a chance and speak, so I just nodded my head in agreement.

"That's better. Now, the last time you were here, I told you to stop drinking and get a job. The officers tell me you're still drinking and although you say you have a job, you weren't able to supply any proof thereof. What do you have to say about all of this, Mr. McKillin?"

I started to answer her and stopped myself. I didn't want to hear the gavel strike again. So, I waited a moment. Then the gavel struck again and I winced. I looked up at her and thought to myself, *she's nothing but a bully, and a wrinkly one at that.*

She yelled, "Answer me!"

"What I have to say is that I do have a job. I work at the tavern up towards the airport. And I have a valid Mississippi driver license. I could have shown the officers if they had just given me the chance. As far as drinking goes, well, I admit that I did drink more than I should have the night before they picked me up."

"That's it? You work at a tavern, but you don't give me a name and you don't show me a valid driver license. Mr. McKillin, what am I to think? What would you think?" she asked.

"I'd think I was telling the truth. You know why I'd think I was telling the truth?" I asked with an attitude rising in my chest.

"No, why?" she asked with some attitude of her own.

"Because I try to always tell the truth, and I believe others should do the same. I don't judge people; I listen to them and hope they're telling me the truth," I said with a truckload of attitude.

"You hope, you said you hope. Well, I'm not in the hope business. I'm in the judge business! You know something, Bobby, you've changed. And I'm not sure for the better. Ok, I'm tired of beating about the bush. I want you to tell me the name of the business where you work, and the address."

I didn't say anything right away, and once again the gavel struck. And once again I winced. She was stuck in my craw and good. She studied me for a moment, and then she screamed, "Now!"

"It's called Sam's Broken Bone Tavern. That's where I work and that's where I live," was all I said before the gavel struck again.

At the top of her lungs she screamed across the courtroom, "I want the exact address, now!"

"I don't know the exact address, but I'd say it's somewhere between Neptune and Uranus."

She leaped up and when she came down she put her hands on her knees and "You bastard," flew out of her mouth. Then she twirled around and glared at the bailiff and screamed, "Jake, do you know where this tavern is!"

Jake, the bailiff, tried to answer her, but he just couldn't get the words to come out. He covered his mouth and nodded his head as he sputtered. He was doing everything he could not to laugh, which I think made things even worse. And suddenly the air burst from his mouth. And he laughed hysterically. I watched the judge reach for the gavel and then her hand came down in a violent blur. The gavel struck so hard the head broke off and flew across the courtroom. Jake, the bailiff, didn't laugh after that. In fact, he barely breathed.

"Take him out to the street, now!"

The bailiff rushed over, grabbed my arm, and started dragging me out of the courtroom. About halfway out, Judge Jones yelled, "Stop!" Jake and I immediately stopped. "Mr. McKillin, where are you going?"

"I, I'm going out to the street like you told me to."

"After that, I'm asking about after you get out to the street," she said in a calmer voice.

"Well, I was going to go see some of the homeless men that live by the Salt."

"No! No you are not. You are to go straight back to this tavern of yours. Do you hear me!" she screamed.

"Yes, ma'am, I hear you. I will go straight back," I said as I stood as still as a tree's shadow.

"I'm going to have a couple officers follow you. If you deviate even one block, I will have you arrested. Do you understand me?" she screamed.

"Yes, yes, I understand. I will not stop. I'll go straight back to the tavern."

She turned and walked away. Then Jake said, "In my twenty-five years on this job, I have never seen her as furious. You must have some special powers that I'm just not seeing. If I was you, and I thank God, I'm not, but if I was you, I'd do as she said."

He escorted me out to the sidewalk before he let go of me. I looked up at the big clock on the front of the courthouse. It was exactly a quarter-to-ten in the morning. I had a long way to go, but I knew I could use some peace and quiet. I put one foot in front of the other and got to steppin'.

54

The hotel/Saturn, Alabama/ Madison's room
I was snoring like a bear when Tommy and Ricky knocked on my door. I looked at the clock and yelled, "I'll be down in the lobby in a half-an-hour."

We ate a quick breakfast in the diner next door to the hotel before we drove back to the Saturn Police station. After a few words with Chief Brown, we headed to 1 Hurtwood Lane. When we drove up to the front gate, I remember looking at the clock in the car. It was exactly a quarter-to-ten. An elderly black man name Riley opened the gates for us. And as we drove down the tree-lined lane to the mansion, I felt as though I was either dreaming or in a movie. The grounds were so gorgeous, every turn of my head was worthy of a photograph. A middle-aged black woman ushered us in to an office that reeked of privilege and money. She was dressed in the traditional full-length black dress, white apron, and gray shawl. Her hair was tightly wrapped in a white cotton turban. She was polite, but in a distant way. Three chairs were set in front of a huge oak desk; I assumed they were for Tommy, Ricky, and me. We stood in the middle of the room for a half-a-minute or so before a tall dark man wearing a black trench coat walked in and stood against the wall to our left. He didn't speak.

Then a carbon copy of the first man rolled a wheelchair into the room. In the wheelchair sat a silver haired, handsome gentleman. I assumed he was Cotton Hurtwood.

"Please, sit down. Nigeriana, you can go," he said to the black woman that had led us into the room.

She gave what appeared to be a short curtsy and after we sat down, she quickly left the room.

"Good morning, I'm Cotton Hurtwood and I'm pleased to meet you. You've come a long way in search of your family member. I sincerely hope I can be of some help. Before we continue, would any of you care for something to drink? We have fresh coffee, lemonade, water, or if you'd prefer we can get you something a bit stronger."

The three of us looked at each other and just shook our heads no.

"Well, if you change your mind, let me know. How can I help you?" he asked in a sincere tone.

Once again, the three of us looked at each other and then Tommy said, "I'm Tommy, and this is Madison." I said hello. "And this is Ricky Reed." Ricky said howdy like some cowboy fresh off a ranch. I suppose he thought howdy fit the situation. I guess you could say Tommy was speaking for our group, and he continued to do so.

"Mr. Hurtwood, your time is valuable so I'm going to give you a condensed version of what has brought us here. I assume you already know we're looking for my nephew, Junior McCool. This is a flyer with several pictures of Junior," Tommy said as he handed Hurtwood the flyer. Hurtwood studied the flyer and looked up at Tommy and said, "I see he's a police officer." Ricky blurted out, "And a darn good one."

Ricky's sudden outburst kind of set the mood for the rest of the meeting. From that point on, Hurtwood looked at Tommy with a chiseled stare rather than a gaze. Tommy sat up real straight in the chair before he continued.

"Someone stole Junior's airplane ticket and used it to fly out to California. This person also stole Junior's luggage. A violent crime took place in California, and we believe Grits Wetmore is the person that committed this crime. While he was there, Mr. Wetmore used your address as his own. So naturally, we're wondering what his relationship is to you. And where he is?" Tommy said in a more assertive manner than I expected.

After Tommy was finished talking, the tension in the room was palpable and rising. The men wearing the black trench coats were each standing against the wall, one to our left and the other to our right. Their eyes danced with emotion. Hurtwood looked around the room several times. Glances and unsaid feelings were being shared and deflected by everyone there.

"Thank you for being so straight forward. We do like to keep things simple here in the south. To answer your question, Grits is my nephew and he has a twin brother named Alvin. We were not told that Grits was going to California or that he had gone; that is until the FBI came to the plantation looking for him. Now, as you may already know, Grits and his brother are missing. We don't know if they have gone fishing or if they're running from the law. You asked about Grits using this as his address. Yes, I'm aware that he has at times used Hurtwood plantation as his home address. He does have a small room in the stables, which he calls the barn. Now as far as him going to California, well, that is beyond my scope of imagination. You see Grits can barely write his own name. He is a functioning illiterate. I was told that he boarded the airplane in Des Moines. So, for me the journey begins and ends there. And trust me, I have no idea how or why he was there in the first place. Tommy, what I've told you is pretty much all I know. Now, I have taken up a lot of time talking and I apologize for not allowing you to ask questions here and there. Is there something you'd like me to go over again?" Hurtwood asked.

Tommy looked at me and I did have a question. In fact, I had several questions running through my head.

"Mr. Hurtwood, you said you have no idea what your nephew was doing in Des Moines," I said before he quickly said, "No, I have no idea why."

"I'm sorry; I wasn't finished asking the question, so I'll continue," I said as I watched the red in his cheeks brighten. "I've talked extensively with the airlines and airport security. Your nephew was seen in the airport with another man. And the description given for the other man was quite different from your run of the mill person. He was described as a mulatto or a light skinned black man. He is of average height and extremely thin. He has medium brown hair which he wears in an afro. This man doesn't sound like someone you see every day. So my question to you sir, is, do you know who this light skinned, mixed race black man is?" I asked as beads of sweat began to appear on his forehead.

He cleared his throat as he stroked his thin white goatee.

"No, I don't recognize the person you just described. He was probably someone Grits met in the airport. Asa," Hurtwood said as he looked to the back of the room. "Does the man this young lady just described sound familiar to you?"

"Well Cotton, I suppose he does and he doesn't. Madison, where you come from, this man may sound quite different or maybe even peculiar. But here in the south, we have lots of men that could fit that description," was all Chief Brown said.

I watched both of the men's eyes dart here and there, a classic physical response to a person knowingly skirting the truth or telling a lie.

"Chief, thank you for being so observant and honest, you have unknowingly proven my point. My point being that this man's physical makeup may be commonplace here in Alabama, but he stuck out like a throbbing sore thumb in Des Moines. So obviously, this man traveled to the Midwest with Mr. Wetmore. And just so that we are all crystal clear on this point, the man I described to you is, without question, from here," I said as I watched Hurtwood and Chief Brown squirm. I asked if they knew who the man was again and, once again, both men lied. So I decided to go in a different direction.

"Mr. Hurtwood, have you or anyone that works for you checked with the hospitals in the area. I mean to see if Grits or his brother have been admitted or cared for?"

"I can answer that Cotton," Chief Brown said as Hurtwood's eyes said no. "Yes Madison, we've checked every hospital in the area. And, I might add, we've checked every day since the Wetmore boys went missing. No one has seen hide nor hair of either one of them. I'm sorry," Chief Brown said as his eyes strayed away from me.

"Ok, Mr. Hurtwood and Chief Brown, have you checked the homeless shelters in Saturn and the nearby clinics? I'm asking because if Junior is here, he may have needed medical attention and gone to a free clinic. Are there any free clinics in Saturn or this part of the state?" I asked in good faith.

Chief Brown stepped up to the plate again.

"No Madison, at present we don't have any homeless shelters. In fact, we've made a concerted effort here in Saturn to move all the homeless from the streets. We find work for some of them and some just decide to leave the area. No doubt it's a problem, but we're doing our best to deal with it," Chief Brown said like an out-of-work politician.

I looked over at Tommy and his eyes said, *let's get the heck out of here*. So I thanked all the gentlemen in the room for their time.

We stood and Hurtwood said, "Tommy, Madison, and Ricky, I hope you find Junior. And don't be afraid to come back if there's something else you believe I can help you with. Asa, will you please show these people out to your car?"

"Sure, Cotton," was all Chief Brown said.

We gave the two dark men and Hurtwood a small Midwestern wave as we walked out of his office. When we got in the chief's car, I looked at the clock and it was exactly eleven o'clock. When we drove out of the plantation, the grounds didn't seem as wonderful as they had on the way in. There was something dirty about the man that owned the place and everything in it.

•

After I left the courthouse, I walked in the morning sun for a long time. And I'd been walking at a pretty good clip. Not a blue streak, but pretty darn fast. But no matter how fast I walked, I felt as though someone was behind me, definitely felt like I was being followed. I turned around so many times I started believing that I was the one creating the feeling. I quit looking over my shoulder. I went straight to Gino's so I could take a break and sip on a cold bottle of pop before I headed over to the tavern. I went ahead and walked in the back door and sat down at Gino's table. I looked up at the clock and it was exactly eleven o'clock.

"Hello Junior, I didn't see you sitting there. Did you fly in here or something?" Gino asked in good fun.

"No Gino, I walked in the back. Hope you don't mind. Listen, I don't have a penny on me and I'm very thirsty. So I'd gladly pay you Tuesday for a bottle of pop today," I said in good fun.

"Sure thing," he said, as he stepped closer to me so that he could have a look at the bruises covering my face. "Bobby, how'd you get all bruised up like that?" he asked, genuinely concerned.

"It's one of those long stories Gino. Ok, if I tell you about it some other time," I said.

"Sure, Bobby, absolutely, here let me get you that soda. Oh, what flavor?" he asked as he hurried back to the cooler.

"Orange," I said. He came back out and handed me a bottle of Orangette and a glass. "Thanks." I took a big drink out of the bottle, I didn't need a glass. He sat down and waited for a half-a-minute or so before he said, "Bobby, I don't know what's going on, but Sam was here looking for you last night. She was awful upset. Are you gonna—"

"Yes Gino, I'm on my way there now. Soon as I finish this bottle of pop, I'll be going. Just need to sit for a minute, is that ok with you?" I said, not in a mean way but in a kind of tired way.

"Ok, you rest for a bit," Gino quietly said.

He went back in the kitchen and left me there to

my own thoughts. I was thinking and I was thinking very hard. *What am I going to say to Sam? I guess I'll just wait and whatever comes out comes out.* I sat for a half-an-hour and at eleven-thirty, I got up, waved goodbye to Gino, and took off out the back door. I walked around the trash cans and when I did, I got a glimpse of someone across the street hiding behind a tree. I said to myself, *you can't let this person know where the tavern is.*

I decided I'd walk two blocks from the tavern and then I'd turn south down that street and run and hide. Then if the person was still behind me, I could jump him. Well, I mean jump out and ask him why he was following me. I went across the street and started walking as fast as I could. I'd made it about a half-a-block when I heard someone behind me start screaming. When I looked back, Pearly had his arm around this little skinny guy's neck and was holding him up in the air. The screaming was short lived. My guess is, it's hard to scream when you don't have any air coming in. I ran back to Pearly as fast as I could. When I got right up to him, I realized the little guy he had the strangle hold on was Diego.

"Pearly, what in the world is going on? Hey, where is your curly cue? How long have you been following me? Why'd you grab Diego like that?" I asked, wondering why Diego would have been following me.

"Diego, you say. Hell wit dat - dis ain't no Diego and I ain't no Pearly. Dis little nigguh here is Grasshopper and I's Odell, and don't you forget it," he said in a threatening manner that I hoped he wouldn't repeat.

"Your name is Odell? Why didn't Pearly ever mention the fact that he has a twin brother?" I asked in complete confusion. Odell didn't say anything. "Odell, do you know who I am?" I asked as he laid the skinny guy's limp body down on the ground.

"Yes, I know who you is, you Bobby. I was dere dat foist day Pearly found yo white ass in de culvert. And I toldt him den ta leave ya dere, but he din't listen. He don't ever listen ta me."

I don't know exactly why, but I suddenly blurted out, "That means Belle is your sister."

Odell looked at me as though I was an idiot. I suppose he had good reason. I mean if Belle is Pearly's sister, then she is also Odell's sister.

"Yes, yo goilfriend is my sistuh. So what 'bout it?" he asked as he smiled at me.

Finally, there was some peace in the air and, like Pearly, it was his twin brother Odell that started the peace process. I stuck my hand out at that point and he thrust his massive arm towards me. We shook hands and it was the strangest thing to shake with someone that had a hand as big as Pearly's. We were sharing a small smile while we looked down at an unconscious Grasshopper, or should I have said Diego? I guess I didn't really care which one he was. I just wanted to know why he was following me.

Diego started to stir a little bit when out of nowhere, a female began screaming bloody murder. I nearly leaped out of my skin and Odell jumped back a little before we turned and looked at Sam. She was running as fast as she could toward us. She had her arms waving from side to side in front of her and she was screaming, "Don't hurt him, don't hurt him, Bobby, don't you dare hurt him."

Odell and I just stood and watched her until she was right up on us. She took a swing at me but missed. She looked at Odell and decided against hitting him. Then she was down on the ground patting the side of Diego's face.

"Grasshopper, wake up. Come on please wake up," she said as the little guy started coming to.

He finally looked up at Sam and I think he thought maybe he'd gone to heaven. He smiled at her and then he looked up at Odell and cringed before he curled up into a little ball.

"Grasshopper, it's ok. Come on, I won't let them hurt you. Get up now," Sam said.

Grasshopper got up on one knee before he looked up at us. I think he felt safe down by the ground so he stayed there. Makes sense if you think about it. You can't fall as far if you're already down on the ground. I wasn't going to wait for him to get up so I hollered, "Why were you following me?" He didn't say anything. "I'm only going to ask one more time and then I'm going to have to knock some sense into you. Now, why were you following me?"

He looked at Sam for protection before he said, "I was toldt ta folluh you by Missuh Hurtwoodt. He wants ta see ya 'bout somepin o othuh."

I guess Sam was so far in the dark she just had to stop all of us at that point.

"Bobby, when did Grasshopper start following you?" she asked.

"Sam, you don't know this, but I was in jail last night. You know why I was in jail?" I asked.

"No, why were you in jail?" she asked.

"Because I had no identification with me. You see, someone took my wallet!" I hollered out of sheer frustration.

Sam looked down at the ground. "I'm sorry Bobby, I forgot I had your wallet."

"Listen, before we go any further, Sam, this is Pearly's brother, Odell."

"What?" she said with a shake of the head. "I thought you were Pearly, you're not Pearly?" she asked.

"No ma'am, I's Pearly's twin brother, Odell. Lots a people confuse us, dat's why Pearly has dat big old curly cue on top a his headt. You know so's folks can tell us apart. It's nice ta meet ya," Odell said as he stuck out his massive hand.

I looked down and Diego was trying to crawl away. I grabbed him by the collar and pulled him back.

"Sam!" I yelled to get her attention. "I was in jail when Grasshopper here introduced himself as Diego. Long story short, the judge let Diego go before me. Then when the judge let me go, I headed straight for Gino's. And this little creep followed me the whole way. I got thirsty so I went in to have something cold to drink. Well, I drank a bottle of pop and the moment I stepped out the back door of the restaurant, I saw him. I was going to hurry down the street and hide and grab him myself, but Odell beat me to the little creep," I said as Sam's eyes narrowed onto Grasshopper.

"Is what Bobby just said true?" she asked Grasshopper.

He looked down at the ground and then he just nodded his head yes. Sam slapped him across the face, and hard.

"Here I was protecting your ass, and you let me - you little turd. Ok Odell, I guess you can finish what you started. Go ahead and kill him, just make it quick," Sam said as she started walking away.

"No, no, I's sorry. I'll tells ya whatevuh it is ya wants ta know, just don't kill me," he said while he stared back at Odell.

Sam walked back and said, "That's better, now start talking."

"Mr. Hurtwoodt toldt me ta find Bobby, cuz he wants him ta come by de plantation. I don't really know why, but I tink he has somepin dat belong to Bobby. Dat's all I knows, for real," he said as he repeatedly glanced over his shoulder at Odell.

Odell looked down at Grasshopper for a bit before he said, "You ain't toldt dem de truph."

We looked at Grasshopper and it was easy to see that he knew what Odell was talking about. Grasshopper started looking around; I think he was considering running. I got right in front of him. "Diego, or whoever the heck you are. If you make one false move, I might kill you myself."

Then Odell says, "Tell the whole truph or I'mona kill yo little nigguh-ass right here taday."

"Ok," Grasshopper said before he looked up into the sky. "What Odell mean is he and Belle done caught me peepin' in her winduh. I followed Belle home from her woik. Anyway, Hurtwoodt wants ta see ya Bobby, I tink he... I tink he knows who you is. Or at least who you uzed ta be. Honest, dat's all I knows, please don't kill me. I'll he'p y'all if ya wants," he said in a halfway believable voice.

The stuff that was going through my mind was more than I could take in all at once. This man that lives in the biggest damn mansion I've ever seen knows a lot about me, maybe even who I am, but why? I was just going to ask Diego a few of the questions that were circling my brain when Odell beat me to the punch.

"Was you wif dem godt-damn Russians when dey went to de Salt and hoit Scootuh?"

"No Odell, I swear I wasn't and I don't know anyting 'bout dat. When did dis happen?" Grasshopper asked in a sincere voice.

"A few days ago. Dem two evil mothuhs done beat Scootuh and killdt Ralphy," Odell said with angst and venom leaking from every word.

"Who Ralphy?" Grasshopper asked.

"Ralphy is or, I should say was, Scooter's dog. What a wicked thing to do," I said.

When I was done talking, Diego fell back to the ground and wailed and cried like the dickens. He was every bit as distraught as I had been when he found out the Russians killed Ralphy. Then, without a warning, Diego stopped crying and sat up straight and looked at us.

"I love animals. Had me a puppy once, but he got runned over by a mean old man. Odell, Bobby, and Miss Sam, I am so sorry dey killdt dat po little dog. Lord, you don't know how sorry I am. Dat little dog never hurt nobody. Lord, when will all dis evil stop? I'll tell ya when, it gonna stop now, taday. If y'all can see it in yo hearts ta let me go, I gives you my woid I will never follow or hoit any of ya. Please, I gots ta go," he said with his heart on his sleeve.

The three of us looked at each other for a moment or two before we decided to let him go. I mean, what else were we going to do with him? We made him promise to never say a word about Belle or where she lived. When he said he would never tell a soul, I believed him. As far as the tavern was concerned, we believed that Diego didn't know where it was.

To me Grasshopper became Diego that day, and I said as much to Sam and Odell. They agreed. After all, it was a lot easier and quicker to say Diego than it was to say Grasshopper. Before Sam and I started back to the tavern, I wanted to know why Odell was following Diego in the first place.

"Bobby, I din't start out to folluh Diego, I was gonna folluh you. I guess everbody in de Salt is lookin' after yo white ass. Seems dey tink you stand up. I guess I do too. I can certainly see why Belle so fond a you. Anyway, I got word dat you was in jail, so I went dere ta keep an eye on y'all. Dat's when I saw dat little high-yelluh nigguh folluhin' you."

"Odell, could you do me a favor and not use that word anymore," Sam asked.

"What woid is dat, ma'am?" Odell asked.

"That 'n' word, it hurts me deep down inside when I hear people use that word. I would sure appreciate it if you didn't say it around me, please," Sam asked.

"Well, I'll be, I hadt no ideya one little woid could cause someone so much mis'ry. Yes, ma'am I s'pose I can try my best not to say nigg... dat woid anymore," Odell complied with a smile.

He turned and looked down the street and started whistling before he said, "Ok, well I gots ta go now."

Odell had walked maybe twenty feet away when he stopped and gazed back at Sam.

"Sho was nice ta make y'all's acquaintance. I'll be seein' ya, bye now."

55

Saturn, Alabama
"Vladimir, where's Grasshopper? We need to keep him out of sight," Hurtwood said.

"Grasshopper was told to follow this Junior person," Vladimir said.

"Oh my God, when you see Grasshopper, you tell him to go to his room and stay out of sight. Christ! I can't believe how damn dumb Asa is. And how did that Madison know about Grasshopper? Why didn't the FBI ask about Grasshopper? Ok, first things first," Hurtwood said just before his office phone began ringing. "Nikita, can you get the phone?"

"Mr. Hurtwood, it is Judge Jones. Would you like to speak with her?" Nikita asked.

"Yes, yes, give me the phone. Eleanor, yes, he did, where? I don't believe this. You're sure, ok, well, thank you. Yes, bye now. Vladimir, it seems that our man, Bobby McKillin, has been right here under our noses this whole time. He is working for one of my employees at the Broken Bone Tavern. Do you know where it is?" Hurtwood asked.

"Yes, I know where it is. This problem will be taken care of. Do not worry," Vladimir said.

"Good, that is very good. Nikita, can you please take me up to the veranda. I need to sit and think for a while. Please bring my morning coffee and my medication," Hurtwood said.

•

Chief Brown drove us back to the Saturn Police station without two words being spoken. Tommy, Ricky, and I had heard enough during our meeting with Cotton Hurtwood to know that there was more to this story, a lot more. When we got out of the car at the station, we declined Chief Brown's offer to take us to lunch. Tommy told him we had phone calls to make so we needed to get back to our hotel. We thanked him and nearly ran to our car. As soon as we left the parking lot, Tommy drove back through town. As he drove, Tommy asked Ricky and me to take a look around, he didn't say why, or what to look for, or at, he just said look. And so we did. It took a block or two before I understood what we were supposed to be looking for.

"Now I understand," I said to Tommy.

"Ok, you two, what am I supposed to be looking for?" Ricky asked.

"Ricky, do you see any of the flyers we put up last night?" I asked.

His head spun around a couple of times before he said, "Well, I'll be. Somebody has taken down every single flyer we put up," Ricky said in a 'how'd they do that' voice.

"I didn't say anything this morning when we were in the station. But anyway, when we were there, I noticed that the flyers we gave the Chief last night were gone. This isn't good, but believe it or not, I'm encouraged. I think Hurtwood and the Chief are afraid someone will recognize Junior from the flyers. And that tells me he's here or, at the very least, he has been here," Tommy said.

"Yes, that makes sense Tommy. So where do we go from here?" I asked.

"We're going back out to the plantation," Tommy said.

"Why?" Ricky asked.

"Because there is someone there I want to talk to," Tommy said.

"Who do you want to talk to?" I asked.

"The FBI, that's who. I saw their dark gray car parked on the side of the road this morning. They're keeping an eye on the Hurtwood place and I want to know what they know," Tommy said.

•

Sam and I headed back to the tavern; when we

walked inside, I looked at the clock and it was twelve thirty in the afternoon. Sam told me Joey would get back from Jersey that evening, so I went up to my room to take a nap. I was exhausted. I think I was already asleep when my head hit the pillow.

I was immediately in the same dream I had when I walked through the four seasons. This time a man was following me in my dream. And he waited 'til Jack Frost had his arms around me before he eased out from the shadows.

•

We drove by the dark gray sedan and then Tommy turned the car around in front of them. I think he thought it would be safer than driving up behind them. When we came to a stop, Tommy said, "Wait here, I'll be right back."

He got out of the car and as he walked towards the sedan, he held up his badge. I looked at the clock and it was exactly twelve thirty in the afternoon. I figured we had most of the day to look for clues that might lead us to Junior. Ricky and I watched as Tommy stood next to the FBI car. He was obviously engaged in a conversation with the agents sitting inside. After a minute or two, he turned and waved for us to come over. All three of us got in the back of the sedan. After short hello's, the black man sitting in the driver's seat said, "I'm agent Lipscomb and this is my partner, agent Cummings. Tommy, you can ask all questions you like, but I can't guarantee you that we'll answer any of them. You understand, don't you," he said more than asked.

"Yes, we just want to help in any way that we can. I'm going to give you a rundown of all we know about this case. And everything we discussed with Hurtwood and Chief Brown," Tommy said.

The agents didn't respond. They just turned a bit in their seats so that they could listen. Tommy started with the tornado that had swept by the north end of Crestfield. He told them every detail he knew about the case. And at no time did they seem interested. That is, they weren't interested 'til he got to the part about the mulatto that was traveling with Grits. It was obvious they had not heard about him. And it was obvious they wanted to know how we knew. So they asked. And Tommy started to answer them but stopped and said, "I think I'll let Madison fill you in about the mulatto, since she's the one that found out about him."

Both agents craned their necks as they turned in their seats to listen to me. Then, the female agent named Cummings said, "Madison, how is it that you know of this person that traveled with Grits and no one else knows?"

"I asked, that's how I know," I said.

The FBI agents continued to look at me with question marks in their eyes.

"Ok, none of your people took the time to go and talk to the people that work in the airport. So, when I went there, I started with the custodians. I found out nothing. Then I went to the people that work for American and United Airlines. And of course, I found out the same thing you did, and that is that Grits purchased only one ticket. I reasoned that there had to be at least two people involved," I said just before agent Cummings stopped me.

"Madison, we're here in Alabama looking for Grits. We're looking for him because we believe he committed a murder while he was in California. The whereabouts of your brother is part of all this, but he has been missing for so long we just figured, well, I think you know what we figured. Have you seen this mulatto that you're talking about?" agent Cummings asked.

"No, but when I asked about him this morning, Chief Brown and Hurtwood both lied to me. How do I know they lied, well, let's just say that is my opinion. Anyway, I think this person might be the answer to a lot of our questions. I know the mulatto exists because Ricky bought some coffee for Junior in the airport. And he and the young lady that sold him the coffee both remember seeing the mulatto." When I said Ricky, both agents turned and keenly eyed Ricky.

"Are you sure?" Lipscomb asked Ricky.

"Yes, I'm positive. Like Madison says, there were a lot of people, but that guy stuck out. At least he stuck out to me," was all Ricky said.

"Ok, well, we have not seen this person, but if he's here, we'll find him. Now, for the sake of our efforts, I want to thank you. We have to check in with our superiors, so if you don't mind," agent Cummings said in an effort to get us to leave.

We didn't have to be told twice, so we got out of the car and said our goodbyes. We were halfway back to our car when agent Cummings got out of hers and said, "I know you're not going to stop searching. Please, be careful. The people that are involved are more dangerous than you may think."

•

"Why didn't you tell them about the stewardess that was on the plane from Des Moines to Saturn with the 'mulatto' and Junior?" Lipscomb asked.

"I didn't say anything because they thought they had some important and unknown information. I didn't want to steal their thunder. The fact is, from the time that plane landed, no one has seen or heard of anybody by the name Jack or Junior McCool. I believe the Russians killed him and dumped the body, end of story," Cummings said.

"Do you think they know about the drugs?" Lipscomb asked.

"No, I don't. And I hope it stays that way. I don't want them to know the drugs are the reason we're here," Cummings said with a culpable tone.

•

"Tommy, where are we goin'?" Ricky asked.

"We're going back to see Chief Brown. I'll go in by myself. I want to ask him where all the flyers went. And he'd better have a good answer," was all Tommy said as he headed back into the police station.

Tommy was in the station for only a few minutes

before he came back out.

"Well, what happened?" I asked.

"Chief Brown has left the building. At least that's what I was told. I was also told they have a city ordinance that makes debris, flyers and such illegal. Said it causes an unsightly trash problem. That same kid named Ricky-Lee told me. When I asked him about the flyers that we gave them for the station, he said he didn't know what happened to them. He was obviously lying. At least now we know where we stand with the Saturn police. Now, I think we should go check the Saturn hospital," Tommy said as he started the car.

56

Tavern

Sam came up to my room and woke me at exactly five o'clock in the evening. She told me that Joey was back and that he wanted to talk to me.

"Sam, would it be ok if I take a shower first. I feel absolutely filthy and for some reason, I can't seem to wake up. I'll only be a few minutes," I said.

"Sure, come on down after you get yourself cleaned up. Go to Joey's office," she said in an edgy voice.

•

We parked in the lot at the community hospital in Saturn. Just before I got out of the Imperial, I looked and it was five o'clock. It was still hot as Hades. I looked around the hospital parking lot and it was nearly empty. I thought, *don't people get sick in Alabama?* We went in and talked with every person we could that worked in and around the hospital. Nobody had seen or heard of the Wetmore brothers being admitted. And they hadn't seen anyone that looked like the photos of Junior on the flyer.

When we walked out of the hospital, I saw a man panhandling for change. I went straight to him and introduced myself. He said his name was Bert. I gave him all the change Ricky had in his little red football-shaped coin purse. Then I sat Bert down on a bench next to the emergency entrance.

"Listen Bert, I'm hoping you can help me with a few questions I have," I said as he looked up at me with his droopy brown eyes.

"Ok, I can he'p ya, but might take a little mo jingle than what y'all done give me. That is if ya wants some real good answers," he said as he held out his hand.

Tommy reached in his pocket and gave the man all the change he had. Then he held up a five-dollar bill. The man smiled real big and showed off all three of his teeth.

"Ok, is there a free clinic anywhere here in Saturn?" I asked.

"No ma'am, there's none here, but if y'all drive a couple mile west a here you can find one. That's where all the homeless go," he said in a matter of fact way.

"You say a couple of miles, is that still part of Saturn?" I asked.

"No ma'am, the clinic is over ta Jupiter," he said in a way that suggested we should know that.

"Where's Jupiter?" I asked.

"Like I said ma'am, it's a couple mile west a here," he said.

"Well, I've looked at the map of Saturn and it goes right up to the western border of Alabama. It doesn't show a place or town called Jupiter," I said, more confused than ever.

"A'course it don't, it don't cuz Jupiter ain't in Alabama. Jupiter is in Mississippi," he said as he looked at me as though I was the strange one in the conversation.

"Oh, now I see. Mississippi never crossed our minds. Can you tell us how to get to the free clinic in Jupiter?" I asked.

He didn't say a word, he just stuck out his hand. Tommy reached and turned the man's hand palm up and laid the five-dollar bill in it. He told us the clinic was across town on Adams Avenue. We thanked him as we started walking back to our car. Then he said, "It ain't open at night. Y'all gonna have ta go there tamarruh. It's not so crowded in the mornin'."

We had struck out, but only temporarily. We decided to go eat supper and then make some calls from the hotel. We would get an early start in the morning. Tomorrow looked promising.

•

As soon as I was dressed, I went down to Joey's office. He had a very serious look on his face, kinda looked like he was mad at me. I was wondering what I had walked into. I said to myself, *maybe he knows I'm a rat.*

He told me to sit down and when he did, he looked at Haystack. It was only a look, but it made me very uncomfortable. Haystack slowly walked over and closed the door. I thought the meeting was just going to be us guys when Sam walked out of Joey's little bathroom.

I was sitting on the left side of Joey's desk and Sam was sitting on the right. And Haystack was right in front of the closed door. I looked at Sam for a hint about what was going on, but she gave me no clue.

"Bobby, I called you down here because we are in a real live ball buster predicament. Sam told me that you know we work for Hurtwood or at least he's who we make our mortgage payments to."

He was going to stop there, but Sam cleared her throat in a way that made me believe there was more to this whole thing.

"Ok, listen, we haven't been completely honest with you about some things. For starters, the motorcycle parts you go pick up every week. Well, there's more in those crates than just parts. Some of the parts have drugs stuffed in them. You know like the gas tanks, and tires, and well, everywhere you could hide a drug."

He could tell that I was about to get real upset for him using me to move illegal drugs.

"Don't go gettin' your underwear all in a bunch," he said as he pointed down at me. "You didn't have a damn thing when you came here. No money, no food, no job, and no place to lay your little head. Fact is, you didn't even know who the hell you were." He stopped with the pointing and sat down. "Bobby, I'm in a motorcycle gang. Do you know what that means?" I started to say no, but he stopped me. "Men in motorcycle gangs' mule drugs to make money. You're not so innocent that you didn't know that. Ok, here's the part that bothers me the most. You see, Hurtwood is a stone-cold drug addict. It's just that he's also rich. So he can do the drugs and keep it quiet. He has others go get the drugs for him, so he never has to worry about gettin' busted," he said and then stopped.

Crestfield

"Joey, how do you know all of this? I mean, how long has Hurtwood been a drug addict? Seems to me that after a while the drugs would kill him. Are you the one that got him on drugs?" I said, more than asked, not really knowing what I was talking about.

"No Bobby, I never got him or anyone else on drugs. I just get them and sell them for him. As far as Hurtwood goes, years ago he was in a strange accident; got hit by a train. And that's a fact. His wife was the one driving. She was killed instantly. The car split in half and he was thrown two hundred feet down the tracks." Joey laughed after he said it.

I was thinking, *that's not funny* when Joey said, "I know it's not funny, but it's true. Anywho, he has been paralyzed ever since. And I guess the pain he felt after the accident was unbearable. So he started with your basic pain killers and they led to stronger drugs. Now he does them all: uppers, downers, and everything in between. I ain't afraid of him, but he's got some mean characters that work for him. He has these Russian twins that, for the right price, would probably kill their own mother. People think they're the only two that he has working for him, but people are wrong. He has lots and lots of men willing to do almost anything, that is, if the price is right. We've got to have a sit down with him, but I'm afraid of what he's gonna say. Bobby, I'm not gonna give you up if that's what you're thinking. You have been too good to us and in return, I feel like I owe you some protection. It's too late in the day to do anything about it now, but in the mornin' I'm gonna give him a call. We'll set up a meet then. Look, I know you have a bunch of questions, you always do. Just wait 'til mornin' and then we'll see which way the wind is blowin'. For now, we're safe because he doesn't have a clue that you live here," Joey said as he walked around his desk and hugged me. I looked over at Haystack and he gave me a black smile. I went out to the bar and Jay-Don served me two beers and one of the awful sandwiches they sell in the tavern. We didn't do that much talking.

Can't Find my Way Home

• Madison

My hotel room creaked and groaned like a rusty gate in an Alfred Hitchcock movie. I battled the drama until the scene playing in my mind became unbearable. It was pointless to fight so I gave in and got out of bed. The clock read three in the morning. I pulled the curtains back and walked out onto my balcony. The coolness of the night air was sublime and I just stood and stared out through the darkness. Several times I said out loud, *where are you, Junior? I know you're close, I can feel your pulse in the air.*

•

I said goodnight to Jay-Don and barely made it up the stairs. I don't know why, but I was so tired I couldn't think straight. I fell right to sleep and was walking through the seasons again when a noise woke me. I looked around in the dark and started to lay my head back down when I heard something downstairs. I got up and peeked out of my door. I didn't hear anything, but I just had to go down and check. I walked down the stairs and I looked at the clock; it was three in the morning. The noise I'd heard was coming from Joey's office. I knocked on the door and asked if everything was ok. Joey hollered, "Yeah, go on back to bed." I went back upstairs and got into bed. I laid there on my back, thinking for a minute or two, before I slowly drifted off to sleep. Then the man in my dream came out from the shadows. The pain I felt was dull at first and then it became sharp as my head felt like it had been split wide open. I put my hands up to protect myself, but it wasn't doing much good. Then my ribs ached with a pain that took my breath away.

I rolled off my bed and the man yelled, "You ain't gettin' away this time. I'm gonna kill you, you sum-bitch!"

I crawled under the bed and I saw him get down on a knee and look at me. He reached for me once and missed, then he reached a second time and he had my arm and he pulled me out from under the bed. I tried to fight him off. He let go of me and groaned before he reared back. I just knew he was ready to deliver the final blow. So as fast as I could, I scuttled back under the bed.

I heard the man from the shadows breathing hard, but when I looked across the floor, instead of two feet there were four, two of the feet were bare. I crawled forward and did my best to get up so I could see what was going on. I heard a loud crack and then all was quiet. The light suddenly came on and I looked across the room. Haystack was there smiling his black smile at me. And at his feet lay the road gang guard named Teerlink. His chest was flat against the wall but his face was turned towards me. His lips moved, but he didn't say anything. I was going to get up when Joey came running into the room. He was bleeding something awful. And when I touched the side of my head, I realized I was bleeding too. Joey got down on his knees and felt for a pulse. Although his neck was clearly broken, Teerlink was still breathing.

Joey squeezed Teerlink's nose with one hand and covered Teerlink's mouth with his other hand. Teerlink shuddered and quaked for a moment and then he was still. Joey jumped up and ran down the stairs; it sounded like he opened the front door and went outside. I heard a car drive away and then Joey slowly walked back up the steps and said, "It was Armstrong, he got away. I know where he lives and as far as I'm concerned, he's a dead man."

Joey looked at me and he asked if I was ok.

I squeezed out, "I'm ok for now, how about you?"

"Yeah, I'll live. That son of a bitch, shit I gotta call Sam and get her over here," he said as he started to walk away.

"Joey, tell me what happened. I mean how did Teerlink get the jump on you?" I asked.

"Haystack and I were putting away the empty bottles when someone started pounding on the front door. Then Armstrong yelled through the door that he had to talk to me. I unlocked the door and we went into my office to talk. He asked me to take him out to see the last shipment of drugs. Anyway, we're walking across the tavern when this son of a bitch hits me from behind."

"What did he hit you with?" I asked.

"Hit me with the same thing he hit you with. That damn truncheon over there on the floor."

I looked over and next to Haystack's bare feet there was a black metal rod thing with a brown wooden handle.

"Haystack, did you take that from him?" I asked, knowing he couldn't hear me.

He just smiled at me and then he looked down at the truncheon and nodded his head yes.

"Yeah, old stupid ass Teerlink forgot about Haystack being under the stairs. I'll bet he shit his pants when Haystack grabbed hold of him. In fact, I can already smell it. Christ what are we gonna do? I gotta call Sam, she'll know what to do," he said as he took off down the stairs again.

Haystack walked over to me after Joey left. He took my arm and helped me down the stairs. He walked me over and sat me down at the bar. Then he put a whole bunch of ice in a towel and put it on my head. First, he saves my life, then he gives me first-aid. The world needs a whole lot more people just like him. I sat and waited for Sam to get to the tavern. And the longer I sat there, the sicker I became. Finally, Sam came running through the door. She and Joey talked right there in front of me and decided that they needed to get me out of there. After I was gone, Joey would call and report the break-in to the police. Sam bandaged up my head the best she could and then put me in her Corvette. We drove into the night; I must have passed out. I woke up when I saw a crack of light come into the room where I was sleeping. I looked at the clock on the wall and it was nearly ten in the morning. Then the honeyed aroma of something cooking wafted my way. That was just before Belle walked into her bedroom.

"How you feel Bobby? Lo'dy, you lucky to be 'live. Why wouldt someone want ta hurt such a sweet man like you. Dis world we livin' in sho is full a wicked people. Bobby, you din't answer me, how you feelin'?" she asked again.

"Belle, I'm sorry, but I feel sick to my stomach. I think I'm gonna be," I said before I pressed my hand over my mouth.

Belle had an old plastic trash can next to the bed and she got it in front of me just in time. I can't tell you how many times I vomited, but I can tell you it was a lot. I was shivering one minute and burning up the next. I slept, but I was so restless. In between fits of nausea, Belle sat and put a cold cloth on my forehead. I was burning up with fever; thank God Belle was there to help cool me down.

•

"Vladimir, what time is it?" Hurtwood asked.

"It is nearly ten," Vladimir answered.

"Nikita, help me get dressed. Why haven't they called?" Hurtwood asked.

"We don't know sir, but they will," Nikita answered.

"Take me down to my office, I need to make some calls," Hurtwood ordered. "And bring my medication."

"Yes sir," Nikita quickly answered.

Hurtwood was dressed and wheeled down to his office where he sat waiting for his morning fix of coffee and something a little stronger. Nikita had just administered the stronger of the two when the phone rang.

"Get the phone, it must be them now," Hurtwood slowly slurred.

"Mr. Hurtwood, the phone call is for you, but it is not one of our men," Vladimir said.

"Then who is it?" Hurtwood slowly slurred.

"It is Joey Lombardi. Do you wish to speak to him?" Vladimir asked.

"What? Yes, hand me the phone. "Hello, and good morning Joey, what can I do for you?" Hurtwood said as clearly as he could.

"Let's see, oh yeah, you asked what you can do for me. Well, for starters, you can kiss my ass!" Joey screamed into the phone. Hurtwood started to object. "Shut the hell up asshole. Good, that's better. I guess you haven't heard anything from your boys, have you? Well, I wouldn't wait by the phone too long because they won't be callin'."

"I have no idea what you're talking about," Hurtwood said, his mind struggling to keep up.

"You know exactly what I'm talking about. And you wanna know why they won't be callin? No, you shut up and listen. You see neither of your boys will be callin' cuz they're dead. When you sent them out here to come into my place of business, you broke all the rules of trust. And now you're gonna have to pay. I mean, you're gonna have to pay big time. Don't give me any of that bullshit; you know exactly what I'm talking about. Now, here are the rules we're gonna play by. I'm gonna call for an emergency meeting of all the men in the Headhunters M.C. There are going to be one hundred and seventy-two men guarding this tavern. That means day and night. Now, if you still try to mess with me, I'm gonna call my dear old dad. Guess what he does for a living? Yes, he's a mademan. There will be mob guys coming at you up from Florida and down from Jersey. They won't hesitate to burn your stinking plantation down to the ground. You hear me, asshole. Our business venture ended last night. So, for now on, you're gonna have to scrounge up your own drugs. Sam and I will not be making any more mortgage payments either. You know why, because you're going to mail me the deed to the property. And if you don't, I just might drop a dime on your lame ass. I'll take whatever the consequences may be, and so will you, you backstabbin' son of a bitch. You hear me, Hurtwood?" Joey spit into the phone after the line went dead.

Cotton Hurtwood had never been spoken to in such a manner. He was beyond angry when the phone rang again.

"It is Mr. Lombardi again; would you care to speak to him?" Nikita asked.

"No, I do not wish to speak with him again. Nikita, please take a message," Hurtwood said as he sat and watched more than listened to Nikita.

After no more than a minute, Nikita hung up the phone.

"Mr. Hurtwood, Joey Lombardi says that the police do not know why your men broke into the tavern. He also said that Bobby has been taken someplace that is far, far away. He says you will never find him. He says this time you lose, so be a smart guy and let it go," Nikita said.

"Vladimir, you and Nikita are stuck here inside. And we can't take the chance of going after Mr. McKillin, at least not right now. But I have a trump card that I'm ready to play. Nikita, will you please hand me the phone," Hurtwood said as a drug induced smirk slowly spread across his face.

●

Tommy, Ricky, and I ate an early breakfast and then we took off to try and find the clinic in Jupiter. It was nearly ten in the morning when we found it. We walked inside and asked to see the doctor that was on duty. A woman came out and said she was doctor so and so. She was wearing a lab coat with the name Reese Miller stencilled on the left pocket. She said she was not the regular doctor. We gave her one of the flyers and she said that if Junior came into the clinic, Doctor Miller would have helped him. She said Doctor Miller was on vacation, but he'd be back in a day or two. She gave us directions to the Jupiter hospital. We left the clinic and drove east on Adams Avenue, which is the main street in Jupiter. Funny thing is, that's the name of the main street in Crestfield too. It's a small world after all. We checked in the hospital and nobody'd heard of, or seen, anybody matching Junior's description. We went back to the hotel with our tails between our legs. We knew we were going to have to sit and wait 'til Doctor Miller came back.

•

I finally went into a deep sleep and it was nearly two days of tossing and turning before I woke up. Belle was right there by my side, and next to her stood Gino and Sam.

"Bobby, you've been burning up with fever for two days now. Here, you need to take these," Sam said as she put four large pills in my hand. "Go ahead and drink this water and swallow the pills," she said in her nurse voice.

I was too weak and confused to talk so I listened as she told me everything that had taken place after she delivered me to Belle's. She said Joey and Haystack drove to Armstrong's home and at gun point made him drive back to the tavern. Joey gave Armstrong the opportunity to tell him the truth. Armstrong was a good soldier and didn't give up any information. Joey shot and killed Armstrong right there in the middle of the tavern. When the police finally arrived, Joey told them Armstrong and Teerlink broke in as a team. So, now the police had two dead men to deal with instead of one. She stopped there and said, "Joey and Haystack send their regards. I'm glad I can go back and tell them you're doing better. Don't worry about me being seen. Gino drove me in his delivery van. Nobody will ever know I was here. We're going to have to move you in a day or two. It's too dangerous for you to stay in one place for very long. Bobby, I wish we could stay, but we need to get out of here." I did my best to absorb all I'd been told as Sam and Gino waved goodbye.

•

Two days had slowly gone by and needless to say, Tommy, Ricky, and I had a bad case of cabin fever. For some reason, when we drove over to Jupiter, the air wasn't as hot and heavy as it had been. There was an unseasonal blue northern blowing across the gulf. When we parked the Imperial and got out, I had a good feeling come over me. Why, well, I'd say I had the good feeling because there was a nice new Buick sitting in the parking lot. It was the kind of car doctors prefer to drive. The moment the three of us walked inside the clinic, we saw Doctor Miller, or at least a man we believed was the doctor. He was a slender young man with light brown hair and eyes to match. He was a dead giveaway because he was wearing the white lab coat with his name stenciled across the left pocket.

"Hello, I'm Madison McCool," I said as the doctor stood gazing at us.

"Hello," he said in an inquisitive tone. "I have a feeling you're not here for medical reasons," he said in a nice way.

"No, we're not," I said before Tommy and Ricky waved and said hello.

"You must be the people that left the flyer of the young man that you say is missing," he said in a not so positive way.

"Yes, we're hoping you recognize him," I said, almost praying he'd say yes.

"Well, the truth is, I work on so many men like him that they all end up looking like the same person. Because this is the only free clinic near the Salt, we get bombarded with folks needing medical attention," he said and then for whatever reason, he stopped talking.

I started to ask him if he could look at the flyer again when he stopped me.

"The problem with the flyer you gave us is that the young man is well dressed and smiling. Well, he's smiling in all the pictures except the one taken in his police uniform. The men that come in here are not smiling. In fact, most of them are either grimacing in extreme pain or they're unconscious. Do you understand? So, I'm not sure I recognize him by his photograph, but I am sure about the way you speak the English language," he said as the three of us shared confused glances.

"I'm sorry, but I don't understand," I said.

"What I mean is the young man on the flyer is only vaguely familiar to me, but the manner in which he spoke is as clear as a bell," he said with a smile.

"You remember seeing Junior," Ricky said before I could get the words out.

"Yes, I do," was all he could say before Tommy, Ricky, and I started hootin' and hollerin' like a bunch of wild Comanches.

The doctor stepped back a little bit to let us celebrate; that was before Ricky ran over and hugged the doctor as though he were a long-lost relative. I'm glad Doctor Miller was a reasonable guy. There are some people that just don't like having others invade their personal space. When we quieted down a little, he turned to us and held up his hand and said, "Don't you want to know how he got here and where he went?" he asked in good fun.

"Yes, yes, of course we do," Tommy urged.

"Ok, he was carried in here by a black man named Pearly Cisco. Junior was seriously injured. If my memory serves me, he had a good-sized laceration across the right side of his head. And his eardrum was probably broken. I'll go back in a minute and look at my log notes, just to be sure. But most of the men and women that come in here don't have a permanent address. Well, Junior didn't either. In fact, he didn't even know what his name was," he said and hesitated for a bit.

"Is something wrong doctor?" I asked.

"Well, I don't know. Listen, he smelled of whiskey when he came in here. Now, he didn't seem like an alcoholic to me, but I have to ask the question. Was, or is, your Junior a heavy drinker?" he asked as he gave us a serious look.

We looked at each other for a moment or two before we started laughing out loud. He was confused by our reaction.

"Doc, I am a recovering alcoholic. Trust me, I know a drinker when I see one. Junior seldom even drinks beer, he prefers a cold bottle of pop. He'll drink anything he considers refreshing, but he hardly ever chooses to drink alcohol," Tommy said.

"Well, I'm glad you told me that. So then there can be no mistake about it. He had been drugged and drugged good. I should say well, but right now well doesn't seem to fit," he said.

"Here's the sixty-four-thousand-dollar question. Doctor, when Junior left here, did he tell you where he was going?" Tommy asked.

"No, he didn't say where he was going," he said with a concerned look on his face.

"Doc, I don't like the look on your face," Ricky said.

"Well, here's the thing. Since he didn't know his name or have a permanent address, he was arrested and taken to jail," he said before he stopped to let us gather ourselves. "No worries, going to jail in this case might be a good thing. At least there will be a record of him at the police station. I mean if he hadn't been taken to jail, he could have floated away in the wind," he said with a bit of a smile.

He was right and we figured when we got to the police station they could tell us where Junior went from there. We started to say our goodbyes when the doctor held up his hand, "Wait a minute, I think I wrote down his name. I'll be right back."

Once again, the three of us were lost.

"The doctor ran back from his office and said, "Good news, Pearly told the police officers what his name is," he said with a bright-eyed smile.

"Doc, we know what his name is. His name is Junior," I said.

"That's what I've been trying to tell you. You know his name, but he doesn't or at least he didn't," Doc said.

"Ok, what is the name Pearly gave Junior?" Tommy asked.

"He didn't give him a name. Pearly said that was his name, oh never mind. Ok, Junior was Bobby something when he left this clinic," Doctor Miller said as he blew out his breath.

"Bobby?" I asked.

"Yes, Junior is now Bobby. I told you he didn't know what his name was when he came into the clinic. I'm sorry, but I didn't write down the last name," Doc Miller said.

The three of us were looking back and forth trying to understand how Junior became Bobby. Then we thought, so what. At least that's what I was thinking. We asked the doctor for directions to the police station and he said we drove right by it on our way to the clinic.

"Doc, all I saw was the Jupiter Courthouse. Didn't see a sign for the police," Tommy said.

"Police station is around back. You can't miss it. Good luck, I hope you find him," he said.

We said our goodbyes and thank you's in a hurry. Then we dashed out to the Imperial and drove back east to the courthouse. We drove around the back of the building and I'll be darned if the police station wasn't right there. We parked on the street and when we walked up, there was a sign that said for the public to use the north entrance. So we walked around to the north side of the building and went in the first double glass doors we saw. When we walked in, it was kind of like a déjà vu all over again moment. The station was the exact same as the Saturn Police station. It was just turned ninety degrees to the north.

We walked in and there was a young man standing on the other side of a glass partition. He didn't have on a uniform, but he did have a big smile on his face.

"Can I he'p y'all?" he said in a polite voice.

The three of us looked at each other and then Tommy took out his badge and pushed it against the glass on our side of the window.

"Can I speak with your Chief of Police?" Tommy said.

"Sorry, he ain't in right now," the kid said.

"Ok, well, how about the person that is next in line

seniority wise," Tommy asked.

The kid scratched his head and then he says, "Don't know what that means, but I'll go get somebody. Wait here; I'll only be a minute."

He was gone for about a minute when he came walking back to us with a tall red headed policeman right behind him.

"This here is Officer Tucker, maybe he can he'p y'all," the kid said as the officer waved to us.

The tall red headed officer named Tucker stepped forward and he and Ricky locked eyes on each other. It was beyond uncanny how much they looked alike. Through the glass he said, "How can I help you folks?" He sounded exactly like somebody that was born and raised in Crestfield.

Tommy held up his badge and said, "Do you have an office where we can talk in private? This is a very serious matter."

The tall officer pushed a buzzer and we heard the door unlock. He waved for us to follow him. When we walked past the dispatch lady, she adjusted her bra and winked at Ricky

"Betty-Sue, cut that out." Officer Tucker said as we walked by. "The conference room is empty, so we can use it. This way please."

We walked by a stairwell and I could hear male voices down below. We turned a corner and the officer stopped and held the door open. He let us walk in ahead of him; I thought, *a gentleman,* as I walked into the room.

We sat down at the end of a large table, and then Officer Tucker sat down facing us.

"I'm Officer Reed Tucker. The chief is on vacation and my sergeant is home sick today. So, I guess you could say I'm the leftovers." He smiled after he said it and sat down.

Tommy introduced us and when he got to Ricky, Ricky stood up.

"Sure is strange how much you look like me. And

what's even stranger still is your first name and my last name are the same. What are the chances? Anyway, I'm Ricky Reed and I'm glad to meet you," Ricky said with a smile and a wave before they shook hands.

The three of us looked at each other for a moment before Tommy looked at Officer Tucker and said, "We're here–" Officer Tucker stopped Tommy and said, "I know why you're here. In fact, I knew the second I laid on eyes on you folks. You're looking for Bobby."

It was the second time in the last half-hour that someone had said Junior was Bobby. And it was the second time we hooted and hollered. We didn't know who Bobby was, but we did know who Junior was. I guess that's all that mattered. When we were done shouting, Officer Tucker asked us if Bobby was the correct name. We looked at him and shook our heads no. Then I said, "We don't know how he became Bobby, but his real name is Jack McCool, but everyone calls him Junior."

"Junior hah, that's kinda strange to hear, because Bobby really does fit him. But now that you say his name is Junior, well, that fits him too. Bizarre how things work out sometimes," Officer Tucker said, mostly to himself.

Then without a warning, Tommy placed one of the flyers on the table and when Officer Tucker picked it up, he stared at Junior and just shook his head. He sat for a long time and then his shoulders kind of drooped and he became noticeably sullen.

"I'm sorry folks, it's just that I feel terrible now that I know he's a policeman. I should have seen through all the surface stuff and realized that from day one. Gosh, imagine the pain and suffering he has gone through. And there's probably going to be more trouble coming down the tracks," he said in a spooky way.

"Officer Tucker, that didn't sound good at all. Please explain," I said as I thought about things for a moment. "Wait, you haven't told us if Junior has a last name or not."

"Oh, yes he does, it's McKillin. Which I thought

from day one was a weird last name. Look, I think I owe you people an explanation or two. Let me start at the beginning," he said before he began telling us the entire story.

He started out by saying that the first time he and his sergeant went to the clinic, Bobby was unconscious. We didn't want to interrupt so we just let him keep using Bobby for Junior.

He said the next day they arrested Bobby and took him to jail so that he could go in front of the judge. He made a special point of telling us that when they arrested Bobby, he didn't know his own name or where he was. Then he stopped and asked us how in the world Bobby came to Mississippi in the first place.

"That is a long story, but I can give you the short version. A man by the name of Grits Wetmore stole Junior's plane ticket and went to California. And somehow this Grits and another man put Junior on the plane and he ended up in Alabama," I said.

I stopped talking because I could tell Officer Tucker had something he wanted to say.

"I know who Grits Wetmore is. He's a thief, a liar, and just plain no good. Did you know that Grits and his twin brother, Alvin, are missing?" he asked.

"Yes, we were told. And that makes finding Junior that much more difficult. Officer Tucker–" "Please, call me Reed," he said. "Ok, Reed, so it was over a month ago that you took Junior to jail. Have you seen or heard from him since?" I asked.

"Yes, that's one reason I may have had a distressed look on my face. You see, just three days ago we arrested Bobby again," he said.

"You did?" I asked.

"Yes, gosh that's awful. If you had been here, well, we…" he stopped talking at that point.

"Why did you arrest him? I mean did he break the law or something?" Ricky asked.

"No, he didn't break any laws; he didn't have any

identification. We're trying to move the homeless people out of Jupiter. I know it sounds like a terrible thing to do, but they do cause a lot of problems. Anyway, I think I should tell you that Bobby was hung over something awful when we arrested him. And it looked to me like he'd been in a fight. His face was all bruised up. Did Bobby drink and get into fights back in... Say, you never told me where you're from?" he said.

"No, Junior doesn't drink or get into fights. I'm sorry, I thought we had told you where we're from. We're from Crestfield, Iowa. You didn't tell us where you're from. You don't sound like you're from Mississippi," I said.

"No ma'am I'm not from here. I was in the army and when I traveled through this part of the country, I liked it. So, I came back and applied for this job and for some reason, they hired me. My hometown is Omaha. I'm from Nebraska. I guess the Midwest thing is how I knew you were here for Bobby," he said as he picked up the flyer again.

We all sat without speaking for a bit as Officer Tucker looked over the flyer.

"Reed, is it possible that Junior gave the judge an address? I think that's where we should start. When you arrested Junior, did he tell you if he had a job or where he lived?" Tommy asked.

"No, he didn't," he said and then paused for a moment. "Oh yeah, but he did say that he had a Mississippi driver license. Yes, when he applied for the license, he had to give them an address. Hang on, I'll be right back," he said as he got up and walked out of the conference room.

Officer Tucker was gone for quite some time. Not exactly sure how long, but when he came back he was shaking his head no.

"I talked with the DMV and the address he gave is twelve-twenty-two Salt Street," he said.

"Ok, let's go there," Ricky said.

Crestfield

"Ricky, there is no Salt Street in Jupiter," Officer Tucker said with another shake of the head.

"Oh," was all Ricky said.

"Ok, how about the judge?" I asked.

"Yeah, he may have given the judge an address, but… remember I told you that our chief is on vacation. Well, so is Judge Jones. Every year, they take a vacation at about this time. And a year ago, the city council decided we could save money by not paying a stenographer during the homeless court sessions. So there's no record of what was said in court that day," he said as he scratched his head.

"How about the bailiff, there has to be a person in court to protect the judge and keep order," Tommy said.

"You're right and I thought about that too. The problem is, when the judge goes on vacation so does Jake. He's the bailiff. There is one other thing we could try, but I have my doubts as to whether or not it will get us anywhere," he said.

"Well, we have to try everything. So what's the other thing you're talking about?" I asked.

"You could go down into the homeless camp by the Salt. The problem is, if Bobby had been staying there, I would have seen him. That's my section of town. And the homeless don't care much for the people with jobs and such. They can get real nasty at times. Madison, I know you're probably not afraid, but there have been a few women go into that camp that didn't come back out. I think the best bet as far as the homeless camp is concerned would be to wait in the park. Yep, that's your best bet," he said in a positive way.

"I don't understand? What park are you talking about?" Tommy asked.

"It's the Jupiter Theater and Family Park. It's right next to the gulf. Anyway, at night a lot of the homeless men go up and hang out in the park. I could take you there myself this evening when I get off work. Would seven o'clock be ok? I'd go earlier if I thought there'd be some of the men there. But like I said, they only go after dark," he said.

"Do you want us to meet you there or pick you up here?" Tommy asked.

"Let's make it easy, you pick me up right here in front of the station at seven. Ok," he said.

"Ok, we'll be here at seven," we all said as we stood up and said our goodbyes.

"Oh, before you go, I think I should set something straight with Ricky. Ricky, I don't look like you, you look like me," Officer Tucker said with a big smile on his face.

We waved goodbye and walked out of the police station with a positive attitude. It was going to be difficult to wait all afternoon and part of the evening, but at least we had a plan.

•

I looked up at the clock in Belle's bedroom and it was seven in the evening. I stretched and yawned and decided to get out of bed for a while. When I put my feet on the floor, I felt pretty darn good. I walked out to the kitchen and something smelled awfully good. Belle didn't see me coming and when she turned to look at me, she was startled.

"Sorry Belle, I didn't mean to scare you. I was feeling better so I decided to get up out of bed. Whatever you're cooking smells great."

"You sho you feelin' up ta bein' out-a bedt? I don't wants you gettin' sick again."

"Belle, as a matter of fact, I feel great. Must be those pills Sam gave me. What were they?"

"Dey was anibotics, sposed ta take away de 'n-fection. I guess dey woikin'."

"Yes, they must be. Belle, would it be ok if I listen to the radio?"

"Yes, dat's a goodt ideya. I likes ta listen to de radio when I's cookin'."

I turned her little transistor radio on and had to ask her to dial in a station. She turned it to the station she said was her favorite. It was nothing but rhythm and blues and soul. Although new to me, I loved it. I sat and watched Belle move about the kitchen while the music played. I was having some feral feelings run through me. She was just plain lovely to look at. Now and then she would peek my way; her dark eyes were hypnotic. She was barefoot and when she walked, it was so soft and gentle that I don't think the floor knew she was there. I couldn't take my eyes off of her. Then a song came on the radio that I love. "Unchained Melody" began playing and I stood up and turned Belle around. She looked at me with so much passion I clutched her and pulled her close. We slow danced for a bit and then I kissed her. Her lips were full and raging hot. She tasted just like black molasses, I think. I unbuttoned her dress and slowly took off her bra and then she stepped out of her panties and I dropped them on the floor.

•

We met Reed Tucker at the Jupiter police station at exactly seven that evening. Although it was still light out, he said we should get going. He wasn't wearing his uniform. He said if the homeless guys saw a cop, they'd run for the hills. Seemed like a strange thing to say since there's really no hills to speak of down by the gulf. Anyway, we got in the Imperial and Tommy drove us to a parking lot next to the park. We sat and watched two young couples walk away and then all was quiet.

"Ok, we can get out now. Let's go on down by the water. We can watch from there. Hopefully, I will know a few of the guys that come out," Reed said.

It was a fabulous night. The air was warm, not hot, and the sky was lit up and painted in what looked to me like watercolors. I guess you have to have a big canvas or a big body of water to make colors like that. The guys walked down the beach and I let them go; I felt just fine sitting right there on the sand. It was so relaxing and it wasn't too long before I watched the sun say goodbye with a green flash. I was going to get up and walk down to the guys but decided to stay right where I was. I watched as two men slithered across the back of the park. They went in what I thought was probably a bathroom. Then, as quickly as they appeared, they were gone.

"Hello, young lady," someone said from behind me.

I was startled and jumped a little. When I turned to see who said hello, there stood an older gentleman with a gigantic beard.

"I'm sorry if I scared ya, but this probably ain't the safest place in the world for a lady to hang out," he said as he leaned on a cane.

I walked to him and when I was close, I could see that he had peaceful, but very sad eyes. And he had a cast covering his entire right arm.

"Hello, I'm Madison. Do you live here?" I asked.

"Hello Madison, I'm Scooter and it sure is nice ta meet ya," he said, as he stuck out his left hand. We shook hands and then he said, "I s'pose you could say I live here, but I sure don't own the place," he said with a small chuckle.

Then he looked past me and said, "Why hello, Officer Tucker. What brings you down here?"

Reed Tucker, Tommy, and Ricky walked up and Reed said, "Hello Scooter, I was hoping I'd run in to you this evening. These folks could sure use your help. By the way, this is Tommy, and that guy that doesn't look anything like me is Ricky." The guys all said hello. And then Scooter said, "Gosh, the two of you could pass for twins. Officer Tucker, is Ricky family?"

"No, he's not family to me, but you could say he's family to Bobby. They've come to find him. Have you seen Bobby?" Reed asked.

Scooter backed up a little and cocked his head to the side for a moment before he said, "Officer Tucker, you sure these people are Bobby's relations?"

"Yes Scooter, they are. You have no reason to be afraid of them," Reed said.

"I s'pose not, but there's been some mean and nasty men come by here lookin' fer Bobby. So, I have to be sure you're lookin' fer all the right reasons," Scooter said.

"Is there a light anywhere near here?" Tommy asked.

"Yes, there's a small light in front of the bathrooms. Follow me," Scooter said.

We walked over and when we were next to the light, Tommy handed one of the flyers to Scooter. His eyes went back and forth and back and forth across the paper. Then he looked up at me and said, "You're darker than Bobby, but I can see that y'all's family awright. Thank goodness somebody gonna help ol' Bobby. He sure is one lost soul. When he stayed here with me, he didn't know I heard him, but well, he cried sometimes at night. He cried for his mom and dad. As far as where he is right now, I don't know. He was here several days ago, but then I heard he was arrested again. Did you do that to him Officer Tucker?" Scooter asked in a not so friendly way.

Reed looked at the ground before he said, "Yes, I did."

Scooter gave Officer Tucker a stare, and then he looked back down at the flyer.

"Gosh, Bobby isn't even Bobby, but he is a policeman. Listen, last week Bobby drove down to the Salt in a big ol' truck. He took a whole lot a men and a few women and children to the new family center. It's out on the Old Spanish Trail. I heard some doctor there was tryin' ta help Bobby find out who he is," Scooter said.

"Excuse me, but this is about the third time I've heard someone say that Bobby doesn't know who he is. Scooter, do you know what caused him to not know who he is?" I asked.

"All I know is that when Pearly first found Bobby, he had been throwed down in the culvert. He was hurt real bad. So Pearly and Odell took him to the clinic. Have you been to the clinic?" Scooter asked.

"Yes, we have. Ok, can you tell us how to get to this new family center?" I asked.

"Madison, I can tell you how to get there," Reed said. "But it's definitely closed at night, so you're going to have to go tomorrow morning. You know, I feel responsible for some of this. So, if you can come by the station again in the morning, let's say about nine, I'll drive us out there."

"You know who could really he'p y'all is Pearly and Odell, but they left taday and said they wouldn't be back anytime soon. They didn't tell me where they was goin'. I unnerstand why they didn't tell me. They're protectin' Bobby," Scooter said.

Before we left the Salt, each of us took out all the money we had in our pockets and gave it to Scooter; Reed did too. I felt terrible when we said goodbye to Scooter. Here was a good person that had somehow lost his way. We went back to our hotel and that night all I could think of was Junior crying for our mom and dad. As a rule, it is seldom that I cry, but that night I made an exception.

●

Joey Lombardi called an emergency meeting of the members in the Headhunters M.C. Every possible idea as to how the situation with Hurtwood should be handled was discussed. The general rule for people, as well as animals, is fight or flight. Well, it was decided that nobody could hurt Sam or Joey if they didn't know where they were. And the members felt that if they let things cool down a bit, they could pick and choose when to fight. So, after the meeting, a sign was hung on the front door of the tavern that read, 'Sorry, closed for remodelling.'

●

"Joey, it's seven o'clock. Come on sweetie, we need to get out of here," Sam yelled across the tavern.

Sam was standing by the front door with her suitcase sitting next to her. And standing on the other side of her was Haystack. Sam started signing something and then she mouthed, "Haystack, are you sure you'll be ok?"

He nodded yes. "Ok, well, you have Chet call if you need us, ok?" He nodded his head again. Sam heard Joey dead bolt the front doors, top and bottom. He locked the back doors and walked out the metal gate in the back of the tavern and locked it before he drove the Corvette around to the front. He looked up at Sam and Haystack and beeped the horn. Sam walked out into the street and stared up at the tavern. For the first time in over a year, the bright blue lights that read, **Sam's Broken Bone Tavern** - did not shine.

Fact is, the whole place was shut down and locked up tight as a drum. Haystack put Sam's suitcase in the back seat and then he turned and hugged her real tight. Sam mouthed, "I love you." And Haystack mouthed back the same. Sam kissed her finger and pressed it against Haystack's lips. She wiped the tobacco off her finger and jumped in the car. Joey eased out of the driveway and drove north, heading for the Bronx.

•

Belle's best friend, Ruthie-May Childress, lives just two doors down from Belle. Ruthie-May had come by and asked Belle if she could watch her crib for a couple of weeks. Ruthie-May was goin' over to The Big Easy to visit with her ailing grandmother. She left at six and at seven, Pearly and Odell moved in.

57

Belle's home

I woke up at nine the next morning; I felt next to me for Belle, but she wasn't there. I sat up and then I heard her in the kitchen singing like a bird; a very happy bird. I walked out and when I looked at her, I thought to myself, *last night was so wonderful.* She looked at me as if nothing special had happened and I immediately started worrying. I just had to ask myself, *was it all just a dream?* The more I thought about it, the more frightened I became. Was it all just a dream? Didn't seem like it, but anything is possible when it comes to dreaming and me. I said good morning to Belle, and she said the same back to me, didn't even give me a hint about anything special happening last night. Then she glided over and turned on the radio. The first song that played was an oldie titled, "Oh What a Night".

"Bobby, I like dat song a whole-lot. In fact, I like everting de Dells sing," she said with a smile.

I had to find out and I couldn't resist. So I walked over and wrapped my arms around Belle and we started slow dancing. Then I kissed her and it felt just like it did last night, I think. Belle looked up at me with her smoldering dark eyes and said, "You know somepin', las' night I felt as high as dose white mens dat landed on de moon dis summer." I thought, *we landed a man on the moon.* "Oh Bobby, you hot and wild az a buck, is you gonna leave my clothes on de flo 'gin?"

My heart skipped a beat as I dropped her clothes on the floor. I carried her out of the kitchen. I don't believe life or love can get any better.

•

We met Officer Tucker at the Jupiter Police Station at exactly nine in the morning. We were hoping he might have found out where Junior was living. No such luck. So we jumped in his police car and took off heading

due north. When we reached what he told us was the Old
Spanish Trail, we headed straight west. When we arrived
at the family center, we parked and before we got to the
front doors, a young lady wearing a lab coat came out and
met us.

"Hello, I mean good morning officer. I'm Nancy, I
work here. Is there something wrong?" she asked as she
looked at Reed and then us, with a concerned eye.

"No, there's nothing wrong. We're looking for a
young man and we're hoping you might be able to help us
find him. I'm Officer Tucker and these folks have come all
the way from Iowa to find their family member. When he
came here he would have used the name Bobby McKillin.
Does that name sound familiar?" Reed asked.

"No, not to me, but maybe it will to the others that
work here. Please follow me," she said.

We followed her in and she pointed to a large table
in the center of the room; I guess she wanted us to sit
down. We watched her go through the files behind the
reception desk. She looked up once and said, "Bobby
McKillin, right." Reed said, "Yes." Then she went through
the center and asked every person that worked there. She
came back shaking her head no, "Sorry, nobody has heard
of anyone by that name. Why was Bobby here?"

"He'd had a serious head injury and could not
remember who he was. He didn't even know how he got
here, etc. and so on," Reed said.

"Well, then I think I can help you. We have a
psychologist slash marriage counselor that comes here the
third Thursday of every month. Was your Bobby here last
Thursday?"

"Yes, yes we believe he was. By the way, I'm
Bobby's sister, Madison. Is there any way you can check
with the doctor?" I asked her before I asked myself, *why
did I just call him Bobby?*

"No, Doctor Cooper moves all around the state.
And I don't know his schedule, so there's really no way to
check with him. But, he does keep records here. Let me go

check his files, I'll be right back," she said as she walked away.

For some reason, we all stood up and milled around in the middle of the room and waited. Must have been ten minutes or so that had passed before Nancy came running back out to us.

"Doctor Cooper did see him. But, I'm sorry to have to tell you they weren't able to figure out who he was or where he was from," she said as she watched our shoulders slump.

We started moving towards the door and Nancy said, "Where y'all goin'?"

Reed said, "I guess we're going to go back to Jupiter." Nancy said, "Don't you want to know where Bobby lives?"

Ricky yelled, "You know where Bobby lives!"

"Yes, Doctor Cooper wrote down his phone number and address. I guess so's he could get hold of him if he found anything out," she said as she pulled a file card out of her coat pocket.

She gave us the phone number and then she said Bobby didn't know the address, but he did say he lived at the Broken Bone Tavern. We looked at Reed and he immediately said, "I know exactly where it is. Let's go."

"Wait, let's try calling first," Tommy said.

"I'm sorry, I forgot to tell you that I tried the number when I was in Doctor Cooper's office, but nobody answered. You want me to try again?" she asked.

"Yes," we all said at the same time. She tried several times, but nobody answered. So, we said thanks and took off racing back to Jupiter.

When we got back to town, Reed drove us right by Gino's restaurant. We had no idea how close to Junior we were. When we pulled into the parking lot at the tavern, the place looked deserted. We got out and as a group, we slowly walked over and read the sign on the door. We went ahead and knocked and knocked, but nobody came to the door. We walked around the back and there was a metal fence. Inside the fence we could see the truck that Junior had used to drive the homeless people to the family center. Everything was locked up tight. We were stumped, but at least we had an idea of where Junior had been living and maybe even working. We didn't say anything to each other, but I know the three of us were having a very difficult time with the idea of Junior working in a tavern. It just didn't fit Junior, but I guess it did fit Bobby.

As we were standing in the empty parking lot, Reed turned to us and we could tell he had something to say.

"I didn't want to say anything, but now that we've come here and the place is empty, I think I should let you know that it was just down the street where Sergeant Detwiler and I arrested Bobby." He paused for a moment and then he said, "The next night there was a break-in here at the tavern. Two men were killed. Neither of the dead men was Bobby, but we believe the men came here looking for him. I think it's safe to assume that Bobby has gone into hiding," Reed said.

"Well, thanks for telling us the whole truth. Reed, I believe you're right. Junior wouldn't hang around if he knew someone was out to do him harm. That's probably why the owners decided to lock the place up. Was the break-in covered in the local paper?" Tommy asked.

"Yes, it was only a small blurb, but it was covered in the Jupiter paper. There was no mention of Bobby, but I'd say the owners of the tavern kept Bobby out of the story on purpose," he said as he started walking to his patrol car.

Reed drove us back to the police station and dropped us off. Nobody said it, but we all knew that we were so close, and yet so far away. We said our goodbyes and thank you's to Reed and he promised to let us know if any new developments came down the pike. We got back in the Imperial with our tails between our legs and drove back to the hotel. We weren't beaten; we were just rethinking how to go about finding Junior. We knew how to get to the tavern. So, we decided to check back at least once a day. Maybe we'd get lucky and find someone there that knew where Junior was.

●

Haystack peered out from his hiding place and wondered what the policeman and those three people were looking for.

●

After his confrontation with Odell and friends, Diego waited 'til it was dark to sneak back to his room. Vladimir was waiting for him and gave him strict orders to stay out of sight. Diego kept the contempt he was feeling for the Russians inside, but the truth, is he wanted them dead. After that night, early every morning, Nigeriana would sneak Diego his breakfast. And every night when it was dark, Riley would deliver supper to him. Diego did what he was told to do. He never turned on the lights and he never left his room.

●

Belle and I felt safe knowing Pearly and Odell were close by. The first night they moved in, Gino came over in his delivery van and picked us up. I thought we were going back to the restaurant, but Gino had a surprise for us. He drove for miles out of Jupiter heading due north. When we crossed into Greene County, Gino pulled off the highway and parked behind a restaurant. We stayed in the van and about ten minutes after Gino got out, he came back with both arms loaded with buckets full of fried chicken. We sat in the back of the van with all the doors wide open and had ourselves a little parking lot picnic. It sure was nice of Gino to have gone through all the trouble and expense. While we were eating, Odell said, "Bobby is it ok if I ax you a quession 'bout somepin dat's kinda personal."

"Sure, what's on your mind."

"Well, it obvious to me dat you in love wif my little sistuh," Odell said, and then stopped and looked at Belle. She covered her face with both of her hands and

Crestfield

giggled. "Ok, well, anyway I was just wonderin' how you even unnerstands her when she talkin'. I mean she not only black, but she talk black too," he said, and then stopped and waited for me to answer him.

I sat and thought about things for a minute and the four of them just stared back at me. I guess they wanted me to answer Odell's question.

"Odell, to be honest I guess I've become used to the way Belle and some others around here talk. And I can tell you that, right now, I don't care how Belle talks, because you were right. I am in love with your sister. In fact, I'm crazy in love," I said, just before Belle moved over and buried her face in my chest. I held her with both of my arms as Odell, Pearly, and Gino stared at me with question marks in their eyes. I decided I'd better continue with what I was saying.

"So, I don't care how Belle speaks, but I do have a question for Pearly, if he doesn't mind," I said as we all turned our eyes to Pearly.

He was in the middle of a drumstick, but he said, "Go ahead, ask away."

"Ok, Pearly, how is it you that you speak so different than your brother and sister?" I asked.

Pearly put down his drumstick and wiped his face with a napkin. The look on his face was not a pleasant one.

"So, you're wondering how it is that I'm able to conjugate a verb? Is that what you're asking?" Pearly didn't give me time to answer him. "Well, I hope I can answer your question. When Belle was just a baby, our dad was shot and killed in a bar fight. They never did find the man that shot him. So, from that day forth to help our mother put food on the table, Odell and I had to work. And when Belle was just twelve years old, she started picking cotton. Picking cotton is a filthy and painful undertaking, but Belle is strong and she worked her fingers to the bone. When Belle began working, I was given a reprieve of sorts. What I'm saying is, Belle made it possible for me to go back to school. Odell could have gone back, but I don't think school has ever appealed to him. Odell and Belle, do you think what I just told Bobby about us is a true and accurate summation?" Pearly asked.

They both nodded their heads and said yes, but the confusion in their eyes said otherwise.

"Bobby, if you're wondering whether or not my brother and sister are smart enough to speak the English language properly, the answer I would give is a resounding yes. Just because they're black and don't speak the Queen's English does not mean they're stupid or incapable of learning. It all comes down to having the opportunity to go to school," Pearly said with a wink to his siblings.

"Pearly, I knows you din't mean ta hurt Bobby's feelin's, but I tink you did. Rememuh, it was Odell dat started all a dis mess," Belle said in an obvious attempt to protect me.

"Bobby, I want you to know that I would never intentionally try to hurt your feelings or disparage you in any way. I was merely explaining my family's past. I'm sorry if you felt it was a personal attack; it wasn't meant to be. And little sister, I'm very proud of you for coming to Bobby's defense," Pearly said as he smiled at Belle.

"Tank you Pearly, Odell, don't you dare ax any mo quessions, you hear me?" Belle said with a smile.

"Yes ma'am, I hears you and I ain't openin' my big mouph again," Odell said with a sheepish grin.

I thought it was time to move past our little tiff so I asked Gino what the name of the place was.

"What place is that, Bobby?" Gino asked.

"This place, of course," I said as the others chuckled.

"Oh, this place is called Happy's. It has been here since I was a boy. They only offer two things on the menu here, fried chicken and donuts. And as far as the donuts are concerned, you have a choice of either glazed or powdered," Gino said.

"If dat's de case, den where is my donuts?" Belle asked before she giggled.

"Yeah, where is de donuts?" Odell said.

"I'll be right back," Gino said.

We ate donuts on the way back to Belle's. And I must say, the donuts were very good, but the company was even better. Belle and I spent the next few days in each other's arms. And for some reason, I stopped wondering who I was. That is, I stopped wondering until the day Belle told me she had to go back to work. When she left that afternoon, I sat alone and wondered. Yes, I did go over and spend time with Pearly and Odell. And even though I enjoyed their company, I felt like I was coming down with a bad case of cabin fever.

Turns out, it wasn't cabin fever at all, it was the real deal. The infection I thought had been cured was back.

I was pretty sick and we were out of antibiotics. So Belle told Gino and he went to the clinic and bought more. When Belle came home that night with the meds, I was delirious with fever. After that, Belle spent her evenings working at Gino's, and her days and nights caring for me.

•

Days had gone by and Tommy, Ricky, and I had learned nothing more concerning Junior's whereabouts. It felt like the earth stood still and the three of us were stuck in some southern version of the twilight zone. We drove to the tavern every morning and then we went back again in the evening. And we kept in constant contact with Reed. We drove back to the plantation two times to check in with the FBI agents. They were reticent to speak with us, let alone share any meaningful news. Agent Cummings did go out on a limb and tell us that everything was status quo, and all was quiet on the western front. She gave me the impression they didn't care where Junior was.

Then early one morning Reed came to the hotel to see us. I was excited when Ricky told me Reed was down in the lobby and he had something important to share with us. I got myself dressed and when I opened my door, Tommy and Ricky were there waiting for me. We ran down stairs and found Reed sitting by himself in the hotel lounge; he didn't look happy at all. He had a newspaper sitting on his lap. And instead of telling us what was written in the paper, he handed it to Ricky.

Ricky carried the paper over to a coffee table, opened it, and laid it out in front of us. Spread across the front page was the picture of a man by the name of Bobby McKillin. I admit it did look like Junior. In bold print, it said he was the prime suspect in a murder. To the three of us, it was all so preposterous we just could not wrap our minds around it. We were stunned.

This isn't verbatim, but the article said that three teen-aged boys had found the bloated body of Alvin L'Roy Wetmore. The body was discovered caught up in some illegal fishing lines near the shore at the southern end of the Tallahatchie River. The Green County Coroner's office said Wetmore's naked body had been tied with nylon rope to a folding metal chair. The article went on to say that Wetmore and McKillin were known to have been in a knife fight while part of a road crew in Alabama. The staff writer ended his piece by saying that the fugitive's whereabouts were unknown and that he should be considered armed and dangerous.

The three of us must have read and re-read the article at least a dozen times. The very thought of Junior actually committing murder was absurd beyond words. Reed left us alone, but he walked over to us when he knew we were done reading.

"Reed, you don't believe this, do you?" I declared more than asked.

"Well, it doesn't seem to fit the man I met. But the powers that be don't care whether you or I think Bobby is innocent or not. They want justice. Listen, I think there's going to be more bad stuff connected to this whole story. Remember, Alvin has a twin brother named Grits that is still missing. And where there's smoke, there's usually fire. Madison, it looks bad, real bad," Reed said as he looked over my shoulder at Tommy and Ricky.

"Reed, do you know who initiated these charges? What I mean is, did the murder charge come before or after the body was found?" Tommy asked.

"I don't know Tommy, but it seems to me that when they found the body, they had to point a finger somewhere. And that somewhere was right at Bobby. I've been told that several men witnessed the knife fight. So I think the detectives on the case believe the fight is the motive for the murder. Least that's my take on things," Reed answered.

"My take on things is that in an effort to steer everyone in the wrong direction, the people that actually committed the crime accused Junior," Tommy said as he looked at Ricky and me.

"You know something Tommy - that makes a lot of sense. I'm going to go try to find out who made the accusations. Listen, I'd never tell you to break the law, but if you do find Bobby, I'd be careful about whom you tell. In fact, if it were me, I'd get him out of Mississippi, and fast. Listen, I've got to get back on duty. Because of the murder, the Chief had to come back early from his vacation. So, I'm going to go tell him about Bobby. I'll show the Chief the flyer too. Try not to worry, bye now," Reed said before he walked away.

Try not to worry. Gosh, I hate when people say that.

•

Gino picked up the paper, looked at the picture on the front page, and drove straight to Belle's. When he handed the paper to Belle, she just stared at the picture of Bobby; she didn't know how to read. Belle took the paper next door and Pearly sat down and read the article to Belle. Then he said, "Bobby doesn't need to know about this, just make him well. He has to leave here as soon as possible."

•

"Mr. Hurtwood, you were wise to tell Judge Jones about Alvin. The police will surely find our Mr. McKillin now and this will all come to an end," Vladimir said.

"No Vladimir, it won't end and I'll tell you why. His family will show the authorities the flyer and the ball will start rolling in their favor. No, we have to find him and make him go away. And then I want Grasshopper to go away. Do you understand?" Hurtwood asked.

The Russians nodded their heads yes.

Nigeriana had taken Hurtwood his morning coffee and after she walked out of the office, she stopped and listened to the entire conversation inside, after which she hurried out to Diego's room and told him what had been said. Diego paced the floor trying to come up with a way to stay alive. He wanted to hurt the Russians, but he knew that the next time they came after him might be the last.

"Nigeriana, does you know how ta write?"

"'Course I knows how ta write."

"Ok, can ya get a notepad and pencil? I got some tings I needs ya ta write down."

"Yes, but I tink it might be best ta waits 'til dark. Den, I will sneak out wif Riley. Is dat ok?"

"Be cuttin' it close, I have a lot ta do taday. But I tink dat will woik, yes; go ahead on," Diego said as Nigeriana rushed back into the mansion.

•

Out of breath after running for hours, Diego snuck back into his room. Riley and Nigeriana were already there waiting for him.

"Riley, what you doin' here so early, it ain't even dark out," Diego said.

"I came out now cuz even a fool know you cain't be ciferin' in de dark. And you been livin' in de dark fo too damn long," Riley said with gusto.

"Yeah, you right 'bout dat. Ok, Ana you ready to write?" Diego asked.

"Yes'm, just start talkin'," she said.

She wrote down everything Diego told her to and she checked her notes twice to make sure they were exactly right. Then she took off like a flash. She had a lot to do and a short time to get it done. Riley left with

Nigeriana, but he never did come back with Diego's supper. He had a job to do.

•

Riley watched and waited before he went up to the second story veranda. The Russians were both there with Hurtwood. Hurtwood had been medicated and he was enjoying the late afternoon sun.

"Excuse me, Missuh Hurtwoodt, but I gots a impotant message fo ya from Grasshoppuh," Riley said from a safe distance.

"What, Nikita, what'd he just say?" Hurtwood asked.

"He says he has an important message for you," Nikita said as he gave Riley a stare.

"Um, Nikita, go ahead and read whatever it is he has," Hurtwood slurred.

Riley handed the note to Nikita and then backed away to a safe distance. Nikita read the note and then he handed it to Vladimir and when he was finished reading, he turned to his boss.

"Mr. Hurtwood, Grasshopper says he might know where this Bobby McKillin is hiding. And who he's hiding with," Vladimir said.

"Let me see this note," Hurtwood said in a clear voice.

He read the note twice before a sly smile spread across his face.

"Vladimir, when do the FBI agents leave for their evening meal?" Hurtwood asked.

"They have been leaving just before the sun sets," Vladimir quickly answered.

"Riley, why didn't Grasshopper come up here and tell me himself?" Hurtwood asked.

"He was toldt not to leave his room," Riley said. Riley was thinking, *he din't come up here cuz he knows y'all gonna kill him.*

"Why didn't Grasshopper tell us this before today?" Hurtwood asked.

Can't Find my Way Home

"Missuh Hurtwoodt, I axed him de same ting. He said he just thought of it. He toldt me dat he and Grits saw dis Bobby person talkin' to de girl dat woiks at Gino's. Den I tells Grasshopper dat de tavern where Bobby live been closed down. And he say, 'I bet Bobby done moved in wif de girl.' If ya tink about it, what he sayin' kinda make sense. Anyway, he say if y'all go where de girl woik at, you can folluh her home and see if Bobby dere. Dat's all. He say it werf a try," Riley said in a confident voice.

"Mr. Hurtwood, what Riley is saying does make sense, it is worth a try," Nikita offered.

Hurtwood stared out into the setting sun for a moment before Vladimir said, "The FBI agents are leaving now. We can follow this girl and see if Bobby is there. What can it hurt?" Vladimir asked.

"How will you get back without being seen?" Hurtwood asked.

"We will not come back until FBI agents leave for their evening meal tomorrow. No one will see us leave and no one will see us come back. If we find our man, all will be taken care of tonight. Trust me, we will not leave any witnesses. No one will ever know we were there," Vladimir said with confidence.

"Well, it makes too much sense not to go and at least take a look and find out. Follow her home from work and see if he is there. And then you can decide what to do. Just be sure nobody sees you, not even a glimpse. Is that clear?" Hurtwood ordered, more than asked.

Both Russians nodded their heads yes.

•

Tommy, Ricky, and I spent most of the afternoon looking for an attorney to represent Junior. The first five told us they couldn't help us because they work for Hurtwood. They reminded us that Alvin Wetmore was Hurtwood's nephew. We finally found a young female attorney that said she'd help us, but her office was in Mobile. We didn't have much choice so we told her we'd meet her there the next day. We didn't know what else to do. We didn't want our family to worry, so we didn't call home. I think we knew we would do enough worrying for all of them.

•

The Russians took their time getting ready. They made sure their silenced Marakov pistols were cleaned and fully loaded with superior American-made nine-millimetre parabellum cartridges. They each made sure to bring four backup magazines; it was the way they were taught.

The sun had just disappeared into the west when Vladimir drove out the south side of the plantation. He headed straight for Gino's.

•

The sun had set and Cotton Hurtwood was ready to go back inside the mansion. When he called for Riley to take him inside, he raised his voice, but only minimally; he was still quite medicated.

"I'll takes ya," Diego said,

Hurtwood craned his neck to see who was speaking. As Diego walked up, Hurtwood did his best to focus his eyes. His best wasn't so great. Grasshopper was still a blur.

"Grasshopper, why are you here, and where is Riley?" Hurtwood demanded more than asked.

"Riley been busy wit chores, right now he takin' dat fix-it note you toldt Vladimir ta write to de carpentuh," Diego said in truth.

"What note?" Hurtwood sharply asked.

"De note about dat loose railin' over on de sout side a de veranda. And I here cuz de Russians ain't. I know dey gonna hoit me, but by de time dey gets back, I will be long gone," Diego said.

"What are you talking about - hurt you? They're not going to hurt you. And what loose railing are you talking about?" Hurtwood asked, dazed and confused.

"In a minute or two I'll takes ya on ovuh to de loose railin' and shows ya. Right now I wants ta talks ta ya 'bout a few tings." Hurtwood screamed in utter disbelief at

Grasshopper's attitude. It didn't faze Diego one little bit. "You see missuh whoevuh you is, befo my mama died, she toldt me de truph about a few tings. Guess what she done toldt me?" he asked. Hurtwood tried calling for Riley, then he yelled for Nigeriana. Neither of them came. "So, I was sayin' dat my mama toldt me 'bout my daddy getting' kildt down in Jamaica, but she also toldt me he was only my make-believe daddy. Guess who she toldt me was my real daddy? Dat's right, she said you my fo-real daddy. All dese years ya had de chance ta have a son, you coulda been nice ta me." Hurtwood mumbled that he was nice. "I knowed you was 'mbearassed a me, but ya coulda been nice. Funny ting is, I growed up wif yo daughtuh, Razuh; she was my closest friend. I din't know she was my sistuh 'til long aftuh we was loveuhs. Ain't it funny how life can twist and turn sometimes?" Hurtwood gagged several times before he threw his head back and howled into the night.

"So, you axed me 'bout de loose railin'. Here, I'll rolls ya on over ta de railin' so's you can see fo yose'f," Diego said as he unlocked the brake on Hurtwood's wheelchair.

Hurtwood gathered all the strength he could and screamed, "Riley, Nigeriana, come help me! Stop, Grasshopper, you stop this instant! Please, I'm begging you. Stop! I say."

In spite of the yelling and the pleading, Diego began rolling Hurtwood around to the south side of the veranda. Once they reached the loose railing, he stopped.

"I know it's dark on dis side a de veranda, but I still tink you can see de loose railin'. You din't have ta holluh and yell like dat. It's disturbin' ta hear ya scream like a little girl," Diego said as he locked the brake on the wheelchair. "See, I done locked de wheels again. You don't have ta be 'fraid a me. I just wanted ta tell ya de truph 'bout a few tings so's you'd unnerstands," Diego said.

Hurtwood was beginning to foam at the mouth. He

sobbed several times before he tried to speak.

"What? I din't unnerstands what ya just saidt ta me. Oh, you wanna know why? Why, cuz you run over my puppy and din't even say you was sorry. Why, you ax? Cuz, you mean and treat nice people like dirt. Why," Diego screamed, "Because you kildt dat po man's dog! Dat's why."

Hurtwood watched Grasshopper kick the planks on the loose railing several times. He broke all of them but one. He listened as they crashed and splintered on the walkway below. Diego broke the last railing off and held it in his hands.

"You know what Daddy, I can't hits ya as many times as I'd like ta. You know why, because den dere'd be defensive wounds. So, you can rest easy cuz I'm only gonna hits just de one time."

Diego pulled the piece of wood back and with a mighty swing, he hit Hurtwood across the bridge of his nose. Hurtwood's head flew back and his eyes blinked as he tried to make sense of it all.

"You know what Daddy, ya din't even ax me how my flight was when I come back from de ayerpote. Ya just talked ta me likes I was some little nigguh boy. Well, I'm nicer dan dat, so I'm tellin' ya dat I hopes you have a nice flight."

Diego didn't unlock the wheels he just tipped the wheelchair forward. In spite of barely being conscious, Cotton Hurtwood held on to the wheelchair with all his might. But all his might wasn't enough as he sailed headfirst to the concrete walkway below. Diego unlocked the wheels and pushed the wheelchair over. He looked down at the crumpled body until Riley walked out and looked up at him. Diego threw the last plank down and Riley wiped away all the fingerprints and blood. Then he threw the plank at Hurtwood.

•

Vladimir circled Gino's restaurant several times before he and his brother finally got a glimpse of Belle as she took out the trash. Satisfied she was there, they decided to take a look at the now closed Broken Bone Tavern. Vladimir drove through the parking lot, turned the black sedan around and parked. They walked to the rear of the tavern and peered through the locked metal fence at the old truck inside. They walked around to the front and Nikita kicked the bottom of the front doors. Then he violently pounded up near the top. He turned to Vladimir and in Russian hollered, "Deadbolts!" He grabbed the doorknob and nearly shook the door off its hinges. He stepped back and in Russian said, "The sissy American motorcycle boys were afraid to fight, so they ran." He and his brother shared a laugh; in Russian of course. They walked across the street together and looked up at the second story for movement. Needless to say, they saw nothing. The tavern was empty.

•

Haystack watched closely from his hiding place in the tool shed next to the tavern parking lot. His instincts told him to kill the Russians, but Joey said to wait...

•

The Russians strolled back to their car and slowly drove to within eyesight of Gino's. They parked the car and sat and waited. At eleven o'clock Gino began turning off the lights in the restaurant. Forty minutes later, Belle emerged from the back door. She pulled her shawl tight around her shoulders and walked out to the street, heading south towards her home. She only made it maybe fifteen steps before Gino drove up in his van and stopped next to her. She jumped in the front seat and away they went.

The Russians were careful not to be seen and followed Gino from a safe distance. When Gino stopped in front of Belle's little home, he walked around and opened the door for her and then as most gentlemen would do, he escorted her to her front door. The Russians arrived just in time to see Belle go in. Nikita pulled a small notebook from his pocket and wrote down the address and then he drew a circle around the number nine. The Russians didn't make a move until Gino had driven out of sight. They slowly exited their car and from a very safe distance, stood and watched for movement inside the little clapboard shanty that Belle called home. The Russians stood as still and steady as a statue's shadow. After Belle turned off her bedroom light, the Russians waited another hour before they looked at each other and nodded. They crept up to the front door without a sound. Nikita took a small kit from his trench coat pocket and as Vladimir held a penlight on the lock, Nikita worked the tumblers. It took him all of perhaps ten seconds to unlock the door. Silently they moved inside. The Russians slithered into Belle's home. The front room and the kitchen were empty. They used only hand signals as they moved towards her bedroom. The door was shut. Vladimir held tight but steady to the doorknob before turning it and opening the door. They crouched, military style, in the doorway with their guns pointed at the center of the room. They waited a reasonable amount of time before entering the bedroom; it was empty. Deflated and confused they stood and pondered. Frustrated, Nikita walked out to the hallway and then into the bathroom and turned on the light. There was a small window above the bathtub, it was wide open. Vladimir stared out the window and could only see darkness. He whispered, "Dermo," to Nikita. They'd been seen or possibly played. Either way, they knew they would not be killing Bobby McKillin or anyone else for that matter, at least not on this night. They holstered their guns and were careful to lock the front door before they trudged back to their car.

•

"Odell, I have a score to settle with the driver, so I will take him," Pearly said with a note of angst.

"Pearly, sounds like you don't like dat man, and it takes a lot ta make you not like somebody. Why you hatin' on dat guy so much?" Odell asked.

"Odell, when I first saw Bobby by the bus stop the driver rolled up on me and treated me like common rubbish. He didn't say it with words, but his eyes called me a nigger. Now do you understand why I hate that man so much?" Pearly asked.

"I sho does, and now I wants the driver too. But, if he called you a nigguh den I feel like his ugly-ass brothuh just done de same ta me," Odell said as he crouched behind the rear passenger side taillight of the black sedan.

Pearly and Odell waited 'til the Russians opened their doors and had their backs to them. The first blow delivered by Pearly would have knocked most men to their knees, but the Russian was not most men. When Vladimir worked his way through the sudden pain and overwhelming confusion, he tried to retreat, but the open door stood in his way. The next blow landed in the middle of Vladimir's face; he caromed off the door and collapsed face down on the front seat. Only just barely conscious, he instinctively reached for his gun. Pearly grabbed Vladimir's right wrist with both hands and yanked his arm out of its socket, then he pressed Vladimir's forearm tight against the doorframe of the car.

Nikita had not fared as well as his brother. Odell ran to Nikita, jumped up, and brought his right elbow down on top of Nikita's head with such force that the impact radiated down through his skull and neck and immediately shattered two vertebrae in the middle of his spine. Nikita lay on the ground in a grotesque position. As quickly as it had begun, it was over. Odell peered down at Nikita for just a moment before he walked around the car and watched Pearly slam the car door on Vladimir's arm, three times. Suddenly, the black sedan and all four men were lit up like the White House Christmas Tree. With his car speaker on high volume, Officer Reed Tucker ordered everyone to lie flat on the ground. Nikita was the first to comply. Pearly threw Vladimir to the ground and then he and Odell lay on their stomachs with their hands out to the sides, palms down. They knew the routine.

Officer Tucker walked up and looked at the Russians for a minute, or maybe it was twenty minutes, before he called the dispatcher and told her he was going to need a couple of ambulances. Before the ambulances arrived, the Chief of the Jupiter Police, Malcolm Nettles, drove up and jumped out of his car. He yelled, "The Russians were obviously attacked. Take their handcuffs off. And do it now!"

"I'm sorry Chief, but that's not the way it happened," Sergeant Ronny Detwiler said.

"I said take those handcuffs off right now!" the Chief yelled.

"I'm sorry Chief Nettles, but from this point forward, the Russians will be in my custody. Please, move away from them, now!" FBI Agent Cummings roared at the Chief through a megaphone.

Chief Nettles looked past Agent Cummings and there were at least three more FBI cars, all of them full of agents.

Agents Cummings and Lipscomb began a search of the black sedan that the Russians had been driving. She instructed Lipscomb to retrieve the car keys from Vladimir's pocket. The trunk was opened and beneath the blanket that had been used to wrap Alvin's dead body, in she found the bloody gag that kept Grits from screaming. Next to the gag was the roll of nylon rope used to tie up the Wetmore twins. And next to the rope, lay the Louisville Slugger, which they assumed was the murder weapon.

Agent Cummings told the agents that were standing nearby to bag and label everything in the trunk. She moved away from the group and looked over the notes that Nigeriana had delivered to her that afternoon. She walked back to the black sedan and opened the glove compartment. Inside she found a key ring full of keys to airplanes, boats, trucks, padlocks, and warehouses. She smiled on the inside and then told the agent nearest her to cordon off the area. A young female reporter was now following Cummings everywhere she went.

"Agent, agent, can you please give me a statement,

please. My job depends on this, please?" Suzie-Ray
Tompkins pleaded. "Agent, it would sure help me if you'd
let me get this story before the guys get here. I work for
the Jupiter Rocket, the town newspaper. I was here first.
Come on, do it for all the girls in the world," she begged.

Suzie-Ray had done a good job. She had gotten
into Agent Cummings head.

"Ok, I'll give you the official statement. But,
you'd better be accurate or this will be the last story you
ever cover," Agent Cummings said.

"I'll only write what you say, so whenever you're
ready," Suzie-Ray said.

"I am FBI Agent Jill Cummings, Southeast
Division. Tonight, Vladimir and Nikita Stoyakoff are
under arrest for the murders of Alvin and Grits Wetmore.
We will also be charging them with a murder that took
place in San Francisco. The name of that victim is Leon
Beauchamp. Our experts will need time to look at the
evidence, but I believe it will speak for itself." Agent
Cummings stopped talking and paused for a bit. She was
thinking about the narcotics charges and decided that it
would be best to hold off on revealing that information.
They still had work to do.

"Agent Cummings, is that it?" The Jupiter Rocket
reporter, Suzie-Ray, asked.

"Yes, that's it for now," Agent Cummings said.

"What about the murder charges that were brought
against Bobby McKillin? Have they been dropped?"
Suzie-Ray asked.

"I think it would be safe to assume so, yes," Agent
Cummings said before she walked away.

Suzie-Ray had a flash camera with her. She wasn't
about to wait around for the photographer, so she started
clicking. She had emptied her entire roll of film when she
was told by the FBI to leave.

•

I was in the middle of a tumultuous sweat-filled
dream the evening Pearly came and moved Belle and me

to Ruthie-May's little home. He said the move was just precautionary. Then late the next night I was almost positive I heard someone outside talking real loud through a megaphone. I tried to get up and have a look, but I was too sick. And of course, Belle told me to lie still and that everything was ok. I trust Belle so I did lay my head down and I fell right back into another colorful dream.

The Jupiter newspaper was delivered to Chet's front porch at seven the next morning; he immediately called Sam and Joey.

•

Riley opened the gate for carpenter, Joe-Bob, at exactly seven in the morning. He rode with him to the back of the Hurtwood mansion. They got out of the truck and walked around to look up at the loose railings. But instead of looking up, they looked down at the twisted wheelchair and the broken body of Cotton Razor Hurtwood the sixth. Riley had somehow forgotten to lock the gate and after he and Joe-Bob drove in, so did the Jupiter newspaper reporter, Suzie-Ray Tomkins.

Riley took Joe-Bob in the house and let him do all the talking with the people at the hospital. And while Joe-Bob talked, Suzie-Ray was taking as many pictures as her camera would allow. She was in the middle of her roll of film when she heard the ambulance coming. And when she was near the end of her roll, the Saturn Chief of Police, Asa Brown, walked up. Didn't say a word; I think he was too stunned to speak. Never even looked at Suzie-Ray; he just stared down at Hurtwood's body. The men in the ambulance rushed up and one of them got down close to the body. He almost immediately looked up at his partner and shook his head no.

When Chief Brown finally absorbed the fact that Hurtwood was dead, he went inside. Then he and Joe-Bob walked up to look at the place where the wheelchair had broken through. Joe-Bob showed the Chief the fix-it note he'd been given the day before. They figured Hurtwood had gone to inspect the damage and had somehow fallen through to the concrete below. It was unfortunate, but from what they could see, it was clearly an accident.

While the Chief and the carpenter were up on the veranda, Suzie-Ray snapped a few pictures of them inspecting the broken railings. Suzie-Ray sat and waited for them to come down and then took statements from everyone. Somehow, she had beaten all the other reporters to both the capture of the Russians and the accidental death of Hurtwood. No one knew, or suspected, that she was Gino's little sister. I guess nobody really cared. She was given a pay-raise and promotion that same day.

•

Pearly and Odell were both released that night and when the police work was finished, Officer Tucker drove straight to our hotel. I heard the knock on my door before someone said, "Please wake up."

I threw on my robe and when I opened the door, the sleepy kid from the front desk nearly fell in the room. I guess he'd been leaning on the door. Right behind him stood Reed. He had a big smile on his face when he yelled, "We found Bobby!"

I made him say it a couple more times before I hollered, "Wahoo!"

I ran and woke up the guys. They hollered up a storm as they danced a happy jig. We called Dad, Dezi, Randi, and Ajax; they were ecstatic. We promised to call back after we went to see Junior.

We got dressed as fast as we could and when we ran down to the lobby to meet Reed, he was fast asleep. I hated to wake him, but I was not willing to wait even a minute longer than necessary to go see Junior. We followed Reed in his police car. He had the lights flashing most of the way; it seemed like the right thing to do. At seven in the morning we parked in front of the little clapboard shanty with the number nine over the porch. Reed knocked on the door and then two doors down a little colored gal with skin so smooth and shiny it looked like black marble said, "We's ovuh heuh."

Crestfield

The closer we got, the more beautiful the little gal became. She had mysterious dark eyes and full ruby red lips and a scarf to match. She waved for us to come in and then when we did, I think my eyes nearly popped right out of my head. Inside the little front room stood two of the largest black men I'd ever seen. I was, for whatever reason, alarmed. One of the two men could see that I was frightened.

"Please, don't be afraid. At first glance, my brother and I do make for a disquieting sight. But the truth, is we're really quite gentle; at least I know I am," the one wearing his hair in a soft serve swirl a foot over his head said as he looked at the other one with a keen eye. "You must be Bobby's family. We are so happy that you have finally found him. Before I go any further, I am Pearly Cisco and this delicate little black olive is my beautiful sister, Mahidabelle; we all call her Belle." He said as Belle gave us a curtsy.

"Pearly, I may be black, and I's little, but I ain't no olive. It plain as de nose on yo face dat I's just a lady," she said as gentle and sweet as anything I've ever heard.

"Pearly always leavin' me out'a stuff, I's his twin brothuh, Odell. It sho is nice ta meet Bobby's fam'lee," Odell said as he leered at Pearly.

We were overwhelmed to say the least, but we said thank you and I believe they felt our intense gratitude. Officer Tucker introduced each of us, but handshakes just weren't enough, so there were hugs all around. When we finished hugging, I looked at Belle and she knew what my eyes were asking. She said, "He in heuh, dis way please." Tommy, Ricky, and I walked behind her into a bedroom; Junior was lying there in bed. He was completely unaware of our presence in the room. He was soaking wet and delirious, at best. He was obviously very sick, but I didn't care. I couldn't help myself; I ran and hugged him with all my might. He opened an eye and then he hugged me back.

I don't know why, and I can't explain, but at that point, all the pain and the heartache were gone and I cried uncontrollably. They were the best kind of tears, because they were tears of joy. Then I turned and looked at Tommy and Ricky; they both looked away. I guess it's a guy thing. In any case I know they were overjoyed, and it didn't take but a second or two before they were hugging Junior too. It was right at that point when I prayed that this was not a dream. I stood up and looked back at the guys and I knew this was all very real.

I looked behind me and Belle cried at least as hard as I did before she ran away. My instincts as a woman told me to go after her, so I did. She ran and disappeared into number nine. I slowly walked in and she was in her bedroom. Belle had her head buried in her pillow, crying her eyes out. I just sat next to her and stroked her back. She didn't push me away, she just continued to cry. I knew why she was crying and I asked her how long she'd been in love with Junior. She stopped crying and slowly turned and looked at me.

"Is it pos'bole ta be in love de moment you foist set eyes on someone?" she asked.

"Yes Belle, I believe love at first site is very real. It happens more often than people would care to admit. This must be so difficult to deal with. I hope Junior has been nice to you."

"Nice, you say. He so, so nice, in fact he de nicest boy I evuh met. And now I gots ta let him go," she said as the tears started all over again.

"Belle, love always finds a way. That's all I can say right now, but I do believe that love will find a way."

I felt someone else in the room and I turned and looked at Pearly and Odell. They were the big brothers that hurt when their little sister hurt. I felt just plain awful. I was so confused. We had been looking for Junior for what seemed like an eternity. And now I was wondering if things wouldn't have been better if we hadn't found him at all.

Then I thought, *better for whom?* Certainly not for us; we would have missed Junior something awful. And the not knowing would have been for most, if not all of us, unbearable. It took a while, but Belle finally got up and dusted herself off; she walked back over to be with Junior. Her brothers and I followed. When we walked back in the bedroom, we could see that Tommy and Ricky had somehow got Junior to sit up. He looked at me and said, "Hello, are you with these gentlemen?"

"Yes, she's with us. She was the one you told us hugged you so tight. Junior, this is Madison, the oldest of your three sisters," Tommy said.

Junior looked at me the way a person would look at a complete and absolute stranger. It broke my heart. But he reached out to me all the same. It was as if we were meeting for the very first time. I hugged him all over again, and when I stopped he said, "Thank you, you are a good hugger."

I was wondering when Tommy was going to show Junior one of the flyers. Well, I didn't have to wait very long. While I was hugging Junior, he was out getting a flyer. He walked back in the room and said, "Junior, your real name is Jack, but nobody ever calls you Jack. This flyer is about you. I hope it will tug at your memory banks a little."

In my life, I've never seen a look like the one Junior had on his face. When I looked around the room, everyone was sharing the same look. It was then that I fully understood. He wasn't Junior; he was Bobby. And the new name and everything that came with it were near impossible for these people to deal with. At least it was too much to deal with all at once. It was going to take Junior, and everyone else in the room, a long time to get things straight in their minds. Then out of nowhere Junior looked up at Reed and said, "Officer Tucker, did you know I was a policeman?"

"No, I just found out Bobby. I'm so sorry; I should have known. You didn't try to mess with us, you were always agreeable and polite, geez, I feel awful about arresting you," Reed Tucker said.

"Say, Officer Tucker, will you and Ricky stand next to each other for a minute?" Junior asked. When they stood next to each other, Junior gave a weak smile. "Gee whiz, you two look like you could be twins, wow, I have a best friend and a guy that threw me in jail, not once, but twice, that look like brothers. Imagine that," he said just before his smile evaporated.

Junior looked around a couple of times and a harried look ran across his face as he cried out, "Belle, where's Belle, I need Belle."

Belle almost knocked him over she ran so fast to his side.

"Belle, did you run out of here a little while ago? Is something wrong? Please tell me," Bobby said.

"No Bobby, everting fine," Belle said as she put her hand to his forehead. "Good Lord, you burnin' up. Gracious you hot, you needs ta lie back down. You sick 'gain," she whispered.

She laid his head down and then she ran out of the room. She was gone for only seconds before she ran back in with a small dish towel with crushed up ice wrapped inside. I looked down at Junior; his eyes rolled back and he was out again. Belle held the towel to his forehead and stroked his face as a tear cascaded down her cheek.

"We gots ta let him rest now, please. I know I'm gonna lose him to y'all, but I gots ta know he well befo' he leave," Belle said as she laid her head down on his chest.

I didn't have to be told twice and neither did anyone else. We walked through the front room and kept right on going. I had just sat down on the porch when I heard someone honk their horn at us. We all turned to see who it was and there was a van with Gino's written on the side parked right next to Reed Tucker's police car. A short roundish man and a slender man wearing a tweed coat and carrying what looked like a doctor's bag walked towards us. I didn't recognize him at first, but turns out the man wearing the tweed coat was the doctor from the clinic. We were all introduced to Gino and then Doctor Miller politely asked to see Bobby. Belle didn't waste any time as she led the doctor in to see him. After a half-an-hour or so, the doctor came back outside and explained to us that Bobby had stopped taking the antibiotics before the bacterium had been totally vanquished. And as a result, the bacteria had become more resistant.

"I can see that you're all worried and that is understandable. Bobby has been put through the ringer. But it's this ability he has to fight back that makes me believe with time and the correct medication, he will pull through this. For now, I think he should rest. I've given Belle instructions and she knows she can come get me again if needed. Now, I have other patients to tend to. It was nice seeing you folks again, and I'm happy you found Bobby. Gino, thanks for the ride here. It's a nice day, so I think I'll walk back. Bye now," Doctor Miller said before he slowly strode away.

When Doctor Miller said he was happy we found Bobby, I wasn't convinced he meant it. Seemed to me he understood that Belle's heart was broken, but there was more to it than Belle's heart; I think he felt his Bobby now belonged here in Mississippi.

Reed finally told us he had to go home and get some rest. After all, he'd been up all night. We understood. Then Gino asked us all to come and eat at his restaurant. We needed to eat and Junior needed to rest. Pearly and Odell were going to go in Gino's van, but Ricky asked them to ride in the Imperial with us. For some reason, I decided I'd go with Gino. I watched the two giants get in the Imperial and it seemed like the car sunk down a little closer to the ground. On the way to his restaurant, Gino filled me in on how he watched Belle and Bobby fall in love. He said it was a love story that should be in a book. Gino reminded me several times of the fact that they weren't the same 'flavor' of person; at least that's the way he said it.

We ate like royalty. I think it was a brunch, but it felt more like a supper. The mood was bright, and the spirits were good; I had several glasses of wine. After we ate, we all piled into the Imperial and drove back to Belle's to see Junior. He moaned and called out names just as he'd done in Crestfield. We sat and told them about Crestfield and they told us all about Jupiter. The places were totally different from one another, but the people weren't. Seems there are good and bad people and some in between, no matter where you go. I was glad we had the time to just sit and talk. It brought everyone a little closer together. Time had flown by and it was late in the day when we headed back to the hotel. We had a lot of phone calls to make, and of course, a lot of good news to share with the folks back home.

58

Plantation

For the most part, Diego stayed in his room, but he did manage, now and then, to sneak a peek at Chief Brown, the ambulance guys, and of course, Gino's little sister. He was ready to come out of hiding when he saw the FBI agents drive their car right up to the back porch of the mansion. He had to move and move fast. He believed they were looking for him. So he high-tailed it to his hiding place in the barn. There is no way that they would find him there, but his heart nearly pounded out of his chest when he heard them walk by. An hour or so later Nigeriana and Riley came out to get him.

"Diego, dey gone now, you can comes out," Riley said.

Diego crawled out from beneath the bales of hay and the three of them sat down on the straw. Nigeriana read the paper to the guys. When she finished reading, they looked at the pictures Gino's little sister had taken. Nigeriana could see Diego was worried and said, "Don't worry, I done toldt dem FBI agents dat you ain't been here in ovuh a mont'. I put dem keys a Hurtwoodt's in de Russian's glove-box like you toldt me. Dose keys is de keys to de hi-way, should keep 'em bizzy fo a long time," she said as the three of them chuckled.

"You know somepin Ana, I tink you right 'bout dem keys. And I knows somepin else too, dem devil Russians is arrested and goin' ta jail. Dey ain't gun bodder none a us evuh 'gain!" Riley said as he shook his head and mumbled, "Dat's right, yes suh, dey got 'zactly what dey de-zoived."

"Diego, I tink maybe you shouldt prob'bly call Razuh now. Wouldn't be right fo her ta hear 'bout dis on de TV. o de radio," Nigeriana said.

"Yeah, you right. Ok, let's us go inside so's I can

make dat call," Diego said not looking forward to what he had to do.

He went in Hurtwood's office, sat at the big desk, and called Montgomery. He had a long list of numbers and eventually someone brought Razor to the phone. When he gave her the bad news, she said she'd already been told by Chief Brown. She wasn't near as upset as he thought she'd be. In fact, she was cold as ice. Diego thought to himself, *dis ain't de Razuh I knowed.* Senator Razor Hurtwood was now a powerful woman. And her first order of business was to tell Diego she expected him to run things 'til she got back. He thought she would hurry home to be with him. Heartbroken, he knew this day would come, he just hadn't expected it to happen so soon. Razor Cotton Hurtwood had changed; she was now for all intents and purposes, a complete stranger. When he finally hung up the phone, Diego knew she was no longer his... anything.

•

Diego was up and walking long before the sun smiled on Alabama. He had a heavy load and a long way to go. Exhausted, he finally made it to Belle's. He saw the Imperial with Iowa plates and decided he'd better lay low for a bit. At least 'til he knew what was going on. He hid behind a tree and watched and waited 'til someone behind him said, "Mornin' Diego."

Diego was understandably startled and for a moment or two considered running, but he knew the load he was carrying was far too heavy. So he just stood up straight, looked back, and said, "Odell, dis is de toid time you done snuck up on me, I wish you'd stop doin' dat."

"You look tired, what you carryin' dere boy? Lands sakes alive, I'd like ta have me a fancy suitcase like dat one," Odell said.

"Mornin' Odell, you and Pearly ready ta go?" Diego asked.

"Yeah, we ready. Don't ya wanna come in and meet Bobby's fam'lee?" Odell asked.

"No, please, can we just go?" Diego asked.

"Ok, let me take dis in and den we'll go," Odell said as he picked up the plaid suitcase.

When Odell walked to Ruthie-May's home, Diego took off runnin'. He didn't run far, just far enough to where he felt safe. He knew there was a chance that Bobby's family might want to exact some revenge on his little ass.

Tommy, Ricky, and I absolutely devoured the breakfast Belle made for us. We thanked her and then single file, we went out to the front room and sat down. We heard the door open and in walked Odell with Junior's plaid suitcase. The three of us were in shock. We knew exactly why the suitcase played such an important role in all of this, but none of the others had a clue. They didn't know it had been to the west coast and back. I think seeing it had the greatest effect on Ricky. After all, he was the one that loaded the suitcase into the trunk of his car, and he's the one that carried it into the airport. After he jumped up and shook his head a couple of times, he hollered, "Where in the heck did you get that! This can't be real, how in the world?"

Belle and Pearly heard Ricky and hurried out of the bedroom to see what the commotion was all about. Everyone was now crowded into the little front room staring at the plaid suitcase. I started to explain when Tommy took over. That is, 'til he and Ricky started talking at the same time. Eventually the three of us explained, and after everyone calmed down a bit, we decided to open the suitcase. As we expected, it was full of Junior's clothes. But what we didn't expect to find was his wallet. Ricky held up the wallet and said, "This is Junior's wallet all right. I was there with him when he bought it at the five and dime in Crestfield."

Ricky opened the wallet and all of Junior's identification was still inside. Ricky gave everyone a nervous look as he opened the part where you'd keep paper money. He started counting and when he got to five hundred and seventy-two, he stopped and frowned as he shook his head.

"Ricky, what's wrong?" Tommy asked.

"I'll tell ya what's wrong. Junior was kinda proud that he'd saved some money for the trip. He had over eight hundred dollars when he left home. That Grits guy that stole everything spent more than two hundred dollars. He was only in California for three days and he spent that much money. What the heck was he doin'?"

"Ricky, it's amazing there's any money at all. We should be happy. This brings everything nearly full circle," I said.

"Full circle my butt! Junior worked hard for that money!" Ricky shouted out of aggravation.

"Say, what's all the yelling about?"

We all turned and Junior was standing there staring at us, trembling. He could barely stand on his own two feet. Belle rushed to him. "Bobby, you cain't be up, come on sweetie let's go lay you back down."

Tommy didn't want Junior getting caught up in what was going on, so he closed the suitcase. When Junior looked at the plaid, he put his arms out to balance himself and then he started wobbling. Pearly grabbed him and held him up. Then Junior's eyes rolled back and he slumped over in Pearly's arms.

"Lord have mercy, nevuh in my life have I seen anyting like dat. Just from lookin' at an old suitcase. Good Lord," Odell softly said.

They, Pearly and Belle that is, put Junior back in bed. None of us knew what to think. Here I was the experienced person in matters such as this, but I'd never seen a reaction to stimuli like the one Junior had. I've heard of it, but I've never actually witnessed it. I thought it best to keep my thoughts on the matter to myself. I looked over at Tommy and he had zipped and snapped the suitcase shut. He looked at me for a bit before he said, "Madison, I'm going to take this out to the car. I'll pick out some of Junior's clothes for the ride home. Then I'm going to put the suitcase in the trunk and leave it there."

Crestfield

We stood around for a bit; I don't think anyone knew what to say. Odell finally told Pearly it was time for them to go. We didn't know where they were going and it would have been impolite to ask. However, Belle wanted to know, so she asked. Pearly softly said, "Belle, we are going with Diego to the animal shelter to adopt a dog for Scooter. Odell found a little female that looks like she could be Ralph's sister. As soon as we deliver the dog to Scooter, we'll head back home. You have two policemen here to protect you, but I believe all the evil that invaded our lives has gone on vacation. And I, for one, am going to enjoy every moment of our newly attained peace and quiet. Bye now," Pearly said as he and Odell walked out the door.

59

Madison

We went home that night, home being the hotel. We called Crestfield and had a family meeting of sorts. It was decided that the longer we stayed in Jupiter, the harder it would be to leave. So, we made up our minds that we would leave the next day. We were going to give Junior the option of going home in an airplane or with us in the car. Either way we had to go.

We arrived at Belle's early the next morning. The moment she looked at us, she knew. She didn't cry or carry on. I guess she had decided to put on a brave face. When we told Junior, he was very upset, but he knew we weren't leaving without him. Then Belle stepped up to the plate, and like a seasoned pro, she hit a home run. She explained to Bobby that she would be waiting for him and when he was better, and if he still wanted her, he could come back. The tears the two of them shared at that moment were the worst tears I think I've ever had to witness. Their hearts were broken, and so was mine. The thought of flying home-made Junior get sick again. So, it was decided that he could sit or lie down in the back seat of the Imperial. It would be a tight squeeze, but the three of us would have to ride up front.

We had to pull Junior and Belle apart to get Junior in the back seat. We said our goodbyes to Belle, Pearly, and Odell and just when we were going to leave, an old truck and a Corvette drove up and parked next to us. Two men with long hair got out of the truck. One guy was big and the other one was gigantic. The lady driving the Corvette jumped out of her car and ran to us. She begged us to let Bobby out so she could give him a hug. We knew we were not getting out of there until we gave in to her. Junior got out of the Imperial on his own, and he and Belle and this other lady all hugged each other at the same time.

We got out of the car and the smaller of the two guys that had been in the truck walked over and said, "Hi, I'm Joey Lombardi and that nut that's hugging the life out of Bobby is my wife, Sam. Oh, and that big fella over there is Haystack."

We looked over at Haystack and he gave us a black smile. Then he looked at Pearly and Odell and narrowed his eyes. The look the three of them shared was a little bit of surprise, mixed with de facto racism and utter ill-regard. It was a very perplexing situation to witness.

This time after all the hugs and kisses and such, we had to tear Junior, Belle, and Sam apart. Belle sat down on her knees with her hands in her lap and sobbed. Sam stood and stared at nothing. We had Junior back in the car and Tommy looked at us and said, "I think we'd better go now."

Ricky and I nodded our heads yes; Junior just gazed out the window. As we were leaving, Reed Tucker drove up in his squad car. Scooter was with him. They got out and waved goodbye. The scruffy little dog Scooter held in his arms gave us a goodbye bark.

60

On the road home to Crestfield

For the first hundred miles Junior talked non-stop. He started with the first day he went in front of the judge and he didn't stop 'til he got to the day he first met us. He still didn't know who we were, but he said he came with us because Belle told him he could trust us. He told us how Sam and her husband had helped him. He told us Pearly's middle name was Abraham and Odell's middle name was Lincoln. And then he suddenly stopped talking. The quiet was nice, but it made me worry. Then out of the blue Junior says, "Do y'all know what the difference is between Sam and Belle? No, how could you? The difference is I was infatuated with Sam, but I'm in love with Belle."

At that point, he completely stopped talking. He laid his head down and fell asleep. We kept driving through the day and night and when we got to Memphis, we stopped and ate at a Krystal drive thru. Junior wasn't hungry and stayed in the back seat. Tommy was too tired to drive anymore, so we switched. Ricky started driving and I sat in the middle. Tommy had a pillow leaned against the window and was asleep before we even got back on the highway. Ricky drove for hours and when he started getting sleepy, he turned the radio on.

We drove for a while and then a song came on that Ricky liked so he turned up the volume a little. About half-way through the song Junior sat up and said, "Could you please turn the radio off."

I turned the radio off and Ricky looked at me. "Madison, I like that song. Why does he want the radio off?"

"Ricky, do you know what the title of that song is?" I asked.

"Um, no I don't. I just like it. What is the name of that song?" he asked.

"You big dummy, the title of that song is, Since I Don't Have You," I said.

"I don't understand," he said.

"Would you understand if I said Belle?"

He started to answer me when Junior said, "You know, I'm sitting right here behind you. I can hear everything the two of you are saying. Please, leave the radio off for a little while."

Neither Ricky nor I said a word; Junior said, "Thanks."

We took turns driving and didn't stop until we drove into Crestfield. When we pulled off the highway, Junior was sweating and moaning again. We took him straight to the hospital.

•

The day after we got back to Crestfield, we had a family meeting in the hospital. We were allowed to use a conference room and a speaker phone. Buck had flown to San Francisco and was with Dezi and her friend, Matt. So, everyone was there, at least in voice. We discussed how to treat Junior. We agreed that he'd been to hell and back. And we knew everything there was to know about Jupiter, and all the friends Junior had made while he was there. In the middle of the meeting Dad said, "If we try to keep Junior from thinking about Jupiter, we might lose him in more ways than one. Like it or not, Jupiter is part of Junior now, and vice a versa."

Dad was right, so Tommy suggested that we mollify Junior, let him relive whatever it was he wanted to. At that point in the meeting, we all made a conscious and unanimous decision, where Junior was concerned, to make sure we were good listeners.

• Junior

I opened one eye just to have a look around. There, sitting next to me was a man and a big black and tan dog. I was going to open the other eye, but before I got it open the dog barked at me. I guess she knew I was awake. Then the man said, "Junior, are you awake? Talk to me, please."

"Ok, sure, I'll talk to you. Do I know you?" I asked.

He told me he was my dad, and for some reason I believed him. He got up and hugged me so hard I could barely breathe; the dog barked a hug. At least that's what it felt like to me. After that, nearly every single day, people crowded into my room. It must have been déjà vu all over again. At least that's what I was told. I could go on and on and drag you through the steps and the time it took 'til I woke up and knew who I was, but there's really no need. We've been through this before. After the same old tests, and what I was told were routine questions, Doc Mayland told me that if I continued to improve, he was going to let me go home. I was excited and just couldn't wait to get the heck out of the hospital. I decided it was time to write Belle a letter.

I'd committed her address to memory, so that part was no problem. What got in my way was the fact that I knew Pearly would be the one to read her the letter. I couldn't say some of the things I wanted to, you know, mushy stuff. So, I wrote a nice letter and I told her that I loved her and how much I missed her. And as soon as I could I would come back down to be with her. I said hello to all the folks in Jupiter that had helped me. I wrote my address on the envelope and on the letter. I wanted to make darn sure she could write back. Dad promised he'd put the letter in the mail for me. I was beginning to feel a lot better, and the letter helped me along the way. Three days later, I walked out of the hospital. And for the next week or so Ricky drove me around so that I could reacquaint myself with Crestfield. It took a little over a month before I felt comfortable enough with who I was to ask about taking a trip back to Mississippi. Dad was dead set against my going, and I think a few of the others were too.

Dad argued that Dezi had worked so hard to help me get back to Crestfield that if I went anywhere, it should be to see her. I knew he was right, so it was decided that's where I would go. All the arrangements were made for me, and we all agreed that this time both Ricky and Randi would drive me to the airport. The day came and Ricky parked right in front of my apartment; he loaded my suitcase in the trunk of his car. To be perfectly honest, I was worried about a few things; like being drugged and kidnapped, but those were fears I had to face head on. We made the same trip to my dad's house before we left, and like the last time, he was worried. We all did our best to reassure him everything was going to be ok. Finally, he said, "Ricky and Randi, you just make damn sure this time you stay 'til you see Junior get on the airplane. Understood?"

They both promised they would, and after a few hugs, we were off to Des Moines again. The sun was shining, but the air was cool. I felt like I was floating in a milkshake, with a smile on my face and a big straw by my side. I fell asleep for a while and when I woke up, I sat and gazed at the countryside; everything looked as it did the first time Ricky drove me to the airport. Then, for some reason, I looked down on the floorboard of the car and saw something bright and blue. I reached down and picked up the wallet that Sam had given me with the motorcycle on the front. I looked inside and my license was right there where I'd left it.

"Ricky, where'd you find my wallet?" I asked.

"Your wallet, what are you talking about? That's not your wallet," he said as he looked at me in the rearview mirror.

"Of course it's my wallet; look it has my name right there on the driver license." I took the license out and read the name, "Bobby McKillin, see it's my name and my license," I said.

I passed the license up to Randi so she could take a look. That's when Ricky pulled off the highway and stopped the car. Then Randi turned in her seat and said, "Junior, you found this wallet in the bathroom at the Rooster Inn the day before the tornado hit town. Did you look at the address that's on the license?"

"No, please give it back," I said as Randi handed me the license. I looked and the address was somewhere in Tupelo. "It's supposed to say Jupiter; is this some kind of trick?" I asked as the turmoil inside of me began to mount.

Randi unbuckled her seatbelt and turned all the way around in the front seat and looked at me. She could see that I was on the verge of either tears or insanity. She reached back and held my hand in hers before she said, "Junior, you know I'd never do anything to hurt you, right."

"Yes, I know that, but this license should say Jupiter. Why doesn't it say Jupiter?" I pleaded.

"Junior, I guess the only way you're ever going to understand is to read this," she said as she reached in her front pocket and pulled out the letter I'd written to Belle. She handed it to me and as she began to weep, she softly said, "Junior, haven't you wondered why no one from Jupiter has taken the time to write back?"

What she'd just asked me was more than I was prepared to deal with. I knew perception and reality were now on a collision course. I thought, *why haven't they written back?*

I stared at the envelope as it quivered in my hands. I finally turned it over and our postmaster, Henry Dillard, had written, 'I'm sorry, but there is no city in the state of Mississippi named Jupiter.'

"If there's no Jupiter, then why'd Dad mail the letter?" I asked in tired desperation.

"Junior, he mailed the letter because he loves you. And I suppose because he promised you he would," Randi softly said.

I looked out the window and there was a little yellow bird in a tree just singing his heart out.